LET ME EXPLAIN YOU

A NOVEL

Annie Liontas

Scribner

New York   London   Toronto   Sydney   New Delhi

Scribner
An Imprint of Simon & Schuster, Inc.
1230 Avenue of the Americas
New York, NY 10020

First Scribner hardcover edition July 2015

For information about special discounts for bulk purchases, please contact Simon & Schuster Special Sales at 1-866-506-1949 or business@simonandschuster.com.

The Simon & Schuster Speakers Bureau can bring authors to your live event. For more information or to book an event contact the Simon & Schuster Speakers Bureau at 1-866-248-3049 or visit our website at www.simonspeakers.com.

Interior design by Akasha Archer

Manufactured in the United States of America

10   9   8   7   6   5   4   3   2   1

ISBN 978-1-4767-8908-8
ISBN 978-1-4767-8910-1 (ebook)

Greek Chorus #V, page 107, references the chorus in *Oedipus the King,* translated by Robert Fagles. Sophocles, *The Three Theban Plays: Antigone, Oedipus the King, Oedipus at Colonus* (New York: Penguin Classics, 1984), 1683–84.

for Sara, my favorite

LET ME
EXPLAIN YOU

PART I

DAY 10

Acceptance

Let Me Explain You Something. We start from the same sea.
This, We shall repeat.

CHAPTER 1

From: SteveStavrosStavrosMavrakisgreekboss1@yahoo.com
To: Chef.Stevie.Mavrakis@saltrestaurant.com; xxangelxx@yahoo.com;
Ruby.Mavrakis@yahoo.com; CarolM@Starbucks.com
Subject: Our Father, Who is Dying in Ten Days

Dear, Family. Daughters & Ex-Wife:

Let me explain you something: I am sick in a way that no doctor would have much understanding. I am sick in a way of the soul that, yes, God will take me. No, I am not a suicide. I am Deeper than that, I am talking More than that.

DEAR STAVROULA, MY OLDEST. Please grow out your hair. It is very very short. This is one little thing that can change everything, you will see what I am saying when you take this small but substantial advice. Sometimes if we are who we are supposed to be on the outside, we are who we are supposed to be on the inside. The hair is the thing to trust and leave alone, and it will take care of you.

Let me explain you something: your father has seen some of the world for it to be enough. There is a way to be for the normal society, and you are not it. The hair says things about you that, yes, they are true, but the hair is not a fortune-teller. The hair is not the thing that has to point the way, like a streetlight.

I am not somebody religious, but this I know: Death is coming. In ten days, I promise you, your father the man will cease, he will be dust, he will be food in the worms. What do we owe our father? This is the question you can say to yourself at this time. Who can deny a dead man—a dead father—the thing that he demands?

No, I am not sick like my brother in Crete, who die with emphysema (this is Greek *en* which means *in* and *physan* means *breath*).

DEAR LITZA, MY SECOND, please go to church. You could say, no dad, you go to church then we will talk about if I go to church, but what I am talking about here are lessons that I should have taken for myself if my father had the wisdom to give me awareness, which I am holding out for you.

Litza, let me explain you something. Litza, you have problems.

Litza, nobody marries for a big wedding and then divorce one week later. When your mother and I divorce, it took years off our life. Litza, nobody destroys property the way when you come here into my diner and smash the dessert case with my own stool. The same is true for your sister, which you take that same stool and break her car window with it, even though you deny this always. Are you on drugs, Litza? Are you the same low-life as your biological mother, Dina?

Litza, you need God in your life.

Litza I see how much helping you are needing, and I know that God has to exist, because he is the only one who can do for you. I cannot do for you. I can only do for you what I am done for you.

And here, I will tell you this secret, that I have questions for God— Are you real? Are you here for me, Stavros Stavros Steve Mavrakis? Am I Your Forgotten Son? What is the meaning of this life that is too sorry for what it could be? Even though I have succeeded more, much more, than any foreigner would do in my country and I have now two diners and plans for selling one of them so that I have a little something for the future, yours not mine since my future is not something I can belong to any longer, and not your Mother since she is a thief, I'm sorry if it is a truth.

I, Stavros Stavros, have ask God to erase the mistakes of my life; and God has answer, in a matter of speaking, That it is best to Start Over, which requires foremost that We End All that is Stavros Stavros. No, not with suicide. With Mercy.

Yes, Litza, you must go to Church. To pray. For your father, yes, and for yourself.

DEAR RUBY, MY LITTLE ONE that I have adoration. It is a

good rule to follow that if the mustache is weak, so will be the man. Look at your father's mustache, which it is a fist! Forget the boys, Ruby, find yourself a man who encourages you get your own education, because you don't want to be one of those woman who takes and takes and does not appreciate all of the way her husband slaves, like your Mother. Don't go marrying some losers. Which you know I am talking about Dave. Why choose a man with the facial hair of an onion? When you can choose instead one of my assistant cooks, who make a decent living and has dreams of owning their own diner the way their mentor has, which is your father.

Otherwise, you are doing OK.

DEAREST MY EX-WIFE, Carol, the Mother, who divorce me one year ago. Which I am still, as a generous person, paying for things like to repair the plumbing. I am talking to the woman who is still my Wife in death, even if she did not know how to mourn me in life: please be the Ex-wife a Wife should be, in sickness and health. Even though you poison Stavroula and Litza against me from the moment I bring them into this fat country, and Ruby from the moment you bring her into the world. That is why I am asking: you should wear only black for the next year. To show a sign of honor for the man who walk much of this life with you by his side.

If you have any confusions, Daughters and Wife, you can email a response. I will answer them all. Such as, what is missing for a man at the end of his life when the path is clear and wisdom is the greatest? . . . the respect and love for the *pateras*!

Signed within Ten Days of Life Left, and a Dying Promise,
Your Father: Stavros Stavros Steve Mavrakis

DAY 9

Denial

CHAPTER 2

Stavros drove away from that Club of Cunts, that Whore House Starbucks where he Fucked Her Virgin Mother. Fuck the Cunt That Threw Her Into This World and ruined his life. His Ex-wife, the Horn Fucker, the Dick-Dinner Eater, who only cared about servicing One Faggot After Another with Cappuccino, rather than care about him. The Fucking Mother, he was finish with her. She could Go to the Crows in Hell with her Divorce and sit there without sex.

He said, "God, if you listen to anything a man say, let her die alone."

He heard himself talking and the words sounded ugly, like bits of fat, which was how he had intended them to come out. He said again, "Alone, do you hear me?" He wished the Ex-wife, the Mother, were here so he could say it to her face. And then, because God was not really paying attention and could not judge him, Stavros Stavros began to cry.

He did not really want his ex-wife to die alone. What had happened was:

Carol refused the flowers. Yellow, with bright red centers, as if they were trying to convince people they had a heartbeat. He chose them for that reason. He bought them for her. In their marriage, Carol had complained about flowers, *Where are the flowers?* when he would bring home bouquets of leftover pot roast. She was too simple; a roast was worth more, much more, than flowers; he had gone a year, sometimes, without roast. In their marriage, she looked at him strangely when he said, *Why would I love you as much as flowers when I can love you as much as meat?* And here he was, bringing flowers to her Starbucks drive-through, being a romantic and a gentleman and a truce, and for the third time she is refusing taking them!

He only wanted to end things the right way, the proper way. None of them do things right. Litza, she is angry and uses her fists to strike empty air, when by age twenty-nine you should move on with life (didn't he?). Stavroula—thirty-one—she is busy, always busy so she doesn't have to be anything else. They all live on Facebook, as if Facebook is Facelife. His little Ruby (twenty-four? twenty-three?), she can't even call back. But Carol gives him coffee. He does not even have to tell her triple macchiato with three packets of sugar; without asking, Carol knows. That touched him. That made him sure that she had to be the one by his side when he was taken. There had to be someone. He might be ready, he might know to expect death in nine days, but that did not mean any man should face his conclusion by himself in a place like crowded New Jersey, America.

Being alone in the last days of life was like being the last star in a galaxy, watching one neighbor star after another blink into nothing, until even the faraway, nub stars are just light-years, just messages from a dead source, and all Stavros is left with is debris from the first cough of creation. And does Stavros look like a cough? No.

A long line of cars was trying to get his attention, but he did not care. He could be Jersey driver, too. He could be spoiled Starbucks exactly like his ex-wife. Out of spite he would let the coffee get cold and the stale pastry more stale. He could stay until six o'clock if he had to, if she made him, because the only thing needing his attention today was dinner for the goat. He could get one of many tools out of his trunk and open one, two tires of the beeping cars behind him, and then the customers would be spoiled like him, in no rush to go anywhere. He could do that, he had very little to lose. Except time—he had far less than she did, actually, and far less than the rest of the drivers making noise behind him, he had nine days left, which made him terminal—so maybe, no, he was not prepared to wait until six. Actually, he was ready now for her to come with him.

He said, "We know each other, twenty-five years. Twenty-five, you don't close your eyes on that."

He noticed for the first time in twenty-five years that her eyes had lightened from the wet-barrel brown of the first day they met to the speckled brown of cork. Her hair, which she highlighted with streaks of red, denied all traces of winter, all gray, which he knew to be her natural color whether she wanted to admit that or not. She had put on weight since the last time they talked. She was full in the arms and face, like a sow holding more milk than her share. Her nails were painted peach, which meant they were painted almost the color of nothing. Her face was puffy at the bottom, but it was bright through all the lines. Like happy, to spite him.

Stavros tried to explain: no man's days were as questionable as his final ones. The days of a man's youth were half days, while the final days were overfull. The very last days told a man, and everyone else, and God, if the days leading up to his last days had been worth living in the first place. Couldn't she see that? And the point he was making? Never mind the car line for cappuccino. Was she listening? He said, "Come with me today, now, Carol."

Carol said, "I can't right now," and adjusted something on her mic. "You want something else? A pastry?"

"What pastry? Duty, I'm talking about." Is no woman going to give him what she should? "We are more than coffee. We are twenty-five years of coffee."

When they first met, he drank only instant—Nescafé, crystals that looked and tasted more like dirt than beverage. Carol made pot after pot of home brew, but he never drank it, and eventually she switched to instant, too. It was better that way. For them both, she whipped the Nescafé and sugar into a froth, and for years this was the only way he drank it. Then she got a job at Starbucks and switched to French press. He got a black mistress and switched to espresso. She divorced him, and he snuck back into the house to steal from her own kitchen the Greek cookbook he had given her on a birthday, because what was the need now for any Greek in her life?

Carol said, "I could get off a little early if you want to have dinner."

He tried again to make her understand what he was actually wanting. It was a very simple, pure thing, which he was confident he could make her realize. All I am asking, he tried again, is that you come with me to some few places *now*. You are always good at shopping; you are like expert at shopping; you are so good, you almost ruin me, you almost take over my whole life with shopping. No, you misunderstand, I am not meaning to fight with the past, I am only asking that you should make some visits with me today, some few arrangements. Very easy visits. We go to this funeral director. We look over a nice plot, something with a lot of grass. Then we share a meal. Not the diner, forget the diner. We go someplace special at the end.

She was smiling in a way that was compassionate and soft, so he thought he had gotten somewhere. She, the manager, would tell the employees to take care of the store, and she would get into his black used BMW and she would be his witness to these very important arrangements. They would eat together one final time. They would talk about where things went wrong and how, after all, he did work very hard in marriage and business and fatherhood, and she would start to understand things from his perspective, which was of a man with some certain troubles. Then he would drop her off at her white used Lexus, which he had bought for her, and they would end, if not as friends, as co-workers in a labor of life. But the soft smile was not for Stavros Stavros. She was talking into the headset and making apologies for him having car trouble. She was saying to the customers that Starbucks would have baristas come directly to car windows, if the customers could only be patient a few moments longer, and she was offering complimentaries to the angriest ones.

This is what a woman, his ex-wife, was like. He could see that to gain anything, he would need to get angry.

He cast the yellow flowers into the backseat, which he had been holding this whole time as if they were proof of his very good intentions. He said, "You want to come or no?"

She continued to talk, not to him. Always talk-talk, not to him. That was what was to blame for their marriage failings, not his mistress. For months, he had had to hear how he was not the man she wanted, that he would have to figure out exactly what she wanted and then become him. But to be that man, he would have had to become Starbucks. She was in love with Starbucks. Starbucks became more important than making him dinner or washing his clothes or having coffee together or going on cruises or listening to the problems of the diner or the daughters; it became a way for her to reinvent herself, which he did not see the point of. It gave her new friends, which he never trusted. It gave her purpose that had nothing at all to do with her children or Stavros. It gave her hope, which he did not understand or believe to be necessary in her case; it accused him as the reason for her hopelessness. He knew, before she had left him, that she would; he had seen the future of their divorce, just as he had seen the future truth that she would make top manager. Now, because of a dream and a goat, he saw the future again, one where he was dead and she making bigger and bigger boss, with all the hard work of their years together wasted!

He said, "You want pay? I pay you. That is nothing new to me." Then, "Or you."

Talk-talk.

Carol of twenty-five years ago would not recognize herself taking orders from strangers in this headset and man's black-collared shirt. She had stopped carrying her body for others and carried it now only for herself. This was admirable, in a way, but selfish, too, and hurtful, because for a long time she had dressed and carried herself as his wife. He put the car in drive and stared ahead. "It's always money with you." This made her push the headset away from her mouth. She started to talk, this time to answer him, but he interrupted. "I am talking about a dying wish, I am asking only a few hours, but you are only, as usual, for yourself. As usual, you are a thief of a man's life."

Carol shut her mouth. She changed what she was going to say. "Whatever you're planning, Steve, don't bother. I don't feel sorry for you."

"You don't believe me because you don't understand. But we don't choose when we go, we just go."

She went talk-talk about how she was trying to be friendly, she would have gotten food with him (food he would have to pay for!) but, as usual, he was only thinking about himself. She was moving her sow body away from him even as she spoke, her hands attentive to the drinks. She stirred someone else's coffee with more love than he had ever seen her stir his. She said, "Venti no-whip mocha."

"You want me to leave, good luck. Now I will just sit here and take as much time from you as you took from me my whole life."

Carol shoved something metallic and heavy, he could not see what. Her mouth was twisting, a sign of danger: you did not mess with her soul mate, Starbucks. He felt nervous, like he was about to receive a punishment he did not deserve, even though his anger was a reasonable thing: he would end up with a lap of something hot. He prepared to be scalded, even as he knew she was not that kind of woman. It took a man to punch holes into walls.

"You have final requests, Steve? Take them to your black bitch."

"Yes, that is where I will go, exactly as you say, and you can go straight to your black-coffee-bitch Starbucks."

Then he was leaving, he was gone from that Venti Mocha Whip-cream White Whore. He was like all those other Jersey nothing-no ones, trying to beat the traffic to the one place that would make him feel like a person that mattered, and that was far from his ex-wife the nothing-nobody Dick Hunter. Stavros parked his car. He adjusted his shirt, which had wrinkled out of anger. He used his palm to calm his hair and mouth. He reached into the back for flowers, still bright, only a petal or two damaged.

Stavros could hear Rhonda typing before he saw her. From the door, even sitting behind her desk, he could see how much space she took up. She was a big black lady. Her arms were the size of his thighs. Always, she had her hair arranged into shapes that told people—told him, the first time they met—that she was not weak. Her hair obeyed her, her hair was solid object. It made him want to touch it, and when he finally got to, it was all he could keep his hands on. *Ela*, except for her big breasts.

If the wife had continued to make herself up like this, he would not have gone looking for Rhonda. If the wife had looked less fat and more fatty, like steak, like ribs melting into honey, he would not be here; if she had just shut up sometimes and talked to him. He, himself, was getting fat, OK, but not too fat for a man of over fifty. The lines in his face like slits where you deposit pity. His eyes and his skin worn, maybe from smoking but more from stress, like maybe God had been rubbing an elbow over him too long. His hair, thinning and gray, like all of his brothers, some of whom were dead. His mustache, it was still impressive because it was not American, it was as Greek as democracy, it was the thing Rhonda first liked about him, but it was also graying. Now it is the tail of a powerful black ox, when once it was the tail of two powerful oxes! Yes, he was becoming old but, look, he could get a young business-professional mistress!

OK, not mistress, because he was nothing with his wife these days, but mistress because what he had with Rhonda still felt like something he had to keep from people.

Rhonda didn't look up until he slid a Styrofoam package onto the desk. "I come to bear gifts," he said. He meant sandwich, which he had not eaten in his rush to get to Starbucks.

"I ate, *malaka*. It's four o'clock."

"I know you. You're hungry."

He stared down at her, waiting to be invited closer. He placed the yellow flowers with the red centers where she could see them. Soon enough she turned her knees. That made him feel good, that he could get her to turn like that. He came around the corner of her L-desk and sat on some papers. He watched her navigating a computer older than his own. He knew she was secretary to somebody, but the way she conducted business, it was as if she were the one to be answered to.

"I don't know how long you expect me to live on Styrofoam for," she said.

The wrinkles in her skirt were deep, which meant she had been working all day. He liked that about Rhonda, that she worked as hard as he did, because if you worked hard it meant you loved hard. Carol only worked hard when her job replaced her husband; Carol had no love for him. Rhonda's problem was that she did not get enough love. She was tired of waiting. She did not want to live with her sister anymore just because some loser left her and their children behind. What she wanted was a big house together, what she wanted was a future for her sons. But the last thing he could give her, at fifty-three, was a marriage and a father. It smashed his heart, but she was not a wife he could take on his arm and walk through town, and the problem was she knew that now.

He pulled out the sandwich, which was soggy at one end. He tore it off for her, took a napkin out of his pocket.

"I deserve cloth napkins. And waiters. And wine."

He put the sandwich down and rested his short, strong hands on her shoulders. He knew what she wanted: to go out. Always, they spent time alone—here, at his apartment, at her sister's house when her sons were at a sleepover. Or else, with strangers, on planes or boats or in hotels. He covered himself with the half-truth that he was still getting used to being on his own. The other truth was that this was new for him, being with such a dark woman. Every time he brought his face to hers, he was surprised by how brown she was. The people he knew, they would see them together, and they would call him the soft white bread of the roast beef special. And was that any way to be seen? For any of them?

She was showing him how good she was at multitasking—typing and ignoring, waiting for the talking parts that would be useful to her. She was pushing her big knees up to the desk.

"What do you want?" he whispered, his mouth speaking into the gold earrings he had purchased. "Do you want another cruise? I can cruise you."

This was not a real offer, of course, but at one time it would have been. In the last year, he had spent much money on her: $10/month for the interracial dating site where they met. $300 here for a necklace, $300 there for shoes and clothes, $400 so she could fly down to her family reunion in Atlanta, $500 to fix her car. How much hundreds on meals together, how much monies for the twins, Henry and Miles, to play Little Leagues and Boy Scout. He didn't mind, because he had always wanted sons, he had always wanted to seem kind to children. He had wanted to like Henry and Miles; he had wanted Henry and Miles to like him. He was a good inspirational man to look up to, for two twin boys. And Rhonda returned what she cost, just like a woman, just like a partner should, not like his wife had been. He would never admit it, he knew it was not the way to think of someone you cared about, but he couldn't help himself: it was a way to see her as his equal. She was proud to be with a smart, successful Greek man, just like he was excited—so excited, he sometimes felt reduced to jiggling, jangling change—to be with a smart, achieving black woman.

He liked wooing her, liked realizing that even when he did not choose big women, he chose big women. Their fourth date, he felt all of her weight on him, letting him know just how gravity worked, reminding him that this way of being pressed down was another way of being held. What he felt with Carol, in the beginning, until it just felt like being pressed down.

He was still kneading Rhonda's shoulders, hoping this squeezy would lead to other squeezy. He was only a man. They had not seen each other in many days; this could be the last time, of his life, that he has sex. He did not like the idea of his organ softening in moist soil, and he was desperate that she should bring it to life. She should treat it like a waterless plant that is arching its stem toward moisture. Thinking about a coffin, which to his mind looked like a wooden crate for produce, and seeing himself lying naked in it, his dandelion losing color and shape after being left in the cold—it made him want everything at once: to be held, to penetrate her, to sob, to feel life dripping out of him, to feel life dripping into him, to climax and die, to confess the dream, to let her in and shut her out.

Rhonda pulled away to reach into the filing cabinet. She said, "You don't want a cruise. You want something cheaper than that." After two weeks, she was still mad with him.

He had taken her to Philadelphia—because all the people who would recognize him were in New Jersey, except for his daughter who was workaholic like him and, no question, at her restaurant—when they ran into someone he knew. It was in the old, cobbled streets of the city, on a road that had purported to be deserted. They were coming out of a cigar shop and the businessman was going in. Rhonda was standing so close to Stavros he could not get away. He could smell her fruity breath and felt the fabric of her coat brushing against his waist. "We work too hard," Stavros told the businessman. "A man should have fun sometimes." As if Rhonda were fun, takeout. As if she were not the woman of his life.

The man, a regular at the diner, gave a chuckle. "I hear you," he said.

Then he looked at Rhonda as if she were leftovers, and Stavros did nothing about it.

Rhonda watched the man leave, then she stepped onto the curb. Stavros, still in the street, was made to look up even higher at her and at the power lines swooping above. "You're about to work a lot harder," she said. She took a cab, would not return his calls.

The businessman idiot, he couldn't keep his mouth to himself.

Stavros was lonely, he missed her; she had a way of walking with him through the world that made him feel as if he had just gotten here; she made him feel like a child, and she was going to teach him how to hold a fork and look at trees. It should have been enough to beg her to come back. But Stavros was not familiar with begging. The businessman, he returned to the diner. Everything between them was the same except for one small order of business. He had always paid his checks, even if it was a sandwich, with fifties; now he had a funny way of paying with only small bills. This is how Stavros knew it was over with Rhonda. Even this late in his life, Death coming, he could not bring himself to be with such a woman. He could not walk with her on his arm or have her at his funeral.

Did that mean he was coward? No. Maybe. No.

He was a man who did not know how to be any other way in the world, even at the end.

Rhonda rolled her chair back. "You know I don't keep my boys waiting."

He had forgotten all about Henry and Miles and baseball practices. "Give them until five."

Rhonda was sliding a binder into a bag. She was putting on her blazer. "You mean give you until five."

Stavros helped her into the jacket with the intention of helping her get it back off. "Not me. Us." He ran his hands up her sides. The produce crate came to him. He buried his mouth into her neck, where it smelled like Sunday. She adjusted her jacket, her message that he was not going to get any squeezy squeezy.

She stopped at the door with her keys ready and he realized that what she was actually telling him was goodbye. He had seen this many times at the diner, some woman looking across the table, telling the man that their relationship was dead; he had faced it himself, of course—twice. But with Rhonda, it felt different. She took her time, never shy with her eyes. This look was the look she might leave on his grave. Yes, she loved him. No, even now he could not return that look. He could not say, Let me give you my remainings of the day.

He said, "Take to them the chicken sandwich, at least." He put it back in its container, happy it was cut in half, one equal part for each boy.

She would not let him walk her out, made him leave while she locked up. He watched her from his car. He smoked, she flipped down the mirror for lipstick. He watched her smooth her hair. She always looked nice for her sons. He hoped God was not too busy to see what a lovely woman she was. The one thing he had always known about her: she never needed him. In that way, she was superior to him.

He thought back to the first time they met, an expensive restaurant an hour away, in Delaware. He got there early, she got there on time. He stood when she arrived, kissed her cheek. That night she was in a skirt, too, and a shirt cut low, which made him order a bottle. Only, he did not like her name, which to him sounded like a man's. He could not make an easy, pretty nickname of it.

"You like merlot?" he asked, waving the waiter over.

"I like it all," she said.

He felt giddy when the waiter filled their glasses. He did not look up at the man, partly to show that he was more society and partly because he did not want to see what the man thought about these two people, one white and one black, on a first date off the internet. She sipped the wine without bringing it up to her nose. He showed her how it was done. "I know about wine," he said, "because I am from the country where all of the songs are about wine."

She asked him where that was. "Your accent," she said, "it's very strong. I like that."

He told her about Greece and enjoyed how her eyes lit up at the emerald-blue water, the islands carved out of marble, the summer lovers, landscapes as early as breakfast and long as sunbathing. Introducing her to this paradise, he felt as if he had been the one to make it. "I will take you one day," he told her. "I can show you everything." Oh, he meant it. Wanted to. He could be one of the Richie Riches and spend money on one good time for them both.

She laughed with her mouth open, like a Greek. He was surprised by her teeth, the space between them, the way he felt he could fit his whole body inside, and how it had made him want her even as it made him nervous, cautious. His wife did not have space between her teeth for him. His wife, even when they first met, when they pressed against each other inside two beers and a crowd, did not make him feel swallowed whole the way Rhonda did. Rhonda talked a lot. She told him about her dream to be a travel agent and her night classes and her nine-year-old sons. She told him she had no time for small men.

"It's all over your eyes. I saw it the minute I came in." She laughed. "Don't be afraid of the bigness, Steve. Sometimes, bigness brings joy."

But a man like Stavros Stavros Mavrakis cannot have joy for very long. His entire life has been leading him toward the end of things. He has and has not written his end into being. His decision on the email letter to his family, it only points at the sun through the clouds. He sees the sun but cannot make it stay through the night, any night, no matter how he tries.

He is not planning his death—that is not the right way to explain it. He is Sweeping Away the Hay and Cockroaches from the Floor of Destiny. He is Thawing the Meat of What Is To Be. He is aware of death the way you might try to become aware of the wolf in the forest, only to understand that the wolf has long been aware of you. He is not sure that God will meet him halfway or any way. So far, it is clear that you take maybe one, two steps with someone, and then you make the rest of the journey alone; it could be that Stavros will make it to heaven to find out that he is the only one there. But would that be so different from this crowded life, where you were left to yourself?

This was it, the final nail in the crate.

Rhonda's car pulled out of the parking lot. Stavros watched until it became confused with all of the other cars. Since his arrival to this country—this state—over thirty years ago, he has never gotten over how many cars can be on one road and how, in those cars, day after day, most people are driving with no one beside them. This, plus the sun quickly moving away from him, reminded Stavros that he would spend tonight alone. Then he thought of the goat.

He parked in the back of the diner, as usual. No one came outside. The goat sat on its curled haunches, as if it were a cat.

"I am home," he said.

The goat did not flinch. It accepted a Saratoga with its long tongue.

"Do you know the evil three, goat? θάλασσα καὶ πῦρ καὶ γυνή. Sea and fire and women."

The goat raised its head.

"Good you only have to worry about number one or two." He squatted in the darkness some feet away. He smoked. "These women, goat, they are killing me to death."

The goat settled down again. This one sympathy was exactly what Stavros needed.

Dusk began to mask their surroundings. It made Stavros feel as if he were in another time—first his childhood, the village, and then, staring at the goat, its head more formation than skull, he could have been a shepherd in another lifetime, isolated on a mountain with his flock and a purse of dried meat, a knife, a flute.

Stavros was quiet. He felt satisfied, for a few moments, that there was no one to talk to.

If We are who We are supposed to be on the outside, We are who We are supposed to be on the inside.

CHAPTER 3

Stavroula answered her father's email: with love.

And food, of course.

In the cramped white office, Mr. Asbury sat. Out of respect, she stood. She could hear blades, searing from the kitchen, the sous yelling about cross-contamination. He was fastidious, which she liked. Under it all, the vacant hum of the nearby ice machine. The middle of a dinner rush on a Saturday, and she had insisted that they talk now. No, it couldn't wait. Her new seasonal menu—her answer to her father—was going out tomorrow. It was printed on cream-colored paper in an embossed font that you expected to taste like crème brûlée.

Mr. Asbury mouthed consonants as he read, his thin legs hooked around a stool. He was all brow and snowy arm hair. His eyes were fin-blue, like his daughter July's, his skin pink. He was a father first, and a businessman second. Never a dictator. Nothing like her own father. Mr. Asbury would have never sent an email like the one she received, but Mr. Asbury also would not have made a good cook, having none of her or her father's bullheadedness and intuition. Mr. Asbury was a wonderful boss. He respected Stavroula, acknowledged her as a person and an artist and a partner. He trusted her to do right by Salt. He had recruited her for his restaurant two years ago. Stavroula had not yet made up her mind about how long to stay—she had a history of moving from one kitchen to the next—but there were things keeping her here. Such as, she had exclusive creative control of her kitchen. Reading the menu, Mr. Asbury knew that.

Like last Easter: the only thing Stavroula would serve was lamb—roasted on a spit in full view of the diners—with Smyrna figs and

htipiti, a feta spread garnished with red pepper. Fixed menu, no altera-
tions, no starchy sides. One long table that seated everyone. Strangers sharing the holiest meal, eating with their hands or they could go
someplace else. And he saw how well that went, so. She got her way
because she did not give up, and because she fought only for what was
absolutely necessary for survival and good food, which were the same
thing. She had only ever lost once, and that time it was July who had
said no, and Stavroula took it. No fish heads in the *psarosoupa*, July, no
problem. But Stavroula would win today. Love would.

For over a year, she had been in love with July. Had done nothing
about it, the only thing in her life she didn't seize. Until now. She felt
for the printed email in her pocket. It was strange that in this moment
of exposure—probable judgment—the email from her father would
come as a comfort. The ice machine trickled, gurgled, which she felt at
the back of her own throat. Not that she'd show it.

Mr. Asbury said in his soft, courting voice, "Even this one?"

"July."

"The spicy pork tacos?"

"July."

"Crab cakes?"

"Late July."

July Angel Hair served alongside Tarragon Lime Bay Scallops.
Roasted July Poblanos with Cashew Chipotle Sauce. Classic Chicken
Salad with Red Grapes and Smoked Almonds: For July. July galette.
That one she would layer with leeks, zucchini, and green chilis, topped
with a creamy, tangy *avgolemono* sauce. It's not just that she added July
to all of the names of the dishes: that would have meant nothing. July
was the inspiration for every flavor combination. *If everything's July*, Mr.
Asbury might say, *then what's July?* But then, he did not understand
the full complexity that was July. For that matter, neither did Stavroula.
For that matter neither did the ex, Mike, who, until six months ago,
had ordered items not listed on the menu and barged into Stavroula's
kitchen and used his fingers around her plates. These days, Mike was
just a customer. He ordered off the menu and didn't come into the

back. That was the first indication that July was done with him. Maybe all men.

Mr. Asbury's lips puckered into an asterisk. No, a whisk. "I don't understand, Stevie."

She did not answer. Which between them meant, *Yes, you do.*

It was Marina who had taught Stavroula about naming dishes— how it was like slipping a key into a lock: most fit, but only the right one could make the door swing open and the eater enter. It was Marina who had taught Stavroula to take herself seriously—what she wanted, what she needed to be. *You can be a vessel,* koukla—she had taught her years ago—*as long as you know what you're meant to carry.*

Mr. Asbury was hesitant, kind, when he chuckled. Telling Stavroula what she already knew without saying it: she was intense. So what. How did he think her food got its flavor? A few months ago when he slipped a little extra pocket money into her apron for her birthday, what had she bought? Japanese salt, one of only thirty-two batches. And did she take it home? No, she used it in his pots.

"Stevie, you're asking me to name food after my daughter?"

"I'm not asking you to name anything, John."

She was doing the naming here. And she did not want to name food after July: she wanted to name her every creation, from now through summer, after July. Maybe into winter. What women want, more than anything, is honest and intent flattery, which means if you want to pursue a woman you have to show her you know her, see her, nothing less. No, that wasn't it. You have to prove that you will try over and over to know her. Understand this: at any time a woman's appetite can change. Maybe she's hungry for more, maybe she's had enough. A woman, like a meal, is a complex, evolving creation.

In the chaos of the kitchen, filling orders, Stavroula showed him a mousseline, a delicate savory composite of pureed shrimp and cream that enhanced the briny sweetness and plump bite of crabmeat. She removed the crabmeat from the bowl of chilled milk, the ice machine still going, but she didn't hear it anymore. She blitzed six ounces of shrimp, plus cream and Old Bay, some Dijon, hot sauce, fresh lemon.

Pureeing the shrimp releases sticky proteins that delicately hold the clumpy pieces of crabmeat together, she told him. Coat in toasted panko, cook patties until golden brown.

"No egg? No filler?" He smiled. "What, we're too sophisticated for that now?"

"There's nothing filler about your daughter."

Only the sous-chef raised his eyes at this. She didn't care, and the rest of them were intimidated by her, they wouldn't dare look. Mr. Asbury blinked several times until he settled on, "I agree." But it was clear he was not agreeing with her. Enough: she would make him eat. Stavroula plated the crab cakes and squirted an accompanying swirl of wasabi-avocado sauce. She used her fingers to confirm what she already knew. Perfect. Maybe some lemon peel. She added a little salt for crunch and also because salt, in Greek folklore, got rid of unwanted guests. Such as her father.

If it were her father she needed to convince, it would have translated into *This door is locked and so is the window.* But with Mr. Asbury, it was more like a fence she could hop over. There were footholds, if you trusted your weight to it. She imagined herself trying to explain to her father who July was, what she deserved. He would turn around and tell her what she deserved. He would say she was doing this to spite him, and in this instance he would be right. *Let me explain you something*, she would answer back. It was time for her to be who she was on the outside so she could be who she was supposed to be on the inside. It had only taken thirty-one years.

Mr. Asbury broke into the glossy crab cake with his fork. His expression was softening, like meat defrosting. Cooking with someone, you got to learn how they think. What he thought was, the menu would sell. Still—"You want my approval on this?"

"Not approval." She made herself—made herself—look at him. Ice and everything. Email, everything. "Your blessing."

Mr. Asbury was first to break away. He tried, quietly, "What about flowers? Her mother always liked yellow tulips."

"I'm not good at flowers, John."

In her life he was the one person who had ever gotten her flowers, roses after she landed him a solid review in *The Philadelphia Inquirer*, and they lasted ten minutes in the vase. Moments later, she was boiling them down to rosewater. She did not try to reassure him that she had been grateful; he saw it in the rosewater pudding she made exclusively for him, after-hours.

Mr. Asbury didn't know how to handle this kind of demand about his own daughter. Or from a woman. He was trying to protect July, but also Stavroula. They had never spoken it aloud, but Stavroula knew that Mr. Asbury must suspect her feelings. She remembered the first time she caught him catching her, though he may have seen it even sooner than that. July had come in to post the new weekly schedule. She addressed the evening's waitstaff in a long black skirt, which exposed her calf, the most Stavroula had ever seen of July, not counting her bare, long, thin arms. The rest of her calf, Stavroula could imagine: white as batter. That was when Stavroula felt Mr. Asbury's eyes on her. She double-checked. Had they taken actual inventory? They had. Did he know? Yes. Stavroula went directly to the ice machine and plunged her hand in. It drained the pink from her face and soon enough her fingers took on the texture of rubbery poultry.

Mr. Asbury had picked up the menu and was rubbing it between two fingers as if it were oregano.

"Stevie, nobody does this. Nobody wants it done to them."

"Maybe they do," she said, drawing back. Then, because it was him, she admitted, "I don't know how to give less."

July at breakfast, July at lunch. July half-price appetizers with a summer ale, when everyone feels relief that the hard hours of the day are done and looks forward to the final amber hours of the evening with gratitude and ease. The waiters would relay to the kitchen: July. Their order slips would be filled with July. Trash cans would be filthy with July, stomachs full of July. When the order was up, Stavroula's assistants would ring a bell and their sentences would all start with July. Stavroula's entire world would be July, as it was already, in a way. July would walk into July and feel—stunned, flattered, maybe desire the size of a pea. Which is all that Stavroula needed.

"If I say no, that means you'll walk?"

"Do you want to say no?"

Mr. Asbury adjusted himself on the stool. "She'll think this is my idea."

"You can tell her it isn't."

"You ought to tell her it isn't."

Stavroula bunched up the side of her apron. "You're right. I'll explain it to her."

The email—that was the thing pushing her, from its place in her white apron that had only ever seen utensils. The letter was this *one small thing that can change everything*. It was this *Let me explain you something* that had been explaining to her, all night, what she needed to do. It had appeared in her in-box some time around midnight, addressed to all of the women in her family, and each time she read it she told herself it would be the last time. At four, she left her bed and her bull terrier, Dumpling. The blankets were a scramble. She started to email him a response. Instead, she rewrote her entire menu.

Fuck her hair.

DAY 8

Denial

God has to exist, because He is the only one who can do for You.
We cannot do for You.

CHAPTER 4

The alarm registered in razor-green flashes, one grinding wail blaring into the next, like spreadsheets opening within spreadsheets opening within spreadsheets, all of them inventorying her faults in a code that everyone tried to read but no one but her actually could. 10:31, she was officially thirty-one minutes late for work. 10:43, Litza answered Rob's call. Of course it was him, who else was looking for her on a Sunday morning? Not her ex-husband—and not her friends, who were too fucked up for her these days, or too stuck on rehab repeat.

Could Rob blame her for sleeping in? No one should have to work insurance on Sundays in an office located on a street called Industrial Complex Row, but Litza herself had elected to work Sundays so that a) she could work from home three other days a week; b) none of the supervisors would be there to correct her when what she was doing was right to begin with; c) how would they know if she was doing it wrong, anyway? d) none of the cunts she worked with would be in to outpace her; e) Sunday was the Lord's day to do with what she wanted; f) Sunday was actually an ambitious track for someone in her field, this was a way to get promoted, fuck her father that he thought she had no ambition; and g) Rob was fun. But this Sunday there were already a hundred E-100s to sort—all the leftover ones from the morning she and Rob went for pancakes.

What she could not handle today was mass denials.

Rob wanted to know, "Yo, you want to come grace us with your unhealthy presence?"

She could have reached the clock to turn off the alarm but didn't.

She said, "I'm not asking for that much, Robby. Just the pending sterilizations."

The pending sterilizations he could do in his sleep, just like her, he joked. That wasn't the issue, the pendings. The issue was it was a gorgeous Sunday. He had made them eggplant parmesan. Well, bought it from Carmen's. She should come in, they'd kill the pendings and walk to the park for lunch. Yo, it was a beautiful day. The swans might be at the lake.

It was almost enough—this surprise of lunch, a promise of swans. It was his wanting that she wanted, the hard work of a nineteen-year-old eager for a woman in her late twenties to notice him, which made her, she realized, not all that different from her father. How could she ever take seriously a man—OK, kid—who wanted only to please her? She said, "You just have to run them as a batch appeal. It's quick." Knowing he'd cave.

She should have been promoted already, a jump from pay scale 4 to pay scale 6, whatever that was supposed to mean. Every job gave you aggravation, but at least here she didn't have to be nice and pray that her niceness would get her somewhere. Here, it was brains and quotas, except that, before too long, here was just like everywhere else and they held off on the promotion when the cunts reported Litza talking on her cell during work hours. Thereafter she had to watch her back, that was the moral of the workplace, any workplace. Rob she could trust, because Rob she knew how to handle. But the cunts, they were the type to complain to the supervisors about how she spoke to customers and how she needed to ask colleagues for things differently, when Litza didn't understand why the question had to be different if the answer was going to be the same regardless. She could say, "Is it pharma 636, cunt?" or she could say, "Is it pharma 636?" and the cunt would have to confirm it was or it was not 636. The dumbest people surrounding her, exactly like the ones who stood up at graduation to interrupt the dean, who was handing out associate's degrees. Litza had been the only one listening to the dean's remarks, she had been paying attention about how to get ahead, because she was smart. Her father couldn't see this. Her father had refused to come.

Watch your back was the moral of family, too, of course, but that she learned early.

"I'm going through some family shit right now, Robby." He wasn't mad—if there was one thing he respected, it was being there for your family. He did whine like a baby for another minute, though. She promised that she'd be able to cover for him when his boys came into town, but knew she wouldn't have to because he wouldn't ask.

She went back to sleep. The second time she woke, it was to push the alarm off its shelf. The third time, it was voice mail pinging at her ear. She sat up to listen: *Litza, ah, you and I have some things. To talk on together.* Pause, laugh. *Are you not answering because you have my email letter there in front of you?* Pause. *I know I have forbid you from the diner, but it is OK now that you come when there is not too much time.*

She should send him a letter of her own final wishes. *Dear Dad: Let me explain you. Don't write me letters, don't leave any more fucking messages.*

But that was not her actual final wish. Her actual final wish would have nothing to do with her father.

A baby.

Even if all she had left to spend with it was ten days. Or one day. That would be enough for her, God. If He—obviously He—were listening. One day is too much to ask? God?

She brushed her teeth. She applied makeup that she did not need. Her unblemished skin made her appear tender, which was sometimes true. Her eyes were smoky brown with flecks of blue—where did those come from? No one in her family had eyes like hers. Often, when she got what she wanted, it was because of those eyes, large and intense and giving the unlikely impression that she was interested in what was spilling out of your mouth. Her hair was smoky, too, her hair was also her own; it surprised even Litza that her hair was not dark like Stavroula's. But, whatever, she was skinny, and her boobs were perky, undeniably Greek. They were the reason every boy she'd ever been with called her his Greek Goddess, and she never confessed that the nickname had been used up already. She threw on a zebra-print shirt, slipped into some heels, added silver hyperbola earrings. The earrings, she had made herself.

One occasion—her wedding—Litza made jewelry for all of the women in her family. Now Litza made jewelry exclusively for strangers, people who, after visiting her online store, thought her an artist. Her family did not know the store existed—did not know she was an artist. At the moment she was into cement, had designed a pair of teardrop earrings that, truthfully, she could see on Stavroula. Before cement, there had been the copper phase, and before that, sterling silver. She liked working at 750-degree temperatures, did not yet trust herself with gold. Her jewelry was simple, modern, surprisingly the least complicated thing in her life and in no way representative of the jumble in her head. If she tried to go ornate, the piece said *enough*, and demanded she loosen up, and she got out of the way. That was why people were willing to sometimes pay for her hobby. Over the last few years, it was this hobby that brought Litza praise—some almost inexplicably generous. Many nights those online reviews were what got her to sleep, and then what got her to wake up two hours before work so she could heat up the soldering iron and discover what shape the next piece would take. The side money she was earning was almost enough to book a flight to Greece, finally give her a break from every fucking thing and person bringing stress into her life.

Litza opened the minifridge. The full-sized fridge had overheated or whatever coils did when they sizzled then crackled to death, and the landlord had posted a note to her door, *Fridge's luxury not necessity, see lease, but you can borrow this for now*, and replaced the refrigerator with what might as well have been a cooler. You could keep eggs, butter, orange juice in it, some leftovers, vegetables, or you could keep, as she did, one bottle of soda and a tray of mealy pasta. She went to the diner.

Her father owned two diners, but she knew which one he meant. Her family always went to the Gala I; it was their second home. She hadn't been to the other diner in years—some unlucky subordinate ran the Gala II and reported back to her father. The Gala I was the only thing going on in town, other than Diamond Lady, the purple warehouse strip joint so infamous that it had been on daytime talk shows.

When they were teenagers Litza's friends had filled out applications to work at Diamond Lady, but Litza had refused to set foot inside even as a joke.

Her drive to the diner took only seven minutes because she lived in the same shitty town. She got out of the car and flicked her cigarette, half-smoked. She winced at the glare from the diner, proudly covered in stainless steel. Her father liked to brag how, of the six hundred diners founded by Greeks from Philadelphia to New York between 1950 and 1983, the Gala I was the best.

The hostess kept her eyes away from Litza's face like she didn't want any trouble, and Litza kept staring her down simultaneously like *a) You're not worth any trouble* and *b) If I want to, I will,* even though the girl looked perfectly sweet. Litza slunk into the same booth where, as children, she and Stavroula talked about eating so much candy that they would be able to replace their teeth with gold ones; Litza had snuck to the front and stolen the metal dish of dinner mints from the cashier, and they packed them into their mouths like extra teeth. No one in America had so many gold teeth as they were planning, until Stavroula gave in to something that Litza did not feel and brought the mints back.

Litza swallowed a half-mg of Xanax dry. The diner was shiny and right. Mirrors all over the place. And, for some reason, a statue of a Greek goat god, which had been here her entire life. The dessert case next to the hostess station was a temple; the glass was clean, not in shards as it was the last time when, as her father noted in his letter, she smashed it with a stool. Cakes were whole, not all over the floor, and Stavros was not instantly on his knees to gather the mess away from the eyes of the customers. That was the image of her father she would take to her grave, him on his knees sweeping all of the wet crumbs toward him, icing clinging to his bare forearms like Spackle. She would die with that vision of him, she was sure of it. What is the point, Dad, of gathering what's ruined?

He knew she was here. He could come to her.

She flipped through the menu so that she did not have to meet anyone's eye. It had gotten longer since she last looked. The menu promised, *We never close, New Jersey! (Or, New York, or—anywhere you are Coming from!) Always, we are here for you, Twenty-four/Seven. Just like home.* Then, page after page of diner items like pork roll, egg & cheese. Halfway through the menu, two full pages of welcome; in paragraph form, her father explained his philosophy behind every dish and its connection to the homeland. *We Eat a Little, We have some Wine (BYOB), We thank the Cook. Sincerely, Your Greek Family.*

That's when Litza saw Toast Delight. Surrounded by self-respecting dishes was the concoction of warm milk and cereal and chocolate, the only meal she had ever actually seen her father prepare at home. It stunned her to see something so private listed at $7.50 and "New!" As children, Toast Delight excited and disgusted them. They forced their way into the kitchen, led by Mother, to gawk as their father poured milk into a bowl of frosted flakes smothered in Hershey's syrup and chocolate chips and graham crackers, topped with refined sugar, and then boiled it in the microwave for a good two minutes. It was more porridge than toast, but porridge to him was white and tasteless. *Toast Delight*, he called it, *because if I say cereal, you think cold.* Toast, they all called it. They squealed. Did he wink at her, at them, every time the buzzer went off?

Litza did not want to admit it, but she had always wanted to try it. She was pretty sure that Stavroula had wanted to try it, too. *Dear Dad: How about some Toast Delight?*

It was Marina, not her father, who appeared at the table with a pot of coffee. She stuffed herself into the booth. Without saying hello, she poured coffee and dribbled creamer into Litza's mug. It was the generic, pale drip that no one in Litza's family drank but Litza. Even Marina liked Greek sludge, so this "American spit" coffee, as Marina referred to it, was something of a peace offering. Marina saying, *No hard feelings*, because this was the first she was seeing Litza since the post–wedding cake display. Marina saying, *It's OK you come into my house and break my things. It's OK you keep the wedding gift even though you end your marriage one week later.* Like all Greeks, Marina loved being in a benevolent position to forgive: it got her off. In the card, Marina had written *To a new life* and included a check for two hundred dollars. It was a significant gift, one that suggested that maybe Marina actually cared about Litza, but that possibility disappeared as fast as the money when Litza cashed the check.

"Your father, Litza, he is sick?" Marina was stirring the coffee like that might make it stronger.

"You would know, you see him every day," Litza said. "I haven't seen him in a year."

With two fingers, Marina summoned a waitress. "The big baby, whining about life again. Let's give a little more work for him to whine over. Two egg plates with home fries. Scramble for this one. For me, fry the eggs until the yolk is dead. If they are wet at all, they go right back. Tell him not to screw it up."

Though she had known Marina all her life, it was the first time Litza had ever seen her talk to a waitress. "You're such a bitch when you order." The first smile.

Marina winked. "You can fix anything in the kitchen unless it's burned or unless it's eggs. Or unless it is your father with his crazy ideas."

Litza felt a prickle with *father*. What were Marina's intentions?

Not for the first time, Litza wished that around everyone's neck was a name tag, and this name tag was in a plastic sleeve to protect it from dirt and spills; and typed beneath the person's name should be a diagnostic code—such as those from the *International Classification of Diseases* (ICD–9), to which she had to refer every day and so knew intimately and irrevocably—and that these codes defined what a person needs and what they're hiding so they aren't forced to say and you aren't expected to decipher. In a crisis, they're just given what they need and you're immediately clued into what the hell is going on.

Marina's name tag would read 401.9 for Hypertension with a few postscripts like Prying Dramatic Hysterical Old Greek Woman and Stubborn Racist Spinster. And Self-Righteous Judge. That, she shared with Stavroula.

Litza said, "Did he send you to deal with me?"

"I send me." Marina's big arms, folded across her bigger chest.

"You saw the email."

"Of course."

"You get one, too?"

"No, no letter for Marina. Add Marina, and the email goes on and on forever. Your father has too many women to keep track of as it is. Marina is just the hired help."

Marina was not just the hired help. Marina was pretending to have no loyalty to Stavros, and everyone—Stavroula, even—could believe it, but never Litza. Marina had her hand in every pot. They both knew why Litza was here. He had called for her, he was going to recite all the problems listed in the letter, all the things wrong with her, and part of her wanted to sit here until he said them to her face, and that same part of her wanted to sit longer, beyond that. Marina was priming her. Marina was sent out to see if she'd break any more dessert cases.

"What is it you want to say to me, Marina?"

Marina took a long sip of the shit coffee. "Is your father right about Stavroula?"

"You read the letter."

Marina waved her hands dramatically, making the air around them talk along with her. "Everybody has to forget the letter, Stavroula especially. You, especially."

"Why?"

"Because it is wrong." Her stewy eyes flicked once, twice over Litza. "Isn't it?"

Before Litza had a chance to respond, they both saw Stavros making his way through the restaurant, eyeing Marina and Litza as if he did not want them to leave before he reached them. He was waving down Kelly the waitress. He was touching a young customer on the cheek and checking to see that Litza caught this. Litza and Marina could have gone back to talking, but they watched him. Until Marina said, "Your father is the kind of man who needs to be cut with cream. Women like you and me, we know exactly how to cut him. You make him forget this dying business, Litza."

At Marina's insistence, Stavros sat down and took over her cup. The waitress came and dropped the plates, and he took over her breakfast, too. He rubbed his knee. He watched Marina head back to the kitchen. Then he turned to Litza. "Want some milk? To drink?"

Litza almost said yes. This close, she saw how bottom-heavy his face had become. His jaw looked like a fossil. Where was the rage of the 301.3 Explosive Personality she recalled so vividly? Where was the 301.3 that had been threatening them all their lives?

"You like the dessert case? Better than the first, even. We call her my Show Off case."

"You never replaced the stool." It had a rip in it. Litza recognized its lightning pattern.

He turned to see the stool, the fat man perched on it, said, "We keep it for memories."

She followed his eyes, which she knew to be as alert as bear traps. She realized his question about milk had been genuine. He writes a letter about her barren life, and then asks if she wants milk? What does he want her to do with milk, when he's never once, in living memory, given her any? The amount of milk he's never offered her, she could spoil in it.

"How is work?"

"I quit."

"Quit? What kind of quit?"

"The kind where you leave and never come back."

"You mean fired?"

"No. Quit."

He grunted. He busied his mouth, then tapped his fork at the edge of her plate. "That is not true. You would have order something bigger if you have no money for food. Somethings To Go." He knew her quitting was a bluff. He smiled to say, Let me in on the joke.

They were eating together. They hadn't done that since the night of the wedding, after which they danced father-daughter, after which he loaded the extra alcohol into the back of the car and kissed her on the cheek. The morning of the wedding, he made her cry over money. But that was not why she smashed his original Show Off dessert case.

"I can see that you have trouble with my email."

She watched him wipe his mouth three times. Finally, he was here.

Finally, so was the Xanax. It spread over her lap like a warm napkin. She said, "No, not really."

"OK, but your face, it says to me you have difficulty knowing what I say. It takes a long time to put my thoughts together, so it is good you come see me in person." He ate some more, nodded. "There is too much of one life to fit in one letter, is why."

"What did you call me for?"

Stavros paused. His forearms were propped against the table, his fists loosely curled. He opened his mouth, closed it. He said, "To have lunch with your father."

He said *lunch* as if it were a weekly occasion, as if they had done this when she were a little girl when in reality he did everything he could not to be around her. He casually mentioned *lunch*. He put together *lunch* and *father* as if they weren't the banging of pots and pans that frightened away strays. Even through the haze that sat on her tongue like a pad of melting butter, Litza felt the anger, the nostalgia for evil words he used to spout. His death, it should have been her idea. But even this she felt at a distance, because of the Xanax. She stared at his sagging clavicle. How was he so weak all of a sudden? She put down her fork.

"Why did you call me and not Stavroula?"

"Your sister, she will come around. But you"—he used his fork to gesture—"I think you take a little more consoling." By consoling, he meant cajoling.

Litza said, "What else could you possibly have to say to me?"

"Nothing about the past, only the future." He said, "After we finish here, I have an *oraio* book for you in the back. Which it is called"—he closed his eyes for the title—"*To Live Until We Say Good-bye.*"

She laughed. *Dear Dad: You are ridiculous.*

He frowned, the first one for her today, which was satisfying. She thought about telling him that the only lesson he had ever taught her, anyway, was that Living was Goodbye, but she was caring less and less. He was getting more perturbed than she was.

"OK," he said, "there is one thing you can do for me." He pulled a magazine from his pocket. It was turned to the Premier Coffin

Selection page. The coffin he pointed to was very distinguished mahogany. "They have coffins made of cardboard, even leaves. They try to sell me one of banana leaf for biodegradable." He chuckled again. "I tell them only the best for Stavros Stavros Mavrakis. Something solid, strong. Who cares about environment at a time of a man's death? They don't understand. My English is not so good for this strange type of thing. You can call them for me, give my order."

He was full of shit, her father. He was not dying. She could not imagine him in a coffin. He would be staring at her the way he was now, waiting for her to acquiesce. She tried to imagine him cremated, but all she got was cigarette ash, and that wasn't right, either. That was too much a daily part of her life.

"Do they know you're making it all up?"

He frowned again. "Listen, Litza, your father, he is not anything if he is a joke."

He got up, crossed to her side of the booth. She was slow to interpret what was happening, did not recognize what he was doing until it was too late, and she was penned in. She had never known him to sit next to her unless they were at the counter and he was ignoring her to talk to customers and associates. Like this, they were as close as they had been for the father-daughter dance, only not touching, and not for other people watching. She did not like seeing the saggy, wrinkled skin of his arms, the way the watch loosened his wrist.

Dear Dad: Don't sit so close.

She used to think about hurting him. She used to revel in what it would be like to put lit cigarettes very close to his eyes, because she thought that he would have done the same to her if it weren't for the two or three obstacles in his way. She had wished his death many times.

She said, "I have to get to work." Coming was a mistake.

"Now listen to me. This is important."

She was embarrassed and alarmed at the tears in his eyes. She saw him look away first. *Dear Dad: Too late.*

Who was this wrinkled, almost gentle person? What had happened to the man who was more volcano than father? Had he gone dormant, reduced to a slumbering mound? Had the dangerous lava become

nothing but rock and, at worst, souvenir? Were there flowers and spar-
rows nesting somewhere on his old, sensitive skin? Was this why he
wanted a funeral? Because he wanted one last chance at Vesuvius, and
otherwise he was some quaint Greek village mountain?

"We can choose these things together," he said. He reached out to
put a hand on hers.

She said, "Let me out." She felt a tear in the shape of lightning run
through her. She was sure she was going to scream, and go for the stool
with the scar, and push off the fat man, and ram its metal legs through
the angelic bakery case.

He saw this. He shifted across the booth's fake leather bench in fits.
She waited until he was standing before she pulled herself up.

He said, quietly, "You want to go to the back? I help you, you help
me a little?" He was rubbing the air with his thumb as if imagining that
it was the back of her arm, just above the elbow; or he was actually rubbing her arm and to her it felt like nothing.

Dear Dad. "You want to know what they should bury you in? A
hole."

She left him to finish his eggs. She buttoned her jacket and kept
buttoning even after it was clasped.

The odor of incense does not tell you what, it tells you when. It speaks to the time when smell will be all that's left of you.

CHAPTER 5

———

Ever since his vision of death, the smell of incense has been on him. It comes at the moments Stavros Stavros Mavrakis least expects it, and then disappears with no explanation.

The Goat of Death was what brought the bad news that death would come. The goat appeared first to Stavros in a dream, which he considered a nightmare, and then the next day it showed up at his diner, even more of a nightmare.

He was in bed, cold, with no woman but plenty of woman troubles, and he was dreaming of home. His Crete, his island, which he had not seen in some months, which missed him as much as he missed it, which was going through a very tough time economically without people like him. At the top of a gray peak was a white church that, from his place at the base of the mountain, looked like a rib poking out of the earth. Next to the church was a white goat exactly the same size as the church. He blinked once and then, because he was dreaming, Stavros was next to the goat and the church; actually, he was beneath the goat and having to stare up at its dirty chin. The goat smelled like dirt and incense. The goat looked out with eyes as lifeless as one-dollar bills and the same green. There were no shepherds on the goat's mountain. There were not even bodies in the graves behind the church.

The goat pounded the hard dirt with its hooves. It was very strange and scraping, a shovel noise. The smell of incense got stronger, and a smoky cloud appeared above the goat's head. All around him, Stavros felt a Stavros-shaped hole being made by the hooves, as well as a God-shaped one because God was not here for him. And while he didn't feel anything of the hooves on his face where they struck, he did feel himself being pushed and buried. The earth opened. His own last breath was coming to him. It sounded like a gurgle, a sound too tiny for his whole life.

Stavros went down shouting, *Wait, Death! You must give me more time!*

The goat listened, the incense hung in the air. The goat struck the ground ten times. It was hard, like stone on metal, blacksmith's work. Ten times, ten days. This was what he was being given.

In the morning, Stavros woke up and said to the nobody sharing his bed, "That is one crazy dream I would not even want my mother to know about." He took care of regular business—bills, phone calls, sitting with the old man who came only for soup six days a week. But all day he was unable to help himself, looking at calendars and at his reflection in the display case, adding up all the hours left between now and—he snorted—ten days from now. But the day wore on, and mostly he forgot. Then Marina, when he was reading today's paper, undid him. Marina, the one person he could never fire, the person who could almost fire him, said, "There is a goat here for you, Stavro."

"Who goat?" He stood. "Don't say the word *goat*."

The Goat of Death was back, on his property. The goat was early!

"You want me to take care of it for you? A nice goat stew?"

No, no, no, he had to take care of it. Stavros said, "Give me the biggest knife you have."

"You, who is afraid of meat when it's frozen. You have to earn a knife like that, Stavro. Get yourself a little trap from the trap store, or better to let Marina handle it."

He was not afraid of meat, frozen or not: he was as much cook as she, almost. But he was afraid of this goat. He could not let anybody know that. "I bring you a new special tonight, goat all ways."

"Goat no ways," she answered back.

She shuffled off from him, insolent. She gave him that slanted bun on top of her head, the wet rag on her arm, the big white exclamation points of her calves in their black work sneakers, which were somehow like slippers. That big fat Greek-woman ass in its gray skirt, like if it was meat product.

On the wide top step in front of the diner's glass doors, Stavros and the goat faced off, only the goat was not facing off, only scavenging. Stavros knew immediately and was calmed: this goat was not his goat. It did have a dirty white chin, but it was black with black ears and a flicking tail. Young, thin, only its horns full grown. A common goat. It did not smell like incense. It smelled like poor men. Strangers were coming in and out, watching to see what Stavros would do, and these strangers would tell their friends and their friends would tell his enemies, some of whom were his friends, and he would lose business and the face of his reputation. So he joked, "Free goat for every happy customer." But he had no joking feeling inside. This was not Welcome-Welcome Stavros with a sweet pear in his pocket for children, even the teens who walked in at eleven thirty and only asked for one fries to share for five people. This was a Greek man with a strong business mustache and ten days promised to him and he was not going to be beat or embarrassed or made fool by just any common livestock. Stavros was not going to be Mr. Nice Diner anymore.

A goat. Today, of all days in his life.

Had he thought about suicide. Yes, OK, once or twice. Especially lately, when things were so lonely and unexpected. But he had not meant it. OK, yes, in some ways he had been praying for death without actually praying. Yes, he was acknowledging that death was an exact solution to all of his problems, which were many woman troubles, because troubles came with women like sore feet came with shoes. But Stavros did not want to die. And, besides, Stavros was not crazy, Stavros understood that to believe a dream about a goat that foretold your death was something only a sicko one would do, somebody like his first wife, Dina.

Still, it was a very difficult thing to see a maybe-messenger of Death eating cigarettes out of your ceramic ashtray.

He lit a Saratoga, and a dirty breath came out. He bit down on the cigarette out of anxiety and business strategy. He had been chewing the same brand for thirty-five years, since age fifteen; all of the butts he threw into the parking lot had enough teeth marks to make a mold of his mouth. "My menu is going to get a lot more meat tonight," Stavros wagered. "You are no Death, Goat."

He should shout or beat the goat with a broom, like any Greek. He should threaten. This, something his brothers would have laughed at him for. He prodded the goat's back leg with the tip of his work shoe. The goat flicked its tail, but otherwise nothing. Rhonda wouldn't want him to hurt it. She would say, *All it wants is a little, is that too much?* even though it clearly wanted very much from him, maybe his entire life from him. His ex-wife, Carol, the Mother, she would want him to sacrifice the whole goat in her honor and feed the shiny meat right to her lips in pieces no bigger than a big jewel.

The goat nudged into his hand. Stavros pulled away. He was afraid that this goat was eyeing his mustache and wanting to eat it. He took a drag to appear calm. Fewer people were looking, but still, some. The goat tried again, for the cigarette. "No one tells you that smoking is wrong, *re*? They never stop telling me." Stavros laughed. It reminded him of his father's farm, the way he and his brothers used to put cigarettes right up to cats' mouths.

The goat licked a gold butt off the pavement. It moved its jaw right-left, right-left, grinding the filters into cottony pulp between its flat old-man teeth. It searched the pavement with its tongue and lips. The busboys hadn't swept the butts up, because the busboys were lazy and Mexican, but there were no gold ones left, no Saratogas. That was true. Stavros pulled out the pack of Saratogas from his breast pocket. It was a beige box, like the leather interior of a car. He flicked out a cigarette and offered it to the goat, gold end first. The goat pulled back. Stavros tried again. The goat ate the whole cigarette, tongue flapping at the tobacco falling from its black lips.

"You think these are chips?" He took out another. The goat ate that, too. Stavros lifted a white butt from the curb. The goat turned its head away.

Huh! he said, a goat that wants my brand only. Stavros Stavros

Mavrakis; Goat Tamer. It made him feel funny inside, like he should be embarrassed by something so insignificant becoming so important. Then, suddenly, the insignificant began to weigh on him and become very significant, more than significant, because he saw this was no insignificant goat. This goat, meant for him, solely for his brand of Saratoga, was no common goat at all. It had a message: death was part of his life. Yes, Stavro, ten days. It was nuzzling at his pants pocket. Stavros jumped back. He did not want it to touch him with its teeth.

What do you do with Death when it comes at you like a goat?

Stavros used the open pack, coaxed the goat to follow him. Stavros took steps and the goat took steps, moving its neck like a chicken's. They made it to the back of the diner, where there was privacy and a rope to tie it up with.

"Goat," he said, "we have two common things together. Nobody wants us, and we're both looking at death between the eyes." He had decided: if the goat was ushering his death, then the goat would be prepared for his funeral. It would be the Ultimate Supper.

Inside, Stavros jingled his keys. "Got him," he said. "Not even a goat can say no to Steve Mavrakis."

Marina reached for her knives and the burgundy apron she wore for butchering. "No one touch the goat," he said, "not even you, Marina."

He would lay out his final wisdoms in a letter, which none of his daughters—in the confusion of their lives—could argue against. Stavroula, too much like Marina, who heard nothing unless it came out of her own mouth; Litza, who made mountains into mistakes. Ruby and his ex-wife, who lived like spoiled twins. They would give many, many tears and, over delicious goat on a spit, go over the ways he was a good man. They would change for the better and make good lives, finally, even that selfish ex-goat-wife. He suspected writing the letter—no, email, he needed to send it out as soon as possible so they could read it right away—might make him sad. He had been in depression for so many days already—but how could he be sad to build the future? How can he be sad to do what he is doing when what he is doing is making it easier on everybody? Wasn't that wisdom? Surely, this must be what God felt after the seventh day—before anyone could appreciate anything, but knowing they one day would—that what would come was love and respect for the father.

Let me explain you something, he began, the way he always began, even at the end.

CHAPTER 6

Stavroula could see that her sister was the only one in the dining room, hands in her lap, texting. Salt was not officially open and Ruby hadn't told Stavroula she was coming, but the waitstaff had let her in because she was the chef's sister. Ruby could have gotten in anyway: she got into most places. Ruby's shift at the salon would start soon, but Stavroula could tell she was in no rush. Her clientele loved her, her boss declared her a waxed miracle, and if any of them were agitated at her lateness, Ruby would introduce a hair glaze that was inexplicably slimming, or demonstrate a new technique with dry cutting—or something else Stavroula had no idea about—and make them fawn all over again. Ruby had an eye for the fine things in life like makeup and accessories and the adoration of others—things Stavroula approached only occasionally. When Stavroula wanted a makeover a few months ago, in large part because ex-Mike was out of July's life, it was Ruby she went to.

One of the busboys near Ruby's table flicked the black towel at his waist. Around Ruby, all men became boys and all boys became flies. Ruby knew how to ignore flies.

Stavroula entered the dining room with a salad for her sister, a frappe for herself. All the décor, tablecloths had been changed to subtly reflect July. The centerpieces were given to thin vases of black sand. The furniture had been rearranged with the single purpose of bringing people together, the way Stavroula liked. Stavroula loved people, the messy noise of them: if she could, she'd have everyone eat out of one large plate. In this way, at least, she took after her father. Litza always chose to sit alone. That was fine by Stavroula. If it were that sister instead of this one in her restaurant, Stavroula would be content to let her eat by herself.

No. No. She wouldn't want Litza eating alone. She didn't believe in people eating alone. At one time, she and her sister would have enjoyed sharing a plate together. They liked the same foods, though Stavroula would've eaten the bigger portion, probably.

Stavroula squeezed her sister's forearm and sat across from her. Ruby had taken their father's black hair and complexion, Mother's long face, Mother's long legs. No Greek nose on this one. Maybe Mother and their father had agreed ahead of time to mix her by hand, bake Ruby like an artisan boule, then fight over the crumbs. At twenty-four Ruby was prematurely lovely, introverted despite or because of years of attention, and dissatisfied with where she was in life. The only people who knew the latter were those closest to Ruby; to everyone else, life for Ruby must be a perfect cocktail umbrella.

Ruby held up the new July menu and said, "Well, this is subtle."

"It's all they talk about around here. Just not to my face." It came out blustery, but Stavroula was squirming on the inside. She wasn't accustomed to being seen like this by Ruby. "You think I should invite Dad for a tasting?"

"Better do it fast."

Ruby used a knife to cut the romaine into ruffled scraps. She ate in controlled bites, never going for the next one without completely finishing the first. Whereas Mother got excited over new recipes every time she came into Salt (her recent favorite ingredient was "crunchy" fennel), Ruby ordered only Caesar salads. Once, Stavroula had tried to teach her sister how to make grape leaves, the little arms of the leaf tucking in to give itself a hug. *It's like rolling weed*, Ruby had said. Stavroula thought they were having a good time and was convinced Ruby was beginning to think about cooking for herself, but she didn't come back for a second lesson. Stavroula saw little culinary curiosity in Ruby, not much interest in the outside world at all—or maybe Ruby didn't know where to begin. Ruby, who worked hard and had a fluency of the body the way Stavroula had with food, Ruby who had enough business sense to run her own salon but was accustomed to passivity. Was that it? Stavroula jumping at the chance to take care of her sister, just like the rest of them, maybe more so. Seven years apart meant that the parents who brought up the oldest were not at all the ones who brought up the youngest. Stavroula was a chef, Ruby was a kid who still lived at home, even if she had been a woman from fifteen. As a result Stavroula was gentler, more forgiving with Ruby than she was with most people. And she was willing to admit she had no idea what her sister craved out of life.

Whatever she wanted, it certainly wasn't to marry one of her father's assistants.

Stavroula said, "Remember the time he got so pissed he threw a plate of spaghetti?" The pasta had stuck to the ceiling, dangled like streamers.

"Yeah, that was the last time Mom cleaned up any food tantrums." Ruby snickered. She quoted their father. "'See all the abusion I take from yous?'" He had been justified in throwing his plate, he said, because he was a hardworking man with no peace, and all these women were taking years off his life.

"Remember when the school asked for donations for the bake sale and he sent scrapple?"

Ruby said, "Remember the first time he brought home a rutabaga, he tried to light it?"

That one was good! "Like a candle." Stavroula said, "Remember Toast Delight?" Disgusting when he nuked it.

"Remember the pink shirt?" It hung in his closet, but it wasn't his, he swore. He didn't wear pink hunkies, meaning hankies, and said it must have belonged to the fruity who lived there before them. That time he got so mad at their teasing, he sent the hunky down the garbage disposal.

Stavroula said, "Remember when Mother was sick and for the first time ever he got her a get-well card? He put it on her nightstand? He didn't sign it or even put it in the envelope? He didn't realize it was in braille? He didn't even know what braille was?"

"You always tell that one."

"It was just a big fat smiley face on the front of the card. No words at all. The only way to read it was to touch it?"

"Yeah, I remember."

"He was like, 'So that's what those little bumps on the elevator mean.'"

"Remember the time he wrote a letter to his daughters about how he's going to die in ten days, and here's everything that's fucked up about them?"

"I remember. Reminds me of the day I got my master's in culinary arts and he called just to read the names of lawyers off his place mats."

Ruby pushed her plate back, and the busboy removed it wordlessly. She'd taken ten, twelve bites max. Lunch was free, of course, but a generous tip for the boys who would arrange for anything more she could want. She never wanted anything.

Ruby said, "I'm over it."

"You're not the only one."

"He's so dumb. A goat comes to him in a dream, and then it shows up at the diner, and now he thinks he's gonna die."

"He told you this? You went to see him?"

Ruby said, "No, he left me a voice mail and told me not to tell any of you."

"This is all because of a goat? Let's just butcher it."

"You can't butcher the goat. He's the goat," Ruby said. "Anyway, next week we'll get emails about how he's starting a fig farm or some-thing."

"Remember the time he planted cacti in the backyard in case he ever got cancer?"

"I'm tired of talking about it, Stevie. He's just whining because no-body's paying attention to him."

"We never stop paying attention to him," Stavroula said.

Ruby smiled. It was compassionate, confident. "I do."

Stavroula didn't believe her. Then she did. It was hard to tell with Ruby. Stavroula was still trying to understand the adult version of her sister. Stavroula had left home early; her father's motto had been I

Made It On My Own And So Should You, and Mother agreed with him. Or maybe it was Mother's idea. All Stavroula knew was that suddenly, at age seventeen, she was alone and angry and taking care of herself in every way. When things got hard and she had no one to turn to, she reached out to Marina—but Marina did not get involved in family matters, that was one of Marina's many rules. When things got desperate, Stavroula went to church—once. What Stavroula got from the one prayer she put together for God was that she was on her own. She stood, made the sign of the cross, and put herself through culinary school. She was grateful for her independence, there was no doubt about that, but those years of self-sufficiency had fermented something in her. She could feel, some days, her very veins filled with vinegar, but that was OK. Because vinegar is potent, versatile. There are a hundred and fifty common applications for vinegar. Vinegar is self-preserving. And if you wait long enough, it makes its own mother.

Stavroula could have gone anywhere with her credentials and experience, but somehow she ended up returning to the area for the evolving Philly food scene. She was slowly working her way back into the family. She had missed all of the years that gave Ruby her nuances. She missed important stuff. Like the time Ruby was thirteen and a pack of waves almost dragged her and Mother out to the Mediterranean. They had to anchor themselves to volcanic rock, and by the time a fisherman discovered them, they had almost no fingernails. Stavroula hadn't even heard this story until a few weeks ago, and the way Ruby told it made her think it happened to a different Ruby, which it did, because it seemed everything did. Stavroula imagined how her father must have handled that scare. Husband, protector, he had been onshore, unaware, drinking coffee . . . after they were rescued, he was still onshore, unaware, drinking coffee.

The morning after their father sent the email, Stavroula texted Mother, YOU IN BLACK YET? Mother had texted back with a picture of herself in a vampiric black cloak, which Stavroula recognized from a costume trunk.

Then Stavroula asked Ruby, nonchalant as she could manage, "Did you show Dave?"

For years, their father had been demanding that Ruby break up with her boyfriend, Dave. The problem with Dave was that since he had been released from the army, all he wanted was a platoon. He spent time with his boys at intramural soccer, he spent time with his boys—none of them even in the same room, mind you—playing first-person shooters with titles like *R3venge*. He rolled with his boys to laser tag and the club and the diner. OK, he was taking a few college courses, but Dave had no real plan. What he said he wanted more than anything—if only Mr. Mavrakis would give him a seed loan—was to own his own business, a bicycle repair shop. What he needed, in Stavroula's estimation, was somebody to give him orders.

"Yeah, I sent him the email. Doesn't matter, though."

"Why not?"

"It's already done."

"What's done?" Though she knew. Guessed, anyhow.

"We eloped," Ruby said. She took a nice long drink of Stavroula's watery frappe.

It was not the email that made Ruby elope. Ruby had eloped *three days before* the email. She did not tell her sisters about it. She did not tell Mother, but Mother found out, of course. Mother was arranging Ruby's things. Ruby did not like anyone to touch her shit, but Mother was an exception. Mother was installing a brand-new closet organizer, because the day before, Ruby, overwhelmed, had said she was going to throw all of her burning, flaming shit off an overpass and into the Delaware. She wanted something different, couldn't she have something for herself and for Dave? That was why Mother was picking up Ruby's clothes from the bedroom floor and sorting them—to alleviate Ruby's stress. Stavroula had dropped by the house but Mother didn't hear her come in. Stavroula was going to announce herself but felt, as the seconds built on each other, that she had no right to be there. She couldn't bring herself to break the silence. Instead she watched unseen as Mother lovingly picked up Ruby's things, stacking the jeans with the seams facing one way. That folding, each pair of pants stacked on another, was how Mother sensed a similar layering happening in her daughter's life. Pant leg on pant leg, hand on hand. Spirit on spirit, voice on voice. The seams in the heap of denim ran together to spell a message: *Mrs.* This was the story that Mother told, anyway, a few minutes later when Ruby called to tell her the news.

"I knew it, goddamnit," she breathed. "He better be ready to give you a good life."

Ruby said something Stavroula couldn't make out. Mother responded, "We can do it together now," and she began listing ideas for a wedding. There would be a harp player. Downstairs Stavroula put the oven on low, warmed up the tray of lasagna that she had baked for Mother, and went back to her one-bedroom in Philadelphia. She wondered if Ruby was pregnant.

Her father was right; Dave could have used more ambition. The way Dave spoke reminded Stavroula of some kind of nut butter—words and thoughts stuck to the roof of his mouth. But, honestly, who would be good enough for Ruby? Something Stavroula and her father had in common, and Litza, and Mother: they wanted only the best for her.

Stavroula said, "Are you going to tell him you're married now?"

"Who?"

"Dad."

"I'm not gonna keep it from him."

There it was, the thing that separated them: if it had been Stavroula, she would have gone along in secret. If the elopement had been a chicken, Stavroula would have plucked its feathers and boiled it down to dumpling. No, Stavroula reminded herself: that was before. Post-email Stavroula was wide open. She was writing poetry about a woman and selling it to the public at mealtime. She was eating chicken and smearing her face in the drippings and wearing the bones like a necklace.

Ruby brought a napkin to her mouth. For the first time Stavroula caught the trifle on her sister's ring finger.

The kitchen was beginning to get hectic, Stavroula could sense it. An order—July's voice—broke through the atrium. Something sluglike smeared itself against Stavroula's stomach and left a slimy trail, like a dog tongue on a window or like okra. July was seeing the menu for the first time. Stavroula stood and asked one of the boys to get Ruby a frappe to go. She put her hands on her waist to give the impression that she was composed but obligated. "Sounds like I'm needed."

A nod, then Ruby took up her jeweled phone. She said, "Catch you at the wake."

Marina had taught her: in the kitchen, there are three kinds of proxemics. Intimate = six to eighteen inches. The people who cook with you, or the people you cook for, they fall within this reach. Often, you're coming into actual physical contact. Sometimes the closeness is too much, and this is when dropping your eyes helps. Stavroula, of course, having been trained by Marina, was not one to drop hers. Social = four to twelve feet—her kitchen vs. the dining room, her staff vs. the waitstaff—the distance at which most precise work takes place over a fourteen-hour shift. At once estranged and familiar, Marina explained, social distance creates the phenomenon that a good waiter senses, without being told, what the kitchen is short on and makes a perfect alternate recommendation. Like a lover loping gracefully despite the darkness. Despite it, *koukla*. But anything over twelve feet was public distance. Supreme formality, plus enough space to escape in case of danger or awkwardness.

And here was plenty of both coming at her. Here was July, a good fifteen feet away, pushing through the prep cooks who knew not to get in the way, staring her down. The dress could have made Stavroula's menu—fuchsia, ripples at the bottom. Two gold earrings like the knobs of a dresser, the white wedges that Stavroula was fond of and that revealed three, almost four painted toes. Her arms tanner than they should be in April and a little too thin. July held them apart from her body, a gesture both welcoming and repelling. A fence, closed but maybe not locked. Her smile, tailored and difficult to interpret. The smile of a hostess, which she often was. She was holding the menu. Clutching the menu?

And July, moving straight through public space and into social—

For the first two years, they had worked at this distance. *How are you, Fine, Enjoy your day off, This your umbrella?* This was mostly because July left as soon as her shift was over and kept her office door closed, and Stavroula was not the friendliest. She felt entitled to her temper, just like her father, because she was good at her job. Ask July if she cared about a chef's petty demands? Or tolerated how controlling Stavroula was? The standoff continued until they both got weary of it, and soon they were the only two women on staff. They started to get a little more personal, but not too personal.

Then came the day they crossed into intimate. A year ago. It was the sun that coaxed them out to the bench on the narrow green behind the restaurant. They peeled oranges. July got up and stretched out on the ground, even though the ground still held the mule cold of early April. She propped herself up with her elbows. She could have stretched out her bare feet onto Stavroula's lap. She was saying, "I don't believe you."

"You should," Stavroula said. "It's something I've just always been able to do."

July gestured at Ramos coming up the alley. "What about him?"

Stavroula punctured the orange with her thumb at the thickest part of the rind. One of her claims was that she could remove the skin in a single peel. The other was that she could instantly tell what someone had last eaten by appearance alone. She called out to Ramos, and he said, "Good morning, Chef."

She said, "You had a muffin for breakfast, didn't you?"

"Yes, yes, Chef, a muffin." Ramos's grin was buttery. "A sweet one."

"See?" Stavroula said. "Unquestionable gift."

"Doesn't count. Come on," July said. "Try me. What did I last eat?"

Stavroula rubbed her thumb across the skin of her orange and it lifted from the fruit in a single spiral. She shut one eye and looked July over. The morning sun fell around her easily. Her long blond hair was pulled back but a few strands hung around her face, and she was wearing the same emerald earrings as yesterday. As if she had slept in them.

"Nothing. You haven't had anything today."

July took the orange from Stavroula, the perfect peel. "That was lucky and cheap."

"I only say what I see."

—driving straight through social and into personal space, and now she and July were face-to-face, intimate, with only the heat coming off the ovens to separate them. July's mouth, a lovely rip, how could Stavroula possibly look anywhere else?

"July Summer Sausage," July said.

"Yes." This close, she could have whispered it.

"Pineapple July and Pig."

"Already one of our best sellers." BLT with rings of grilled pineapple for tomato, inspired by the ham and pineapple pizza that July had Stavroula make after the kitchen was already broken down. And then she proceeded to eat only the pineapple and pancetta.

"A Whole July Rotisserie."

"A Whole July." For the time that Stavroula watched her eat an entire chicken by herself. This one would be accompanied by watercress, yogurt, and lemon.

The joke was fading from July's face, if it had ever been there in the first place. "July's July. Really. You put that on there."

"Of course: a plate of blackberries drizzled with extra-virgin, creamy feta on the side."

"As Apple Pie—"

"—As July."

July was keeping her voice down, but just barely. She was not the manager of Salt for nothing. "An entire plate of blackberries? You expect people to order that?"

One look at Ramos told Stavroula that the kitchen staff had been waiting for this: food fed you, but kitchen gossip made you take big bites. It didn't matter. Stavroula was showing July instead of talking, using her hands, which were becoming a flowery purple by the second, pulling in some pickled red onion, a dash of crushed pepper, large torn leaves of mint. She placed the dish in front of July, added a generous handful of feta with her cupped hands. July's July. The blackberries were a peal of bells hanging in a church tower, moon unveiling their shoulders. If she didn't say so herself.

"They won't be able to help themselves," Stavroula offered, a little breathless. "We'll sell hundreds."

Like that time they—she and July—bungled the produce order and got six times the amount of blackberries they should have. What had happened was, she posted a note for blackberries. One of the other cooks posted a note for blackberries. Mr. Asbury posted a note for blackberries. July posted a note for blackberries. Stavroula approved the order for blackberries when she was "multitasking." Inexplicably, the producer left them two more crates on top of that. By the time they realized, a return was out of the question. They froze some, they unloaded some to other restaurants, they made ice cream and pie, they delegated to glazes and marinades, they served a complimentary compote to guests, they still had a thousand blackberries left, it seemed.

The look July was giving her now didn't match the delicacy that was July's July. Rather, it was like the last day of the berries, when she and July surveyed the damage, the hundreds of blackberries overripened into saccharine mud, the dull and damaged skin, the loose, erupting drupelets. The soft, fine-haired mold that spread like a diseased cloth. That day, it was not exactly disgust that July expressed when she said, "Is it too late for sorbet?" but an exhausted humor that implicated them both. Instead of throwing the berries at each other or pushing one another into the sliding, skating fluids of the fruit, as Stavroula fantasized, they used a mop. They took turns wiping and rinsing, even though they could have had one of the boys take care of it. They talked about their fathers.

"Try it," Stavroula said. She held out a fork. "You don't like it, I'll take it off."

With her fingers, July took a berry with some onion.

"It's good, right? Take another."

July slid the menu across the counter. "Change it, Stevie, the whole thing." She walked off in the white wedges.

Because the entire kitchen was already part of this, and because

Stavroula knew it would expose her as much as she had exposed July, Stavroula called after her, "Next week we add Sorbet in Hot July." It gave the staff permission to laugh.

Marina had taught Stavroula, this is how you learn who a person is. First, you ask, What was the happiest moment of their life? Then you ask, and you keep asking until you get the real answer, Was it worth it? Stavroula had yet to have her happiest moment: that would come with July, when July was ready.

Wouldn't it?

Stavroula had slept with a few women. No one she had been serious about. No one worth risking anything for. Everything.

Age five, that's when she fell in love with the first woman: Mother. Ba-ba's new wife, who, along with Ba-ba, got them out of Greece, brought them back to America, raised them. As a child, Stavroula knew intrinsically that if you were hungry, you ate what was on your plate—so she had always been grateful to Mother. She adored Mother even now, with everything that had come between them and all the ways Stavroula had been left to fend for herself. If it weren't for Mother, she'd be married off to some Greek who expected her to clean his fish of the faintest bones. Mother was the first to say—even before Marina—*In this country, you can be whatever you want.* She had been the one to teach little Stavroula, coming off the couch after an episode of *Love Connection*, about prenuptial agreements—and little Stavroula responding, "Maybe that is for me." By which she meant, what women wouldn't want that?

Another thing: if you were hungry, you paid attention. This is what Mother likes—butter not margarine, television shows where women drift from one room to another, not realizing that some other woman has convinced their men to go away on a trip. This is the way Mother catches the little horse that lives at the end of your hand (your fingers are the legs, the middle one is the head, sniffing around her nightshirt). This is Mother eating burned toast and lukewarm tea, since you haven't figured out cooking yet. Mother eats as much of it as she can, because Mother loves you. This is what love looks like.

But not at first. At first Stavroula had to earn Mother's love, just like she would have to earn July's. Which felt right.

At first Mother said, "If you want to go back, we'll bring you back." Because Stavroula, anytime she got into trouble, would cry to go back to Greece. Ba-ba fell for it, but Mother knew that no little girl actually wanted to return to the orange dust, or to the farm roosters that called *ruku, ruku* at all times of night, or to motherlessness. So, three weeks of these fake Greek tears, and Mother took out a suitcase. The same brown shell that Stavroula had entered the States with. She began to pack Stavroula's American things. Stavroula, who could not speak English, had to guess at what was happening. She said, "My clothe." She removed them from the suitcase and pushed them back into her drawer.

Mother watched until all the clothes were in the drawer and then said, "You want to go back, so you keep saying." She took out the clothes, put them in the suitcase again. "You get what you ask for here. No one's making you stay. If that's your home, we'll send you there."

Little Stavroula felt a bundle of panic, and it rose to her fists. The first step was the packing; the second and last step was being put on a plane and forgotten. She began to wail, she dug at the clothes in the suitcase. She put them in the drawer, quickly, then blocked it with her whole body. She could do this all day, whatever it took to stay with someone she loved—loved so much it hurt—and who maybe loved her. "Mother," she said. Not asking: pledging.

"You sure?" Mother said. "You want to stay with Mother? *Etho?*" Which meant *here*. One of the few Greek words Mother knew.

Stavroula said, "Here." She opened the drawer and folded the crumpled clothes the way Mother taught her. She put them back in her drawer. She was not letting herself cry, and this may have been the reason that Mother did not take her into her arms.

"The next time you ask to go back to Greece," Mother said, "I will bring you there myself."

Stavroula nodded, grave. "You. I, here."

Mother did take her, did hug her.

It did not take Stavroula long to figure out what Mother's happiest moment was. March 2, 1988, 11:08 a.m., the time of Ruby's birth. And, in all fairness, that would have been Stavroula's, too, had she been Mother. Stavroula knew that there was something wondrous growing inside of Mother before Mother and Ba-ba told her about it. There was a small swelling on Mother's stomach that Mother pet and pet, and Stavroula knew that Mother had been waiting for it for a long time. Maybe even as long as Stavroula had been waiting to come home to America, which was most of her life.

Stavroula could tell that whatever was inside of Mother would be more deserving than Stavroula, and it would be worth keeping forever. Stavroula understood that she and Litza were secondhand. They were someone else's children, dragging around someone else's problems, while the little girl growing inside of Mother was as miraculous as spit, which is natural to the body. Stavroula felt Mother start to withhold, and she hated it, and yet she knew it was absolutely right. No, she can't have more new clothes, the baby will need some new clothes. She can't crawl into Mother's lap and pretend she is a snail and Mother the shell, because the baby is the snail. The baby is the snail for now, Stevie, OK?

Mother was still pulling Stavroula toward her and calling her Little Yia-yia. It's just that there was something between them now, something that felt like Mother but something she couldn't throw her arms all the way around anymore.

She should have hated Ruby. She hated Litza.

For as long as she could, Stavroula kept the growing Ruby from Litza, to protect Litza from knowing, and to protect them all from Litza's knowing. But when Litza finally realized what was happening, she got excited. Litza was five years old, the baby only weeks away, and she should have long forgotten Greece. But what she said was, "Just wait. After Mother loses all of her leaves, they'll send us back."

They were alone in their room, putting away their toys in the bins that Mother had organized. They were speaking their own special Greek—a version that their father would not have understood because it did not exist for anyone else. Stavroula said, "What leaves?"

"On Mother. A big pile of them, in a trash bag under her shirt. You can barely make out it's her beneath all those leaves."

"They're not leaves. They're little babies."

"I know what's under there. I've seen it."

"We're not going back, Litza. There's nothing to go back to."

Litza was not helping to clean. She was sitting on the bed with her knees to her chin, thinking in rough cuts the way only Litza did. Stavroula threw two more dolls into the bin. They were stupid toys—she preferred monsters with strange faces but couldn't get the adults in her life to accept that. She joined Litza, put a hand on her leg. Litza jerked away.

Stavroula said, "Mother is nice. She's always been nice to us. Don't you think?"

"Nice doesn't last forever."

"We just have to work harder."

"You are such a stupid *koukla*. Only a foreigner thinks like that." Something they had heard Mother's family say about their father.

"At least I'm a good *koukla*. That's why Mother loves me and not you."

"She loves those leaves more than she's ever loved you." Litza's eyes were wet, but not like crying. More like victory. "That's what mothers do, they have to give up their children for the leaves."

Stavroula felt a clog in her throat, the same one that appeared when Mother took out the brown shell suitcase. Litza was wrong, she was bad. That was why she couldn't understand Mother's love. She had never wanted to. It didn't matter how much attention or punishment Litza got. Litza didn't feel Mother's love like Stavroula did, because Litza didn't deserve it.

Litza, no longer trying to be mean, said, "Yia-yia was nice, and she was also home. That's why I'm going back."

If Litza got them to send her back, they would send Stavroula, too. Litza did not realize everything they would lose. Only Stavroula did. She barely remembered Yia-yia. Yia-yia was the one made of leaves. Greece was what was made of leaves. Stavroula tried something new. "Well that's why you have to be nicer to Mother. So she agrees to send you back. You have to make a deal."

"Is that what you did?"

"You make an agreement and you never, ever talk about it."

Slowly, slowly, it came to Litza. Her body began to rock on the bed as she put the pieces of logic together. She was approaching what Stavroula already knew: If I'm The Way They Want, I Get What I Want. Litza began to rock faster to get to the idea faster.

"You have to be nice to her and to whatever's inside her, and they'll let you go back."

Litza looked up. "You'll come, too?"

Stavroula nodded. "We go together."

"You promise?"

Stavroula solemnly nodded. She could promise. She had been taught by adults that a promise was something you said today to make a child do something for you, and tomorrow it was their job to understand why you had to break it.

That lie, that was one of the worst moments of Stavroula's life. It kept after her with the question, *Was it worth it?* For a long time, Stavroula expected Litza to bring it up, but she never did. It wasn't that Litza had finally adjusted to life with their new family. Litza didn't get over anything, she was just storing it up.

Driving home from her restaurant, Stavroula let herself wonder about how the email had hit Litza. How would she make him pay for it?

Listen, and We shall explain.

*Survival is Our instinct, passed down from a long line of
hunched farmers
who coax life from the most insignificant seed; who received it
from foragers of berries and sticks and names; who got it from hands
of tribes scratching the dirt; who got it from wild, hunted men; who
got it from animals trying to stand upright; who got it from all
fours scurrying the earth; who got it from, who got it from . . . where
it originated in amoebas frantically searching for a way to reproduce
all by themselves without saying the same old thing, without having
to share a single resource with even one other cell.*

CHAPTER 7

Stavros sat on a cinder block, smoking far enough away from the adopted goat where he would not be bothered for cigarettes. He took a big-fat-self drag. The goat rattled its chain, but Stavros was not in the mood for sharing cigarette butts with a filthy animal. All the sharing he had been doing these days, and what did he get back? A goat messenger of Death hanging around the diner and scavenging his brand of cigarettes. A family of women who does nothing except take and take from him, giving him no real answer to his final wishes. He told himself, very clearly, that he did not love them, having never really loved them. Let them go on thinking they are dealing with a butcher who doesn't give store credit, the bitches.

Had his been a suicide email, he would have written, *Nobody is to blame, only the poor foreign bastard with the rope in his mouth.* A suicide note had no honor, whereas his letter—it was blessed. What did he have to do to convince them of that?

The paper from the funeral director asked about military honors and if he was in the American army. No, he was not. He was Greek: Greek army. There was no box for that. Did he wear glasses? No, but he had checked yes, because he thought it might make him look on the outside how he was distinguished on the inside. Who would help him choose the silk shirt they would bury him in? Who would throw in the final rose with the dirt? Maybe his ex-wife would throw in a headless flower? This form, it was not enough for him. There were other arrangements to be made that this form did not address. He pressed the ballpoint pen into the pad that rested on his knee. He wrote in Greek, HOW TO SAY GOODBYE. Then he crumpled up the paper and threw it to the goat, who ate it as a second favorite to the cigarette. Like all of them, the goat has no real love for Stavros and takes trash and gives back nothing: and that is why Stavros keeps all of his cigarettes to himself now. Something he should have done from the start.

Stavros crushed out the cigarette, which it smelled to him like his own fingernails, and lit the next. His pants and also his socks were orange from the dirt of the lot; he could count the number of days he had sat out here on this very cinder block.

Stavros started again, on a clean sheet. Every man deserved a clean sheet, didn't he?

He started, with Greek, SONG TO SAY GOODBYE, Τραγούδι για να πω Αντίο. This satisfied him and made him think maybe his first ideas were not always the best, but eventually he would come up with the right ones. He took in a deep breath of the cool air. He was still alive so was able to make mistakes.

He wrote, on a new line, THINGS TO DO BEFORE DEATH.

1. Fix ice machine
2. Fix *G* in Gala sign so that it is lit up like on the first day we open
3. Cancel vendor for seafood because he is dishonest druggie
4. Finalize will, give it to the lawyer so no one selfish or conniving will make any changes to it
5. Call Hero
6. Write obituary to remember Stavros with respect
7. Which clothe do I want to be bury in (a shirt with pocket for the picture of Rhonda and me)
8. Find picture of Greek Agora

Then—

~~7. Which clothe do I want to be bury in (a shirt with pocket for the picture of Rhonda and me)~~

~~8. Find picture of Greek Agora~~

He began to replace the scratched-out #7 with Picture of Carol and Family but scratched that out, too.

9. Leave message on voice mail for Carol, which explains what ruin Family and Marriage: If a person is good to me, I would be a hundred times good back to them.

But with the liberation of the women comes forgetting about the man. The man went out to make, and the woman? She wait for the man to come home so she could take what he makes: then she gets a job to go make some more because enough is not enough. That is why the Family dissolve. And the children become selfish and have no thought for the father, only themselves, the same as the Mother. And we can't blame the man for that, sorry.

The goat snorted. Proving a goat is no different from family. Or, if you look at it another way, they are all goats not to care that their father is dying in seven days!

What else can be done in only seven days?

10. Send package to Greece
11. Make final decision on the executor
12. Make final payment to Gabriel for funeral service
13. Make final wishes heard
14. Make bakery case shine

Enough. The list, it can go on forever. There is too much to do. He still has to have a talk with Marina, who will keep his diner alive after he is done for good but who refuse to listen to anything he says, even more so now than ever. He still has to decide what happen to all the property, the house and business, which he made from scratch. There is goodbyes to be written to the one or two people of his life who mean everything to him—the people who knew him before he was a success. Then there is the goat.

Then there is Stavroula, Litza, Ruby. There is his fat ex-wife.

Seven days is still seven days, it was dawning on him. And the last seven must be the most important. What he has left may not be enough days to get all the spoils, but it may be enough days to get some. Seven days makes him all of a sudden into a very busy man. Before too soon, it would only be six days. Then five. Then four. Then none.

If the world can be made in seven days, in seven days Stavros can retake his life!

He folded up the paper, slipped it into his pocket. He smashed out the cigarette.

He looked at the goat. The goat was not lazy or stubborn, it just did not know any better. The goat ate trash, for peace sake! It was waiting for him, for his wisdom and charity. And Stavros, being the nice man he is, cannot look at a hungry goat and give nothing. He must offer mercy, for the goat knows not what it does. So, on the way up to his apartment, he takes up the two butts and tosses them where the goat could reach: with mercy.

DAY 7

Anger, Rage

CHAPTER 8

Litza watched from her car as her father climbed the rickety stairs of his snake-hole apartment for a nap, a Greek custom he had never kicked. She saw that Marina was outside, on the side of the building, sharpening knives. She knew she had time to break into her father's office unseen. It would be easy. She had years of experience of walking through the back door of a place as if she belonged there; they wouldn't think twice if she pulled out a key. They wouldn't think, isn't this the one who smashed the bakery case? They wouldn't think, she's looking for her father's will.

It had been gnawing at her since her trip to the diner: if he was picking out coffins, he was drawing up a will.

When she was twelve years old, Litza found herself at a major league baseball stadium for the first time in her life. Who knew why her parents let her go, maybe to get her out of the house, maybe because Mother hoped that if Litza spent some time in the world as a kid, among children with no agendas, Litza would start to act more like a kid and not like the falsely accused in pursuit of vindication. Mother gave her an extra five dollars with encouragement to have fun. That, and the game lights, seen at a distance from the school bus window, made Litza feel warm. Special. It was nice, and some instinct suggested that she always ought to feel this with Mother, but then the feeling flickered and cooled. It rubbed her, having to watch it fade. She returned, as she always did, to the dankness of the feeling's absence. She decided Mother wouldn't be the one to make her feel special; none of them would. She'd make her own self feel that way.

What was it that the first security guard gave in to? Was it her

smoky eyes? Was it her persuasive, kid-boxer personality? Was it
that she innocently attended to his body language and his need for
entertainment, while the other preteens gave all their attention to lip
gloss? Her refusal to be kicked back to the nosebleeds? She slipped
her hands into the back pockets of her jeans, which hugged her hips
like a skin soon needing shedding. He gave in to her charm, was able
to acknowledge that she had power for a twelve-year-old. He whispered, "Tell them you want to use the photo booth on level two." She
did, they let her pass Gate 2. She did not see the guard again. She left
the hangers-on at Gate 1 with the lie that she'd be back for them. She
cruised past the box seats. She kept calling, "Dad? Dad?" as if she were
just rows away from her father, and no one answered, and no officials
stopped her to check her ticket for the Field Level. This taught her that
all you have to do is get close enough, and act as if you belong, and no
one will suspect you—but ultimately this was a lesson for someone like
Stavroula, not someone like her, who didn't want to belong if she wasn't
wanted. She hung her arms over the fence. She watched the players
come down the sideline. Orange cake on their spikes, clay dusting
their knees; she imagined herself being raised on their shoulders, being
taken for pizza and soda in the locker room afterward with the winning game being dedicated to her. She called to an ump. Who knew
why he came all the way from shortstop? How did she convince him
to give over the black Magic Marker tucked into the breast pocket of
his striped uniform, resting near his official silver whistle? She might
as well have asked for his belt. But he indulged her, they all indulged
her, they didn't know how not to. And then the baseball player winked
at her, among all those other people—who had a right to be there, who
had bought tickets and did not scheme their way down to the cush-
ioned, special seats—among all those cute, much cuter kids. She got all
of their signatures. She did not care about baseball before or since, but
on the way home she made sure the students and teachers saw what
she did.

   Litza entered her father's office, leaving the door open just a crack
so she knew what was going on out there.

   Through the waffled glass blocks, more portal than window, no one could see her rifling through his papers. She began her search for Who gets the ring he uses to crown his pinky/Who gets the used BMW/Who gets the used diner/Who gets the money he has undoubtedly hidden in undisclosed accounts? Will he give it all to his black girlfriend, who never had to suffer through him as a scaly, angry man? who got him in his lame years? who never understood that, not so long ago, he wanted to shake and rattle, to crack all of your plates and saucers so that you had to lap your milk from porcelain shards? Or was he going to leave everything to the fucking goat tied up outside?

He wasn't going to die, but if he thought he was, the first thing he'd reach for was his money. He liked to say that he had come to this country with fish bones in his pocket and intended to leave with a whale. He'd settle the will before any other business, she was sure of it, and she wanted to see if she was in it. She was entitled to whatever she could melt his estate down to, she was Big Daughter Bank to his defaulted parenthood. She was owed a future and security and a family of her own. With this will, her father would look at everything he built in the last thirty years (she could concede that he had built for himself a successful life) and decide how the seed would be scattered. In the will he would become mortal, and also immortal, and while these thoughts flapped in and out of Litza's mind, too wild to be ensnared by understanding, she knew that she would see, once and for all, who mattered and who didn't, who he loved and who he didn't.

Plus, Litza needed a new car.

She scurried around the office, quick and decisive movements that made her look, and feel, raccoonish. That made her scurry even more. She was manic, the best she had felt in a long time. Her father's desk gave up addresses, phone numbers, an account of vendors. No money in the drawers or in the freezer of the minifridge, which is where she would've kept it. He kept his in a safe. She doubted, though, that he had locked the will away. It was the kind of thing he'd want them to find.

The desktop was password locked. She stared at it, thinking it could tell her something. She tried DINER, GALA, then GREECE. The computer was as forthcoming as he had ever been.

After SARATOGAS, GALAKTOBOUREKO, CRETE, MONEY, $$$$$$, RHONDA, RUBY, GOAT, she tried MORI, a pet name he had thought to use until she turned seven and then he didn't bother anymore about pet names. She typed MALAKA, left it on the screen.

There was a space between the desk and a cabinet, and she felt there. She found a brown leather portfolio. In it was a brochure for funeral caskets. She also found a torn sheet of paper that told her,

The depression is on me like a wolf tooth.
The wolf may take you by the throat,
but it is not the wolf that take you whole.
God is on the snout for Stavros Stavros Mavrakis.

And then, folded and taped, his Last Will and Testament. Today's date.

I, Stavros Stavros Mavrakis, being age of majority, being of sound mind and memory, not acting under duress, under influence, fraud or menace, declare this. He revoked his prior will, and he revoked his prior marriage with the typed line, "I am not currently married." He revoked his children, too. The section called Gifts was blank, as was Residuary Estate, as was Executor and Executor Powers. No indication of where his money and possessions and remains and estate would go. It was a blank will, or it was the wrong one altogether because the real one was elsewhere, or it was his doubt that he was really going to die, or it was telling her something that Litza couldn't quite figure out. Or he was just going to rewrite it after his nap.

The photograph slipped out of a side pocket in the portfolio. It curled at the edges. She did not recognize this picture, and it took some minutes for her to realize that she did know the little girls in the photo. Her, her sister. Ages four and six, a close-up. They were swathed in pitchy white dresses, which, like the rest of the photograph, had faded to the color of concrete. Their hair was pulled into pigtails. Litza traced the red ribbons at the collars and wondered who had had the imagination to tie them on. The girls' faces were as round and fresh as hard apricots, except there was sleeplessness in Stavroula's eyes. A child has dark circles under her eyes? Stavroula, her smile a little cocky even then, face and shoulders imperceptibly ahead of Litza's, which should have served as a warning to Litza that she'd better sit up. But Stavroula's hand, on the back of Litza's neck: it said, Here we go, together. Here we are, and you can take us both or you can leave us both. The cocky smile, maybe, but still the hand on Litza's neck saying, No matter who comes: it's us together.

"Looking for something?"

Litza's heart kicked like a hoof. Her sister, finally.

When Litza was eight, ten-year-old Stavroula was standing just like thirty-one-year-old Stavroula was now. At the door, simultaneously wanting to know and not know what Litza was doing in their parents' room, the nervousness in her close to curdling the fun because Stavroula was always obsessed about getting caught at things she was barely doing. The tone accusatory, but also curious, wondering. And what did Litza show her then? A wooden man made of clothespins, which her father, as a little boy, had first bound together with laces from his own father's work boots until his father surprised him with a smear of glue, kept warm in his pocket between two sheets of wax paper. And what did Stavroula say when she saw the wooden man? *Are you going to break it?* And what did Litza do? Break it. And then what did Stavroula do? Tell. She went running with her mouth open for telling. And then what did Litza do? What did Litza do? When she heard Stavroula running with her mouth open to Mother? Break it even more, that's what she did, so that the wood became pricks and sawdust. And then what did their father do? Punish her. But in the privacy of his room, he moaned a little, she saw him when she was supposed to be sitting on the bottom step of the attic, grounded, she saw the way that mourning and sadness and an inability to gather the shards of days you can't remember, still feel close to, could turn his cheek into something that bobbed and gulped, like a frog dipping up and down in his home pond. And what did Litza do? She glued the man back together. And what else did she do? She buried the man in the backyard. And what did Stavroula do? She made their father a new man from clothespins and said that it was from both of them. But it took years—not until the wedding, really—before Stavroula would conspire with Litza again.

This was a moment when one could have asked the other how she was, but Litza didn't do it because Stavroula didn't. *Dear Stavroula: I'm fine, how are you?* Stavroula, the control freak, everything on her terms.

Litza slipped the photograph beneath sheets of paper on her lap. "You lost weight."

Last time Litza saw her, Stavroula's hair was long and stringy, and she was fat, and she accused Litza of doing something she did not do. OK, she took a stool to her father's bakery case, but did that mean she was automatically at fault for her sister's car window? Weren't there thousands of other people capable of petty vandalism? Why did Stavroula have to leap to blame her? Yes, the younger, dumpy version of Stavroula loved to deliver judgment on Litza. Was this the same Stavroula now? She wasn't sure. Her face, which drew to a point at the chin, seemed not so serious the way Litza remembered it. Stavroula had changed how she dressed, or how her clothes fit, so that her pink sleeveless shirt and jeans made her seem a year younger, not older. She was wearing earrings, though not the ones Litza had made her—generic, lifeless hoops, from a mall, no doubt. Stavroula's hair was short, shaved in the back and lightly curled on top. The way Stavroula looked said she looked this good because she hadn't had to bother with her sister in many months. Stavroula was like a divorcée who had realized, finally, that she was better off. Litza was the one who aged in the last year. Sure that Stavroula was sizing her up, too, Litza hoped that Stavroula did not catch this, and then she hoped that she did and felt responsible. Wait, Stavroula was wearing eyeliner? She knew how to do that?

"And you look like you're up to no good," Stavroula answered.

"I'm looking for his will."

"What do you need to see his will for?"

Stavroula, the goody-goody. She suspected Litza was looking for money. On top of all this, in her hand was a brown bag full of medicine for Marina. That was why Stavroula was here on her day off. Litza knew this from when they used to be friends, sort of, around the time of the wedding, and got lunch in the city. Had she come at this time on purpose, hoping she'd run into her sister?

Litza said, "He's changing it."

This had an effect, though Stavroula was hesitant, suspicious, weary, all the things she had been in the final days before they stopped talking. "You've seen it?"

Litza nodded.

She thought that Stavroula might sit in the metal chair. She did not. Litza thought about switching to the metal chair so Stavroula could take the office chair, but then it would look like this was Stavroula's idea, and Litza didn't know how to say, Don't worry, I'll say it's me, which it is, which it always is, even if it's you, too. She wanted to give the impression of ease, that she would confront their father for the both of them if he came down suddenly.

Dear Stavroula: Everybody deserves a second chance.

Stavroula closed the door.

Litza rolled the photo into her jacket pocket so Stavroula couldn't see it, then brought the papers to the desk. Litza pointed out the missing information in items one through four and explained how this new Last Will and Testament revoked his old Last Will and Testament. She could feel her sister softening. A cricket chirped in Litza's chest, too noisy with pride and fear at having something her sister, who wanted nothing to do with her, might now want.

She could let this dangle, if she wanted to. She could make Stavroula fucking beg for a second chance, see how she liked it.

She could feel Stavroula leaning in, learning, and it reminded her of the last time they were this close—Stavroula lifting the long train of her wedding gown as they circled the altar three times for holy, holy, holy matrimony. And Litza, encircled by her husband and her sister— in that moment, they were the two people who could understand her in a world of people who couldn't, and then the priest stopped his chanting and the spell broke and she remembered that no one, actually, understood her. But right now, as Stavroula's brow furled, Litza felt again that they were joined.

"We have to come back," Litza said, "as soon as he finishes it." Her breath was caught in her throat.

A little tuft of air escaped Stavroula's lips. Her eyes, stupidly wide, the way they had been on the wooden man, thinking that Litza was going to break it when she had no intention of doing that, only wanted to cup him in her hand to see how much space his full body would take. Only wanted to touch it, to hold something her father cared about.

But, right now, Stavroula wasn't running to tell. Stavroula folded the sheets, placed them back inside the portfolio. Litza put the portfolio back into its spot. Their eyes met solidly.

Stavroula said, "What the hell is he doing?"

Pause. "What, you want me to smell my fingers and tell you?"

Stavroula let out a loud laugh. Then Litza laughed. They were quiet for a second, and it began all over again. One stopping, then the other getting her going. Laughing with their mouths full as if they had stuffed them once more with those after-dinner mints, stuck them to their little-girl teeth, the mints dissolving into a fluoride-tasting paste. The laughter was like that—the kind of fit that children fall into and can't get out of—and it only got worse when it gave Stavroula the hiccups. It hurt so much, Litza felt tears. *Dear Stavroula: Smell my fingers!* A Greek idiom, a favorite of their father's that was supposed to mean: Am I a mind reader?

A beat, a door opening and closing, something in her telling her this had to end now. And their father was entering the office. "What is this?" he said, looking from one to the other. "What are you doing?" His hair was crushed from where he must have been lying on it, his eyes a little crushed, too, from sleep. He didn't sound angry. That stunned them both to silence, then back to laughter. He laughed because they laughed. This had them laughing more.

He realized the laughing was not with him, but still hopeful, said, "Are you here to visit with me for the final wishes?"

Litza's eyes shot to Stavroula. She felt herself pleading for Stavroula not to tell. Her sister's mouth, turning like a knob. Her own mouth preparing to say, Be on my side for once.

Litza's mind raced through a catalog of items her hands had picked over. She spun the chair and grabbed at the pile to the right of the desk. She picked up two copies of *To Live Until We Say Good-bye* and held one out to Stavroula. "We came for these. They're for us, right?" Litza forced herself to keep her arm outstretched. *Take it*, Litza said to herself. *Dear Stavroula, Take it.*

"Yes, a gift. One each," her father said, a little surprised, also gleeful.

He was not concerned that Litza was in his office unattended. Or maybe he thought Stavroula was her supervision. Or maybe he'd like her to stay in his office the rest of the day, reading *To Live Until We Say Good-bye*, telling him why it was such a good gift. He was smiling.

Stavroula took the book.

He said, warming up, "The three of us, we can have lunch. We can talk all this unfinished business."

Litza shook the book as if it contained coins. "We already took care of business."

She got up. She got out as fast as she could. She took the photo from her pocket, and she tucked it into the car's visor as if it might bring good luck, which maybe it did. She threw the book under her seat.

CHAPTER 9

When Stavroula and Litza came to the States, Carol taught them how to take a shower, how to zip a baggie, how to turn on a TV set, how to flush the toilet, which they already knew. She taught them English words that Ba-ba didn't—*leaves, underwear, sandbox, McDonald's* (which they already knew). She taught them that *jeans* did not start with a Z. When Stavroula got *elephant* wrong on a quiz in kindergarten (*Carol, what is elephant?*), Mother turned her arm into a trunk and trumpeted. Stavroula, delighted that *elephant* was something she knew now, did it, too. Litza did it, too, without knowing what elephant was; she did it because Stavroula was doing it. Stavroula learned that American food tastes like paper and is served on paper; children are fed but do not actually eat because what they eat looks like toys, not food. Also, she was shown how ketchup is not sauce for spaghetti, a lesson she would never forget. Because Ba-ba came home late, Mother put the sisters to bed each night, which meant letting them curl into a pile on the couch until they got drowsy. She stroked their backs. Stavroula could tell that Carol wanted them to be lulled but never forget that it was her doing. Carol whispered, "Call me Mother when you're ready to." Stavroula did right away. Litza took longer.

Their second month back in the States, starting on Monday, Litza's freckle was the size of a pin: only a mother who had spent long days staring at a child's face would have been able to spot it, so no one spotted it. On Tuesday, it was the size of a pencil eraser. On Friday, Litza woke Stavroula up because her face itched. The entire left side of her face was surly with pus. Mother was panicked, couldn't get the child—who was growing exponentially more infected cells than little-girl ones—into shoes fast enough.

Stavroula did not understand why they were not bringing her to the doctor's office, too. She knew Litza's likes and dislikes, her real cries from her phony ones. She knew that Litza slept on her side with her arms shoved between her legs, as if she were hiding a pork chop she wanted to save for herself. Stavroula knew Litza better than anyone, and if there was something wrong with her, Stavroula would be able to translate. She said to her father, in Greek, "I have a question for you, Ba-ba. To help Litza." By question, she meant she had some knowledge for the special doctor. But Ba-ba was putting on shoes that meant work. The cigarette on his lip tipped up and down, in time with his speaking. He gave Mother money and a kiss on the lips, Stavroula a touch on her face. Litza cried because he gave her nothing.

Stavroula was patient for her sister and Mother to get back, even though she was with Mom Mom. This was Mother's mother, whom she was supposed to call *Yia-yia*, but Mom Mom could not be anyone's yia-yia, for yia-yias were gourdish, plump with age. Mom Mom was bones crisscrossing a body, plus a wardrobe of pants that made shushing noises when she walked, and glittering shirts that kept her far from the labor of feedings and farm. The scarves around her waist weren't for wiping noses or keeping two-three eggs safe until they made it back from the henhouse. In Mom Mom's ears there were holes, as if a mouse had been nibbling there; from the holes hung gold hoops that Yia-yia would have placed only on the shrine to her dead parents. It was these mouse holes that made Stavroula feel most nervous around Mom Mom, and was the reason that she did not cry while she waited. Also, her hair was as pretty as a horse's. Also, she smoked cigarettes. She said things that Stavroula didn't understand, such as, "Don't trust boys" and "If it has anything to do with his cannoli, don't believe him. Just 'cause they're cream-filled don't mean they're dessert." Because Mom Mom laughed, Stavroula laughed. But Mom Mom did not like that Stavroula and Litza called Mother *Mother*. She wanted to know why Carol wasn't good enough, even after Mother had explained that the girls could only manage Carl. "I brought them into this country," Mother

said, "that makes me more than just their babysitter." Stavroula understood enough to feel her chest glow with loyalty. Still, whenever Mom
Mom was in the room, Stavroula avoided saying *Mother*. She tried not
to say it now, as Mother pulled up. She rushed to unlock the door, even
though she was not allowed to unlock the door. Mom Mom had to
compete with her quick, ineffective fingers and finally said, "Don't they
have doors where you come from?"

The doctor prescribed an ointment for impetigo, an infection of the
skin.

Stavroula waited for her infection to come. She looked every day
for the cloudy blisters that would turn into sores. But Litza was very,
very careful. She did not want her sister to have a slippery face, too; as a
result, Litza was the only one to suffer through it. It was the first thing
they had not gotten together.

For days, Litza's face ruptured. The drain ran from the meat beneath
her eye to the side of her mouth. The scabs would not heal—perhaps
Litza kept opening them—and her face was constantly blubbering.
Litza did not cry. Mother said, "*Oxi*, don't scratch. If you scratch, it gets
bigger." To distract her, Stavroula and Mother made a game of English
words. Stavroula said "nose" and touched her own nose for Litza, who
was not allowed to touch anywhere above her neck. She touched her
lips, so Litza could remember there was a new, better way to say "lips."
When Mother shouted out "Cheeks!" both little girls puffed up their
cheeks the way Papous used to do, but only Stavroula was able to clap
all of the air out of hers. Mother gave Litza sticks of spaghetti to break
into little pieces so that Litza would have busywork for her hands.
Stavroula broke the pieces, too, and when Mother wasn't looking, she
scratched Litza's chin with an end of pasta.

Stavroula had Mother tie her cooking apron around her waist and
insisted on serving Litza the orange medicine. Mother followed with
a damp cloth to blot out the itches. Stavroula leaned forward on her
tiptoes. "Can I do it?"

"Not this part." She folded the cloth into a neat square and brought
it to Litza's face.

"I want her," Litza said.

Mother reached in again with the cloth. "She's too little for that, Litza. This is what mommies do."

Litza pulled away. She threatened to scratch off the bloated welts. "I want her."

Stavroula reached for the cloth and said, "I can do it, I am good with her."

Mother stood. She said, "You pat, you don't rub." She monitored Stavroula for a minute, then went to the kitchen.

Stavroula knew that Mother would do a better job, so she went slow, every tap purposeful. Everything she did to her sister registered on Litza's face. "Does it hurt?"

"It tickles." Litza probed at her cheek with her tongue, but Stavroula reminded her that Mother said not to. She said, "Mother knows how to make you better."

This went on for a few weeks, the scabs hardening and then opening again, her skin weeping and forgetting what it meant to be dry. Every time it seemed she was getting better, another river opened. It ran down to her neck. Litza was scheduled to start preschool but would have to wait until she was no longer contagious. For Stavroula, kindergarten was starting. At first she thought she could do both—take care of Litza and go to school, but then Mother corrected her. School in America was a privilege that village girls in Greece didn't get, so she had to take advantage of it. Litza would go when she was no longer suffering.

So, every day, Stavroula woke from the couch, where she was quarantined, and ran in to ask, "Is she suffering anymore?"

"A bit," Mother said, brewing water. "But she's a little better today." She turned off the burner and brought down a packet of instant oatmeal.

"Is she suffering enough for school?"

"Not yet." Mother smiled.

"Then I am not yet, too."

Mother poured the steaming water into a bowl of oatmeal. The oats sucked in the water, then more water. "If you were the sick one and Litza were starting school, wouldn't you want her to go?"

Stavroula shook her head. She groped for the right English. "We do together."

Mother put the bowl in front of Stavroula. She added a spoon with peanut butter, the way Stavroula liked it. Today, the oatmeal looked like her sister's lumpy face. "You'll see, it's fun. You'll want to go."

Stavroula ate the peanut butter, left the oatmeal. She inspected Litza in her sleep. She poked her awake and said, "If they ask, tell them you aren't suffering anymore." But how did the first day go from being many days away to being one? Ba-ba waved at them, not touching either child. "Be very good girls today."

Mother pulled Stavroula to her lap and stroked her hair. She glanced up at Litza. "We'll be waiting the whole time, won't we? We'll be first in line to get you at twelve-oh-five."

Stavroula kept her body very still so that Mother would not know she was stopping herself from crying. Then Mother said, "Litza and I will have all kinds of fun together," and Stavroula didn't want that exactly, either. The best would be if they just let her stay. Even after Mother left the kitchen, Stavroula resisted crying.

Litza said, "They can't make you if you don't want to."

Stavroula repeated, "They can't make me," but she was not so sure. So far, they had made her do all kinds of things.

Mother brought her to school the next day. Litza stayed in the car while Mother walked her to the line. Stavroula looked back but could not see Litza. Mother carried her brand-new purple backpack for her. It was filled with a lunch pail that she had packed herself, and a notebook with lines thicker than her fingers.

Mother said, "Just remember that everyone else is nervous, too."

"What is nervous?"

"It feels a little bit like ants are crawling in your stomach."

Stavroula nodded. She knew what that was like. She stayed in line and didn't speak so that none of the children would ask why there were funny words in her mouth. At the last minute, she turned around and saw that Litza had snuck out of the car and was standing there in bare feet. The bell rang, the line moved, the car left, school began.

Stavroula was determined to hate school: she loved it. She loved the way the teacher pointed at the letter *A* as if to say, *We will do this letter by letter, together.* As if to say, *It is the same as Greek, only it's English.* She liked being placed in line, and then getting compliments at how she didn't even fidget (what is fidget?). She liked how she could mix different colors of clay together—a little of this, a taste of that—to create something new, even a color the other children found grisly. When Mother came at 12:05, Stavroula tried to look sad. She tried to look the way the sores on Litza's face looked. She touched her chin to her chest and dragged her backpack behind her the whole walk back to the car.

Mother said, "It's OK if kindergarten makes you smile."

There was dinner, and Mom Mom came, but Ba-ba worked. There was cake. Litza ate two pieces. Her face was crusting over, no new sores, which put her in a good mood, all of them in a good mood.

When they were alone that night, Litza said, "Carol made hot dogs today."

"What's hot dogs?"

Litza shrugged. She pulled the blanket to her chin.

They were quiet. Stavroula sat on a plastic chair next to the bed. They only had a few more minutes before bedtime. She still wasn't allowed to sleep with Litza. She said, "Did you let her touch your face?"

Litza shrugged.

"Did you?"

"One time. But not two times." Litza smiled. "She wanted to."

Stavroula whispered, "Was she nice to you?"

"The nicest."

Stavroula did not expect that from Litza. She had the feeling that Litza wasn't sure about Mother, like a toy she picked up to play with and then put down and then picked up when someone else wanted to play with it. She wanted to ask how Mother was the nicest. She wanted to ask where Mother took her today (the bank for red lollipops? the grocery store? the park for chasing the birds that she could not figure out the English name for?).

But Litza wasn't thinking about Mother anymore. She said in their special Greek, "Soon I will be allowed to have fun with other children, too."

"School isn't supposed to be fun. It's like the doctor checking you. It's just something they make you do."

"It looks more like a ride on the plane." Stavroula tried to look less guilty, and then Litza said, "Just tell me."

It rushed out of her, the first chance to speak to her sister about her day. "It's nothing like a plane. With kindergarten, you never expect to fall out of the sky. And they serve snacks, which you can eat outside."

Litza asked about the colors, and Stavroula gave them. Litza asked about the children, and Stavroula described them. Though she was not supposed to, she was holding her hand by the time Litza said, "Tell me more about the snacks."

In the bathroom that night, Stavroula poured cup after cup of water over her face. She told herself it was because she wanted to be clean for school, but really she wanted to know what it felt like to have an infection running down your face. What it felt like to not be in school. She did her best not to reach for the towel as water soaked the front of her shirt. She wanted to remember what it was like, being alone with the wetness, having her shirt stick to her flat chest. But the next day, picking out pictures of vegetables with the rest of the class, the feeling slipped away.

CHAPTER 10

It was the end of Day Seven. Stavros was here at his goodbye party, with good spirits and hope. He sat in the king chair at the biggest, roundest table, with candles that he lit and a Special Menu that included what they each liked to eat—or what he thought they ate. They were adults, how was he responsible for knowing what they ate? He didn't know what they ate when they were children, either, but that's because children never know what they want, they only want what they can't have, and his job was not to feed children it was to make a living and support a family. His children, which they were adults by now, had nothing to complain about because they were not even here yet to eat, anyhow. Neither the sow ex-wife.

Wait, here she was—

Wait, no. That was not his sow, that was somebody else's sow. The thing this sow had in common with his sow was reddish brown hair, like his ex-wife likes to wear in public. Probably now all the divorce women wear that style thinking it will get them some poor *malaka* with a life savings.

This was Stavros Stavros Mavrakis's Last Supper, and he was at it alone. His plan was to make mends with his family and very close friends. In Greek, the verb is *epanorthono*. What the politicians do when they want two very different parties to sit together over a treaty and agree that the past is the past. Only now is for the taking and changing, only the future—επανορθώνω. Cousin to the Greek word *protokollan*, which means *first glue*, which it comes from the act of gluing a sheet of paper in front of a document, which says this is Official. Such as, This Faccbook Invitation to His Last Supper is Official or Else.

But he sees, yet again, that they are suckers one hundred percent, which means he is a sucker times one thousand. These women. What did he expect? They would not even accept his generous offer for lunch, Stavroula and Litza, who came only to snatch a book and snoop around his office while they thought he was sleeping. He gives them the book, he wants them to have it, of course. But do they want a book and nothing else to remind them of their father when he is gone? Don't they want an evening to look back on and say, That Last Supper of Our Father's Explained Everything? And why not? For some moldy-oldy grudges? Some things that happen so far away ago?

Everyone wants to live in the past, but Stavros wants to live in the now. Maybe their life is all old memories and Facelife, but his life is here and today in the flesh. His life is six more days.

No: he must be patient. They will come. Won't they?

The doors to the diner opened again: and here was Hero, Stavros's oldest friend and some would say only friend, which if you look at who comes to the Last Supper dinner party is maybe true. Hero's hair was gray now, but when he was a young man it had been blond and thin, like fibers. Hero was the kind of Greek who looked like a Swede. His face was not strong like a Greek face, it was more flat, and gentle like bread. His skin was pink, like a ghost or a flower. Most of all, he was a very big man. His hands and shoulders, his chest, they all said, *I dare you to prove that I am Greek, you can't do it.* And the years in America had even softened his accent. On top of all this, he adored his wife like an American or Northern European would.

They shook hands and called each other *malaka*, which established that things were all right between them even if they had not talked in many weeks, was it months? The last thing Hero had said to Stavros was, "I'm sorry you're having a hard time," and Stavros had said, "The only hard time I'm having is with your wife," and Hero did not like anybody to disrespect his wife, as Stavros knew, and Stavros did not like his compatriots to see him having a hard time and publicly acknowledge it. So—here they were, *na epanorthosei.* They called to the waitress Kelly for some *mezedes.* Stavros specifically asked for crunchy pickles, a favorite of Hero's. That was the first thing in mending, the right food.

Hero said in Greek, "I got your message on the Facebook."

"It looks like you were the only one." The message, sent to all of them, had said, The Last Supper with Stavros Stavros Steve Mavrakis.

Hero surveyed the five other place settings. "No daughters?"

"No daughters."

"No Carol?"

Snort. "Of course not."

"Who is the fifth seat for?"

Stavros leaned over and tucked the fifth place mat beneath his own. "The fifth was a mistake."

"Well, you did only send the invitation out today. Maybe the girls had plans."

"That's right, but you're here. Doesn't that prove that also they should be here?"

"It proves nothing more than I like a free meal."

Hero sat back. He accepted Stavros's little pour of ouzo. You poured a little, because it said, We Take Our Time Here. And it said, There Is Much More to Come. We Are Only Just Beginning to Connect over Conversation, Which Is Nonthreatening. He and Hero sipped a while, listening to the no-imagination lyrics of soft classic rock sung by a bald middleman singer that Stavros had heard many, many times and did not want to hear again before he died. Stavros hoped that whoever put the next dollar in would pick a song by a woman.

Hero said in English, "Are you sick, Steve?"

Stavros shook his head. Listening more to the music than to his friend. "I am dying."

"Dying how? This is incurable?"

"It is incurable."

"The doctor, he told you so?"

Stavros stroked his powerful mustache, which it was more powerful than Hero's naked but heavy lip, hoping Hero would get the point. "We are beyond doctors here, Hero."

Hero pushed the sleeve up on his right arm. Underneath, on the skin, was a single stitch. "You see this, *re*? It was a mole, and before it was a mole it was a freckle. They took it out because that mole grew horns and ate the freckle and all the other moles around it."

Stavros waved his hand. How could you compare a freckle to what was coming for him?

Hero said, "You want to know what I think? I think you're not dying any more than the rest of us."

"Oh no? And suddenly you are an expert also at dying?"

"Ela, Stavro. What is upon you is *xenitia*. You are suffering because you forget who you are. Your girls, they forget who they are, too. You miss your homeland, you pine for it in the way only a foreigner knows how. Maybe you need some little vacation—go back to see the relatives, reconnect with your roots. You have become in exile not just from your country, but also from your family."

"Don't talk to me like I don't know *xenitia*. I know *xenitia* naked from her inside out. Not like you, Hero, who turns his back on his own motherland." Which was true and not true, because Hero had assimilated quickly, willingly, enjoying a success in the United States that allowed him to return to the old village three, four times a year just to act the celebrity. But did he have real relationships with family anymore? No.

Here it was, that itchy silence between the two longtime companions that had caused them trouble in the first place.

This Last Supper was going all wrong. Every time Stavros tries to have a goodbye, he makes an enemy. Hero is his best friend. He needs to somehow make him realize that these are precious minutes being wasted and that what he has summoned Hero for was to say, Thank You for Being More than a Friend: For Being a Possibility in My Life. And what is he doing instead? Pouting. He is pouting over Hero, while Hero is very aggressive with his crunchy pickles, and taking the little seeds in the pickle broth and mashing them with his thumb into his mouth.

Hero shrugged. "You don't want to know what I think. So, let's instead order a few plates from your special menu."

Stavros brightened. Yes, food, how could he forget? The way to mend all things. We break the back of our individual sufferings over bread. He said, "I'll have Marina send out her duck. Hero, it is like tasting a young bride."

Hero shook his head. "Doctor says no fatty meats. And no young brides. Anyway"—he tipped more ouzo into his glass—"don't you know they force-feed those birds to make them so fat?"

This was incredible from Hero, for whom he had reserved the duck especially. "No duck?"

Hero licked his finger. "Birds are not supposed to be fat in nature. We have to stick to the natural order of things, Stavro. Such as, do not count your death before it hatches."

This time, Stavros knew to be patient and make his way in. He spoke to Hero as if Hero were a child who did not know what he wanted. He said, "You do not understand, Hero. You have never understood, because your life is a dream. I have to accept what my life is and what it isn't."

"My friend." Hero clapped him on the shoulder. He stared dead into his eyes. He was crunching on the crunchy pickle, but everything else about him looked at Stavros in serious friendship. No, even more than that, like Stavros was the king and Hero was consoling him about his kingdom's deficit. "You are depressed, and you should see somebody."

"Hero, this is not what I call you here for. You come to my place to say this to me?"

"You are a lonely man, Stavro. That is all that is happening here."

Stavros was sorry before he said it, but his eyes went red. He saw only the man at the door with the puffed-up umbrella, the couple feeding money into the jukebox to pick more middlemen to sing to them, the waitress expertly pouring coffee into a mug across a business meeting, the cashier accepting small bills, a family eating a simple dinner, people giving orders in his establishment. And a smell so sharp, he could not recognize it, but it was filling him inside and outside. All this and more made him say, "I may be lonely, but nowhere near as lonely as your wife."

Hero grinned, but it was the way glass grins when you break it. He patted Stavros's shoulder twice, like he was the child. He said, "Let me know when the next supper is."

Stavros watched his friend walk out and wanted to call to him. He knew it was that easy and simple, if he could just reach for Hero with an apology. You didn't mess with Hero's wife. You honored her the way Hero honored her. But if this was his Last Supper, should Stavros have to make himself into a whimper? Wasn't mending mostly about forgetting? Such as, *Hero, forget what I said and remember only my intentions.*

It was breaking his heart, his friend's back to him.

It was bringing him knowledge of the smell that had appeared so suddenly it burned his nose hairs, and brought tears to his eyes, and made him say the worst thing. It was incense he was smelling. But the thread of incense was disappearing as fast as it came, just like his old friend Hero.

Hero, You and I Are Countrymen! Hero, You and I Invent a New World Together! Hero, I Did Not Mean It. Hero, You Are a Great Man. Hero, Come Back. Hero, I Want to Drink and Remember All the Ways We Made It Through the Rough Life Together. Hero, Who Will Be with Me at the Final Goodbye Now?

There was nobody left.

DAY 6

Acceptance

As for Us, We keep our watch and wait the final day.

CHAPTER 11

Dear Dina,

I have written letter on letter to you. It is not because I am not a person of letters, but because writing, it is not satisfying. It does not get close enough to what must be said. I write one draft that blame you for everything; I write another draft that save you of everything. Neither is true.

We enter life in the same way that we leave it—unsure what is happening. All we can ask is those who have know us, our friends and enemies, to witness. You and I, we both start from the same sea. You remain sand—every time you think you escape a wave, it pull you back in. Not Stavros. Stavros becomes glass. The sun shines through the man you once knew as only a speck on the Beach of Life.

Marrying you was the devastating decision of my life. You ruin me and you ruin my children. This is why: they hate me. It is unnatural for girls to hate their father, and that is why they live unnatural lives. But daughters are not only daughters but also adults, and hate is something you choose, not something of inheritance.

If Stavros Stavros as a young man were here with me, he would say, Do you open your mouth for the birds to circle back and shit in it? He would say, Why don't you also give Dina your *arxidia* so that she can smush them into bits the way she did to headlights, taillights, windshield, back window, rearview mirror of the car you love more than anyone in the world. Remember thirty years ago? Remember, Dina, I could not escape you and you could not escape me? What a difference the world was? I am no more this young man, and neither

are you, and we are no longer young and understand that a person
can escape almost anything?

The truth is that you and I, in many ways, begin life together. And
so we must end life together. That is why, Dina, I ask: you be my
executor.

A rap on the windshield. Stavros jumped. His heartbeat zippered
through his body, shot up his arms and into his legs, and continued to
radiate, as pain, from his shoulder. The papers crumpled in his hand.
Was his heart having an attack? For a moment he imagined the long
angel of God with his farming tool come harvest him a few days too
early. God and his angels did not fly you home or cart you up to heaven
in some bassinet. They picked through the rock and dug you out of the
earth, because you were potato with too many eyes made dull from
being far underground too long; and you were dirty, you were blind,
and you could not return. The gloved hand rapped again. A black
umbrella obscured the knocker's face, and he mistook it for a cloak of
death, and then a potato sack of death, and he felt very afraid. It had
Stavros crying, "Not yet!"

A woman's voice, muffled, said, "Get out of my parking spot."

The woman moved menacingly closer to his driver's window.
Through the ribbons of rain, he could just make out her face, and understand it was not death come for him but his ex-wife. Unless, in life,
death took the form of your ex-wife.

"Dina," he said, and rolled down the window enough for his voice
to get out. "What are you doing in this rain?"

Hearing her name shrank her back into a woman, but then she
puffed herself up again and said, "What are you doing, *malaka*? This is
my house."

By house, she meant apartment. The buildings were joined and
identical, including the rusting railings, and there was communal trash
and assigned parking spaces. The pretend brick façade was yellow-
brown, which did not to him look like a color but like a color with mud
on it. The Dina he knew belonged here.

He was not sure what to answer. He thought about asking her to let him in and then he will make himself known. He also thought, maybe just hand her the letter and drive away? But that was not the plan. This was important enough to be here in person. The letters did not work on their own: apparently they could be misunderstood or ignored. The calls following the letters, the Facebook invitations to a Last Supper dinner party—these did not work. With his family, nothing worked. His campaign was failing. But with Dina, he would get an explanation, a face-to-face, a conversation that could make him heard, even if that had never been exactly true before. Because she owed him. But more to the point of because—for the second time in their life, he was picking her; and he knew that for Dina, nothing mattered more than being chosen. And knowing Dina, he would need to go over some paperwork with her to make sure she is doing his wishes right. One thing he had never figured out was marrying women who were good with wishes or business.

He said, "I am going for a coffee. Would you like a coffee also?"

Dina stared at him. "You show up after fifteen years for coffee?"

"Or we go for a smoke."

The water running down his window helped him see her both as she was now and as she was when they first met. Her face not so hardened, though even then it had been too much like clay. Her big red lips and uncontrolled mouth, which always reminded him of live wires. Her Greek nose, long and pointy and now darker than the rest of her face. The black ugly short hair, which even when it had been long had seemed mannish. The lazy eye—he called it a slow eye because it was only a little lazy—that had made him fall in love with her, even though he was left with the impression that she would have lived a much happier life had she been born without it. At one time the eye had been a thing he wanted to cradle, something he found very appealing in her; but then she learned how to control it, and there was nothing vulnerable left, nothing in her he felt compelled to protect. Dina stared him down through the window, and he could barely see any problem with her eye at all.

She said, "No, we're not going for coffee. Unlock the doors."

He did, and expected her to come to the passenger seat, but she got into the back. Dina, never doing things as a normal person. She shook out her umbrella, but still, water got onto the seats—good thing he chose leather. He saw that the umbrella had a little gold brain on the top. To say what about her, exactly? She leaned forward enough that it made her look taller than she actually was, and as if she was seated both in the back and the front. She looked very fit, not eating so much sweets. Why were all his exes deciding to look pretty now that he was done with them?

"What's this about, *malaka*?"

Before she had scared a little death out of him, he had been speaking the words of the letter to himself, intent on fixing them to memory in a way that made them sound eloquent and like the wise thoughts of a man who has suffered with time. His decision had been: he would recite them to her, impress them on her, and Dina would be moved. Not out of pity or obligation or being forced to, which is what his family thought his final wishes meant, but because it would become important to her. He would make it so. He hesitated now, because he did not want her to react as Carol did.

"I will say first: please."

Dina scoffed, but it had her interested. They both knew that he had never started a conversation between them with this word.

He looked at the crumpled letter. He bit his cheek, which he knew put a fold onto his face.

"Well, should I read it?"

He said, "Yes. If only you don't get out before we have a chance to talk."

She took the letter from him, and he realized how warm his rehearsal had made the pages. Her eyes moved too quickly to appreciate what he was saying, and he tried to keep up in his mind with what flashed across her face in the rearview. He took a breath. He might have to interrupt if her face got too dark. He needed her to say yes.

He said, "I want you to be my executor."

Dina laughed. "You should have asked me years ago."

Having only ever heard the word *execution*, this is how he pronounced it: EX-ecutor. It made perfect sense: the man in the hood who uses the double ax to separate your life from your body, your neck from your chin, is the one who is responsible for what happens to your body after death. Stavros's body was also his estate.

Stavros turned completely around in his seat so she could understand him. "The one who manages the will," he said, "to make sure it is correct."

Dina, his last resort. Why not Marina, at least? Because Marina had already told him no. She had said exactly this: A chicken doesn't shit in your bed if you don't tuck it in. Marina did not believe him about his death, and that hurt his feelings. Besides, Marina might not agree with his final decisions regarding his will.

Dina looked down again at the page. He winced, because he knew what would come next. "Am I in your will?"

"Picture yourself as me," Stavros offered. "I need a person who can think about my death without confusion on the brain." Then, when she was quiet, he said, "We were too long ago, anyway."

"I don't care, really," Dina said. "It costs too much to be in your will."

He nodded, gravely. He saw she was going in the direction of Carol and Rhonda, but also that maybe she was not. It was this: something still connected them. There were the daughters, of course, but also, they had made their home in America together. Brother and sister, not ex and ex. Which, if you think about it, he thought, is truth, because people who marry and then divorce and recognize each other thirty years later are more like siblings than man and wife.

He said, "I need someone who can take care of the girls when I am gone."

He meant this, even if he did not mean that she would be the one to do it. He would never pick her to do it, because she had never done it, and actually it was a point of pride for him that he had done it, on his own.

In the beginning of their relationship, he was crisp Apple, she was Core. Then he was summery Peach and she was Pit. Then he was luxurious Pear, and she was Core again. He could cut the ripe parts of himself from her and did, that was the only way to survive, but he always noted the parts that were missing. If he had been Mask, he realized, she would have been Eyeholes. If he had been Dog, she Tongue. If Chicken, Liver. Fifteen years of hating the Core, then another fifteen pretending it did not exist, Stavros had finally, only yesterday, come to acceptance that you could not have Stavros without Dina.

She said, "Tell me something. Why wasn't I invited to the wedding?"

The question was ridiculous, because nothing could be so obvious. Who was invited to a wedding when no one wanted them there? Who was invited who was not friend or family or business associate or caterer? Who was invited who did not understand it was wrong to sit in the backseat and make someone turn themselves in the chair to address you? She was reminding him of a story his grandmother used to tell him, sing to him of the old village witch who became jealous and rageful when she was not asked to the wedding of a farmer she had helped, and after that she blacked him out of growing anything but roots— roots of tomato, roots of squash, nothing ever surviving aboveground. The food that saved his family? The potatoes.

"You want to be invited to a horse show to watch how much a horse can piss?" Stavros asked. "*Ela*, Dina, we all knew it was over before it was beginning. She is already divorce."

"That didn't stop you from going." She added, "I'm the mother." She said this with her neck, in a way that gave it muscles. She had an army neck.

"Yes, OK, maybe," Stavros said. "But I am not the one to ask about this. Litza is the one who refuse to make an invitation."

That, at least, was true. Litza had told him of that decision, which had pleased him, but he had never had to be the one to say, No. Instead, they had used the slot for one of his vendors. He did not like that Dina looked so hurt about it, but it gave some small satisfaction that being uninvited had served as punishment for years of neglect and low-life behavior.

Dina turned her head to look outside. The rain was not so heavy now. "OK, Stavro, I will do this for you." She looked him dead in the mirror. There was no slow eye on her. "If you're here, it means you've got no one else."

Here was the condition by which she was agreeing to give him her cooperation: not denying it. It made him feel grateful and seen, and, yes, some resentment. He opened his mouth to say, Good, excellent, I knew you would, here is the way we proceed with the terms, which if you look at them . . . He said, "Thanks."

She nodded, which made her look away, but then she was back at him, in the mirror. "I want a seat reserved for me, front row."

He nodded. This pleased him. It would look, to many, as if she were sorry for all of her ruinings. Funerals were where people apologized, sometimes just by showing up.

They sat together a minute longer. She was silent, would not meet his gaze in the rearview. Lonely Dina, a nearly forgotten memory which he was forcing himself to bring to the present; she resembled him more than she ever had, except for that one day, long ago, when he took her by the hand and they left his parents' farm.

Dina smiled. "Do I get to give the eulogy?"

"The eulogy," Stavros said, "I have big plans for."

CHAPTER 12

From across the street, Litza watched Dina get out of her father's car. Litza knew it was her because she walked through puddles rather than around them. It had been some years since they had seen each other in person. The last time Litza went looking for her, she found Dina's profile online. Occupation listed as Spiritual Wanderer, company as Mother Earth. These two, these parents, that's what she had to choose from?

It was crazy that her father was here. It was crazier than his email. He hated this woman more than anyone in the world. Whenever he wanted to hurt Stavroula or Litza, he compared them to their biological mother. Nothing until now had made Litza think he believed in his own bullshit, but this forced her to pause and take him seriously—if only for a moment. He was here because he was afraid of death and had nowhere else to go? More likely he was just delivering yet another belittling letter.

All through her childhood, Litza yearned for Dina, whom she recalled in blurs that more resembled bruises than face. She and her mother must have the same wild hair. They must have similar noses. She did not know what else she had gotten, though her father said it was a conniving personality. No one spoke Dina's name. Litza wanted to. She tried with Stavroula. There was no need to talk about their mother when there was a mother right here, was how Stavroula saw it. For Stavroula, Dina never happened. For Litza, she was always happening. She was always close. Overhearing adults, Litza learned things about Dina. Dina had the eyes of a rabid dog. Dina had replaced the skin around her vulnerable, membranous throat with an animal's pelt.

Dina made decisions that other adults did not make, because Dina had taken one look at the adults around her and decided, wildly, to not do anything they did. Dina did not remarry. Dina said no to men.

It made her all the more tempting.

Litza picked up leaves that might have resembled Dina in certain moods, or that Dina herself might have stepped on. She carried them in her pockets, where they disintegrated into small flecks. Mother got her a plastic envelope to store her leaves in. Litza crammed unimportant leaves into the envelope, which Mother kept for her on the refrigerator, and she kept the ones for her mother hidden. In the backyard, she lit a fire and tried to spell *Dina* with the smoke.

Then, the miracle happened. When Litza was in fifth grade, Dina showed up at school.

Litza went out to clap erasers against the fence, even though she wasn't supposed to do it that way, and there was Dina. Standing in the teachers' parking lot with a long black coat on. Around her neck, an animal. She was too far away to hear, but she spoke as she advanced. Litza tried to make out her blotted face. The bell rang, and children flooded the pavement.

Stavroula got to Litza first, and before she could tell her to get the erasers back to the classroom, Litza said, "It's her." She couldn't stop herself. She pushed many young children with backpacks. She tried to shake off Stavroula, knowing that her sister would keep her from her mother. Litza broke into a run. "It's her, it's her." The parking lot was full of moving cars now, and adults pushing their way through children, too, and teachers putting keys into cars and leaving. Dina was nowhere to be seen. The long black coat was gone.

Litza still held the erasers, and when Stavroula said, "Mother's picking us up at the corner," Litza whipped an eraser at Stavroula's face. The other she smacked on her teacher's windshield.

Mother made her walk back to the teacher's car, but the car was gone, so Mother made her write an apology after dinner, which was something Litza could do easily from memory. While Mother was watching TV, Ruby in her lap, Litza punched in the numbers, even their tone familial. Dina Lazaridis, phone number, street address. All available in the phone book for anyone wanting to know. Anyone brave enough to look and memorize, almost brave enough to call.

"Hello?" her mother said.

Litza breathed into the receiver, hoping she would recognize her just by the way air went in and out of her body. "It's me," Litza said.

"Stavroula?" she answered, just as breathless, "It's you?"

"No, no, no," Litza said. "Me." This she said only to herself because she had hung up immediately.

The next day at school, Litza gave her teacher the apology. She pleaded for one more chance to show she could handle the eraser job. The teacher read the note, but she still said no. Litza went outside anyway, when the teacher was addressing three squabbling girls. She walked out to the parking lot, and some parents who recognized her waved, but she did not wave back. She circled the building in case Dina was waiting somewhere else. The closer it got to the last bell, the more agitated she became. She wanted to get to Dina before Stavroula did. She imagined them arriving at the same time, and she imagined Dina hugging Stavroula first.

Dina did not come.

The next time Litza called, she left a message. And it was this: I will be at the McDonald's at 8:10 a.m. on Thursday.

She saw Dina before Dina saw her. It was the lazy eye—to Litza, this was the kind of feature someone was given in a fairy tale to indicate they were crucial to the story. Plus, Dina's hair was not at all like hers, it was black like coffee—no, crows. Her nose was big and beautiful. But she looked like she couldn't decide if she wanted to be a man or a woman, a young person or an old one. Litza decided she did not want people thinking this was her mother. She decided she did not understand the lazy eye after all—how could she be sure her mother was truly seeing her?

Dina sat down, which meant she had to push the table away from the booth. She took Litza's hands. Maybe because she was staring so intently at Litza's face, the lazy eye went away; this made Litza's heart hop in her chest. Still, Litza felt nervous having her hands held; she was nervous to take them back. Dina rolled her thumb over Litza's knuckles like she was wanting to smooth them out.

"I'm your mother," Dina said. "Do you know that?"

Litza nodded. Litza would have petted a rabbit the way her mother was petting her. Her mother's hands were not as rough as they looked. A little rough, the way a nest must be.

"I've been waiting for you your whole life, Litza."

Litza felt her hands relax into Dina's. She told herself, *This is my mother.* "Everybody thinks I'm at school," Litza said.

Dina got them hash browns, three each. She ordered Litza a small orange juice. Litza sipped it slowly. She felt shy. If Mother caught her, she would want to know, again, why Litza was being bad, and again, Litza would not know how to answer except to say, I had to.

Dina was watching her eat a hash brown and take sips of juice. "Sometimes I see you walking home in the afternoons."

"You see me?"

"I live close, just a few blocks from here, in an apartment. I can show you, if you like."

Litza would like that. Litza wanted to see her house, her car, her pets, which she must have—

"Slow down," Dina said, "you'll get sick if you eat too fast."

"I always eat like this."

Dina was not eating at all. She said, "I want to know everything, all the time I missed."

"You missed basically all of it."

Dina tilted her head, but this time the eye drifted left, which Litza did not like. She said, "I've been paying for my mistakes. But it doesn't have to be like that. You, me, your sister. We're going to be happy together."

This was not the plan. The plan was two, a train, airport, then a plane for Greece. All her clothes are new, all her extended family is happy to see her, her mother's mother. They buy her Nirvana CDs, which are selling like gyros even on the island, and she goes to school and is good at Greek, and in a few years when everyone has calmed down, she and Dina come back to America, and Dina's eyes never stray, and she starts high school. "What if Stavroula doesn't want to?"

"We'll persuade her." Dina rubbed just the one knuckle on Litza's hand, over and over, with her thumb. The longer it went— It did not feel good. Litza pulled back her hand. She said, "I have to get back to school. I'm already in trouble."

"I will do everything, whatever it takes. I can protect you."

"How?"

"I'm your mother."

Litza nodded. She reminded herself that adults say all kinds of things if you let them get away with it. If they think you'll believe them. She was not yet sure about Dina, so she said, "I'll walk myself back."

Dina said, "Take these," and fumbled to pack the remaining hash browns in a paper bag. Litza zipped the paper bag into her backpack, knowing that Mother would smell the food and want to know where she got it. Dina said, "Do you have lunch money?" She took some bills out of her pocket and squeezed them into Litza's hands. Dina kept squeezing her hands with the money in it, not saying anything, so that the quarters jammed against Litza's fingers.

Litza walked five steps before she let herself look back. Dina was standing at the table, watching her.

And was she watching now? All Litza saw, through the rain, was the ruffle of a curtain in one of the apartment windows, all identical, and perhaps someone staring back.

CHAPTER 13

Stavros sat outside the diner on a wooden pallet gazing at the startled sky. He could hear the sounds from the kitchen winding down the latest hours of the day and winding up the morning. Marina would be in soon. In the meantime, the night cooks would keep the travelers awake with sandwiches and pie. They would break everything down so that Marina could start all over again. But for now, at least, the stars were kind, and it was cold. For now, the tree branches nodded with sleepiness. The goat's head was in his lap, and they were both chewing cigarettes. Only Stavros's was lit.

He would die in five days. Less than a week now.

Stavros had trouble with sleep. He walked in slippers from his apartment. The slippers were the color of camels, and they had spills and holes at certain places and made his feet look like humps. He looked at his feet when he said, "Have you ever seen any man more pitiful?"

A sigh so gloomy from the goat. Stavros, too.

It had been hours since Stavros had spoken. He had been with himself only and he did not like that feeling when he could count the hours he had left to live. Even Marina had left early, because he had lost his temper and she had kept hers. Always, always she kept hers, and was that really fair? Was it fair that the only person who understands him is the funeral director? *We will make this as easy for you as we can*, the man said over the phone. *We will make it comfortable for your daughters.*

I am not paying for their comfort, Stavros said. *I am paying for mine.* But what he meant was, Comfort does not mean understanding, and more than anything, the daughters must Understand the Father.

None of his daughters had answered his calls tonight.

The goat nudged his hand. Stavros came back to the dwindling night. "Do you know what is Fatherhood, Goat?" he said.

Fatherhood is you holding a little tape; and the tape is sticky, so it follows you everywhere. Your hands are never clean, they are always sticky. You run, the tape flies after you, it is stuck to your little finger. You do not pay too much attention, because it is just tape. But then something happen: you, the father, realize what you have been holding is not actual tape. What you have been stuck to this whole time is a flypaper strip; and this many years you have been catching flies. You realize you are just a stupid idiot, and God has tricked you into trapping flies. What can you do? You cannot do one thing about the stuck fly. You cannot take off the fly legs from the fly or the flypaper. It is too late to try and change things but still you try, and nobody cares that you try, not even God, who is just sitting on a stool in the corner telling jokes about fly shit.

The goat nudged Stavros's hand again.

"Soon it is all over for us," he said to his friend. "Our mistakes will no longer have our names on them. No more, you fat *kri-kri*. Do you hear what I am saying, Goat, about how there is never enough time?"

At least the goat's head on his leg was a solid feeling, a light pressure that confirmed they were together. It was atom and atom, Stavros and goat.

Stavros looked up at the sky, said, "Could you make a noise, maybe so I know?"

Nothing. Nothing. It was a black night like he hadn't seen in his life, even with the stars. The wind rustled the grass that was more dirt than grass. Stavros could sense every blade trembling, as if about to blow away, and he kept expecting them to. He thought the smell of incense would come with the wind, but it didn't. He moved his hand from the dirt to his goat. He stroked the goat's buckled forehead, where the hair felt like straw.

"Ah, Goat, why not get fat?" he whispered. "*Ela*, we will have our Last Supper, just you and me, and talk a little." The goat lifted its head. "What, you say 'But *patera mou*, it is midnight and we have nothing to eat?' Goat, you should see the nothing we eat in Greece, my family and I, growing up so poor."

Stavros took out his cigarettes, and one by one he fed them to the goat. He lit the last one for himself. A feast.

"You know the first drachma I made, Goat? It was from a tourist who had lost his way. He asked which was the right way to go and I, Stavros, showed him."

He pushed smoke through his nostrils and made a sound like *humph*, because he was thinking of that first time he had ever been paid. Everything until this point in life had been slave labor. But no one in the world, not his brothers, surely not his mother, knew about the drachma that suddenly belonged to him. He could swallow it or buy a *glyko*, it was his choice. He was too young to know what that meant exactly, but the ability to choose felt important. He felt the coin in his pocket; he took it out and examined it in the sunlight. The coin winked at him. It had found its way to him.

Like a dummy, Stavros spent that drachma. He couldn't even remember on what. Did he regret it now? No, not really.

The goat grunted. Stavros petted his head again.

"You want to hear another story about Stavros growing up? If you promise not to tell, I will give you a funny one.

"My brothers and I, there are so many of us growing up that we share beds. Not two to a bed, I am talking four big boys, one bed. I am not the smallest, but I am not the biggest, either. Therefore, Stavros is stuck all night in the middle where it is warm. There is just one small constant problem which makes his brothers so mad: Stavros pees the bed."

Stavros laughed.

In retaliation, Kostas, Manolis, and Nikos had tried to set Stavros's penis on fire. Stavros ran, but his pants snagged around his ankles and the brothers pinned him to the ground. Orange dust caked his mouth and nostrils. Marina, the daughter of the *pappas*, the village priest, watched from the fence. Stavros could see her hand on the single wire that keeps the goats from wandering. She was not smiling or laughing, which would have made her seeing this OK, no; she was taking what was happening seriously. This was bad, a girl giving him pity with her eyes. Stavros spit in her direction, and this excited his brothers. Nikos brought the lighter to his crotch again. Stavros, afraid he was going to lose the most important piece of him, and in front of the *pappas's* daughter, became so hysterical that his sobs could have been mistaken for gobbles. Only then did his brothers let up, laughing so hard they nearly peed themselves.

"That gave me my childhood nickname, Goat. *Galopoula*. It means turkey. I hated it for years, but now I am OK with it."

Little Stavros yanked his pants up and gobbled after his mother, who was bathing the neighbor's three children in a metal bucket because it paid for her boys' schooling and their shoes (the left ones, at least, Goat). The children couldn't all quite fit in the tub, and one of them stood with a foot in the dust.

"At this point I am so afraid my *pouli* is gone, I can't even look. I can't touch it, only point."

His face was shiny with snot. "What, Stavro, what?" his mother asked, but she was not paying attention, she was ordering the children to raise their arms. She went across, scrubbing all three chests and throats. Stavros Stavros ran to the other side of the bucket so she would have to look. "Nikos burned it!" he shouted. Stavros Stavros pointed to himself, but still she did not get it. "Burned what?" she said, and Stavros Stavros pointed at the *pouli* on the little boy in the middle of the bucket. Little Yannis stopped dancing in the water. Katerina, washing the children's faces, wrestled Yannis's chin with her pink hand. In frustration, because what else could he do to make his mother understand, Stavros Stavros pulled his pants down. His *pouli* hung there, a sun-shy worm. Katerina roared into laughter. Finally, she understood. She splashed her son's lap with bathwater. "Don't worry, *agapi mou*, it's still there. It's just *mikro* for a while."

"Worst of all, who is still there staring the whole time? The *pappas's* strange daughter Marina. She looked sorry for me, like it was her fault. But also, Goat, it was like she was insisting on seeing the shame of Stavros Stavros Mavrakis. So what do I do? I pour out the bucket of dirty water close to the fence, and I splash her feet. What does she do, the strange *keftedaki*? She takes off her sandals and hangs them on the post and follows me with her eyes until I finally go away."

Stavros took a drag. "The things we think of at the end of our life."

He wanted that last comment to come out as a joke, but it didn't. It was too mournful for that.

He dragged his half-smoked cigarette against the pavement to put it out, and then he fed the last of his last cigarette to his friend. He closed his eyes. He tried to be here, now, with the goat's head on his leg. He listened to the wind.

A lullaby came to Stavros. One that no one had ever written, but one that every Greek knew because it had drifted down to the islands and farms from mountainous Kastoria, and it carried with it the diminutive "little," which was spoken with deep affection, the "akis" of his surname. The lullaby had come down to him years ago, like light, and he had only just received it. Stavros sang, his voice unaccustomed to singing, but he kept going. The goat breathed out its listening and stayed with Stavros and did not ask for anything other than this.

Nani, nani, my child
Come sleep, make it sleep
and sweetly lull it.
Come, sleep, from the vineyards
take my child from the hands.

Take it to the sheepcote
to sleep like a little lamb
to sleep like a little lamb,
and to wake up like a little goat.

The lullaby rose up with the wind to lift the weight from his shoulders, up to the stars to take its place in their glinting faces. The lullaby dusted itself clean. The lullaby, which Stavros felt come from the loneliest part of him, the part that was forgotten and far away, the part that wanted to be held and wanted to hold, that lullaby came and made family out of the words.

In the morning, Stavros Stavros Mavrakis was gone.

DAY 5

Bargain: Beg

CHAPTER 14

Stavros Stavros Mavrakis was gone: but not before one more story, Goat! Don't you want to know how the boy became a wise businessman?

On the main square in the village of his island of Crete, two *kafenia* faced each other: one red, one blue. Twelve-year-old Stavros Stavros opened the door to the red *kafenio* owned by the fat Onus. In the cool white room, customers sat on broken stools and played *tavli*, one of them debating louder than the normal loud Greek. The black hairs on his forearms were long, groomed. The other man shoved back, and the table rocked. Onus did not intervene because this happened every afternoon. One of them would lose money, the other would buy him ouzo, and by the end they'd be boasting that they fucked one another's sisters behind the church. The only harm was spilled drinks, which was no harm to Onus at all.

"What do you want, *mori*?" Onus asked when he spotted Stavros Stavros.

"I want to make money," Stavros Stavros said.

"I don't hire children," Onus said.

"I want to work."

The man with groomed forearms took his hat off to scratch his bald, damp head. "You're wasting your time with this cheap crook, Mavrakis. He wouldn't give his dead mother a job."

Onus did not deny it. At night he sawed off the tops of all his glasses at an angle. But today he poured a free shot of clear *tsikoudia*.

"Hey, crook," the groomed man said, "what's the Mavrakis *agori* going to do with that, water my squash?"

"He's going to swallow it like a man," Onus answered. "And then I'll give him work."

Stavros Stavros ignored all the well-deep eyes that followed him and took a sip. It tasted like it had been strained from a goat's coarse ass hair. His tongue pushed the liquor out of his mouth. Onus wiped Stavros Stavros's face with a stinking rag. "Tell your father that if he wishes to be a rich man, he should sell me a hunk of that nice land."

Stavros Stavros pushed away and left, face wet. He did not go home. Instead, he crossed the road and entered the blue *kafenio* owned by Takis. He didn't know what he would do, but he did know it would take more than a fat Onus to keep him down. Inside, the *kafenio* looked exactly like the one across the road. The customers were identical to Onus's—deeply wrinkled, hiding grassy ears beneath dark gray caps, counting worry beads beneath waxed white mustaches. Even Takis looked like Onus, except he was skinny and there were dark patches below his eyes.

Without addressing Takis, Stavros Stavros picked up a towel and began to wipe down the weatherworn tables. Takis paid no attention. He continued to slice a loaf of rough bread. When Stavros Stavros began to sweep out the lizards curled like bits of dry fat, Takis interfered. "What are you doing there, comrade?"

Stavros Stavros did not look up. "Cleaning."

"Don't bother. We like things here the way they are."

"You've got spiders."

"You leave those spiders alone. Those spiders are socialists. Good friends of the establishment." Takis put a wedge of bread into his mouth, followed by a hunk of white cheese.

"I'm just doing my job."

"Comrade," he laughed, "there are no jobs."

Stavros Stavros continued to sweep. He picked up the dirt with his hands and dumped the pile into a wastebasket. He wiped his hands on his pants and looked up. He was disappointed to see that Takis didn't look impressed.

"Who sent you, Mavrakis? The government sent you to spy on me?"

"Nobody," Stavros Stavros said. "I came myself."

"Onus sent you? He sent you to my shop?"

Stavros Stavros hesitated. A nod. Takis slammed his hands on the table. "That fascist wolf," he roared. "He thinks he can hire a peckerless runt to take care of my establishment?" Stavros Stavros's eyes darted to the door, sure that Onus was coming to clip his knuckles with a wooden ladle. "My brother, ignorant animal that he is, does not understand that one crow does not poke out the eye of another. Crows do not behave this way, so why should men?"

Stavros Stavros was nervous when he spoke. "I told him that your *kafenio* is the most respected in the village, but he says your shop gives his business a bad reputation."

Takis pulled a blue handkerchief from his pocket, drew it around Stavros's arm. "That cheap goat thinks he can get his hands on my shop. Let's see how he likes it when I take care of his."

Stavros Stavros, emboldened, said, "He told me you wouldn't even hire your dead mother."

"I wouldn't hire *his* dead mother. Now go show that goatfucker who you really work for."

Stavros Stavros ran across the street. He peered into the window. Onus was smoking a cigarette. He saw Stavros Stavros's head of greasy black hair and came out.

"Κακό σκυλί ψόφο δεν έχει. What do I need to do to make you go home, mangy pup?"

Stavros stood there. He was afraid of Onus a little.

Onus chewed on his cigarette. He peered into the dusk. "What are you trying to show me, *mori?*" Stavros Stavros stretched out the arm with the blue handkerchief. "My brother gave you a job? That poor bastard can't even afford the water he's stealing from me."

Stavros, still afraid, saw this as a chance to get back at Onus for embarrassing him. He said, "Takis says the youth of Crete won't be corrupted by fascist wolves." This was a favorite phrase in the village.

"Sure they will. How would you like to make double?"

Stavros Stavros thought about it. He nudged his chin at the red

handkerchief tied around Onus's pudgy neck. Onus pinned the cigarette between his front teeth. He untied the handkerchief and slipped
it over Stavros Stavros's arm, above the blue one.

"There, Mavrakis. Now you look almost like a man and less like a
socialist donkey."

Young, ambitious Stavros reported to both *kafenia* from then on.
He washed glasses, dusted chairs, poured alcohol when the brothers
were too drunk to do it themselves, learned the alchemy of Greek coffee. Within a year, Takis was training Stavros Stavros in the kitchen;
not to be outdone, Onus let him take over all of the cooking. By age
sixteen, Stavros Stavros was feeding all of the village men. His *mezedes*,
especially the *sardeles pastes*—fresh, salted, skinned sardines—were so
good, the locals said they were sweeter than maternal love. Να τρώει η
μάνα και του παιδιού να μη δίνει, they confessed: A mother would
eat it and let her child starve. No longer a boy, Stavros had become a
businessman with an eye for a profitable future.

Greek coffee, forever it would be the smell of his childhood, the
smell he hoped to be buried with. The long-handled brass *briki*, the
thick grounds, the golden froth that cooked slowly to the top. It was
prophetic—it spoke of a life better than this one, with riches to come.

DAY 4

Acceptance

CHAPTER 15

For the third time this week, Litza was on her way to the diner. She was going to make him finish the will in front of her while she drank glass after glass of milk. She was going to make him recite the letter from memory—she had memorized it, and so must he. She was going to make him tell her what he wrote to Dina. She was going to order him to leave Stavroula alone, Christ, couldn't he see the inevitable, hadn't he seen it coming like the rest of them? She would tell him he was *the wolf crying wolf*, just as he used to accuse her of being when she was young and *running with the pack, pretending to be one of the animals, crying wolf! wolf!* She would eat a big piece of carrot cake, slowly, while he confessed . . . whatever. She wanted to imagine the dense white icing changing her insides, like primer, while on the outside she stayed exactly the same. The question of the will, it wouldn't let her concentrate. She hadn't slept all fucking week.

Marina came out and told Litza that her father hadn't been to the diner in two days. This was unheard of. A thrill went through Litza, a whisper that said that maybe he was dead—and if her father's death were true, it made everything else in the letter true, too.

"He's not in his apartment?" Litza asked.

"It's not Marina's place to go looking. But, no, I don't think he is up there."

Litza went up herself and saw that he was not there. Marina said, "I always know where he is. This is the only time in twenty years that I don't."

"You don't sound worried."

"You aren't worried, either, *koukla*." Marina shrugged. "We both know—your father, he likes his own fireworks."

Litza knew that better than any of them. He was probably crying in a corner about poor Stavros because none of them had come to his stupid Facebook dinner, and he was gearing up to do his next mean-spirited thing. He'd return in a day or three days or a week.

Litza went to her father's office. Instead of calling Rob, she dialed the main number. She got through to a supervisor, a real 608.89. The *Urethroscrotal* asked her a number of annoying and personal questions until Litza exaggerated the problem and crafted a scene that involved her father's becoming disoriented on public transportation. Yes, they had filed a missing person's report, which she could get to them as soon as possible but, as she anticipated, the *Urethro* 608.89 told her that wasn't necessary. To make her feel bad, Litza said, "My mother's hysterical right now. I'm the only one keeping it together."

The supervisor backed off, and suddenly Rob was on the line. "What's going on, Lizzy?"

"I told you, Rob, family shit."

"You want me to help you look for him after work?"

This knocked her off guard. Did he mean it? She imagined the two of them stopping at Wawa to hang up Missing Father flyers, then cruising through the neighborhood, Rob's curly hair looking dirtier than hers. She imagined his eyes flicking back to her whenever she spoke, seeing the points of his canines whenever he laughed at her jokes about her father, because Rob sort of had a lynx's face, too playful to be a real predator because he was still so young. Too young to have to repeatedly submit forms for reimbursement for 300.02, *Anxiety*, which was the thing that kept him from really making anything of himself. If she said yes, she and Rob would end up in the backseat, and she'd let him go down on her, which she had only let her almost-ex-husband do. Then she'd stop Rob because it was too much, and tell him all she could smell on him was fried chicken. Spending the day with Rob would be a day of nothing, with no results, because the only way she could ever expect to confront her missing father was alone.

"Yo, I can leave early if you want," Rob was saying, eagerly grabbing up the silence.

"No," she said, eyes closed. "No, thanks, it's just a family thing right now."

Then she hung up and convinced Stavroula to meet her at the diner.

In Marina's story, the widow is so sure she can bring the dead back to life that they find her lying on the cots of the recently deceased; the village hospital bans the woman and yet she finds her way to the stiffening bodies and lies with them, fully clothed. When challenged, the widow says, "Death is only a temperature." This, told to her by a castrated angel.

"Does the village shun someone like this? No. They go to her for business advice."

When Marina told the news of home, she wanted a rapt audience and ice tinkling in a froth-necked Nescafé frappe. While she talked, she knitted something amorphous. It was not clear whose third cousin this was. Just because Marina was talking about the woman did not make her Marina's. Marina's news came from her father, the *pappas*, who sent emails about the whole village, and neighboring ones. Marina never called home. She pretended that this was because of the seven-hour time difference. Marina did not visit. She had tried once, in the early nineties, for a wedding. What happened was a lot of rain, and flooding, and the ferry Marina was supposed to be on sank near Chania. Though she had a ticket, Marina had not boarded. She refused, for no reason, or for reasons only clear to her, in her heels and black dress and pearl bracelet. *Something came to me*, Marina said afterward, *a sign. And Marina was smart enough to recognize she was spared.* The sunken ferry was her old life, and she could wave at it from a dock. Or the airport, which is where she told the taxi to go. Having flown seven-plus hours toward her family, she flew another seven away.

Over the years, Stavroula probed the question like salt on her tongue—no, more like salt on a sore. Did Marina ever want to go home? Did she miss it? Did she feel guilty? She kept the deaths of her two brothers private. Stavroula found out about the second-oldest brother's death—and existence—only when Marina created a new recipe, Unadorned Grilled Snapper with Pear Slices and served it for a day only (Name Day, Minos). When she served another recipe for one day only, Unadorned Grilled Dorado with Pear Slices (Patrikios), Stavroula realized that there was another brother and Marina had lost him, too.

Marina told her no one but Hero had shown up for the Last Supper. But Marina wasn't worried. Was she? Stavroula herself kept thinking he was at the casinos, charming old ladies into thinking that he was a good man and the thing that was missing was respect for the father.

"This fat woman lies on a man who is narcoleptic, to the whole village's knowledge, and still everybody thinks she has cured him of death." No, Marina was not worried. Marina was thinking of her own father, and how the village thought however he thought, even in these modern times. Marina pulled one loop of yarn through another. She could sense Stavroula's distraction. Behind her glasses, eyes like swift clouds. She said, "You have your own story you want to tell?"

Stavroula moved the straw in her glass. "No story yet."

This morning, after agreeing to come, Stavroula showered and made sure her face looked bright. She took the tag off of a new shirt and settled on a shiny black belt that was the point of the outfit. She knew Litza was going through her own version of this at home. Stavroula wanted to look professional, not open for nonsense. Then, Stavroula called out of work. July picked up.

She hated talking on the phone, was awkward with anybody. At least if it were her boss, she could say one, two quick things: *John, I'm taking a few days.* And not feel so off about it. She had never taken a personal day before, and July answering made her feel like she didn't have the right to now. Like maybe July would judge her for someone who didn't follow through. Someone who flinched. She didn't want July getting the wrong idea. She said, "This has nothing to do with our conversation from the other day."

"I know that. It's not really your style to avoid uncomfortable situations."

Stavroula took a breath. July was joking, but still. What else was she thinking?

July said, tentatively, "You're just not feeling well?"

"Oh, I'm fine," she said. "It's family stuff."

Stavroula heard her switch the phone to her other ear. "Everybody OK?"

"Yes." If OK was inheriting your father's last wishes, followed by your father going missing.

"Take your time," July said. "We can cover you for a few days."

"It's my father."

July was quiet. She didn't know about the email, but she knew about Stavros from Stavroula's stories. The most recent one was about *smell my fingers*, which the kitchen staff had picked up delightedly, relentlessly.

"Is he OK?"

"Probably," Stavroula said. "You can expect me tomorrow."

"Don't come in tomorrow. We'll be fine."

She was feeling a little braver now. "You wouldn't know what to do without me." That came out of her mouth? She was awful on the phone.

They were hanging up, and July said—"Stevie? Call me, OK, if you need anything?" and she gave her, for the first time, her not-work cell.

Stavroula saved the number in her phone. Then told herself that she'd never use it. July would call her first, so. Not that she was being proud. Just that July giving her her private number was a kindness, a friendship, but July calling Stavroula, now that would be an intention. That would be something.

It was a mistake, that hope.

Maybe the real mistake was giving in to Litza in the first place.

Stavroula hadn't come to the diner because Litza called to say their father was missing, or because, as Litza explained on the phone, it was Marina who discovered he was gone. No, since she had seen Litza— was thrown by the sight of her in his office—Stavroula had been going over and over the email. Not the part addressed to her. Rather, the part she had purposely avoided before now. *Litza, you have problems. Litza, I can only do for you what I am done for you.* She could imagine her father writing, reading it back to himself; then Litza reading, speaking it back to herself. It was like being in a car accident with someone, your sister. And realizing that even though you are bleeding, she is bleeding much more than you are. Or maybe you are just shocked at her blood and realizing that your parent is behind the wheel.

"What are you two digging for? A map to your father's whereabouts?"

Marina's question, the knitting needles clicking. The story about the third cousin must have ended without Stavroula noticing. Stavroula explained, "No map. We found his money trail, and proof of the mistress. But it all stops the day of his disappearance, the trail runs out."

Marina said, "Trust me, he is not with the girlfriend. That is over." She got up, gave Stavroula a quick peck on the forehead to emphasize her point, and left the dining room.

Stavroula and Litza had been going through his stuff when Stavroula's phone, sitting on their father's desk, rang, vibrated. In their thrill, both she and Litza jumped for it. Litza got to it first. Stavroula snatched at it, but Litza held it just long enough to read Stavroula's expression. Bubbles seemed to float from Litza's fingers up through her body, until they popped in her eyes. She did not even say, "Who's July?" or something equally direct to demonstrate that the call was inconsequential to them both. She handed the phone over—was that a smirk on her face?—and kept looking through papers.

Stavroula made an excuse about needing to contact some of her father's vendors, because she did not want to endure her sister's scrutiny. It would come, invisible but unmistaken, like the burn of onions. She went out to the dining room, drank a glass of ice water. She tried her voice—it was even. She redialed July. She got her boss; what July had been calling about was her approval for some menu substitutions. Stavroula's heart had leaped at nothing, she had betrayed herself in front of Litza for no good reason.

Now Litza was in front of her, sliding into the booth. Their booth. The clatter of nearby silverware was so loud, the rubbing of knife, fork, knife in her chest. Stavroula trained herself not to look away from Litza's gaze.

Litza said, "Check this out." She pushed a paper in front of Stavroula.

It was a deed. The proprietors of Tolley Cemetery exchange for good and valuable consideration, the receipt of which is acknowledged, so on. Address and other fields filled in. Plus,

(1) That the Plot of <u>Stavros Stavros Mavrakis</u> shall be used for the burial of the dead;
(2) That the Plot of <u>Stavros Stavros Mavrakis</u> shall not be enclosed in any manner nor shall be divided;
(3) That the Plot of <u>Stavros Stavros Mavrakis</u> may be adorned by one monument or stone memorializing the dead;
(4) That no tree, shrub, plant, or flower be planted on the Plot of <u>Stavros Stavros Mavrakis</u> without permission of the proprietors.

"He's got a burial plot?" Stavroula asked.

"Yeah, but people live their whole lives with a plot. It's real estate." Litza pointed to the date. The purchase had been made years ago, not two days ago. Not because no one came to the Last Supper. "It's probably the only thing he's held on to since his first marriage, other than us."

Stavroula read 1 through 4 again, looked up. She tried to take in what Litza was saying. All she could hold on to were the words "burial of the dead" and "stone memorializing the dead" and "without permission."

Litza leaned over and helped herself to some of Stavroula's Nescafé. Not gingerly, not politely. She drank from the glass as she might have in the past, when they took sips of one another's beverages.

We enter as if this is a tomb that does not have death in it but will soon—or into the house of an innkeeper who sweeps out lamentations daily and discovers that it is children, children he does not recognize as his own, who have been leaving behind their lamentations. And he eats the children and picks his teeth with their lamentations. We look again for the will, but it is gone. We decide to look for something else. We find years and years of credit card statements. She knows where to look; I do, too, even more so, but I let her go first. We read where the money, for years, has gone (not to us!). We see it goes to Atlanta, though we know no one in Atlanta. We discover there was a monthly subscription for an interracial dating service—We laugh. We imitate his voice—stupit eediot! We say, black women? We say, Remember him refusing to sit in his gray recliner for an entire day because our boyfriend Ricardo sat in it? Stupit eediot! We laugh, we laugh. We flip through the credit card statements as if they are a flip book of animations, and they are. We feel the Saturday-morning feeling of choosing our own entertainment. We feel the disoriented minutes of sibling companionship, free of gravity, before a parent returns to remind us we exist in zero sum, thus biologically and domestically programmed to root for each other's demise. We forget we were exiled to different worlds. We laugh. We search and share the next ridiculous artifact. Did you know he liked the movies? we ask. Did you know he ate brunch? We become a single, excited chatter born out of exploration and the revelation that someone, your father, is not who you thought he was: So how can We be who We think We are?

DAY 3

Depression

CHAPTER 16

The text from Litza said—
<GOING TO THE FUNERAL HOME.>

That there was punctuation meant she edited before sending. In the past, messages from Litza were unbridled boxes of dense text without periods or commas, often screeching and incensed. She had told Stavroula yesterday—when they seized their father's records—that she was going to see the funeral director. Stavroula had been reluctant to confirm she'd go along for the visit. It was only Litza's text, late last night, which said <DON'T YOU HAVE QUESTIONS?> that convinced Stavroula, ultimately, to come.

Stavroula wrote back—
<ON MY WAY>

Litza knew not to suggest that they drive together, so.

Stavroula was about to dial Mother, to inform her of their father's disappearance, to invite her to accompany them. She didn't. Why didn't she? She was pretty sure Mother and Ruby didn't know he was MIA. Should they know?

Stavroula hit every red light on the way to the funeral home. She drove past the Harwain, the theater that, when they were kids, charged $2.50 and that Stavroula stopped going to once Litza left to go live with Dina. She passed by the water-ice stand that they used to visit on scorched days in June.

The afternoon following the Facebook dinner, Day 6—why was she keeping count?—Stavroula had stopped to see Mother at Starbucks. Mother was gleeful; she had just received word of a promotion. Stavroula brought lamb burgers and kale salad by way of congratulations.

Over lunch they talked about the dinner nobody went to, Stavros's final wishes—all but his demands for Stavroula, which she skirted, which Mother let her.

"While your father was having one last pity party, I was celebrating," Mother said. "What did you do?"

"Kind of the same thing."

"He's so needy. That was always the problem with your father."

"Yeah, well, I can't imagine being married to him."

"I can't either, anymore."

"You'd think he'd want to stick around," Stavroula said. "There's a lot to celebrate these days." She meant Ruby, which Mother understood but did not confirm. Stavroula did not ask Mother how she felt about the elopement. She did not want to debate Dave behind Ruby's back. If he weren't ready for marriage and fatherhood, Mother would make sure he got ready. The only thing she was more dedicated to than Starbucks was the idea of a grandchild. Stavroula knew if one came along, Mother would be like its second mother.

"Maybe your father's onto something," Mother said. "Maybe we should all be writing our final wishes." She smiled. "Mine would be a cruise just for us girls. How about you, Stevie?"

This was an invitation to be honest, because it was obvious Mother knew about Stavroula and had probably even heard about the July menu from Ruby. The letter was, if nothing else, an opportunity. But Stavroula wasn't sure how much of herself she was ready to share with Mother. Maybe she just hadn't found the right expression of herself. She was still a little raw, when what she wanted to be—aspired to be—was medium-well.

Stavroula said, "No final wishes. I'm too young to think about dying."

Mother said she, too, had a new lease on life.

"If there's a funeral, are you gonna go?" Stavroula asked.

"If I'm not busy. You think your father will be there?"

"You kidding? Everybody, all in one place, paying their respects? It'll be like his birthday party."

Then Stavroula brought up the will, nonchalantly. Did he have one? Had Mother seen it recently? They were divorced, of course, but was Mother notified of any changes? Did that happen with wills for, like, legal reasons?

"Why are you asking?"

"He's got to be thinking about it, right? Knowing Dad?"

She did not express that his will had been on her mind since she caught Litza in the office a few days ago, or that she and Litza had found the incomplete version of his Final Will and Testament but that it subsequently disappeared from the office, like he knew they were coming for him.

"Your father thinks he's a pharaoh, Stevie. He's going to be buried with his money. I don't need a will to tell me he won't leave behind a cent."

Finally, Stavroula arrived at the funeral home, a building with columns and rosebushes and a sign on the lawn inscribed with gold lettering. She pulled up next to Litza, who had her window down, music off, and was checking her teeth in the mirror. Somehow she did this without looking self-conscious. Litza wore a pair of copper earrings, a light brown faux-leather jacket. It looked good on her, as usual: even Stavroula could admit that. Her sister had always been a brazen kind of pretty, just another way Litza confounded Stavroula. Stavroula could remember, when they were eleven and nine, Litza convincing a fifteen-year-old boy that she was older than him simply by how she hooked her legs around a railing, her hair trailing down her arm. Stavroula felt envious, though it had nothing to do with how the boy looked at Litza.

Litza's long fingers with their long red nails twitched as she spoke; they had a way of trembling when a cigarette was in them. Litza was flicking her tongue over her bottom lip, dark purple, as if feeling for a bit of paper. She was excited, Stavroula realized. Why? "At least this guy might be able to tell us something," Litza said.

The welcome mat was woven out of something green and still alive. The door, unlocked. Litza wandered around the small lobby and peered into vases, rubbed a plant to see if it was real. Stavroula stayed on the

red oval carpet intended for wet feet. The attendant did not come for
some minutes, though Litza had an appointment scheduled and there
were no services in session as far as Stavroula could tell.

Their father was not dying. Stavroula knew that much. But over the
last ten years, something had been breaking his body down. Standing
in the funeral home, she could not shake this thought. He had been
strong, if stocky. His arms had once been muscular loaves. As a little
girl, Stavroula remembered wanting to trace the inoculation scar just
below his shoulder, which looked like it might have been left by the
fine teeth of a melon baller.

Litza was in the candy dish, unwrapping a butterscotch and putting another in her pocket. The man who shook their hands gave four
names, but all Stavroula caught was Gabriel. He wore a three-piece
charcoal suit, a pale tie, and shoes that could have been passed down
from his father. He smiled through a pencil mustache and wrinkles
that seemed carved by many years of crying along with the bereaved.
He had no body fat, as if that were a luxury in this business.

"Please let me offer anything in the way of your comfort," Gabriel
said. His voice was like the skin of a tree after the bark has been peeled
away. That alone might have encouraged him to become a funeral director. His accent worked in his favor, sort of like her father's.

Gabriel showed them into his office. Instead of sitting behind his
desk, he sat in a plush chair. They sat on the couch, Litza closer to him.
Stavroula could tell why her father had chosen Gabriel and this place.
You were ushered into eternal rest here. Bright cream walls and French
tapestry. A heavy, gold curtain separated them from the other rooms,
cinched at the center so that they could see only a sliver of what was to
come. The fireplace crackled—a solitary log—and at her elbow stood a
bowl of cherries that she thought were plastic. A second look told her
they were unseasonably ripe. It was the first time she had ever mistaken
real food for fake.

On the coffee table were two mugs, a kettle, and a platter of shortbread. Stavroula picked a piece up and began to nibble. She missed what
Litza said. In response, Gabriel was saying, "I see. That is strange. What
might I do to ease the anxiety for you and your sister?" He was leaning

into Litza, which was what Litza was able to get most men to do: even this dignified funeral director was attracted to the messy hair begging to be tamed at this difficult time, the knee-high leather black boots with buckles. Stavroula had to hand it to her sister, she knew what she was doing. Stavroula started a second shortbread. Sweet, with some rock salt. Relieved, because Litza was taking care of all the speaking.

Stavroula did not want to be here, why had she agreed to come? She kept her ankles crossed and tried to appear like Litza—on the verge of bereft. Litza could get away with stories, or prying, or whatever this was.

"I'm just looking for answers," Litza was saying. "It feels like we've lost him already." The words came out puckered. Stavroula appreciated how Litza could make herself into a mourner. Maybe had always been one.

Gabriel cupped both hands over his knees, where his fingers ran down to his shins. Stavroula found herself believing the gesture. On second thought, maybe he was not responding to Litza's body: or maybe he was responding, but only in a way that saw what she was trying to do with it and gently, gently rejecting her. "Ah, you poor girls. This must be very disorienting for your family."

"He's proud, you know? He doesn't want anyone to see him suffer."

"Yes, we die the way we live, is how the philosophers explain it."

"Some days I wake up and I think, There's no way we're going to lose him. Some days I think, He will go back to being the father we once knew."

Gabriel poured tea. The cups tinked as he placed the saucers in front of them. His eyes insisted on meeting Stavroula's, then Litza's. "The terrible truth," he proffered, "is that we get only one father. And when he is gone, however he goes, he leaves inside us a hole that tells us we were very much loved."

Litza seemed prepared to reply—then, a feeling took over the room—like something being dropped and then caught, midair. Litza couldn't recover, it seemed, and there was an untenable silence. Stavroula watched Gabriel take Litza's hand in his. It was a clean hand, unblemished. Everything about it seemed cared for, even the three dark strands of hair close to his wrist. She could imagine his fingers crumbling dry chamomile.

Litza interlaced her fingers with Gabriel's.

Stavroula lowered her eyes. She returned her half-eaten biscuit to the plate. She waited. She heard a scratch in Litza's voice. "You can't tell us where he is?" she asked.

He said, "I do not know."

"What's going to happen?"

"What will happen is the sun will come out for your father, or the clouds. There will be music he loves. You and your sister will tell stories about him that people have forgotten, and those stories will carry you forward, each time giving the memory of your father a new life. What is going to happen is that you will consider your father's final wishes, and you will honor his best days on his last day."

"Please," Litza said. "We just want to know his plans."

Gabriel walked to his desk and brought back a book bound in leather. A silk bookmark kept the page of their father's funeral—marked in pencil, open-ended. Gabriel turned the book so that they could read it. He said, "Your father and I have been speaking often. I will be making arrangements with the place of disposition as he requires. He is choosing, himself, to arrange for clergy and musician honorariums elsewhere."

Litza studied the notes. "So the funeral's not here?"

"He is still considering his preferences for public memorial. Only the private family funeral will be held here, when the time comes."

Litza leaned back. She said, "How much will it cost?"

Gabriel smiled, which deepened the creases and the look of compassion. "Your father did not want to burden you with those worries."

"So he's paid you for private services, for some time in the future, and he's got a public service that will be held at some undetermined location?"

He nodded. Gabriel gently tipped his attention to Stavroula. "Please, if you can, Stevie, explain."

She shook her head, Explain what?

"What you are feeling?"

Stavroula unhinged her mouth. He was shifting his gaze from her eyes to her mouth and back to her eyes. She said, "I don't know."

Gabriel shut the book. "That is also how I felt about my father's death, and that is still what I feel." He guided Stavroula's hand to Litza's and said, "Your sister, she may not know what she is feeling, either."

Stavroula kept her hand there a second, took it back as soon as she could.

He led them out. He said, "If your father is found, please call us at your earliest convenience." He shut the door with both hands, a soft click. He was still in the window when Litza caught up with Stavroula.

Stavroula took several breaths. She couldn't get enough air, she felt sick. Like the time she had to skin frogs—the only kind of butchery she could not handle, the only kind of meat she did not eat. There was something wrong about a frog without skin—it wasn't itself, it looked too much like poultry. That green skin was all it had and it knew it, because it wouldn't let go. You had to work your finger between muscle and skin, peel it from the flesh.

It was getting a little better, the farther they got from the funeral parlor. Her heart was hers again, she did not feel so panicky. She realized how stifling it had been, how strange Gabriel was, how he seemed to read their minds. How much—truly—he reminded her of a skinned frog.

"Should we pay the mistress a visit?" Litza asked.

All Stavroula had on her mind was a shower, sleep, to wake up to an annoying voicemail from her father saying he had lost everything in the will in a single round of blackjack just to spite them, and to return to life before the letter. Whereas Litza was treating this like it was a scavenger hunt. Go see the mistress? What did Litza expect to get out of that?

"I don't want to see her," Stavroula said.

"OK, how about lunch?"

No. No. How had she put herself back in this position? That familiar, sinking feeling that Litza was wanting too much from her, was skinning her. Isn't this why she cut her off in the first place?

"They're expecting me at work."

"Just come for a few minutes, I'll show you this last thing."

"What is it?"

"It won't take long."

Stavroula couldn't tell what was happening with Litza behind those glasses. Litza was already lighting the next cigarette. Stavroula got into her car and rolled down the window for Litza, who was still standing there. She was about to say that Litza would have to do the rest of this on her own, Stavroula was going home, but there was Litza's shaking hand, just inches from her face. Litza said, "Wasn't Gabriel sexy for an undertaker?" and then got into her own car.

Twenty minutes later they were drinking coffee in another diner in another town.

A version of Marina comes out of the kitchen doors, and a version of their father—Asian—greets the customers. There are pastries and cakes and menus that flip open like invitational brochures. There is a shimmering bakery case, the shelves rotating. Cutouts of colored eggs and rabbits taped to the glass. The locals call to each other across the tables, but customers who are just passing through treat their booths like private, enclosed automobiles. The diner feels like a version of the Gala that has been sold and remodeled, under new management. It occurs to Stavroula that when that happens—whether that's this Sunday, two days away, or years into the future—all evidence of her father, except her, maybe, and her sisters, will disappear from the world.

Litza is taking as much sugar with her coffee as she pleases. Five, six packets. She pulls something from her bag for Stavroula to see. It is not typed, like the others. It is not sent out through email or posted on Facebook. It is real. It is unfolded. Stavroula reads too much, which is one word, the salutation, and then every line. Despite herself, she reads the whole letter. For a moment, she believes that the letter has come to them from beyond the grave. It spooks her.

It is as if she has seen her father's naked back at a moment he is attempting to cover it. She feels her father trying to arrange his face so that his children do not see the weakness in him—inevitable, like dropping fruit. That's when Stavroula realized that if something actually were wrong, Litza would be making the case that it wasn't. Nothing would convince Litza that their father might be innocent enough to be weak or aging or mortal. If he were in a hospital bed. If the deed were an autopsy report. If this letter were sanctified by God and anointed him a prophet. And then, a strange thought. If there were a difficult decision to make—whatever, whenever that might be— Stavroula would be the one to make it. If someone had to say, *He's dead*, it must be her.

Then the thought comes to Stavroula: this is wrong. Knowing how Litza will react, she slides the letter back.

Why is Stavroula here? She comes out of love. She comes out of obligation. She worries about her sister. She wants to know what is happening to her father, which until now has been a joke. This, she understands, is the source of Litza's excitement. Finding the will, tearing through his records, it felt like stealing old doughnuts out of the diner Dumpster when no one was looking, and stuffing the hardened sugary masses into their sleeves to eat at night after they brushed their teeth.

But, why is Stavroula here? She comes to see Litza without having to admit she misses her. She comes to recapture the fun of their childhood, faltering as it was. She comes to not learn what's happening to her father—a deed, a will, these papers and arrangements are useful distractions. Close enough to the question without actually being the question. She comes to not think about what she is capable, or incapable, of. She can be so cold, with veins of vinegar. What if she does not mourn him at all when the time comes? What if, after years of shutting him out—his words, his cowardice—she has shut him out forever? What if she is colder than her sister, who at least has anger for grief? She comes because she denied him his Last Supper. She comes to know that her father is not actually dying.

This letter, though. Like breaking apart the doughnut only to discover what's inside is not filling or custard, but maggots.

"You shouldn't have taken it."

Litza's face falls. Whatever fun they were having, it is over. Litza is outraged that Stavroula might treat their father's pain more seriously than her own. Stavroula knows this is what's going on, because this is what's always going on for Litza. Reluctantly, Stavroula knew Litza better than Litza knew herself.

Litza says, "Suddenly you feel bad for him?"

Stavroula can't help it; Stavroula does.

A waiter appears with a slice of pie and two forks but knows not to interrupt. He places the dish on the corner of the adjacent table, within reach. He is slim, with fingers probably suited to play the piano, but he is here, wasting that talent. Maybe he is the owner's son.

"He wants to bully everybody into forgiveness, and you're dumb enough to fall for it."

"This letter, Litza. He means it."

Litza snatches the letter, scrunches it up. "Did it ever occur to you that he actually wants us to find this shit? That he's leaving it like crumbs, which is what he always leaves us?"

"Where is he, Litza? Why hasn't anyone found him yet?"

She wants the question to hang in the air, like the smell of something frying, as it does for her. Litza snorts. "You know when we'll find him? When he wants to be found. This is what he does, he disappears when it's convenient."

"Then why bother looking for him? Why have we been searching through his stuff and going to funeral parlors?"

Litza refuses to say. Her reasons, it seems, are private, or she just doesn't want to give Stavroula the satisfaction. Somehow, she is looking at Stavroula dead-on and also watching her from the corner of her eye. Something Litza does when she readies to pounce. "Would you mourn for me, too? If I were missing?"

"Yes."

"And they think I'm the liar. You wouldn't have even called out of work." Litza shifts her coffee mug to the center of the crumpled letter. When she picks up the mug again, it leaves a brown ring. "Nobody knows how weak you are, Stavroula. Not even you." But it does not come out like cruelty. It comes out like pity. Litza's eyes swell, and for a moment Stavroula believes she will be forgiven.

Then Litza is down the aisle, still holding the mug. Yelling, inexplicably, all seven digits of July's number.

Stavroula wants to yell back, but Litza is through the doors. And what's there to say? No one tries to prevent Litza from doing what she wants to do. People, even strangers, even sisters, have the instinct of caution. Sooner or later, every interaction becomes a forgone conclusion—the way food turns to shit.

Stavroula watches from inside the diner. Litza, seething, heads toward Stavroula's car, which is across the parking lot. There are no cars near it, even Litza's is four, five spaces away. Litza launches the mug, and it smacks against the driver's-side window. The ceramic breaks apart and drops to the asphalt. Amazingly, the window does not break. The coffee runs down the glass like muddy rain, dribbling onto the door handle. On the table is the letter with a brown O in the middle.

Dear God,

It is me: Stavros Stavros Mavrakis.

Do you know, all these times, I have been writing love letters—to my daughters, my wives.

No one understands that the entire life of Stavros is a love letter with no possible translation. So it is to you, God, I write my final letter, which this is a letter of heartbreak. And I hope that you answer with mercy, which when you think down to it is what love really is.

Did you realize, all these times, I address to you in English? But I think it is the only way, God, You, will listen. Greek is the language of my beginning, and English the language of my end. Two lives, two languages. Also, God, you see how much I am with improving my writing. A man spends his whole life trying to say it better.

An egg, you remember, because you Created it, is the smallest of all living matters. It can understand only its small, warm self. The egg cannot see, only feel. Inside the shell, the heartbeat is the constant belief. There is a Truth in this: in the history of the world, it is eggs that have change everything.

Why could I not be this egg, God? Why do you have to crack Stavros Stavros Mavrakis?

I have seen you make scramble of the lives of Litza and also her mother, Dina. For Marina, for Stavroula, you boil life until the wet egg is becoming not egg, but almost meat. Then there are eggs that are laid by golden geese, like Ruby, Hero, like men who are famous and rich. How is this fair and equal, God, to give for some?

My ex-wife, she is the rotten egg.

But for Stavros Stavros Mavrakis, you have made me over hard. The Chef does not care that I have been cooking too long. You, the Chef, hold me to the pan. You, the Chef, ruin me, because a man, like an egg, cannot be change back to what he once was or what he was never meant to be. Once an egg is cooked, it cannot be forgiven.

Some may call my letters the letters of a suicide or a crazy man, or some even the prophet. And maybe those are the fates of Stavros Stavros Mavrakis. But Here is the Actual Truth:

Stavros Stavros has cooked himself.

He is a weak man.

I can confess this to you, God: I feel the broken in me, the white parts of me so cook they are almost fry. I could be better and want to be. But my whole life, I am too afraid to be something special, like omelet or cake. I think being an egg means I can be only yolk.

I wish to go differently in death.

Dear God: Make the life of Stavros Stavros Mavrakis over easy.

CHAPTER 17

Litza parked at the 7-Eleven, as usual, so Father Panayiotis wouldn't see her coming. She stamped out a cigarette and entered the church through the cafeteria doors. Without people in the room, her heels made the floor sound much harder than it was. The floor sounded like Stavroula. Nobody saw her cross into the cathedral, which was bright—chandeliers, the windows splintering into stained-glass scenes. Her favorite was a mountain cracked open so you could see the body of Jesus lying beneath it.

Litza was doing everything her father was asking of her. But he was never going to know. He could die today, he could call up choking on his own bones, and she wouldn't tell him.

She crossed herself and popped a Perc. Out of respect, she looked away from the saints, all of them brushed with actual gold because everything precious, even God, is made from gold. She felt like God did listen to her, sometimes, that was why she came, but in the rushed way you listen when you have somebody else on the line, or how a customer representative listens when she knows she's got many more nearly identical calls to take. Still; He listened. This was what she needed, all the saints staring down thinking only of her. She was not made of gold, but she was trying to be a better person. Couldn't Stavroula see she was trying?

Above, Mary held baby Jesus and blessed everything. Mary, the clueless bitch, lucky to have her baby.

Having children was a little test that she had given to her body and to the universe, and they had both failed. Here was another thing stripped away, another thing God did not want her to have. It wasn't her ex-husband that was the problem—it was her. She had gone to the doctor and he said, yes, unfortunately it looked like 628.2, yes, there could be trouble conceiving. It might be genetic. Stavroula, for all her condescension, she could be 628.2, too. Imagine—they might suffer from the same condition. Stavroula could be exactly like Litza, only not know it.

Even when she had run away from all of them—Dina, too—and was getting into some serious trouble, Litza had believed she'd make it right by one day having a child of her own. The decades she had spent on her own. The shitholes she lived in, she eventually realized, were on the inside. She wanted to show them—her family, who never came looking for her—that she had survived despite them all, and not only survived but thrived—because look at this beautiful baby girl.

Litza, you need God in your life.

Litza rolled a candle between her fingers, not so much that she'd put out the flame. The flame seemed very sure of itself. It knew it was a source of pain as well as life.

Once, when they were new to this country, she and Stavroula had sat in a Catholic church together. They were told to go and kiss the feet of Jesus and had come back laughing, because it was strange to be in a place where the appropriate gesture of faith was kissing a dead man's plastic feet. That day, they accepted shame together. If only she had a daughter, she wouldn't need a sister. Her sister, who could only guess at what Litza was. Her sister could kiss her Greek ass.

She squeezed the top of the candle, where the wax was hottest. It burned until she did it enough times that the wax protected her. The buttery wax hardened into a new, clean skin that immediately began to crack. She brought her finger back to the flame and held it there. Her fingertip reddened but she did not take it away.

What the letter really said was, *you are a nothing, a loser, a woman, a no one.* He used up his final words with words he had used all her life. And he was right, because she could not even do the one thing that all women could.

Yes, she destroyed the bakery case. It was like shattering a crystal. No, an angel. She wreaked destruction on a Sunday, and no one saw her coming. She came the day after the honeymoon, when all should have been calm and her husband was napping with a pillow stuffed beneath his ear. Yes, her father warned, the fiancé is a loser, had turned into one the way that sometimes turns into always; he had lived through it with Dina and he didn't want that kind of life for her: she could walk away from the wedding today and no big deal. Yes, he walked her down the aisle. Yes, she was a stunning bride, with baby's breath in her hair and a waist tight as a knot. Yes, cousins came from Greece that she had never even met, all of them to celebrate her, and, yes, there was both a band and a DJ, and they threw dollar bills at her feet and her father's as they danced; and, yes, her father rented a van and took the cousins to the Saratoga horse races to show them a good time, and yes, he paid for their hair to be styled on the morning of the reception. Yes, it was a wedding of abundance, an abundance she had never known. Yes, Stavroula gave a toast that promised a fruitful marriage borne of friendship. After only one week, Litza left her husband. Her father was right about the man she had chosen to spend her life with: he was not worthy of her.

She took shards of the bakery case with her. She put them in her pockets, slicing two of her fingers.

Yes, she came for destruction on a Sunday.

She sat at the counter, she ordered black coffee. She felt the hot liquid go all the way down. How could it scald what was already scalded? But it did. She slid her hands down the cold metal bars of the stool—she felt like she was lifting the heavy bottom half of her own body—and she rammed the stool into the delicate cake case. Everything shattered. Her father was there instantly, making *wh–wh–wh* sounds—after all he had given her—and he was not even separating her from the stool like she expected. The icing stuck like Spackle to the floor, his arms. She dragged the stool out behind her. Yes, she could see it in her backseat, yes, she bled, yes, she knew all the while what she was allowing herself to become. She drove to Stavroula's place of business, and nobody saw. She held the stool over her sister's car for a long, long time—no one, no one, to save her from herself—she came down with all of her strength. Her sister's window blowing out; the scream she had been holding in forever. Yes, she needed God in her life. Yes, she had problems. But who was the one who broke their promises?

The cathedral was blazing sunlight. She was doing that with just her thoughts and feelings. Litza pressed a palm to her arm. It was wax. Her legs were wax. Her nails were not nails. Her fingers could break off one by one if she wanted to. Her heart, animal fat.

Her legs lifted off the wooden pew. Her feet went first, her feet tipped toward the sky. Jesus was inviting her up to be his personal best, and all the icons could watch. These were not angel wings, she was more like a moth, easily torn and shredded. Really, she didn't need wings to get where she was going, heat was making her rise. Mary's eyes tracked her ascent. Mary's eyes moved in the paint and said, *I have, you want*. Litza slapped at the domed ceiling. She went eye to eye with the saints, whose tongues did not sit like pudding in their mouths.

She looked down. Her body was dripping, hitting the floor, and curling into rind. The candle dropped for a very long time, extinguished itself.

She fell down to the blue carpet that loomed beneath like an ocean. She dropped headfirst. No one to grab her arm, no one to turn her upright. If her father had been in the sky with her, he would have watched her pierce the clouds, then the water. He would have kept going. But he was not even there to do that.

Litza ran down the aisle. Her heels sank into the carpet, but she got to the doors before anyone saw her. She hit the weak sunshine, still warm but shaking, and lit a cigarette.

CHAPTER 18

Marina stood at the chopping block in the black slippers Stavroula had always known her to wear. The wisps of hair at her neck were matted with sweat. The three assistants around her worked hard to keep up. She was cutting carrots. The carrots were huge, the size of a child's forearms. Marina did not do wimpy carrots. Stavroula dropped the brown bag at her elbow.

"More medicine already? Pretty soon I will be eating medicine breakfast, noon, and with coffee." But she smiled when she looked into the bag. Inside were two vials, plus a cupcake, which was forbidden by Marina's doctor.

Stavroula accepted the knife from Marina and remembered that a knife was not a knife when it was also a hand—one of the very first lessons that Marina taught her. She ran the blade against the carrot. Orange disks whirled onto the board. She felt the tension in her body release whenever the blade sank. These clusters of cells would be broken down so that other cells could live. One of Marina's 107 lessons.

"You're busy," Stavroula said. She hoped it did not come out a question.

Marina ran her hands along a line of peppers, removing seeds from their sockets. "You wait. Marina is going to take her own little nervous break, then we will see where Stavros disappears to."

What did Stavroula expect? They weren't ones to talk family problems, so. When Mom Mom died, Marina gave fifteen-year-old Stavroula a new recipe to try and a honey bun; the next week, Stavroula returned with a recipe of her own. That's how Marina coached her to deal with loss, absence. There was something to it, of course. And it was, in part, why Stavroula loved Marina like no one else. The more Stavroula chopped, the more it began to feel like her father was fine. She made a pile of the orange carrots and swept the greens off the board. It was nice, this kind of grunt job—something she didn't do that often anymore. She wiped her knife on a clean towel, one that had no smell. Habit.

Then, uncharacteristically, Marina came out with, "You are worried about your father?"

Stavroula shook her head. Kept cutting. Could cut forever.

"You are troubled by something?"

"Everything's good."

Marina went back to the peppers. But she gave some errands to the assistant closest to her, so they could be alone at their station.

"*Koukla*, have I ever told you the story of the milk jug?" Marina asked. "A story of my childhood."

"You had a childhood?"

Marina smirked.

Stavroula once heard Marina say of Greece, "For a woman, it's nothing except a country full of dirty plates. That's why I got out before they could marry me off." She heard Marina tell of the *pappas*'s near-perfect run: "Fifteen sons and then a Marina—fat little girl, always riling up the chained *skylos*." And she knew how fat Marina, spring after spring, snuck into the neighbor's hut to hold the baby rabbits, even though they hadn't yet latched to the mother; as a result, the neighbor flung the babies onto the roof, where they were food for birds. Did this deter Marina from touching the baby rabbits? It did not. This was all that Stavroula knew of Marina's childhood. Marina's stories rarely had anything to do with Marina.

"When Marina was three or four, she dropped a jug. A big glass milk jug. The bottom cracked, all the milk poured out. Her father, the beloved *pappas*, was not pleased because there was not very much milk in the village, the village goats were sick with a vengeful bug. It had taken days just for this little bit of milk sap, which had taken the *pappas* lots of friendly talks with herders. The *pappas* was angry. So what does Marina do?"

Stavroula's eyes moved to Marina's chin, which was covered in soft hairs. "What does Marina do?"

"I pick up the jug, which is perfectly perfect except for the hole at the bottom. I say, 'No worries, it's only broken at the bottom.'" Marina laughed now, just as little Marina must have made them laugh then, even during a national depression.

Stavroula knew where this was going. "What's the lesson?" Number 108.

"The lesson? No lesson. Except in this scenario, you, *koukla*, are holding the milk jug. You walk around wanting to believe that you are whole when actually you are pieces."

Stavroula said, "I'm not the broken one." Litza was broken. Her father, with his letter and demands, was broken. Stavroula knew what broken looked like, because that was everyone around her.

Marina dried her hands on Stavroula's clean towel, and pepper seeds clung to the cloth. "I think maybe I have spent a lot of time teaching you how to be strong and not enough how to be open."

Stavroula picked up the knife again. She went slowly through the nearest carrot, cutting thin slices. They both knew there was nothing soft about Marina. How can you teach what you don't know? Besides, Stavroula wasn't interested in vulnerability. Vulnerable couldn't command a kitchen. Vulnerable was always the quietest voice in a room. Or, at least, the first one silenced.

Marina swept Stavroula's carrots into a pot using her bare arm. After some time she said, her back to Stavroula, "Your friend stop by today."

"What friend?"

"Your friend, a woman. I went out myself to meet her." Marina turned, holding a bowl, wiping it slowly, slowly with the towel at her waist. "She slips off her shoes while she eats. This is your friend?"

"We work together." Stavroula's heart was pounding, making her feel very young. The chopping helped, she stayed with the chopping. She was not a child, she was a chef. Even in Marina's kitchen. She told herself so. "How long did she stay?"

"Not long." Marina put the bowl down. Marina standing there, not cooking, not moving, which did not happen in this kitchen. The assistants toiled around them, pretending to hear nothing. Marina took a folded yellow paper from her pocket.

When Stavroula was a teenager, Marina refused to serve a gay couple, saying, *I know what goes in a mouth like that, and it's not my food.* About two lesbians who often came to the diner she said, *It must all be mush, like cake with no egg.* She wouldn't have cooked for these people if it weren't for Stavros making her.

Stavroula said, "She asked about Dad?"

"What else? Your friend expressed concern, and I tell her it is too early to worry." Pause. "So she is not worried about him. Instead, she worries about you."

The knife, that was the thing Stavroula had to hold on to. Her eyes down on the carrots. "What did she say?"

Marina unfolded the yellow paper. Flicks of water dampened the page.

Once, Stavroula summoned enough courage to ask Marina why she had a problem with these people. What was she afraid of? *Not afraid, Stavroula. Only, it makes me uncomfortable.*

Marina, seeing Stavroula's face, made a sound like *chick-chick.* She waved her hand, and the kitchen emptied. All the orders that had to be filled, and it was just them. And the July menu. Marina patted the yellow paper twice as if it were a misbehaving child. "Your friend has decided to leave this for you because she thinks you aren't going back to work for a long time."

July had annotated the menu, in light pencil, with notes like *They really are the best,* and *If you ever tell anyone about the whole chicken, I'll tell them about sausage.* But also, *These spices sound right, but they're not—they miss entirely.* And, *I lied when I said I liked this dish.* It looked like, in the course of only a few days, July had tried everything.

Marina said, "Where did you come from, with this menu?"

That was exactly what she said when Stavroula cut her hair—*Where did you come from, with this hair?*

Stavroula kept chopping the carrots. The carrots would never run out. But her eyes were full of tears, her vision was orange threaded with silver. She held on to the tears, would not let them fall. She was trying to conceal herself from Marina, and she was trying to make herself known. She was fifteen all over again, shaking and hoping no one and everyone could tell. Marina, the person Stavroula had admired since she was a little girl, Marina, the person she loved most. The reason she has hidden all this time. There wasn't a word in her father's letter that Marina agreed with, except for what it had to say about Stavroula.

All Stavroula needed to say: This is who I am, *thea*. If I am who I am on the outside, I am who I am on the inside. But she couldn't. Thirty-one years old, and this was her answer:

A slip of the knife.

Blood on her finger, dribbling over the other fingers and onto the cutting board. Blood on the carrots. Who knew how many, they'd all have to be thrown out. That was Stavroula's first thought. The second was, *You did this*, but then whatever insistence there was in Marina's face faded. She was stricken, panicked. She pulled the towel from her waist and thrust it onto Stavroula's hand. She was clumsy, wrapping it around the injury.

Stavroula said, "I got it, I got it."

Marina fiddled with a first aid kit. Doubtful she had ever opened one before. Shocking that she knew where it was stored. "You keep that tight."

Stavroula wiped her face on the towel wrapped around her hand. It smelled like garlic, like her birthdays with Marina. Inside, the finger pulsed. There must be a lot of blood coming out. She had seen the slit the knife made, like a cat eye, an almond.

Marina brought Stavroula to the sink, and they ran water over the finger. "I don't know, I don't know," she said. Funny, the way Marina was fussing. Stavroula had never seen anything like it.

"You feel like it's coming off, the finger?"

Stavroula laughed through the heavy crying. "No, it's not coming off."

They figured out a bandage together. Not stitches, after all. Stavroula wound a piece of medical tape tightly around the gauze. Her finger felt safe hugged in like that, but blood was soaking through. She'd need to change it soon.

"Are you crying because your sister is always angry and your father selfish, or do we blame the carrots?" She said, "Or do we blame the broken jug. Or do we blame Marina?"

Stavroula said, "Carrots." She met Marina's gaze for the first time in minutes. Marina's eyes, the slick exposed skin of onion. All this time, she realized, Marina had been rubbing her arm, massaging it as if to make sure the blood knew where it belonged.

Stavroula could not take it, losing the one person whose love had felt as everlasting as bread. There was no reason to fear her father's letter, except this.

"You stop this now. Crying only makes food bitter."

"That's blood. Crying doesn't do anything."

"Exactly, crying doesn't do nothing, so what is the point?"

She was fifteen. What was the point of crying? Litza was gone for good, and Stavroula was forced to take a job in her father's diner. To teach you a lesson, her father said. What she wanted to know was, What lesson? He said, Life lesson. She did not fight him. Somehow, with all the lessons she had been learning lately, the fight had gone out of her. "This is another kind of school, the Slop Room. You will learn important things, and you will learn them behind a sink, like your father. You will come direct from school. You will eat what only kitchen people eat, which is whatever we have much of. You will finish homework on your break, and then you will go to bed by ten o' clock." She wanted to know how long she'd have to work. He said, "Until your lesson is learn."

He fired the dishwasher. So she was dishwasher.

She wore elbow-length blue gloves, like a knight or a superhero. But it was awful work. Ingredients in sink form—starched noodles and congealed sauces and curdled batters and gluey fats and wilted fruits and creamed lunch meat—are the opposite of food. It got to be so that water looked funny without a film of cooking oil clotting the top. The Slop Room told Stavroula, not for the first time, what kind of world she was living in. The stuff on the pan, the pan itself, all that shimmery water, the soap bubbles, the blue gloves, her own skin—it was all the same. Trash, life, it was all the same. She saw a brown cloud over everything. She could not rinse the brown cloud. All her father said was, What is this about a brown cloud when we are cleaner than most people's houses?

She did not know what day it was. Eventually, she realized that breaded chicken meant Monday. Vats of goopy *avgolemono* soup meant Thursdays. All days meant without Litza, because Litza had gone to live with Dina. Had been forced out? Had wanted to go, all along? Stavroula wasn't sure.

"You finish schooling," Stavros said, "you become a lawyer and a doctor, and you don't ever wash pots again. You don't ever put your hands in a full sink. You see my hands? A stranger sees them, he thinks I'm professional." He flashed his pinky ring, its face the size of a quarter. It was an actual coin. The jeweler had customized the gold ring using a Greek drachma, a gift from Mother. "You see Marina there?" her father said. "You keep getting As the way you're getting As, and you don't look like her."

Marina flunked a cleaver into bone. She said, "Your father, for one time, is half right."

Marina was not pretty. When her hair was up in a slanted bun, which was always, her head looked like a ham hock. The skin on her face, in places, was the texture of fried cheese. There was a softness to her speckled quail eyes, and the wisps of hair around her temples were light, like whipped egg white. Her voice was the voice of a woman who knew who she was and had stopped apologizing for it long ago.

Stavroula did not want to look like Marina. She didn't want to go home smelling like Marina. The weak womanly business of preparing meals—she wanted no part of it. She thought her father had done Marina a favor by hiring her. Marina, Stavroula decided, was a slave to someone else's kitchen. She was not smart or strong enough to get herself out. But Stavroula would get out, out. And once she was brave enough to do that, she would be brave enough to go get Litza. Bravery would make her into something she wasn't: loyal.

But Marina was no woman. She was a priest, like her father the *pappas*. Marina respected blood. She demanded that all meat be butchered on premises, and because it was cheaper to bring in whole pig and lamb, because she had a connection that would transport the animals at almost no price, and because the meat was clean and fresh this way and she did the butchering for free, Stavros agreed. Marina claimed that bleeding the neck was a spiritual experience, and she burned incense as she hacked into the hoofs and attached the animal to a tree in the back lot through the leaders in its legs. Stavroula watched from the window. Marina was strong. Once they had the animal up, she could do the rest herself.

But, Marina said, she wasn't going to let just anyone watch her butcher. She wasn't going to let any Stavros off the street see her hands deep in the warm, yolky blood of a calf. She needed staff, she said, with good hearts, hearts that hear. Once, she had refused to work because she didn't like the assistant that Stavros hired—he had vulture teeth.

"Vulture teeth?" Stavros said. "He is not a bird, he is a man."

Marina didn't care. If the vulture was in the building, then Marina was not.

And this was not all. Marina could spear her own octopus, pull apart the tentacles, gut it, clean it, hang it to dry like a man's collared shirt. And then the smell—oh, the smell! like God's oven!—of octopus grilling over charcoal. But that would come later.

Marina did not pay attention to Stavroula in the beginning. The first day, Marina yelled orders and when she realized that the boss's daughter didn't take orders (having lost her Greek), Marina did the work herself. The number one rule for dishwashers was stay out of Marina's way. The kitchen belonged to Marina, the Slop Room was Stavroula's. Good, then, she would stay in the slop. Washing dishes, talking to nobody. Never talking to Litza, because Litza was gone and Stavroula was not brave enough to find her. Stavroula tuned out the Greek music that came from her father's cheap radio, which sounded exactly like her pots and pans. She didn't wink back at the busboys. She played games to get through the day. How many pans could she wash in five minutes. What was the chance she could finish the load before a new load arrived. If she was a leftover, and her sister a leftover, would they be the same leftover?

From the slop, she watched Marina. For someone who was a slave, she looked very much in charge. Stavroula could see how good Marina was at her job, and she could tell when Marina was having an off day just by how viscous a sauce was. Marina, for her part, grew to respect Stavroula's system, that the large boiling pots went to the bottom of the trash can so they could prop up the other pans. Also, Stavroula liked homemade chicken and lemon potatoes, which Marina made for her.

"The Mexican vulture was a dishwasher," she said to Stavros, where Stavroula could hear. "This one, she's a cook."

"No, she is not a cook. She is what I say she is."

He left, Stavroula stopped the water. She hung her apron on his office door and grabbed her schoolbag.

Marina had a paring knife clenched between her teeth. She flicked the knife between her second and third fingers so she could speak. It was like watching a pickpocket take something of yours, right before you mistake it for someone else's. "Where are you going?"

"Home."

"You want to quit, you do it when the dishes are done, and you do it to his face."

Stavroula stopped on the edge of the Slop Room. "The dishes are never done."

"You'll have to start a union, The National Society of Daughters Who Are Sick and Tired of Dishes but They Have Bosses Who Do Not Care What You Think, Only Care What the Boss Thinks." She laughed at her own joke.

She watched Marina trim, in quick swipes, one particularly fatty place. Marina said, "*Koukla*, for a Greek, your father is not so bad. Only, he thinks protecting means controlling." Then, "You leave it to Marina, we'll get him out of the kitchen."

Stavroula yanked her apron from the knob, back to the sink.

Next day—three months into slop and a Christmas without Litza—one of Marina's assistants got the flu. Quiet, dependable, the way Marina liked them, but Riley was not immigrant stock. Only vegetable stock. Not so strong, not so immune to fluffy American diseases.

"Dishwasher, put down the dishes and come out of the Slop Room," Marina said. "You have real work to do."

Stavroula tossed the blue gloves at the sink. She rubbed her wrists. She tied on a clean apron, a white one. She saw that the newest busboy had been chosen for the washing. He was putting his hands into the moist pockets of her gloves. His face said she was gross.

"Hold here," Marina said, and Stavroula did. "Line the pan with these," Marina said, and Stavroula did. "Rub this spice mixture onto the fat backs of the chicken, and beneath the skin," and Stavroula did. The tasks were simple, repetitive, not so different from dishwashing. Still, it was amazing to grab the pans while they were clean, to fill them, to put them in the oven, making something instead of discarding it.

Stavroula was put on potatoes for the rest of that day. The second and third days, she was put on onions. So many onions, Marina gave her goggles to wear, and then tied a scarf over her face. The scarf was Marina's, smelling of melon rind and meat. Stavroula politely declined. "Ha," Marina said, "you would rather soupy eyes than deal with an old woman's stink."

The crying. So many tears wet her face that the goggles slipped off. She sobbed so hard that the busboys, her friends, said, "Boss, she need a break," and Marina said, "That's exactly what she's getting." Her face, puffy like fruit, her eyes raw. The first cry since Litza left. She cried even after she stopped chopping, she cried on the way home and through dinner and in bed. At the end of the third day, when she could take no more, Marina took up Stavroula's knife and finished her onions.

After that, Stavroula started to really pay attention. After that, it was Marina who had her heart.

Marina liked things quick but neat. Countertops were always wiped down. Stavroula did her best to be clean. On day four, she dropped a drumstick on the floor, and Marina made her put it in the pocket of her apron so that Stavroula would feel the weight and remember not to do that again. "The worst crime you can make is a crime of waste," Marina said. "Waste nothing, and you will make the right kind of cook."

Stavroula said she would be careful, she would be mindful, and she would try not to waste any more. If these three things kept her out of the Slop Room, she would do them all day long. If these things kept Litza out of her head, she would keep drumsticks in all her pockets.

The assistant came back on day five. Stavroula returned to dishes. It did not bring her numbness, like it once had. She stared into the kitchen, hating even more the sour steam that wafted out of the basin.

"You think I have money to run down the drain?" Stavros asked. "You are done here. Marina needs extra hands." That was Stavros's version. The real version, the one that Stavroula eventually learned, was that Marina had demanded it.

He had nagged her in the Slop Room, but now! This is boiling, this is cooling, this is burning, this is beeping, this is dry, this is soggy, this is messy, this is runny, this is ugly, this is no good. This is not going out. *This* is not going out. Where's the honey, flavor, seasoning, friendly? Where's the order? What are you doing so wrong? The dinner rolls should be Greek hospitality. A paying eater asks for the rice pilaf, he better taste country. I was twelve, I was doing this better than you; a hundred times faster, and a thousand times right.

"I thought you said she was a cook," he said to Marina. "All she can make is beans."

"Beans are not easy. You of all *malakas* know the truth about beans." But when he left, she said to Stavroula, "*Koukla*, you work like you're still in the Slop Room. A griddle is not a sink."

"I know that."

"I don't think so. Just because the food is going into someone's gizzard doesn't mean it goes down a drain. You can't cook and daydream. You have to be here with the eggs when they're frying."

"I am here."

"No, you're leaving the eggs to fend for themselves. You have to come back, wherever you are."

Be Present, that was the first lesson, and Marina did not mean show up. Someone could show up every day, Marina said, and still never be present. Do you hear what I am saying, *koukla*? You must be mindful, be now. Be the spatula, be the heat, be the cheese sizzle in the pan. The past is true, but the present is truer because it's all we have. The second lesson, *Be on Time*, but that did not mean clocking in. It meant getting a feel for traffic, it meant knowing when someone was going to come in hungry. Anticipate the waitresses, who had personalities like cats. Have a sense of urgency that has nothing to do with lunch, which has just passed, and everything to do with dinner, which is facing us down. *Be Prepared.* That didn't mean pens and school-rulers. It meant understand what the customer is going to order before the customer orders. It meant have the resources inside to imagine the future.

"That's impossible."

"That is how Marina cooks."

Stavroula learned one lesson after another. This kept her from the slop, and it kept her from Litza. Except for the awareness, which snuck in every now and then, which said: Litza, wherever she was, wasn't getting this. Dina was no Marina. Stavroula had been curious about her biological mother, sure, despite her feelings for Mother, but she was wary, too. Stavroula once agreed to meet Dina for hot chocolate, not lunch, but left with the feeling that she had been with someone her own age and who would never get any older. Dina would never be a good mother, Stavroula knew this instinctively. Litza was alone, while Stavroula—suddenly, the eggs weren't being sent back. Suddenly, Marina could trust her to take care of the specials. In exchange, Stavroula got to learn real cooking. Her heritage made sense. It was seductive. She did not tell her father how much she enjoyed making *gigantes*.

He tried to tell her. "Out of everything in this place, the Greek menu is the thing that lives!"

In her gut, she understood. Whipping together cucumber, yogurt, garlic, mint for the immaculate *tzatziki*. Tucking slim-boned quail into golden pans of olive oil and oregano, or wrapping the bird in a dough of water and red earth until the mud bakes hard, or cooking it in a hulled aubergine. Grilling squid stuffed with fingers of feta cheese. Marina taught her the words—*gemista, kotopoulo, petimezi* glaze, which had been passed down from the Ancient Greeks—but no one had to teach her what they meant.

"This is the beautiful secret of your father's business," Marina said.

"This is why I work for him. There is cheap American food to lure the Americans in, and then there are the irresistible Greek dishes to turn them into lovers of Greek."

Stavroula had friends at school, but they did not understand her like Marina.

After they had served the customers their cheap, comforting dinners, Stavroula finished homework. Food did not taste like it should after you stood over it for a whole day, so sometimes, they had only cucumbers for dinner. Marina asked her to read aloud math problems and then tried to solve them in her head. She did the computation with a finger, licking it every time she added.

One night, Marina picked up a sheet of paper. She scanned it. "This is something you have to do tonight? This is homework?"

Stavroula nodded. It was the course request form from the guidance counselor. English, math, science. Her electives for next year were Law I and Law II. Her parents liked her choices. She liked being on a track that meant she'd be somewhere else in four years. Which felt like forever, but still.

"You are not taking this culinary class?" Marina asked. "There is no check mark."

Stavroula shrugged. "What do I have to take a class for?"

"What does anyone take classes for? To become better."

"I am getting better. You're teaching me."

"All we are fattening you up for is to be a wife."

Cooking, Marina said, is the thing that has oppressed all Greek women in the history of the world who have come before us. You know how long it takes to lay out one sheet of phylo dough, then to brush it in a warm butter bath? Do this fifty more times, a hundred more times, and all you are is a Greek woman. Feed the family, and the whole village, too! Is that what you want, to be one of these? Like Marina?

"What do you mean?"

"Today is your lucky day, teenager." Pause. "Your father and I had a discussion. Your life lessons are over. No more kitchen."

"But I like it here."

"You know how to work a knife like a hand now, and not a knife.

You take some culinary class, you go be a professional, and you can do this for people who can get you ahead. You make money, a life for yourself."

"I only want to work with you," Stavroula said. Marina was sounding like her father. Stavroula wanted to hear that she mattered here. She wanted Marina to admit it, feel it. Marina was what got her through. But Marina only looked like a chicken picked apart. She was pulling at her own fingers like they were feathers.

"He won't let me take culinary class, he wants me to take law," Stavroula begged. She was keeping the tears in her throat. Adults did not treat children's tears seriously. Right now, Marina was showing herself to be an adult.

Marina stood. "All I can give you is a job. You need more than what I can give."

"I'll fail." The very thing that would disgust Marina.

But she was not disgusted. She looked sad. "*Koukla*, you couldn't if you wanted to. You are too smart and too good."

"Why do I always have to be good? Why can't I do what I love, instead?"

She meant, be with people she loved.

Marina untied her apron and let it hang defeated in front of her giant chest. Her eyes had turned from teaspoons to soupspoons. She said, "We forgot one last lesson, *koukla*, number sixty-three." She tossed the apron with the other soiled ones. "We will have to learn it tomorrow."

Stavroula watched Marina shuffle off in her black slippers, never turning around or bothering to check on Stavroula, inexplicably, as always, carrying a full glass of water.

In a metal censer, incense burned. The sun was shining. Two pigs were staked to the ground, their legs bungeed to the carving tree, their heads removed. The middles were hollowed out; they were surprisingly dry and firm and clean. This was how Stavroula felt, now that she saw she was about to lose another person she could not imagine losing. Together, the pigs looked like a cold uninhabitable pink tent. The area directly beneath the tree was stained with old blood but other than that was clean. The grass was growing heavy, nurtured by guttings. The patio that led to the kitchen was spotless. It got washed every night. What police, what inspectors? Nobody knew about this. Except for the carcasses, it could have been the setting for an afternoon picnic.

Marina started by holding up the heart-shaped kidney, darker red than blood. There was a shallow cut running down the middle. "Delicious, but the Americans don't like it whole, so I sneak it into recipes." Yes, Stavroula had seen Marina do that.

Marina handed her a knife and an apron. "The last rule is: Don't Let Anyone Tell You How to Cut Your Meat."

Stavroula's arms were crossed.

"Pork is the big special tonight. You don't do it, no one's eating."

"Marina will do it."

Marina picked up her own knife from the stand. "I do mine, you do yours."

Stavroula was squeamish about cutting into an animal. Pig, especially. But also, she wanted to. She poked its skin with the tip of the blade. It felt like a thick layer of butter. Marina kept going, expecting Stavroula to catch up. Stavroula held her breath and pushed with the knife. It was like entering a fleshy door.

Marina sliced, Stavroula followed. Marina pulled off the pieces meant for lard, and so did Stavroula. Marina cleaved at the hock, and so did Stavroula. It was heavy, but Stavroula used her body to move it to the wheelbarrow. Little by little, the huge shape broke off into little shapes that Stavroula could recognize. Pork chops, ribs. Stavroula was panting from piecing away the animal. Her neck was slick. But there was something satisfying, the pig untucked from its bones. After a while, it was not pig.

"Don't get cocky," Marina grunted, "or you get sloppy." They kept going.

Stavroula looked and saw that she was keeping up. Just about. They were both accessorized with flicks of pig skin and gore. She did not need to pay attention to Marina. Her knife knew where to go. It found depressions on its own, moved into natural grooves.

"You know what, sophomore? Only a real cook butchers like that."

"I just followed you."

Marina swung the cleaver and sank it into the tree. "Admit what you are, finish them both."

CHAPTER 19

Rob beat her to the last chicken nugget. She wrestled it from his fist with her mouth; apparently he did not like a tongue driving into his clenched fingers. He slapped her away. She squeezed his nostrils with her fingernails so that he had no choice but to spit out the chewed-up nugget. He threw the last swallow of soda at her, getting it in her hair, and she rubbed her face dry on his knee. People getting into and out of their cars were staring, which was what she wanted. She was more panting than laughing, but laughing, too. Rob was aggressive the way a man is when he doesn't really want to hurt you, only leave an impression.

They were hanging in the parking lot of the Wawa about half a mile from the diner, Rob now leaning on the bumper of his car, Litza standing far enough away where he couldn't grab her. They had not gone looking for her father. Not like Rob had any real thought about going searching for Stavros Stavros Mavrakis—what he was after was something else, which was exactly why Litza had called him up. When they met here, he asked if she was hungry because he was starving, and instead of giving him the opportunity to take her to a nice place—and instead of giving him the opportunity to suggest someplace disappointing—she insisted on McDonald's. The McDonald's where, as an adolescent, she met Dina in secret. The McDonald's that her father had never once stepped foot in. He condemned what they were eating as *junk food*, not really being able to appreciate that, for once, he was using an appropriate phrase. What she and Rob had been doing for the last hour was getting high, not too high, in this Wawa parking lot and scarfing the kind of *junk food* that could not be ordered at her father's diner.

A thirty-five-year-old cop walked by, belt jingling, hand on his firearm like he might revert to using it. Rob pulled his hat over his eyes, casting a purplish shadow over his face. She knew he had nothing to hide and just wanted the cop to think he did. Litza said, "Hey, Leo." The cop entered the Wawa without answering. Rob was surprised she knew him.

"You tell him about your daddy?" Rob sneered, threatened by the possibility that she might be interested in the officer, clearly not realizing that the officer scored a 099.9 in her book. *Venereal disease, Unspecified*, and it was the Unspecified that freaked her out the most, not to mention that he was married with one on the way, and that kind of man she did not respect and did not give it up to.

"Leo? No. He's still mad at me."

"For what?"

She bit Rob's knee, and he kicked her in the stomach, lightly. Enough to catch her breath. She sucked her teeth. "You never kick a fucking woman in the stomach."

Rob snorted. But then he saw that she was serious, and he changed up and was calling her *yo-baby*, which she wanted to roll her eyes at but didn't because that would have quickly unraveled the evening. No man wanted to get corrected when he was sniveling for forgiveness. What she knew about men was, they were in love with the way they laid out sorry.

She was here, refusing to do a damn thing about her father's disappearance.

Now that the streetlights were coming on, the parking lot was flooding with a weak yellow. She came closer to him, nicely. He was half sitting, half leaning on the trunk of his car. She put her hands on the metal bumper between his legs. It was perfect that Leo came out of the Wawa right then with his coffee and soft pretzel, saw them, got into his cruiser but didn't pull away. She eased between Rob's knees, which she could tell he liked, because his whole body was paying attention. She brought her lips to his ear but didn't do anything yet. He squeezed her hips with his thighs, telling her what she was in for. She had played this game before, with men who really had been giving her fair warning, so she knew she could answer in a number of persuasive ways that would make Rob—blah, blah, blah, blah.

She whispered, "You know I can't get pregnant, right?"

She pulled back in time to see the look pass over his face, one that changed him into a little boy. His eyes were saying, *Shit, really? 628.2?* His eyes were reading her eyes, mouth, hair. She had picked him tonight because he was low risk. What harm could he do after what she'd been through this week? But also maybe she knew that Rob would offer comfort at a time when she couldn't ask for it and no one in her life would offer, anyway. She regretted it immediately, that look on his face. She shot him a look that said his pity was pathetic, which caused him to change his expression, too. He said, "Awesome."

But still, he had her by the wrist and was massaging it lightly between his fingers in a way that was tender and bothered her. This kid was only nineteen, what did he know? No nineteen-year-old anywhere is barren. Barren was not how she felt; how she felt was capable of giving birth to a storm. The doctors were wrong about her. When her body was ready, it would give her a child. She would be a loving mother, make her child strong like her. Being a mother was what Litza was meant to be.

It was a shame that the moment was slipping from them. Not that she couldn't get Rob started up again, easily, in fact he was already getting himself worked up, but she was no longer in the mood. It wouldn't help, getting lost in a new body for a little while when that body was going to hold her like she was damaged. Unless, without realizing it, that was why she had called him?

"I have to go look for my dad," she said. That was not what she was going to do.

Rob straightened. "Your dad's really missing?"

"Yeah."

"Shit, I thought you were making it up to get out of work for a few days. I was like, 'Me, too, my dad's missing, too.'" He laughed.

"It's not funny," she said. She knew he didn't think it was.

He dragged his foot over some pebbles. "He just, like, vanished?"

"He wrote a goodbye letter."

Rob was quiet. She knew he was thinking *E950, E951, E953,*

E955.4, E956, E957—all the ways her father might have killed himself. But the truth was that she and her father, in this one respect, were too much alike. They were both stubborn, and they wouldn't give anybody the satisfaction.

Rob was rubbing the hood of his car, unsure what to say.

"He'd never hurt himself, he only hurts other people," she said.

Yes, that was it, that was the way to understand his disappearance.

The disappearance, like his email, was meant to shame her. When he was the one who should be ashamed, because he was a liar and he had never been there for any of them—truthfully, none of them—and all of a sudden he wanted some kind of golden martyrdom named Fatherhood? All of a sudden he wanted to go away and have his life immortalized as worthy? *I have seen you make scramble of the lives of Litza and also her mother, Dina*; when he was the one who made the scramble, had started it, anyway, and once you started a scramble, how could you stop it? Marina had said it herself: you can fix anything in the kitchen but eggs. This disappearance, like that email, was arrogantly trying to rewrite history—and thereby erase what brought her to today, what she fought through and succumbed to, and that meant leaving her with all responsibility for her life when in fact she had been given an inheritance. The things he had given her, he could not take away. Her very life was evidence of what he had caused. The fact that she was here, still kicking the world in the teeth, was all her own creation.

Rob asked her, "What did he do?"

This question, so direct and plaintive, freaked her out. It made her want to tell him to mind his own fucking business, but—Rob was not asking out of pity, that wasn't the look on his face, he was asking because she had led him to this asking; he was asking because he saw it was hard for her to erase the look on her face without breaking, which meant that what she was saying was true or at least what she perceived to be the truth; he was asking if she wanted to talk because it was the right thing to do, at a time when you've shared food with someone, and maybe before sex, even if the food and sex are nutritionally equivalent to junk food.

Stavroula, if she were here, which she wasn't, would have thought Litza incapable of answering honestly. She would have thought her too weak. But Stavroula misjudged her.

Litza could tell Rob at least one thing he did.

When Litza was twelve years old, Stavros came after her. She shoved her weight against the closed door, but he rammed through with his shoulder. He banged his head against the door frame, so intent he was to get in. He got in. The skin around his mouth was wet, expanding, as if it belonged to a whale. But then it got tight like a fist. She told herself not to be afraid, but this was her father and she knew his anger before she knew anything else about him.

Litza could not get away from his body. She went the only way she knew, which was down; her legs buckled beneath her, and she slid down the wall. He was shouting in her face, little flecks of spit. His mustache was like an angry black animal.

Where did Stavroula go? Deeper into the clothes hanging in their shared closet.

On Litza's upper arm, his middle and ring fingers digging in like rodents. He said, "You want to tell everyone how bad a father you have? You think that low-life will save you?" The pink ribbon of his lip curled beneath his wet mustache. "Let me explain you something: I should have left you there, to live like an eel."

She did not answer. He stood to full height.

"I save you. *I save* you." He kicked at her foot, not too hard, and her shoe swung back. He kicked again, harder, and she pulled her leg close to her body. She reminded herself of a snail.

He turned to Stavroula. "Pack her bag. She goes today."

It was out, finally, this thing they all knew he was capable of; he almost surprised himself to hear it. Litza, however, had been expecting this for a long time—since she got here. This thing that had been determined, since their return to this country, every hour of every day. This threat that made her and her sister into who they were, as different as they were.

If he would not fight for them, who would? If he could let them go, who would take them in?

But she did not think—had never thought—that he would make Stavroula do it.

Stavroula did not move. She was swallowing, again and again. There were many questions trying to get out, but it was also as if the questions were bees and Stavroula was protecting them both by keeping her mouth closed. Maybe Litza was not alone? Maybe Stavroula would be with her, sit with her? She would say to their father, *She's not going anywhere. We're sisters, we go together.* Together, they would get real loud, louder than him, because they were two and he was one.

Stavroula knew, didn't she, why Litza had to be loyal to Dina? No, not even that—why she had to be loyal to herself? Stavroula pretended not to see her, but she did, actually, didn't she? She saw who Litza was, deep down, because, really, could they be all that different?

Their father had gone quiet waiting on Stavroula. He propped himself against the wall with his left hand. His right, swinging against his body as if it were weak. She knew it wasn't. She looked up at the arm pressing against the wall. It was as wide as her face, wasn't it?

"Your sister, the eel," he said, almost slurring, "she is putting my two feet in one shoe. She betrays her family."

The three of them, they knew it was true.

His breathing picked up. "The police come. She did that. She and Dina got the police on your Mother. The woman who raise you."

Stavroula was not moving. Was she thinking about how the police had come to Mother with legal papers that called her a bad mother? How Lady State had asked the two daughters questions about how they were treated and, concluded, looking around the house, *This is a nice big dream your parents have?* Or was she remembering what Litza was remembering? The two of them sitting on a park swing, singing *eeska deeska bella.* They had lost their Greek, the language had become nonsense to them, but it was OK—the words *eeska deeska bella* they held on to. They kicked, swung, sang their nonsense. They pushed off the earth as if it were a sure thing. They swung together, like this, their faces cast up to the sky, their feet touching down at the same time.

Stavroula pulled out a duffel bag and unzipped it, put nothing in it.

"They will come for you next, Stavroula," their father said, his voice rising. "They take first one child, then the next. That's how this country deal with accusations like this."

Stavroula dropped a shirt into the bag. The sleeves hung over. She was being slow, not careful.

Litza got to her feet. "He doesn't care about us. Only himself."

Her father reeled, so far back she thought he had lost his balance. His hands came up as if he were going to grab on to her, rather than the wall, to steady himself. He did not steady himself. He took a sharp breath no thicker than a cracker, and he spit into her face.

She shut her eyes. And then she pushed *him*, made her nails into claws, but he was laughing. She yelled for the police, for the neighbors. Dina, the police, they would get him, they would get him.

"They get me? For what? For what?" She stopped thrashing. The look on his face, mean. Like he could crush her, and would. "What they get me for? Explain me, what you think happen?" He looked at Stavroula. "You see something happen here?"

Litza's ears pricked for Stavroula's voice.

"Something happen here?" he said.

"No," Stavroula, from inside the closet.

"*Ela*, what you see here?"

"Nothing."

"That's right," he said to Litza. "Nothing here except a waste of life."

Litza opened her mouth—

"Scream your face off, then I don't have to look you no more."

She screamed at the wall long after he left. She screamed through him saying to Mother, *That one? She is the biggest mistake of all.* She screamed until she heard him say to Dina over the phone, *Take her out of my life.*

Then she was quiet and faced Stavroula, still cowering in the closet. For the remainder of her life she would never feel bad for Stavroula, but in this one moment she did. Because Stavroula did not yet understand what kind of man their father was.

PART II

STAVROS STAVROS MAVRAKIS

Stavros Stavros "Steve" Mavrakis is survive by women, many women, but also: his beloved diners and many customers. In the place of flowers, please bring stories to share so that he will not be forgot.

Most people will say that what they remember about Stavros, or Steve, is that he is a kind man who works hard to make only one life for his children: the best. What he will most be remember by is how he creates this new life in America out of nothing. He is preceded to heaven by his brothers Stavros Yannis, Stavros Nikos, Stavros Markos, Stavros Petros, and his two parents, Katerina Mavrakis and Stavros Constantine Mavrakis.

Stavros Stavros Mavrakis, born in 1959 on his home island of Crete on a farm near Iraklion, was number eight of twelve sons.

Seven years older than the youngest, seven years younger than the eldest—regretfully, Stavros Stavros's birth was mostly nothing. The day after, Katerina attached him to her nipple and returned to the fields. Heavy rains threatened the vines; gray rot had already begun to creep over those closest to the ground. So many fungal spores settled on the grapes. Katerina only had to put her hand out to know that it was alive, with its thick eyebrows and coarse leg hair. And like the Greek women who had lived through the war, there was nothing gentle about this fungus.

In 1950 the Rockefeller Foundation concluded that Cretans had a potential need for everything, and no one knew that better than the Cretans. Greek soil had been cleared of Turks, Italians, and Germans, but occupation and civil war had made the land arid. Families that could grow only rocks stripped the bark off trees for boiling; children sucked on olive stones long after the meat was gone. This was not the glorified fight of World War Two, when Cretans ran out of their kitchens with knives and walking sticks to club parachuting Germans to death. This was not the Andartiko of the Second World War, which took triumphantly to the mountains. This was not the Resistance, which abducted the Butcher of Crete, General Heinrich Kreipe. This was cruel, shameful, emasculating hunger. And Katerina knew, as late as 1959, that if they lost the grapes, they lost everything. A new child, even a son, was not worth all that.

Once Katerina dropped Stavros Stavros among her other wriggling, insistent boys—all of them reaching up for something all of the time—she forgot about him. There were just too many other troubles (her older, louder children; her husband, who farmed from four until four; her blind mother; the checkbook she balanced every week, raising a family out of zero). In the morning she counted twelve boys, at night she counted twelve boys, and if Stavros Stavros was a needy little piglet with short hair, short legs, she barely noticed. He managed to walk, talk, engrave pee lines in the dirt. His mother seemed permanently out of reach until one day, squinting into the sun, Katerina caught him climbing out of caked dust onto the back of a bull. He was wearing the last good undershirt to fit him and Stavros Sakis. Katerina pulled Stavros Stavros down and whipped him until purple grapes blossomed on his naked bottom. It was a formal initiation into the family.

Like all of his brothers, Stavros Stavros was named after his grandfather. But while the other boys had been assigned unique middle names honoring an uncle or a *klepht*—a Greek bandit who fought for independence—Katerina neglected to give one to her eighth-born. By default, he became Stavros Stavros. Stavros Stavros insisted that it was a sign: not even Nikos had been twice honored with the name that meant "victorious" and "crowned." Stavros Stavros obsessed over the heroes his grandmother sang about and decided that he would become brave. A guerrilla, like those of the Second World War who wielded scythes in battle and subsisted on mountain weeds and wild tender *kri–kri*, a goat so elusive that it had once been worshipped as the pale, hairier, lustful incarnation of Zeus.

His brothers, however, insisted on referring to him only as Stavros, and somehow that meant he had less claim to life than the other eleven boys who shared his room. At home, Stavros Dimitrios, Stavros Stefanos, Stavros Kostas, Stavros Manolis, Stavros Yannis, Stavros Nikos, Stavros Markos, Stavros Petros, Stavros Sakis, Stavros Tasos, and Stavros Alexandros answered for Stavros and got his share of the honey-drenched *kadaifi*. At school, they intercepted love notes and walked home with the girls who had been somewhat curious about Stavros. On his name day, they set off all the fireworks while he sat locked in the chicken coop, staring at the wasted bursts of yellow and red.

Stavros Stavros was determined to escape this village life. He would go live in the caves of Malta. He would learn to squeeze water out of limestone, fight the ghosts of Ancient Romans, train hawks to shit on his brothers. His mother would climb the mountain in bare feet, confess that he had always been her favorite because he was strong and clever and self-sufficient, just as her own father had been. Every day, she would come with a basket. She'd feed Stavros Stavros with her own fingers, but he would take none of it. He wouldn't need to, being so resourceful in the wild. She would wash his feet, out of respect. And his father, his father would ask for advice on harvesting grapes. Illiterate, he would learn from his son. Like, for example, how it was wise to plant rosebushes next to grapevines. Roses and grapes are sensitive to the same pests: the roses show rot first. (That one he had heard from the neighbor, and now that he thought about it, his father had, too.)

But at age twelve, after a tourist put the first drachma in his hand, Stavros Stavros abandoned the caves of Malta. Far from wanting to remove himself from civilization, Stavros Stavros decided to get rich and his family could watch. He would be an entrepreneur among men, in the business of coffee.

On the main square, two *kafenia* faced each other: one red, one blue, both with whitewashed doorways to invite peace and discourage ants. The *kafenia* were the core of men's lives, thus the core of village life. A center for Greek politics, because talking politics was as Greek as mathematics, as Greek as Ancient Greece. A place for business and dark coffee and afternoon plates, for mail and cigarettes, for worry beads and news. A substitute for the pews their solemn mothers and wives knelt before. If you wanted a bricklayer, a harvester, a lawyer, an arbitrator, a salesman, you need only visit the *kafenio*.

According to the government, all Cretan coffee drinkers were nationalists, united under Greece's blue and white flag (colors of protection and purity). In actuality, the *kafenia* separated conservatives from communists. Babies born to conservatives were suckled on stories about cousins exiled to Makronisos for patriotic reprogramming; those born to communists were nursed on tales of martyrs who had fought for Greece's liberation only to be tortured and slaughtered in the countryside, where herds outnumbered doctors by the hundreds. Only Stavros, who worked for Onus and Takis, was permitted entry into both *kafenia*. Stavros—and Marina's father, Pappas Emmanuel.

Every night, the *pappas* went first to Takis, whose customers bought him glasses of ouzo, and then to Onus, whose customers bought him more ouzo. When asked which was better, his answer remained, "Your mother, rest her soul, would be very proud." When Stavros Stavros saw him coming—or, rather, heard, because the *pappas* always sang as he moved through the village *kentro*, his high black chimney-pot hat and wide-sleeved *rasso* collecting dust as he walked—Stavros Stavros prepared a drink for the much-beloved *pappas*. He waited for him at the door. The *pappas*, himself, confided that Stavros Stavros cooked better than even his own wife, but this was not the only reason Stavros Stavros loved him. The *pappas* was different from everyone he had ever met. He talked about things he knew without making it seem as if he knew too much. He said that God had enough love for everyone and that man was created in God's image, ergo man had enough love for everyone, only man had forgotten *philos adelphos*, brotherly love. If man could remember compassion, the old resentments and sins would turn to rubble. Also, other wisdoms, such as:

> *Why did God give you two balls? Because that's what all the donkeys got.*

and

> *How does a smart man keep his wife satisfied? He lets the neighbor do the dirty work.*

The *pappas* Emmanuel was the one to get Stavros Stavros thinking about a long-term business plan. "You have something going here," he told him. "Give it a few years. Finish school, let your balls drop, and then get your father to help you open up a little shop of your own."

"Onus and Takis are going to set me up when it's time."

"They are good guys," the *pappas* said, "but they're no sheepherders. You do all the work, they get the profit. In the Greek Church, that is called a fuck-over. It happened to Jesus."

Stavros Stavros crossed his arms. "That won't happen. I'll get them before they get me."

The *pappas* slapped Stavros Stavros's arm. "You Mavrakises, always so serious."

Four years later, in 1975, sixteen-year-old Stavros Stavros had saved enough money to open a quarter of a *kafenio*. He went to his father about a loan, but Stavros Constantine said he was too young. "I only went to the fourth grade," he said. "Don't follow my mistakes, which are the ones of a peasant." So Stavros Stavros continued to go to school, continued to work, saving for the day his balls dropped and he could hire his classmates to wash his floors. At eighteen, he approached his father again, this time with enough to buy more than half a *kafenio*. "I have a business proposition," he said. "Sell a small piece of land to Onus. With the profit, we'll buy a restaurant and you will be half owner. For two years, I will work for free. Only give me a hundred dollars to go out on the weekends, and money for ciga-rettes."

How many tourists were trickling into Crete, all of them looking for a place to drink, meet locals. He had gone dancing with plenty of European girls who wanted to know how real men—Greek men—fucked. He never told his family about them (especially not about Greta, whom his grandmother would have hated for a Nazi, rest her soul) but he knew that if he opened a place for tourists in Iraklion, he'd triple the investment within two years. His brother Tasos could run things while he completed his mandatory service in the army. His mother would kiss him in the middle of the market, in the middle of the streets, she'd feel such pride.

Stavros Constantine said, "We will go to your mother tonight." The land, passed down from her family, was in her name.

ζ

Katerina was preparing dolmades when her son and husband entered. Dropping clumps of cooked rice into the center of blanched grape leaves, she listened without interrupting. Every time Stavros Stavros identified a benefit of the plan, she rolled a leaf and tucked its arms inward, as if it were giving itself a hug. At the end of the conversation, she had lined up seventeen grape leaves.

"*Oxi.*"

"But you are giving Kostas money. You are giving to Yannis and Stefanos."

"You are too late for any money. There is no more money. I have two sons about to be married, another going off to military, another in the field, another building a house. And even if you had come along first, you would be getting nothing right now."

"*Yiati?*"

"This is why," she said, and she dropped each dolma into a richly oiled pan as she ticked off her reasons. "You want to carve up your grandmother's land so you can open a shop for foreigners."

"It could make us a lot of money, *mitera mou.*"

She went on. "I allow you to work for Takis and Onus never expecting a drachma, and yet here you are bragging for money. Where did it all go, you tell me."

"I have it here," Stavros Stavros said. He pulled a faded slip of paper from his wallet. For five years, he had been carrying it around. It listed all of his deposits.

Katerina would not look at it. "Last year, for no good reason, you quit school. One year away from being finished, and you simply give up. And do you come here asking for help with something that a mother could be proud of, no. You come and beg to spend money in Iraklion, which is filled with only whores and beggars.

"And you, Constantine, should have known not to come to me with this *skata*. I will never share family land with strangers. Never, never."

His father leaning on the wall, saying nothing, the big dumb farming tool.

Stavros Stavros couldn't understand the power of many, many
drachmas until Onus and Takis and the *pappas* showed him that a
man is respected—a man is a man—when he is working, when he is
earning, when he is imagining a life better than his father's, when he
is proving his brothers wrong, when he is making something his own,
when his children don't make their toys out of wood. Money meant
that someone could reinvent himself. Money meant that someone
could buy himself a wife, a family, a girlfriend, a name, a middle name,
a business. Money could buy a man community and country.

And Stavros Stavros would get none of it. He'd probably end up
working for some *malaka* he knew from elementary school. Stavros
Stavros couldn't help himself. He swept the pan of dolmades off the
table. He watched it clatter to the floor.

Katerina bent down. She picked up the pan. The grape leaves stuck
to the bottom. Only one had fallen out. She was furious. She pointed
the wasted dolma at him like a finger. "What kind of son are you?"

"You stubborn woman," Stavros Stavros said. He should have been
apologizing. "Keep that land until it buries you."

With every step he took, his shaking legs willed him to turn around
and beg for forgiveness. Stavros Stavros kept going. He went all the
way to the *taverna* for sunflower seeds and beer and came home loud
and drunk through her kitchen. The next day, while the rest of his
brothers ate sides of pork, salad, and dolmades, Stavros Stavros was
served a single grape leaf—the one that had fallen to the floor. He sat
through dinner without eating, and then he met his friends for a gyro.
The following morning, instead of warm rice pudding and Nescafé, he
received the same grape leaf, and once more at dinner.

"What are you trying to prove? That I can't even ask my own
mother for help?"

Katerina cut the grape leaf in half. It was brown now, wilted. "I gave
you birth," she said. "For the rest of your life, you should be wanting to
make up for that."

Stavros Stavros shoved his plate back.

"Don't go, Galopoula," Stavros Stefanos called, eyes shining. "I have your potatoes right here." With a firm grip, he grabbed his *arxidia* and shook them.

Stavros Stavros flashed an open palm, flipping him off. Then he packed a bag, determined to watch his family kiss his Greek ass. He was too young to stay buried under his mother and eleven Stavroses, nothing new in life but the name of the village whore. Whatever he needed to do to get out, he would do it.

He got as far as Kalanakis's Taverna, where he ran into Yannis Fafoutakis.

"Why so angry, Galopoula?" Yannis asked through loosely spaced teeth. He was well on his way to drunk. "Have a drink, get happy. We are so young still."

Yannis had graduated two years ahead of Stavros Stavros, and though he was closer in age to Stavros Petros, the two met often at the *taverna* for table soccer. Yannis was a man bothered by nothing, but once the ball dropped, he was all wrists and concentration. No one in the history of the village had ever beaten him. For years Stavros Stavros had salivated over Yannis's inevitable defeat, but tonight Stavros Stavros did not care about table soccer.

"I'm going," he said. "I'm not spending the rest of my life making coffee for old men who play with their stale balls."

"Where will you go?"

"I don't care."

Yannis pulled a chair up to the table. "You want to go to America?"

"I am not telling jokes, Yannis."

"Neither am I. You remember my *thea* Irene? She moved to New York. She has a daughter, Dina."

Stavros Stavros vaguely recalled Dina. The last time he had seen her, they were eight, running around with all the other village kids on Easter, lamb in their hands. "So?" Stavros Stavros said.

"So they're ready to marry her off to a nice Greek boy."

Stavros Stavros snorted. "What, she's ugly?"

Yannis cupped his hands across his chest, mimicking breasts.

"American girls are never ugly where it counts." Yannis would talk about his own sister like this if he were drunk enough. "What do you say, my friend?"

"I have a girlfriend."

"What, Poppi, the skinny rabbit? Come on, *malaka*. Everyone knows you've got one hand up her skirt and the other on your tiny prick because she won't touch it for you."

Stavros Stavros chewed the corner of his lip, which he did whenever he was thinking something he knew he shouldn't.

"I tell you what," Yannis said, "you don't like her, you don't take her. Anyway, it means a free ticket out."

Stavros Stavros stared at the sudsy liquor that slid down Yannis's glass. In that moment, he began to belong to the masses who dream America, the land too good for peasant Greeks. Like all the other villagers, he had always fantasized about it from a distance—sneaking into the only theater on the island to watch Hollywood westerns, lying about his knowledge of the Big Apples. But what better place to be a man? To work, to earn, to imagine a life richer than his parents', to prove his brothers wrong, to make something his own, to make children who would honor him and gratefully inherit his fortune. What better place to reinvent himself—to reinvent the world? To make it bigger? To make it big enough to fit Stavros Stavros Mavrakis? In America, he would open a *kafenio*, hire Americans to clean the floor, buy crates of blue jeans and ship them back for all of his brothers, especially Stavros Nikos. He would send back dollars, not drachmas, so they understood who he was.

By 1980 he would be twenty-one years old, living in America, where everyone was as good as everyone else, and he would work hard to prove that he was better.

"OK," Stavros Stavros said. "Let's go be big apples in the Big Apples."

Dina landed in Crete in May of 1979, a month before her sixteenth birthday. Stavros Stavros walked to the Lazaridis house with a good sack of coffee, to pay respects and check out Dina. He was disappointed. In the photo she was wearing a dress and her hair was combed, but now all he got was straggly hair, an oily face, this left eye—what lazy eye? He did not remember a lazy eye from their childhood, could it be possible that America had given it to her?—and stained blue jeans. But she was shorter than him, which he liked, and her *kolo* could have belonged to one of his father's sheep. The meeting didn't last long. He and Dina didn't talk, except to say their names. Their parents would make the rest of the arrangements.

The next day, Stavros Stavros discovered Dina on his father's porch. She was bent over a row of plants. She didn't notice him (or maybe she did) because she kept picking the compact, purple-bellied leaves. She tossed back ones she didn't want, probably because they were too small. She was very picky, Stavros Stavros thought, and wasteful. But maybe that meant she had taste. Not everything was good enough for her, just like not everything was good enough for him.

"I will have to charge you," he said.

"Take it out of my allowance."

Stavros Stavros pushed through the screen door.

She looked up. "Does your hair always look like that?"

He didn't think that someone looking the way Dina looked should judge him, but he smoothed out his hair. "I just woke up." Her hair was different today. It was combed, pretty, the way it stopped at the tops of her shoulders. He wished he weren't wearing farm shorts.

She said, "My mother told me to go to the market."

Stavros Stavros plucked some oregano and added them to her feathery pile. "The small ones are better. More tender."

She nodded.

"Like me," he joked.

Nothing. Not even a smile.

"You want to go to the beach today?"

"I don't like the beach."

"Me neither," he said, "but girls always want to go for tans."

"You just end up dirty." She scrunched her nose. "Sand everywhere."

Stavros Stavros grew excited. "*Nai*," he said, "that is exactly the problem." He rubbed a leaf between his thumb and forefinger and it warmed. He wanted her to stay, he realized. To get to know her, if they were going to be married. "Want to get a frappe?"

The only vehicle available was his father's farm tractor, manufactured from motorcycle parts with a bench seat for transporting animals and manure. He changed into blue jeans and they walked. Stavros Stavros escorted her through the market; he got good deals and told her so. They passed the *kafenia*, which she could not enter, but everyone acknowledged Stavros Stavros and called to him from inside the shops, and he made sure Dina saw. When they arrived at the *taverna*, it was dusk and the clouds matched the pink water. They sat in a corner, where they could look out at the shore without having to step on the beach. Stavros Stavros ordered two iced coffees, sweet and frothy. When the owner wasn't looking, he called for the doughnut boy, and through the open window they traded half a drachma for a sugared doughnut the size of a wheelbarrow wheel.

"I can't wait to get out of this place," Stavros Stavros said. "Away from my parents."

"Me neither."

He looked out at the tourists beginning to cover themselves up. "America must be nice. So much going on."

"Not really."

"What are you talking about?" His elbows tipped him forward.

"It's nothing special."

"Nothing special?"

Dina jostled her straw. She did not look at him. "Not for me."

"With me, things will be better."

She did not react at all. He wasn't sure she had heard him. He saw she had left him half the doughnut and said, "Go ahead, finish it. I've had hundreds."

The next night, they strolled through the *kentro*, guided by large glowing bulbs that hung from poles. Power would be cut by midnight, but until then, *gerakos* strummed their instruments, sang without shame to single women the same age as their granddaughters. Stavros Stavros wanted to sing, too, but he was nervous in front of Dina. He was grateful to sip from the bottle of ouzo he had swiped from Onus.

"Want to go pick some fruit? I know an old blind farmer who can't tell if he's growing cantaloupe or rocks." He led her away from the lights, the singing men. They walked through the darkness without speaking, only the slosh of alcohol and the hoot of night-callers. When they reached a rusty wire fence, Stavros Stavros offered his hand. Dina hesitated, and he dropped it.

"I'm not marrying you," she said. "I'm just here to get away from my parents."

Stavros Stavros was surprised. Until that moment, he had not quite decided if he was going through with the arrangement. But hearing this, it made him determined to change her mind. She would be marrying him. He offered his hand again. "*Nai*, OK."

Dina let him partly lift, partly push her over the fence. He was lucky enough to cup her *kolo* when she went over. He pulled himself up, looking strong.

"I'm not staying in Crete. I'm going to Nepal," she said. "I'm going to meet Angelos."

He dusted his hands. He did not know what Nepal was. "Angelos?"

"My cousin."

He nodded and offered his elbow, which she took. She also took a long drink. He took one, too. He liked the way the ouzo made the moonlight into something liquid. Something he could run through a strainer. He liked that he knew the way to the *peponi* patch. He liked that he had an American girl with him that he could change into wanting him.

"When my father bought the tickets, I knew I'd be coming only so I could leave."

The ouzo was making her friendly, honest. She told Stavros Stavros how she was going to hike the hippie trail to Istanbul, through Syria and Jordan, Iran and Pakistan, not stopping until she arrived at Freak Street in Kathmandu. Angelos had told her about the cheap hotels, the stalls selling enlightenment, the prayer flags that stretched across the city like clotheslines. In Nepal, even garbage smells of sweet incense, Angelos said. He would be waiting for her.

"This is your cousin?" he asked.

She nodded. "He was my best friend in America."

Stavros Stavros wasn't sure what questions to ask. He would never chase any of his cousins through Asia. But it did not really matter. Her parents would make him her chaperone, and he wasn't going to let her get anywhere near a Freak Street. These were girly dreams, the kind that would be replaced by her sixteenth birthday.

They reached the patch. He knocked a *peponi* against a rock until it cracked in half. "I also wanted to run away when I was young," Stavros Stavros said, scooping out the slippery seeds with an old spoon he kept hidden in a nearby tree. "I wanted to live in the caves of Malta."

"I don't want to be in a cave," Dina said. "I've been in a cave my whole life. I want to be with people. I want to be enlightened."

He picked up the fruit, took a bite. His face disappeared in the *peponi*. His chin came back dripping. He held the fruit out to her. She took as large a bite as he had. Then he loosened some of the flesh with the spoon so they could get at it with their fingers.

"Forget Nepal. You should go to California." He smiled at the idea of it. California.

"California is boring. It's like America's version of Greece."

"No, California is beautiful. We can go together if you want," Stavros Stavros said, "after you get back from India."

Stavros Stavros was eager to show Dina how American Greece was. He wanted her to see that he and his friends could big-party-party. Same as New York. Since the early seventies, kids had been growing their hair, listening to rock and roll through US military radio stations and local ones that were not supposed to exist. But he also wanted to show her how Greek Greece was, how proud. He took Dina to a *bouzouki* joint.

"You will love this place," he kept saying.

Yannis Fafoutakis greeted his cousin and bought drinks, until a tourist caught his eye.

Stavros Stavros was feeling great. A second good time, arranged by him. He could tell she was loving this. They were getting lots of attention. He was a popular guy on the island with some people. Her lazy eye, it was kind of cute now. It was like a little practical joke between them.

"You have LSD?" Dina shouted against the music. "Hashish?"

"Sure," Stavros Stavros lied. He kept dancing. He was a pretty good dancer.

He was naïve about drugs. There wasn't much in circulation unless you were from the mainland, a musician, or a member of the US military. When he rebelled, when any of his friends rebelled, it was with movies, alcohol, music. Drugs were too Europe, and Greece was many years away from being Europe.

"Can we get some?" she said.

Stavros Stavros passed Dina his glass. "We can do that later."

"Why not now?"

He watched her hips. Proud hips, hips that nodded yes to your questions. Her ass, her waist, her tits, they all moved like they had done this a hundred, thousand times before. A nose to match his, in some ways bigger than his. More sure of itself, maybe, in America, a country of unsure noses. Her hair was gluey with sweat, and there were dark circles beneath her eyes. But right now, all he saw were those Greek hips.

"You don't want to dance more?"

She shrugged. "I want to have fun."

"OK," Stavros Stavros said. "Let's go have fun."

He brought her up to Yannis Fafoutakis's place. Yannis lived with his grandmother, but she was asleep and could sleep through tanks. There weren't many places to sit. A single chair. A bed. They sat on the bed.

"You ever hear Dionysion Stavropoulos?" Stavros Stavros asked.

"No."

He lit up. "*Ela*, how does a Greek not know the hero of Greece? You've never heard 'Dirty Bread'?"

"I listen to Led Zeppelin."

"Me too. This is better." He played the album for her.

He put his arm around her shoulders. He sang into her ear. He wanted a chance to see her nipples, just one. He liked nipples. He liked to touch them. He didn't know how to do much more. Really, he had only fucked one German tourist, and if he were honest about it, she had fucked him. Some of his friends, the ones with bad girls, put their penises between the girls' thighs, just above the knees, and rubbed themselves into goodnight-goodnight. Sex was not a possibility for Greek girls. Dina had to be a virgin the night they married.

Dina got up, opened Yannis's dresser. She pulled out a scarf and tied it around her neck. "What do you think?"

His buzz and his interest in her body made him grin like a big cat. "Better on you than that anteater." He wished he had said something funnier until he saw she, too, was smiling. No one else on the island had made her smile—not her parents, not his brothers, not her cousin, not the *malakas* on the corner. Him.

"Hey, look. *Ela*." She pulled out a thin strip of wax paper. She unfolded it. It was marijuana.

Stavros Stavros came over to inspect. He nodded as if he approved of the quality, but really he was shocked. "What are you going to do?" He almost added "with it" because he wasn't exactly sure how you did marijuana.

She laughed. "What do you think."

Stavros Stavros watched Dina pick up a can from Yannis's floor. She bent the can in the middle, poked a couple holes, turned it so the marijuana could sit atop the holes. "Got a light?"

Stavros Stavros watched her suck smoke out of the drink hole. She passed him the can. He was clumsy holding it, she had to show him how. He took too big a hit trying to make up for his clumsiness. He coughed harder than he had ever coughed before. She laughed every time he tried to talk, because it made him choke. She poured them rum sodas. He drank his like water. He kept clearing his throat. She took another hit. He tried to get hold of himself, change the music, get serious. He leaned in to kiss her. He ended up coughing too close to her face. The coughing made him nauseous. He went to the bathroom, stared himself down in the mirror.

"You all right?" she called. She asked it from a faraway place, like America.

"*Nai*," he said, but he wasn't. He promised himself he'd never touch the stuff again.

Three dates, all of his spending money, not even a kiss good night.

The engagement was announced on Dina's sixteenth birthday.

The church was scrubbed. The day was set, changed, set again. Money for the wedding and the *pappas* and the food and the wine and the band, but also money to build another bedroom for the distant cousins and aunts and uncles who would come to the ceremony. Money for the cousins' boat ride, their clothes, their haircuts. Stavros Stavros didn't complain. He spent freely. He wanted everyone to see what he was about to make of himself.

The *pappas* visited Stavros Stavros twice before the wedding. First at Takis's, during midday. Except for the pulse of cicadas that drowned out the napping men's snores, it was quiet. The *pappas* asked Stavros Stavros how he felt about entering into the heavenly, holy vow of marriage by saying, "You know Greek women grow new teeth after they marry, don't you? A sharper set, ones that will whittle your little pizzle to nothing."

"That what Presbytera Maria did to yours?"

The *pappas* chuckled. "*Re*, it isn't so bad for me because I started with more than enough. Not so with you."

There was no beating him. The *pappas* was well versed in scripture, art, the ancient civilizations, and shit-talking. The *pappas* gestured for more ouzo with his pinky. "What is it you like about this girl?"

Stavros Stavros dipped a crust of hardened bread into the ouzo, the way the *pappas* liked. "She comes from a decent family. She wants to have kids."

"Mm-hmm, and you have a pleasant time together?"

"We have an all right time."

"Just not too pleasant."

Stavros Stavros grinned. "No, Father."

"Too bad. There are ways to have pleasant times without nosy priests finding out."

"Don't worry," Stavros Stavros boasted, "when I get her to America, she'll have such a good time even the president will hear about it."

"America."

Stavros Stavros nodded. "No nosy old priests there. At least none to spy on me."

"Tell me, Mavrakis"—the *pappas* leaned in, ouzo shining from the corners of his mouth—"what kinds of things would you keep from the priests?"

Stavros Stavros, unnerved, examined the mugs. They had browned over the years like the teeth of the men who drank from them; they could get only so clean. "Nothing," he said.

"You have worries about this girl?"

Before Stavros Stavros could answer, a rustling came from the corner of the room. The men were waking. Soon they would demand sweet boiled coffee, toast. The *pappas* stood. "We'll talk again, Mavrakis. I'll have to ask around about your America."

Stavros Stavros did not know how to tell the *pappas* that Dina was strange. OK, she was American. OK, maybe he didn't understand American girls. Sometimes they were nice, fun, happy to climb fences and talk about California, interested in his music, wanting to dance close for everyone to see. Other times they cried over nothing, got angry at their innocent fiancés, then demanded to go to disco. While Greek girls got fixed up, put on earrings, American girls didn't even shower regularly. When he told Dina he liked her hair to be nice for his friends, she went into the kitchen and sawed off large chunks with a meat cleaver. He watched her raid her grandmother's medicine cabinet.

"What are you looking for?"

"Medicine."

"You're sick?"

She cackled. "Can't you tell?" She found some pills, swallowed them without water. Stavros Stavros felt something hard, like a drachma, going down his own throat.

It's not like he could back out of the marriage—it would be a disgrace to his family name. He just wanted Dina to know that, when they got to New York, party time was over. Not that he didn't like to have a good time, he liked to have a better time than any of his eleven brothers, but once they were married, they would need to go after things that mattered.

"Work, succeeding, a house, a business, children to carry on the Mavrakis name," he said. "That's what matters."

She smirked. "Why?"

Stavros Stavros was stunned. "What do you mean? What else is there?"

She didn't answer.

"What else matters?"

There was a pause. "I don't know."

That, to him, proved two things. First, she was too young to know what was important. Second, he could show her what mattered. She'd love him even more for it.

"The only thing in the world that matters to me, to anybody," he clarified, "is respect."

She said nothing. He took that as a good sign.

"You'll see," he told her. "It will be a good feeling when your family sees they were wrong. It will make up for all the bad feelings that you had on the way."

The second time the *pappas* came to see Stavros Stavros, he was working behind Onus's counter. It was late, the place empty. Pools of light swam in puddles of drink. Stavros Stavros flipped the chairs upside down so that they could rest, because tomorrow morning meant another day of sweaty thighs, flatulence. He lined up a row of near-empty bottles. In their bellies waited drips of clear *tsikoudia*. His job was to catch them.

The *pappas* removed the wooden slat that closed the front door and entered without knocking. He caught Stavros Stavros with his middle finger deep in a bottle's mouth. "You practicing for your wedding night?" he asked.

Stavros Stavros let go of the bottle. It made a relieved popping sound.

"Better keep practicing. If you do it that way, Mavrakis, she might retaliate."

Stavros Stavros wished he could laugh about it, but he knew the *pappas* could see the shame roasting his ears. He would make Dina hide behind a pomegranate tree whenever they passed the *pappas* or his father on the street, that was how prudish he was.

The *pappas* took off his hat and placed it on the counter, his thick damp black hair uncurling. Without the clerical garb, he looked like an uncle come to visit. "How about some of those fat green *elitses* Onus likes to keep to himself?"

Stavros Stavros dragged out a stool and climbed up. He reached behind the jarred tomatoes. The *pappas* did not request bread or cheese, he liked the purity of the fruit. The *pappas* bit into an olive, his three fingers wrapped around its slick body. "They cannot have olives like these in America."

Stavros Stavros popped an olive into his mouth, pushed it to his cheek. He liked the way the juices squeezed out of the flesh. The *pappas* was right, this kind of ripe was pure Crete.

"What is it about America that makes you willing to give up your home?"

Stavros Stavros said, "Everything will be different there."

"You will be a foreigner there. Do you know that? Are you ready for that?"

"I'm a foreigner here."

The *pappas* tucked two olives into his cheeks. Without force, because he knew how young men resented a priest's opinion in moments like these, he suggested, "Why not stay in Greece for a year or two? That way, if you ever need it, help is nearby."

"I can handle my wife, don't worry about that."

"Of course you can," the *pappas* answered, "all Greeks can handle their wives. Greeks were born for that. All I'm saying is that America will still be America. Whenever you want her, she will be waiting just on the other side of the water."

"The whole point is to get off this island."

"I know," the *pappas* said. "That is what concerns me."

Stavros Stavros said nothing.

"Have you thought about the possibility that you will get there and have to come back?"

"I won't be back, you can bank on that."

The *pappas* touched Stavros Stavros's knuckles with his greasy fingers, but only for a moment. "You are marrying yourself into a kind of trouble you know nothing about."

This, he never expected from the *pappas*. Until now, he had always treated Stavros Stavros with respect. He had never before seen him as a fool. "I know what I'm doing."

The *pappas* plucked another olive. "I am going to counsel your parents about this engagement. I don't believe in it."

He would do it, Stavros Stavros knew, and his parents would call it off. All of Stavros Stavros's plans would collapse. He took away the bowl just as the *pappas* was reaching for the last olive. It was an insult, more so than throwing a drink in the *pappas*'s face, but he was done with being treated like a child by every backward villager. They stood in the silence of his disrespect.

The *pappas* held a pit between his front teeth and flicked it into an ashtray. "You are too stubborn to see what you're doing," he said, "but you will learn. The rest of the world can be just as stubborn as a Greek." He tucked his hat under his arm and pushed back the stool. "You will find out that when you get into the chicken feed, Stavro, you get pecked by chickens."

The two-hour ceremony would have ended forty minutes earlier, except that the *pappas* stopped to pray for a herd of untamable *kri-kri* to bust through the wooden doors and interrupt the exchange of vows. Yannis Fafoutakis, best man, stood jolly at Stavros Stavros's side. "I'm jealous, Galopoula," he whispered, breath buzzing like a wasp. "You're the first of us to get out of this termite hole."

That night, the whole village watching, Stavros Stavros finally proved his manhood: on the dance floor. With the pomp of the traditional *syrtos* that suggested respite before battle, the resting of the soul, he rejected the *pappas*'s interference, his mother's control, his father's weakness. When he felt like showing off, he showed off. During one of the counterclockwise dances, he vaguely felt Dina next to him, linked by nothing more than a white handkerchief. He saw her only through the haze of warm wine and public attention. Him, Stavros Stavros Mavrakis, in front of all of the bachelors, in front of all of his brothers. The way it should be. They had to wait for his every step, his every flourish, before they could move a foot. A toe, even, because any premature moves would trip the next person. The *pappas*, feigning intoxication, did not lead any dances, but Stavros Stavros did not care if he did not get the priest's blessing. The *pappas* refused to lie, even with his feet, but what did that matter when Stavros Stavros was leaving in just a few days?

Stavros Stavros was fat and full at the end of the night. He had ruled the village, his family, and it made him feel virile. All he needed now was to deflower a virgin.

Everyone knew it was a man's right to unmake a woman. Everyone knew it was their right to see proof of the unmaking. It was customary for the groom's parents to drape the white sheets of a newly consummated couple against the house, the copper crop visible from way down the road. In the history of the village, few women had ever failed to bleed (a cripple, a slut, a rape victim) and that was because women were pure, women were pious, women were chaste, and, when they weren't, women were shrewd enough to cover up their bloodlessness. Even their boyfriends, who panted themselves into premarital sex with their soon-to-be brides, were always satisfied when the warm rusty liquid bubbled up on the night of the wedding. Concerned with shame and self-preservation, these women knew to tuck pouches of sow's blood inside themselves. Dina, who hadn't been from the island in years, knew nothing and did nothing. She just lay there beneath her grunting, fat, full husband.

Stavros Stavros coached himself to keep going. The first time was always difficult for the woman, especially if the man was more shovel than man. Which he was tonight, especially. Then he realized the problem. He scrambled off the bed.

"There's no blood."

Dina pulled her underwear up from her knees. "You said you wanted an American."

Stavros Stavros yanked his shorts on. "Not this American," he said. "No, no, no." He couldn't believe this was happening. The night had been perfect, everything as it should be. Now, he was facing clean sheets. Stavros Stavros ripped them away. "You aren't going to sleep. You're going to help me figure this out."

Dina spun and pulled the sheets free, too fast for him to anticipate. "There is nothing to figure out. You got what you got, just like I got what I got."

His chest heaved. He wanted to shout, tell her what a *sixameni* she was—there had never been a dirtier bitch—but that would send his mother running. Here he was, waiting for their wedding night like it was something special, something needing patience and honor, and meanwhile Dina, *poutana*, had taken all those dirty pipes and swallowed all that dick-food. But he couldn't let that thought overwhelm him right now. Right now, he had to resolve this before anyone discovered their shameful secret. Stavros Stavros tore the sheets off Dina. He saw her, as he shut the door, at the bottom of the bed, a crumpled person.

In the dark hallway, he tripped over a potted plant, scattering dirt. He bit his cheek to keep from crying out. If anyone woke now, he would be a joke. Stavros Stavros Mavrakis, shoeless, pantsless, with a broken wife and a broken toe. His big toe complained that he was a fool, alone in his misery, but he was not going to stand here and be ridiculed by his family or his own foot. He limped to the porch, balled up the sheets beneath the stairs leading to the roof. Then he limped out to the chicken coop.

In the moonlight a line of chickens squatted on planks. They perked up when he pulled a sack off the wall, thinking it might be a second feed time, something that happened occasionally to encourage fowlic euphoria and the production of eggs. The chickens clucked but when no kernels appeared, they bobbed their necks in suspicion. This was not Stavros Constantine, they realized. This was not feed time, when the bright orange bowl fills the sky and signals to their ovaries that it's time to release egg cells. This was a fox or a dog.

Stavros Stavros stepped over damp, shit-smelling hay, his eyes on the smallest bird. She had her head tucked in a wing but shook awake. "Don't worry, little *kotopoulo*," he whispered. "I only need one leg. Not even one leg, one toe. You will not miss it."

The chicken squawked. He lunged. She flapped her wings, half-flew to a higher beam. He ran after her, sack raised over his head. Loose feathers, old-lady clucks, a frantic instinct to get out of reach. Which they all did. Stavros Stavros was panting. What he needed was a knife. A big knife. A butcher knife from his mother's kitchen that no chicken had ever said no to.

The porch light was on: it had not been on before. He walked slowly. He debated about climbing through a window. But there was no other way to get to the kitchen. He decided to go forward; he had no choice. If it were his father, he was probably passed out at the table. If it were Dina, he would make her come out to the coop with him.

It was his mother, sitting with a cup of tea at the table, face and hair still ensnared in sleep. On the table was a fork and bowl of lemon potatoes, his favorite.

"It's late, *mitera*. You should be asleep."

She chuckled. "My son, telling me about my empty bed when he is out of his." She tossed him a pair of sandals. He did not put them on. "I know your feet must be ice blocks. You hate to go barefoot."

"Why are you having tea by yourself in the middle of the night?"

"That is a good question. Here is a better one. You have a bride, but you are out molesting my chickens."

"There was a stray dog. I chased it off."

"Oh, so you left your first night with Dina to check on the animals. She must have been pleased."

Stavros Stavros said nothing. Katerina stood, walked around the table, and led him to a chair. She slipped the sandals onto his feet. Even when she scrubbed the floors, she did not kneel. But here she was kneeling before him on the one night he did not deserve it. She speared a potato on the fork. He took a bite, the potato melting on his tongue. She had warmed them.

"You think your mother does not see what is going on," she said, "but that is because you have the milk-eyes of a newborn cat."

Stavros Stavros ate another potato, and another.

Katerina pulled the bundle of sheets from beneath the table. "Tell your mother," she said. "She will help you fix it."

He tried to take another bite, couldn't. The tears were coupling, falling. "It's not your problem."

"Oh, no, Stavraki. That is exactly what it is."

He began to sob. He knew she would label him impotent, cuckolded, just like the rest of the village. "She's a whore," he said quietly. "You had me marry a whore."

Katerina did not ask Stavros Stavros to acknowledge that the arranged marriage had been his idea. She reached across the table. "The best thing to do with rotten meat," she said, "is send it back. Not cry over it."

"It's too late," he said. "There is nothing you can do."

"There is a saying," she said, standing. "'It's the old chicken who has the juice.' And I, Stavro, have plenty juice left."

Within minutes, six of them were seated in the visiting room to discuss the problem. Dina sat with her chin on her knees. It was not satisfying, because she would not raise her head to receive their judgment.

Mihalis Lazaridis was stern looking in wide, tinted glasses, someone Stavros did not want to come up against but not someone Stavros feared. His dark hair flat against his head, only the strands near his forehead daring to break free. His huge nose, which might have appeared clownish on another man, gave him the look of an animal that lived close to the ground, made to scrounge. Two deep frown lines cutting down his face indicated that smiling was a trial.

"We've had a difficult time with her in the States," Mihalis apologized, uncharacteristically. "We thought things would get better once she found a husband."

"Three thousand drachmas," Katerina answered, "or she goes back alone."

Stavros Stavros looked up in surprise. What was she doing? She had said nothing about money.

Irene Lazaridis cringed. "You ask too much."

"What is too much is that you allowed your daughter to spoil, then you give her to my son pretending she is fresh enough for marrying."

Stavros Stavros saw now that the potatoes, the sandals, the kneeling were just business. His mother cared about his honor only if it mattered to her pocket.

Mihalis raised his hand to Irene. "It is fine," he said. "We will honor it."

Dina's eyes flicked from one person to the next, reminding Stavros Stavros of the crazed chickens in the coop. He suddenly felt like one of those chickens, too. She said, "I'm not going back with him."

"It will cost you the three thousand," Katerina said, "and you will buy his airfare."

Irene threw her hands up. "No. That is the line for me."

"There is another saying," Katerina said. "And that is that when you bring a chicken to the table, somebody has to pluck the ass."

Mihalis's mouth became very tight. As a Greek man, it was his prerogative to explode into expletives when being robbed, but he understood that this was a sensitive situation. "Yes," he said. "We will do it."

"I won't," Dina said. She looked at Stavros Stavros. "You see what's happening? They want to get rid of you as bad as they want to get rid of me."

The *sixameni*, the liar. He should have known not to trust her the minute he saw one of her eyes wasn't trustworthy. But Stavros Stavros looked to his mother. Was it true? Were they trying to get rid of him?

Katerina, in response, came to Dina. "*Koukla*," she said, "do you know what your first mistake was?"

"Marrying your son."

"Before that."

Dina, sullen. "Coming back to this goat-fucking country."

"Before that."

"Being born."

"Being born a woman," Katerina corrected. "A Greek woman." And she went out. She returned with a chicken. It clucked in alarm, knowing instinctively that being in a house meant danger. This was her big plan all along? His plan? "Yes," Katerina said. "And it will work." Everyone present would swear to it.

Stavros Stavros was pulled into the kitchen. They stood at the sink, where Katerina gripped the bird by the neck. Mihalis held the sheet.

Stavros Stavros dumbly took the knife from his mother. He looked at Dina, who stood as far away as she could without stepping out of the kitchen. Her feet were inexplicably dirty. She seemed to blend in with the pile of potatoes that had just been dug up. No, he and his wife were not the same. He closed his eyes.

Katerina stopped his elbow. "One leg only. I don't need a bloodbath. If there is too much, the gossips will know."

"Am I doing this or you?"

Katerina looked at him for a long time. She stepped back.

Stavros Stavros kept his eyes open this time, ignoring the clucks that sounded too much like his wife in their marital bed. A deep red gash appeared on the bird's leg, and she cried and flayed her feathers. Much-desired drops darkened the sheet.

Katerina turned to Dina. "*Ela etho,*" she said, and right there in the kitchen she smeared some of the chicken blood onto her daughter-in-law's inner thighs. It was as if Dina didn't feel it happening until it was already done, because she slapped at Katerina's hand just as she was pulling away. Katerina ignored it. She instructed her not to bathe in the morning. If anyone demanded proof of her virginity, it would be there.

Stavros Stavros wanted to run from the farm, from the red in the sink that was suddenly the price for America. Watching his mother shove her hands between his wife's legs, he felt sick for them both. He saw Dina's eyes when his mother handled her and understood she was suffering. Maybe she deserved it, but it was shameful, sad. He turned now to look at his pitiful wife with eyes of ripped cloth. This was real now. He was bound to this marriage. There had been an arrangement and a wedding, yes, but this clandestine act was what joined him to Dina.

It was five, just enough time for the Lazaridises to get home before the herders brought their goats to graze. The village would not be surprised to see Dina at home with her mother. They would understand that she had gone to Stavros as a dutiful, loving, urgent wife and now returned to her parents' house to prepare for America.

"Try to keep track of her for tonight, if you can," Katerina called at their backs.

The chicken was released back into the coop, her leg bandaged. She would walk with a limp until she got cooked into a soup.

The next day—September 3, 1979—Stavros Stavros left the farm for good. He experienced the tipping of a plane at takeoff. The food was *skata*, the coffee was *skata*, the bathrooms were *skata*, but he loved all of it. When he called his brothers, he would tell them it was like driving an air-conditioned tour bus through clouds. He was not happy with Dina, but he could not pay attention to his anger with America so close. Everything new. Everything different. No one in America would know about his wedding night. She would promise never to tell. She would make it up to him. He would forgive her. He could be a good husband, a good person, in the modern world.

From Stavros Stavros's window, America rose both big and small. The cities, the pastures. He realized how many times as a child he had created this exact world—out of plants and sticks and bones and coffee grounds. Stavros Stavros had already made America. This knowledge gave him confidence, strength. It pushed away the nervousness that tasted like beets. But also, America was big. It was very, very big, even from far above. It stretched like the sea. So many houses, so many buildings, all of them proud, one taller than the next, all uninterested in their neighbors, all unconcerned with the way things have always been. A building wanted to be 86 floors, it could be 86 floors. He wanted to be America like that. Recognizable, respected, the best, the biggest, the only. He decided, in that moment, to make a singular decision.

"Dina," he said, shaking her awake. "From now on, I'm just plain Stavros."

Dina opened and shut her eyes.

Stavros wasn't sure if she heard him, but it didn't matter. Soon, everyone would learn his name: Stavros Mavrakis. Because where he was going, there was only one.

DINA LAZARIDIS

They did not know each other. They had nothing in common, if nothing meant being Greek. But Dina had told herself she could overlook his weak lips and the way he swung his arms as if he were a much larger man. He was proud—what Greek wasn't? He was short—what Greek wasn't? When his eyes grew wet with pleasure, it was not because he was looking at her; it was only that he was boasting or drunk or both. But Dina had not cared that he did not love her, because she did not love him. Now he wanted her to settle down, give up her life. For that, she could have stayed home with her parents. She had mistaken Stavros Stavros for an out; he was more in than her father. Her previous life, he couldn't even dream it into existence. He did not know that before Stavros Stavros, she had been an astronaut, a spy, and a meteorologist.

When she was eight years old, Dina was told she that was going to the mainland to see the circus. This was something that could never come to her in Iraklion. There were no monkeys on the island, no lions. If she wanted to see animals, she had to be satisfied with goats, donkeys, rabbits. Maybe the occasional octopus—but she never saw any octopuses do tricks or wear sequined skirts. They were food. Dina packed and unpacked her suitcase. When circus day came, she wanted to make sure it looked full enough so that her mother wouldn't add another dress to the pile but spare enough to fit a baby elephant. Her *papous* had taught her that the last time elephants were on the island of Crete, they were the size of pigs, and the world was covered with glaciers.

The night before the flight to Athens, after she had been put to bed, Dina heard Papous and her father arguing. She could not make out much, only that her grandfather was saying, "Tell her, tell her or I will."

"She's just a child. There's nothing she needs to know."

Papous's voice rose. "She *is* just a child, you stubborn *malaka*. This will change her whole life."

Dina smiled. Yes. The circus would change everything. She would be the only child in the neighborhood to own a three-hundred-pound pet. She imagined making a leash out of strings of lights, so her elephant would glow during their walk to school. It would wait for her outside, and when the teacher wasn't looking, she would slip it ripe red *karpouzi* through the window. It would eat the *karpouzi* whole, seeds and all. Dina was so wrapped up in the fantasy, it took her a moment to realize there was shouting from the kitchen. Some words she couldn't make out, then a plate, silence. Someone was coming down the hall.

Papous entered her room. He stared at her through the darkness, and she couldn't help but wrinkle her face into a smile. He came over and sat on the edge of her bed. A big wide nose, heavy eyes, and a gummy mouth made him look like a camel. She loved him for it. She loved him for lots of reasons.

"Bad girl," he said. "Always up later than even the adults." He put her pink doll on his lap, stroked its curls.

Dina sat up. "Why are you crying, Papous? Is it because Ba-ba didn't get you a ticket to the circus?"

Papous wiped the doll's dress against his face. "I don't want a ticket," he said.

"Don't worry, I will bring back a present for you. A big one that you can keep on your land, and all of the kids will pay you to come and see it."

Her grandfather smiled. "*Koukla mou*," he said, "I would keep it only for myself." He collected her in arms the color of saddles and buried his stubble into her neck until she collapsed into weak laughter. When he said good night to her, and good night to her left eye, which he had nicknamed Sleepy, the tears came back.

Breakfast was bread and some cheese wrapped in cloth. Her father tried a paper cup of American coffee, threw it out. Dina kept looking out the window at the taxicabs, which were taking people away from the Athens airport, but her parents ignored her when she suggested that they get rides, too. Then there was an announcement, and they were running, there was a *connecting flight*. The phrase made Dina think of twin birds rising from a mountain, their wings hooked together. She tried to keep up. She was panting. Her mother had stuffed at least three more dresses into her luggage, and it was too heavy to hold. It kept knocking against her ankles, making her stumble. "We'll miss the circus, Ba-ba," Dina said.

Her father lifted Dina's suitcase, added it to his pile. "There will be lots of circuses in America."

America! The word, it glittered. America was stickers and television. It was Mickey Mouse and more Coca-Cola. There was no school in America, only things to be curious about. There would be lots and lots of circuses. She could get two elephants—one for her, one for Papous. They could raise them together, ride them up the mountains instead of the donkeys. Dina let go of her mother's hand so she could run alongside her father.

He was pleased. "So you like America?"

Dina grinned. It felt good to have him look at her that way. Like Papous.

It wasn't until they boarded and the plane was pulling away from the gate that Dina realized she had been tricked. She looked at the luggage her father was stuffing into the overhead, counted the suitcases (1, 2, 3, 4, 5, 6) he had checked. She thought of all the family members and friends who had come to see them off, and she realized they were going to America for good.

Her mother was in the middle seat with her eyes closed. All morning she had been nervous, uptight, the way she usually got on trips to the bank or doctor. Dina whispered into her ear, "When is Papous coming to America?"

Her mother did not answer.

Dina reached over her and tugged her father's arm. "When is Papous coming to America?" she asked.

Her father wiped sweat from his forehead and tucked his kerchief into his jacket. "Your *papous* is not interested in America."

"But I will be there," Dina said. "Does he know that?"

Her father nodded, stiff. He glanced over at his wife. "Not everyone gets to go to America. Only the very best."

"Papous is the best," Dina said.

Dina's father shook his wife. She did not respond. He pulled out a cookie and handed it to Dina. "You want a *glyko*?"

Dina took it. It was soft from his pocket, but she ate it anyway. The plane was getting hot. The old man behind them sneezed. At the front, pretty women in blue uniforms were checking on passengers. "When do we go back home?" Dina asked.

"America will be our new home," her father said. His eyes too were shut now.

"How far away is it?"

"How far away is America?" He smiled. He looked over at her. "It is years into the future."

Dina did not understand what he meant, but she didn't have to. She would not see Papous three times a week anymore, she would not pick green beans with him or scrape the dirt from his work shoes. Papous— she swallowed, an elephant bone in her throat—would be years away. Dina fought back the only way she knew how—with a tantrum. She screamed, she kicked the seats, she pounded her fist against the window, which felt more like concrete than glass. Her mother sprang up, but Dina was going to let everyone on the plane know that her parents were liars.

"Shut that little girl up," someone grumbled in English.

Dina's scream carried into the fuselage chamber. The propellers spun in sobbing circles, the wings flapped their mechanical flaps. Dina's rage, not the propulsion units, pushed the plane forward. The pilots felt something overtake the controls. The passengers felt it, too. Grief thrust the aircraft into the air. Dina's scream took them out too far, too fast. Oxygen masks dangled from overhead compartments. She drove the aircraft farther, farther, into the thermosphere. Just shy of crossing the Kármán line, the thin airless boundary between atmosphere and space, Dina looked down. Her beloved Crete, remote as a quasar. Her *papous* not just years away, he was ten billion light-years away. She shut her mouth. The scream stopped. The plane dropped. Unable to overcome orbital velocity, Dina plummeted to the earth: a crash landing in New Jersey, 1971.

For four and a half years, because she no longer believed anything her parents told her, and because she missed Papous, and because she was a foreigner who was treated like a foreigner, and because the kids at school made fun of her lazy eye in a way the villagers never had, Dina rebelled. Adults watched her with suspicion, and she learned that she was not pretty enough, not quiet enough, not obedient enough, not worthy, not gentle, not good, not smart—but she was certainly shrewd. By twelve, she was practicing espionage, and she and Angelos had them all fooled. Before his arrival, Dina had been too unworldly—having traveled only to the edge of space—to know about transnational deception. Now she was cosmopolitan enough to be guilty of treason.

Angelos, a third cousin of her father's, was a chemistry student. None of the Lazaridises had ever met him, but according to the stunted, artificial intimacy imposed on immigrants, they were family. Anyone Greek, anyone from the island, was family. Mihalis was obligated to help. His invitation was warm and heartfelt: Angelos's father had supported Mihalis's sister when she was ill and no one was able to pay for her hospital visits. Angelos was not charged rent. In return he fixed the refrigerator, cleaned the furnace, and tutored Dina in science.

"You like chemistry?" he asked. He glanced at the D on her quiz.

"We don't do that in seventh grade." She avoided looking at him.

"What do you do?"

She did not want to say, because she didn't want to sound stupid. "Boring stuff."

He broke off a piece of his chocolate bar and pushed it across the table. She put it in her palm. It was half melted from being in Angelos's pocket. "Maybe it wouldn't be so boring if you had a fun teacher," he said.

She shrugged. He passed along another square of chocolate.

She put it in her mouth. "Last year we learned about kingdom, phylum—" She paused.

"Class," he said.

"Order," she returned. "I forget the rest."

He smiled. "Family."

She got an A on her next quiz.

Before Angelos came, she had nothing to look forward to—wool skirts, long division, desk inspections, which she always failed. Changing for gym class, the girls told her she smelled like their mothers; something about her was like an old woman pushed into a girl's body, mournful and dumpy. It didn't matter now, she had Angelos. She loved Angelos. It was not a difficult thing to do. He was nice to her, he nicknamed her left eye Sneaky, and he had a nose that reminded her of the Fonz. His wavy auburn hair he kept in a loose ponytail that Mihalis disapproved of and Dina adored. He grew a brown beard that made her think of Jesus; he could have passed for a Greek priest, but Dina could tell his thoughts weren't about God when he daydreamed. Nearly thirty, Angelos had been to college, and he was starting his PhD in the fall. He had traveled to San Francisco, Paris, Geneva, Bangkok. He knew all about the world, and he was going to share it with her.

Every day, Angelos met her at the corner after school, and they walked home. She told him about what they were reading, imitated the humpbacked secretary. He asked about the dirty words the kids used on the playground and laughed when she was too shy to say them. He helped her with homework. Once, he even let her cut his beard. She held it in her hand as if it were a defenseless rabbit. She trimmed the edges, unaware that she was holding her breath until she realized that he was holding his, too.

Her favorite was watching him work on her father's car, which was always breaking down. He named the car parts for her. He opened the hood. He pulled a wrench from his pocket. Her eyes followed his hands. So firm when he held the clamp in place, so tender when he cupped the twin cams.

That evening, after Dina took a bath, she lay down to think about nothing but Angelos's hands. He held forks as if they were instruments, spoons as if they were sensitive scales. She could imagine him in the lab—fingers poised to grasp the beakers or glass tubes or whatever it was that chemists used. His hands could fix anything. They could even fix her, and had once, when she scratched the back of her leg hopping off a fence. She remembered the warm pads of the fingertips that gently pinched her calf when he rubbed a streak of iodine over the cut. This is good for you, he explained; she winced. Iodine is a halogen, like chlorine and bromine and fluorine, only it's much more gentle. Your organs, like your skin, soak it up every day. Trust me, he said, squeezing the back of her knee. Your body needs this.

Dina pushed off the blankets and crept through the hallway. Her father's snores were all the permission she needed.

His eyes were open as if he had been waiting for her. There was a book lying on his bare stomach. Loose gray boxer shorts, and nothing but a single tangled sheet beneath him. "You come for a math lesson?"

"I couldn't sleep," Dina answered.

"Me neither." He sat up. The book fell to the mattress.

She was suddenly nervous in his space, surrounded by his things. Everything was slate-blue. The closet open, she could see his collared shirts hanging. On the desk next to his bed were a stack of magazines, batteries, an old plate, a can of paint. She had never been in his room before, not even in the daytime. "It smells in here," she said, not bothering to whisper.

He shifted to the edge of the bed and grasped her by the wrists. His hold was not demanding, only guiding. He placed her in front of him. He moved to the edge of the bed. Their knees were nearly touching. "Don't talk so loud."

"What are you reading," she asked, unable to look into his face.

He smiled. "You wouldn't like it."

"Why not?"

"It's not really for kids," he said.

"I'm not a kid. I'm almost thirteen."

He took her wrist and rubbed it against his stubble. "It's confidential."

He must have sensed her tensing, because he stopped, began to talk. "It's about spies in the fifties. The Russians have the bomb, the Communists are invading South Korea."

"Like 007?" Voice shaking. "That's stupid."

She was pulled onto his lap, which was warmer than the rest of his body. She laughed in surprise, embarrassment, but stopped cold when he wrapped his arm around her waist. He stroked her back, drawing her in so that she could face him. She could feel her heartbeat in her teeth. "What's so exciting about it," she said from very far away and also up close.

He nuzzled his beard into her neck and said, "Oh, everything. Everything."

There was surveillance. There was bugging. There were dead-letter drops, arranged so two spies could transfer materials without ever meeting. He kissed her earlobe. He raised her nightgown above her waist. There was wetwork. There were honeypots. He flicked his thumb over her nipple, and Dina realized that no one other than her mother had ever seen her breasts before. The KGB thought that Americans were sex-obsessed. They trained girls to be swallows. Their job was to seduce secrets out of CIA officers.

Angelos's tongue slipped over her collarbone, and Dina was dragged down into the molten core she never suspected in her body. She knew she had to leave, and then a moment later, less than a second, knew she had to stay. She didn't recognize his hands when they grabbed her because they were so rough, and yet at the same time she knew they could not have belonged to anyone else. She was suffocating, she was more afraid than she'd ever been in her life, but she could not be anywhere else. It felt important, what she saw in Angelos's eyes.

His fingers crept under the elastic of her underwear. They found the small tuft of hair and slipped easily inside. Dina gasped, her heart pounding. Then his entire body was inside. In a shock, she saw that he was too much, she was too full of him. It hurt. She tried to pull away, but he clenched the small of her back and pushed deeper. Her eyes teared. She was cold from the pain. Just as she began to sob, terrified that her body was being torn apart, it stopped.

Dina was trembling, unable to move. Angelos sighed. He shifted her weight to his right leg. She could feel his heart beating. He was shaking. She believed he was scared, more afraid than she was, and her own panic receded. She rested her chin on his damp shoulder and pressed her hands against his back. She listened to his heavy breaths, they matched hers. "Tell me more," she whispered.

He was quiet. Then, "There were the Rosenbergs. They were the most famous of all. They loved each other so much, nothing could come between them. Not even death."

"What happened to them?"

Angelos fixed her underwear, nightgown. He prodded her to her feet. "They were executed for selling the Russians classified information about the atom bomb. They were scapegoats for the government."

"They were married?"

He nodded. "They sang to each other through the thick concrete walls of Sing Sing. Ethel and Julius, loyal until the very end."

Dina smiled.

He pushed a jolt of black hair from her face. "You won't betray me, will you?"

"I would never," Dina said and she meant it, though she did not know what it meant. She would do anything for him, she wanted to say.

He lay back down and gestured to the door with his chin. "Don't worry about the blood," he said, voice throaty, tucking a pillow behind his head. "That only happens the first time."

Dina crept to the bathroom to wash. In the morning, when she was sore, she did not worry. He had prepared her for that, too.

One of the things Angelos taught her was how to evade suspicion. This started with her left eye, which could reveal her at any moment. He showed her exercises: he stood behind her and, with his own palms, cupped each eye. She put her hands over his and interlaced her fingers over her forehead. They stood like this for five minutes, ten minutes. She wanted it to be romantic, but what she felt was self-conscious; she worried he was laughing at her. But she trusted him. When he brought her home an eye patch, she wore it faithfully, even though she would have burned it had her parents been the ones to insist on it. She started to feel proud of the eye. She started to feel like it was why he picked her.

One day, missing Angelos like crazy even as she sat next to him, she took out a pen and wrote a note, slid it across the table. Angelos continued to read his book. She pushed the note again. Mihalis flicked his paper so that the corner bowed low enough for him to see her over it. "Let Angelos work," he said. "Go play."

She waited for Angelos to defend her, but he just turned the page.

Late that night, she went to his room. It was locked. At breakfast, she swallowed a pastry that tasted like paste. When Angelos came in, she offered him some just to see how he'd react. She even said, "Try it, it tastes like glue," in a voice that was stronger than expected. He smiled at her the way the school principal did and said, "Just a coffee." All was lost. Then her mother said she wasn't feeling well, and could Angelos walk Dina to school today?

"Sure," he said, but the answer had everything to do with her mother and nothing to do with her.

Dina followed Angelos. He carried her bag over his shoulder. She wasn't sure if that was a good sign or not. It could mean he forgave her for whatever she'd done, that he would carry her and her things with him forever; or it could be a knapsack of pity to let her down easy. Dina couldn't help it. She started crying. She walked ahead so that he wouldn't see.

He caught up, stopped her by the shirt. "Listen, *koukla*," he said, "you have to be smart about this. You can't just write notes with everyone looking." Not everyone was as evolved as they were, not everyone would understand. Some people, some parents, were old-country.

"OK," she said, eyes still wet, "but it's hard."

He told her about a case—a spy who searched the daily paper for an advertisement that read "Dodge Diplomat, 1971, needs engine work, $1000." If it was printed, that meant that his contacts overseas needed to reach him. Dina could do something like this—they could have a special sign—if she really needed something. "But you have to promise not to be so obvious," he said. "You have to get stronger. You have to do your eye exercises. You have to be cunning." Dina liked that word, *cunning*.

But Dina did make a mistake. A big one.

Sometimes, Dina's mother made Angelos do work that was beneath Angelos. Dina had to watch him scrub garbage cans (garbage!), clean chicken (clean!), wash dishes (dishes! A Greek intellectual doing dishes!). Irene didn't want Dina helping him, just made her sit at the table and wait for him to complete his chores. And the whole time, Dina's mother talked to Angelos as if they were close. As if he didn't think she was a fat, ignorant, backward peasant with peasant manners and peasant hygiene.

"You miss your home, Angelo? You miss your mother?"

"My mother is a saint. I would call her every day if I could."

Dina kicked the leg of the table. "Ma-ma, we have work to do. Science project."

Irene turned around. Her hands were in yellow rubber gloves, and she was sponging down the face of the refrigerator. "Angelos is almost finished, and then you can start."

"Ma-ma, he isn't a slave."

"What slave? All he's doing is giving his aunt a little help. It doesn't trouble him anything."

"To tell you the truth," Angelos said, "it's a nice break from all the thinking."

"Fine. I can dry." Dina was already up, pulling a towel out of the drawer. She took a plate from Angelos and let herself touch the wet ridge of his knuckle.

Angelos pulled away and, in an instant, cinched her wrist. His grip was unrecognizable—disciplinary. He looked up at Irene, smiling, and dropped Dina's arm. "Listen to your mother, *koukla*," he said. "I should have more often listened to mine."

Irene looked to Angelos's hand, hanging by his side. "My daughter was never so excited for extra chores before you came."

Dina was quaking. "It's not chores," casual as she could. "It's helping."

That night Angelos opened the door, but he wouldn't let her in. He said he barely recognized Dina anymore—she was sloppy, whiny. A double agent. A brat. "I warned you," he hissed.

Dina cried, apologized. She said it was her mother. Her mother made her crazy. Her mother didn't know when enough was enough. Angelos said Dina was the one who didn't know when enough was enough. Teach me, Dina said. *Teach me*, she begged. Too loud, her parents' room too close. She did not reveal that, between dinner and bed, she overheard her parents talking. Her mother saying, *It's something wrong, a man and a young girl alone in a house so much*, and her father answering, *He's a good boy. He is family.*

Angelos pulled her into the room and told her to shut up. Then he said, You won't question me? You won't doubt my methods? Every form of subterfuge? Every expression of concealment? You won't make stupid mistakes? You won't act like a baby?

Yes. I'm ready. I'm ready to learn.

By the time he was done with her, he promised, there would be no mistakes. There would be nothing she couldn't do. "Sometimes spies don't have to speak to one another, even when they're face-to-face," he instructed, untying the drawstring on his pants. "They talk in code."

"Morse code?" she asked, letting him draw her to her knees.

He nodded and scooted to the edge of the bed. "That's right. Let me show you."

He showed her how to transmit information using rhythm. Under his guidance, she listened for the short and long gasps, used her mouth to send out continuous waves of current, honed a message with pulses. She never spoke, but he understood her loud and clear. He could barely suppress the dots and dashes that escaped his lips as "dits" and "dahs." It was the only time he broke his code of silence, muffling cries into her hair.

It was nearly four in the morning. They lay in the sallow light of his desk lamp, Angelos's arm hanging over his chest. She said she could hear his heart, even though she couldn't. She sat up when Angelos reached over to the night table and slipped a white pill out of a textbook. She had seen the white pills before. He hid them in socks, swab boxes. Angelos maintained that they were medicine to help him study, but then why hide them in such weird places? It hurt that he was keeping part of himself secret, but she knew it would only be a matter of time. Maybe he just wanted to make sure she was ready.

Angelos didn't want her to leave yet. He lit a cigarette and she took a drag, entwining her middle finger in his wiry beard. She didn't want to leave, either. She wanted to tell him how beautiful he made her feel, but she couldn't bring herself to talk like that. Instead, she said, "You should see the girls in my class."

"Oh yeah?" he said.

"None of them are Greek."

"What do they look like?"

"They have blond hair."

"They are probably just skinny crows with bird legs and no tits."

Dina clapped her hands over her smile. "You wouldn't say that if you saw them."

Angelos propped himself up on his elbow. He took another puff, and the smoke filled his mouth. "Maybe that is true. When I was your age, I chased after the obvious girls."

Dina's smile receded. "Tell me about them."

"There was only one." And he confessed that, for a while, he had been in love with the Red Spy Queen.

"What happened?" Dina asked, hating this woman already.

"She revealed my true identity."

"She's a stupid dog bitch."

Angelos frowned. "Sooner or later, they'll get to you, too."

"No they won't."

The frown behind his beard became a grimace. "Your father will. He'll get you to defect."

Dina scowled and yanked the cigarette out of his mouth. "No he won't."

"Swear to me."

"I swear."

"No," Angelos said, his voice hard. His Adam's apple rose and fell. He sat up. "Swear to me."

Dina's annoyance disappeared. She had never seen him so close to crying. Her eyes swept over his face. She twisted the edge of his beard in her fist and yanked him toward her.

Angelos's eyes lit up. He chuckled, kissed her on the mouth, then the eye. Then he took the cigarette back. "My beautiful Ethel," he said, exhaling a loom of smoke.

It made Dina feel like she was the most important, most-loved person in the world.

A month later, Angelos was not at the corner. Not once had he been late. Even when he had an interview in the city, he returned in time to meet her, necktie in hand. Dina waited five minutes, ten, and then she began to run. She stopped when she saw her father's car in the driveway. Dina walked into the kitchen, making sure to appear calm. Her father had only just come home, Dina calculated, because his hair was still curled with sweat, and he had yet to shower. He was wearing work pants, a yellowed undershirt. A cigarette, the same kind Angelos smoked, held between two fingers like he didn't know what to do with it. He did not look at Dina. Her mother did.

Dina opened the refrigerator and poured herself some milk. She coached herself to stay silent. When people are nervous or guilty, Angelos had instructed, they talk. They need to get things off their chest. Stay quiet as long as you can: to slow their suspicion. They might know the Reid technique, and then a single twitch of the cheek would set them after her like the CIA on Perseus, the spy who tried to steal the atomic bomb for Stalin.

Mihalis ashed out the cigarette on the tabletop. "You can start your homework," Mihalis said. "Angelos is not coming."

Dina waited one, two seconds before answering. "What do you mean?"

Her mother said, "Angelos does not live here anymore."

This was just falsified evidence. Angelos would never have left.

But maybe her mother wasn't lying. Maybe Angelos wasn't coming back.

Her stomach started to turn. She imagined milky tea curdled by a squirt of lemon. Angelos had been the one to teach her that you couldn't have both. You have to choose lemon or milk.

Dina couldn't help herself. "He's coming back. He would have said goodbye."

"Oh yeah, Miss America? You know so much about him?"

"He has nowhere to go," Dina said. "We're his only family."

Irene came around the table to face her daughter. She took her hands. "He is not your family," Irene said. "He is a nobody."

Dina realized her legs were shaking. But most important, she had to stop herself from crying. Crying meant guilt. An innocent person, at this stage, would scream, deny, refuse all accusations no matter how rigorous the interrogation.

"You went to his room," her father said, "at night."

"No I didn't." She could feel her eye wanting to look away, but she kept it as close as she would have kept Angelos. She met her mother's gaze evenly.

"Your mother saw you coming back to your bedroom in the morning."

"I was on the couch," Dina sobbed. "It was hot."

"You slept on the couch when you have a nice big bed?"

"I didn't feel good. I had my period."

Mihalis faltered. He glanced at Irene. Very quickly, he realized he was in foreign territory.

Irene gaped. "She doesn't have that. She is too young."

"No I'm not." She sank her hand into her pocket and pulled out a pad. She had found it in the girls' bathroom a few days before. Now, she grew instantly confident. Being a good spy meant thinking fast, using resources. "I'm not your stupid little *koukla* anymore."

Irene scoffed, but there were tears in her eyes. She took Dina's face into her hands. "What did you do, Dina *mou*? What did he make you do?"

It was unexpected. Dina felt a rush. All of a sudden, she wanted to fall into her mother's arms. She felt a coming release, relief, as if she might shake off all of the dirt that had been packed over her mouth and chest for as long as she could remember. Then Dina glanced at her father's face, and she understood: this was all a trick. What her mother was doing was Pride and Ego Down: through niceness, she was trying to get Dina to betray Angelos.

"He made me smarter," Dina said forcefully. "Isn't that what you wanted?"

Mihalis pushed Dina into the hallway. He shouted at his wife. "From now on, you are here with her every day after school. No phones, no boys, nothing but learning how to be a good girl."

Inevitably, this was what all Greek fathers forced upon their daughters. Judge, jury, and executioner, Mihalis could detain her indefinitely. "This is not justice," Dina shouted, pounding on the bedroom door. "I hate you."

She yelled until she was hoarse. For half an hour, she cried into her pillow. She had not felt this kind of loss since leaving Papous, who had also left her behind (for heaven). Now Angelos, too, was out of her life forever. She would never see him again, her parents would make sure of that. And then, very suddenly, Dina's tears stopped. She sat up. Angelos would never have left without giving her hope, a sign.

At three in the morning, Dina snuck out of her bedroom. The bathroom light was on, her parents' door was open, but her father was snoring again. Her mother had not cleaned out Angelos's room, thank God. The slate-blue, the smell of him, it almost brought Dina to gagging tears. Their first night in that bed came rushing back. But she had to pull herself together. She didn't know how much time she had.

There was a necktie hanging from a corner hook, and for a moment she thought that was it. She put it up to her nose. She rubbed it against her chin and lips. She slipped the tie on and kept looking. Patches of rug, lightbulbs, beneath and behind dressers—everything was clean. Then she unscrewed his lamp, plugged her fingers into the hollow neck, and pulled up a matchbox. She slid out the drawer. A bit of wax paper. Gingerly, she unfolded it. Inside was a single oval, flat-faced blue pill.

A little blue pill.

There were two possibilities. Either he had left her some of his medicine, knowing she would find it, or he had left her cyanide, knowing she would follow. She tried to think like Angelos. If he had left her medicine, his message would be about trust, about how they could be close in this one experience even if they couldn't be close in life. If he had left her cyanide, the message was that he wanted to be with her forever, in death if not in life.

Cyanide, she decided.

Angelos had taught her everything so that, when the time came, she would not be afraid. Iron cyanides, he had said, were first discovered as components in the dye Prussian blue; the color had not even existed until the 1700s—might never have existed had it not been for a little contaminated potash. This is natural stuff, he insisted. It's produced by certain bacteria; traces of it can be found in cigarette smoke, in the stones of apples, mangoes, peaches. Cyanide smells like almonds. Even the name is familiar, he coaxed—*Kyaneos*, Greek for dark blue.

She had to put it in her mouth.

He had told her about Eva Braun and Adolf Hitler, who bit into a cyanide capsule together just before the pretty young wife was incinerated in her navy silk dress. Yet she did not have to be afraid, because she knew if Angelos had left her one pill, he had taken the other.

She bit down.

Nothing happened for an hour. Then she began to feel happy. Cheerful. Confident. She was alert. She knew exactly what was happening to her and around her. She saw clearly, for the first time, how sad her parents' lives were, how they had never known love and never would because they were unable to love. She had only just turned thirteen and already she had a vision they could never hope to possess, because they were close-minded peons.

The blue pill was not cyanide. Angelos had introduced Dina to amphetamines.

Dina made friends. She met Dill at a party she wasn't supposed to be at, and he brought her into his van so she could "taste a little of his paste." Dill was loud, rude, fat, unromantic, unsubtle. Dina didn't love him, but she spent every day with him in the shed behind his grandmother's backyard.

Dill had rigged a stovetop, and there were a couple of blowtorches in an unplugged refrigerator. She watched him mix baking soda, insecticides—substances introduced as dilutants—into the batch. She had no idea what it was. He combined drain cleaner (sulfuric acid) with salt, lots of salt, to get hydrogen chloride gas. Table salt—he said as he gave her a hit—the most pure, most basic ingredient. It's all over the fucking world. It's in the water.

Over the next couple of years Dina became, like Angelos, seriously committed to science. Meteorology was part of her history, after all: as early as 350 BC, Aristotle had described the hydrologic cycle in his writings. The Evaporation Experiment. *Step 1, Record the air temperature of the room.* Is Dill feeling generous today? Is he moody? Will he give her a little more than Alice? *Step 2, Wet a hand towel and hang it with clothespins in the shade.* Dina is the wet towel, Dina is hanging in the shade waiting for the sunshine to come; she takes whatever he's burning in a little foil of aluminum and sucks it dry. She is not nearly as clean and white as her lungs and her brain and even the soles of her feet. *Step 3, Check the towel every five minutes until it's completely dry, determining wind presence and humidity.* For some reason, Dill is blowing into her mouth, which makes her laugh, which makes him do it more. He is squeezing her wrists. Then he is squeezing his body into hers while Alice pretty much just watches. She must be the control. Or Dina is the control. She's so evaporated, she can't tell.

Other experiments. Temperature and Heat Transfer, Finding Dewpoint, Pressure Change and Weather, Snow to Liquid Ratio, and, best of all, Making Thunder. Every time she discovers a new finding, she thinks, I wonder if Angelos knows that this is what I'm like. Every time she feels a new sensation, she imagines him feeling it, too. Even three years later.

At some point Dill gives her a horse tranquilizer, and she goes blind for a few hours.

It's time to find Dina a husband, Mihalis says.

Irene, unable to imagine any other solution, agrees.

But Dina, who at fifteen has been an astronaut, a spy, and a meteorologist, is not about to just give up and be a nice Greek bride.

STAVROS AND DINA MAVRAKIS

They landed in the City of Philos Adelphos, brotherly love. Three hundred and twenty dollars in his pockets, he liked to tell people. And not a brother in sight.

The Lazaridises did not live in New York like Yannis Fafoutakis said, they lived in New Jersey. There were no American girls with *karpouzi* tits and *karpouzi* ass waiting to suck his big dick. That didn't matter, Stavros told himself, party time was for the island. He was here to become important. Instead, he was given yellow rubber gloves and Brillo pads at the Acropolis Diner. The big office job Mihalis had promised didn't exist.

A man wearing three gold rings emerged from the big-man office where Stavros's pay was being withheld instead of handed over each night. "Who would have known," the three-ring man said, "a Mavrakis scrubbing my pots."

It was Andonis, a boy from the village. Instead of telling him *ai gamisou*, Stavros Stavros smiled and said, "You got fat, Andonis. Too much American food."

"Not just me," Andonis said. "My pockets, too." He flashed a bloated black wallet.

Never had Stavros felt less of a man than he did during the three months he worked for Andonis. Like all of the other dishwashing Greeks, he was called Goatbanger and Flease—short for flap grease, which was said to build up on uncircumcised pricks after a lifetime of working in kitchens. After one of the cooks froze grease into his shoe while he was out shoveling snow, Stavros quit. If he had wanted to be shit on, he could have stayed in Crete. A man had to have pride. If not, what was the point of life?

The next day, Mihalis called Stavros into the living room. They shared a bowl of potato chips, a poor substitute for *mezedes* and nothing to dip them in. The two sat facing each other, listening to the other chew. They were like male goats battling, and whoever ate the most would win.

"What do you think foreigners do? We clean dishes. You think you can get better work so soon? You barely know English."

"I know English," he answered. "More than you, Mihalis."

The old goat snorted. "You, Mavrakis, you want what you want whenever you want it. How do you expect to pay rent now?"

"Rent?"

"Three fifty a month."

Stavros launched to his feet. He was shouting. "You want to charge three hundred fifty dollars a month? I didn't come here just to make you a rich man."

"This is no free ride. You want to live, you pay."

Mihalis was not smiling but he looked victorious, and Stavros realized that this was how he planned to get back the three thousand drachmas his mother had extorted. Stavros stormed into the bedroom. He began to shove their belongings into suitcases. All he had were a few shirts and pants, two kinds of shoes (one smelling of bacon), an electric razor, and half a bottle of Old Spice. He packed Dina's clothes.

His father-in-law opened the door without knocking because, as they both knew, it was his right as the head of the household not to be shut out of any room. "When you pay for them," he said, "you get to take them with you." Mihalis yanked Dina's suitcase away.

Stavros followed. "What do you think you're doing?" he cried. He lunged for the luggage but was too late. Mihalis threw it into the bathtub and turned on the shower. The dresses, some of them still attached to price tags, were soaked. Mihalis was panting. "You want them, take them."

Stavros reached into the tub and flung whatever his hand touched. A pair of sagging panty hose hit Mihalis's oversize nose with a smack.

If a man had been staying in his house and treating him like this, Stavros would have slaughtered him with a spoon. But this old goat just stood there, breathing his offense.

The moment Stavros got into the driver's seat, he felt calmer, in control. The starter resisted until he kneed the ignition, and then it turned over. Whatever he wanted, the Vega would do it. It was the only thing in the world that truly belonged to him. From the front, the 1970 Chevrolet Vega could almost pass as a Camaro. The bottom was rimmed with rust, which the previous owner had covered with latex paint; it flaked off in little sheets anytime someone brushed up against the side; it wept off in the rain. But the Vega responded to him, it answered to only him. If he decided to stop, it stopped. If he wanted to accelerate, like he did now, with Mihalis shouting into his windshield, it would do that, too.

Stavros pulled up to the sandwich shop where Dina worked. He was still seething, but when he saw Charlie—the owner and one of the few Americans Stavros knew by name—he made himself into someone relaxed and easy to talk to. He did not want the man to think badly of him.

"I am speaking to her just for one minute, please," he called from across the room.

Charlie was sitting in a booth, a stack of bills spread out in front of him. He waved Stavros over. "Have a soda."

Stavros did not take off his jacket, his sleeve still wet. Wanting to convey profound thanks for hospitality, which most Americans did not express, he sipped his soda through a straw. That was how it was served to him, so that is how he drank, but he despised it. He did not understand why straws were so popular in America. It was like trying to enjoy a nice cool drink through a piece of garbage. At home, he demanded glass.

Charlie paged through his checkbook. Thin gray hairs hung over his face. "You're just in time to pick her up."

"I think she is working into ten tonight?"

"Oh, no. She's fired."

Stavros clenched his jaw. He knew "fired" from the last job. Here they were without a place of their own to live, him pushing his ass to find work, and she was playing. While he had to clean up after people who had half his brains.

"To explain please, Charlie."

"She's a kook. She scares the customers."

Stavros stood and dropped some coins on the table. "I'm sorry, Mr. Charlie."

"Keep your money," Charlie said. "With a wife like her, you'll need it."

"No, because I pay my debts."

Dina was leaning against a Dumpster, smoking a cigarette. She could have been waiting on the curb, but she chose to be close to filth. He had come here to tell Dina that her father was a blood thief, but now he was going to have to face garbage.

She spotted him. "You hungry?"

"No, I'm not hungry."

Dina shrugged. "We ordered pizza."

She never pronounced it like he did, *peesa*, which made him sour in this situation.

"You had a good job, *re*, and you threw it away with the trash."

Dina flicked the butt of her half-smoked cigarette at his feet. "You threw away a good job, too." So her father had told her.

"I won't be anybody's slave. You, Dina, only want to have a good time instead of working."

"I never wanted a job. That was you and my father."

"Six months. That's all I asked you for. Then you can stay home every day."

Dina muttered something he couldn't catch.

"What you say to me?" he stormed, but she refused to answer. He followed her to the car. When she opened the passenger door, he shut it on her. "You don't get in my car until you answer me." Dina turned on him. Never before had Stavros felt such hatred from anyone. Her stare made him feel insignificant, and who was she or any woman to make him feel like that?

"*Gamoto*," he swore. "This woman is more trouble than children."

This did not faze her.

He forced her into the backseat, pushed her in when she tried to climb up to the front. He started the car to ignore her screaming. He drove. She kicked his chair. In the rearview mirror, she looked wild—all except for her eyes, which were zeroing in on him with such hate, both of them. Fuck your mother in her mouth, she shouted. Fuck the Virgin Mother, you gay Jew, you cunt hair. You chief of assholes with the testicles of a faggot. You *malaka* and your little dick. You fucking peasant.

Stavros threw his elbow back and caught her in the mouth. He hadn't meant to, but oh it was satisfying to feel his bone smash against Dina's face. She sank into the seat, clutching her chin. For a moment, all he could hear was his ragged breathing and the erratic thumping of the vehicle. He thought about pulling over. Then she bit his ear.

Stavros grabbed his ear in pain and the car swerved. She had broken the skin, and his fingers came back with blood. It alarmed him, then he was furious. "You camel," he shouted, and in that moment he was absolved. Any woman who acted like a man he would treat like a man. He lunged with his arm, trying to grab her, but she pressed her body against the side of the car, out of reach.

Pushing his finger into the bite marks, Stavros realized he had been played for a fool. Everyone was in on it—his mother, Dina, Mihalis, the *pappas*, and especially that faggot Yannis Fafoutakis. Yannis, the gambler, the liar, the snake who had swindled him without ever taking his bet. And Stavros, like a *vlaka*, had made it easy for them: he had agreed to marry this girl.

Now Stavros cursed Yannis, cursed Yannis's mother, cursed the goats that were screwing Yannis's mother. "Yannis Fafoutakis," he shouted. "If I ever see your ugly face again, I will crush your withered hairless balls. I will fuck your sister from behind." He spat at the sky. A bit of saliva stuck to the windshield.

Stavros woke before Dina. Rent was due, and he did not want to have to admit that there was no money. Especially because Dina—since the biting—was like a lamb to him, a lamb who ignores you more than cowers but always remembers who carries the knife. He folded up the last of his last bills, singles, drove fifteen minutes to a diner. She could go ahead and think he was coming home with pluses in his pockets, which she would take and turn into minuses.

He missed his *kafenia*, missed his *mezedes*, missed eating warm foods in the company of aggressively friendly countrymen. And now that he was jobless, where else was there to go?

Stavros sat at a booth. He opened the menu so that people could think he was reading it. Funny, how there was always a book to get through before you ordered at a restaurant here, rather than someone shouting out that A is your option, or it is C because the chickens haven't laid enough eggs yet for B. One thing he did love about America, though, you could get pancakes anytime. For Americans, pancakes were common as toast. You could have pancakes with eggs, pancakes with breakfast meats, pancakes with milk shakes or ice cream. He got his with fruit on it. He made sure to smother each bite in blueberries and syrup. He chewed each one like it was his favorite.

Too soon, the pancake as big as a face was gone. Around him, people were having as many as they pleased. He could sit here longer—the day was still a huge stack of pancakes to get through, the sun a pat of butter just starting to melt—but that would mean spending his last nickels on diner coffee. Americans and their coffee, so sour it could have come from the sweat in his shoe. No, he would need to find someplace that brewed coffee he could chew through. Stavros dug into his pocket, pulled out money to pay for his pancakes, and stopped.

At the counter, a waiter was cutting a nice wide slice of *galaktoboureko*. Stavros watched him carefully lay it out onto a white plate. "Excuse," Stavros called to his waitress. "Can I have this, please?"

The waitress brought his portion to him without a word, which was what he wanted. He did not ask how much, he did not know if he had enough. All he knew was that the moon-tinted custard had spread itself out like a smile, and the top crust was so shiny in its syrup it was like a joke the whole place could enjoy. He had not seen one so pretty since Greece.

Oh, the *galaktoboureko*, it was two o'clock on a Greek afternoon with the *pappas*, it was twenty years ago running through the fields with his arms stretched as wide as grapevines, it was sugar if the past were made of sugar, it was semolina-sweet with teardrops of lemon. The first bite was not too sweet, and it made him cry. He did not expect it, he could not help it. The *galaktoboureko* tasted like his mother's fingers. It smelled like her apron. It was exactly like the *galaktoboureko* she used to make, it was the twin of her *galaktoboureko*, and it made him wish for home. It made him want to burrow his head into his mother's thigh like he did when he was a small boy, to make the bucking sounds of a ram until she relented and threw her arms around him and smeared butter on his neck and snuck him a little taste with her own fingers in a way that her other sons could not see. It gave him back memories he did not know he had. Any minute, he expected his brothers to come and fight him for the prize. Any minute, he expected the *pappas* to join him and steal precious forkfuls of the dessert, only so that he could turn around and order them another.

But no, Stavros was alone. He was in a booth, in Xenitia, in a country where *galaktoboureko* was nothing more than syllables and cream.

Stavros wiped his tears with a diner napkin softer than any pillow. What he was doing without realizing it was making *galaktoboureko* into something foreign: from now on when he thought of *galaktoboureko*, as a father or an old man, he would not just remember *galaktoboureko* in Greece. He would have to remember *galaktoboureko* in America. He would have to think about *galaktoboureko* on a white plate at this diner. It would not just be his favorite dessert from his childhood, which he hid from his brothers, or his favorite dessert from his adolescence, which he made at the *kafenia*. It would be the dessert from this morning, when he went for pancakes instead of work, when he cried in front of strangers who did not mind him crying because a Greek newcomer did not matter one way or another.

Without being invited, someone with his own plate of *galaktoboureko* sat down across from Stavros. He pulled a fork out of his sleeve and began to eat. Stavros wiped his face into a friendly smile. He knew that strangers did not just appear at your table and start to eat with you. This was a countryman. His nose was Greek enough to spear a fish, the eyebrows needed mowing, the teeth in his mouth faced any which way as if they were old men at the village center. Stavros ate for some minutes without offering his family name or island or asking the other if he was from the mainland.

When he finally spoke, the Greek's voice was the consistency of the *galaktoboureko*. It was not just that Stavros was warmed to hear Greek spoken by someone who wasn't Dina or her parents and their acquaintances. It was that the man sounded as if his parents, his family, were all made from honey too sweet to come from bees.

Hero Karmkambasis said with his fork, "Mainland or island?"

Stavros cleared his throat. "From Crete."

"Crete, I should have known. You have that stunned look of a *kri-kri*."

If they were still in Greece, Stavros would have taken this as an insult. Here, being compared to the famous goats of Crete was camaraderie. He said, "Is this a place for Greeks?"

Hero ran his fork along the plate to scrape up custard. "Greece is the only place for Greeks. But this is a nice second. You see them come around when they're homesick."

Stavros saw that he was the only one.

"Every week, I get twenty Greeks crying over my *galaktoboureko*," Hero said. "They all tell me how much it tastes like their mothers'."

"You made this?"

Hero turned his face as if about to share a secret. "*Ela*, you can say Hero's is as good as your mother's. I won't tell her, or your dead *yia-yiu* either."

"It is better than my mother's," Stavros answered. "My friend, better." Because it was here, and his mother's was not. Because Hero was here, and his mother was not.

"When I first come to this country, the boss says to me, '*Oxi*, Hero, you are no chef, you are a mechanic.' And he is right. In Greece I had been trained to work with hard stuff only, not this soft butter and dough, which falls apart in my hands. It doesn't take me too long to get the idea, though. All it takes is the boss's wife going into labor, and Hero the only one left in the kitchen." Then Hero said, "Since you like it so much, friend, you can have this one for free."

Stavros opened his mouth to refuse, and then he shut it. In other circumstances, he would have felt wounded in his pride, which stretched over his whole body like a second skin, but here he couldn't. Stavros could tell that Hero was not pitying him. Hero had been at this place before. Someone had given him a slice of *galaktoboureko* when he was down, when he was just starting. With his *galaktoboureko*, Hero was offering him entry into a brotherhood. It was his first invitation in this new place.

Stavros's eyes looked to the crumbs on his plate, where the tears were falling. "Thank you," he said in English.

Hero stood so that Stavros would not be embarrassed, and he dropped the wet rag from his shoulder onto the table. He picked up his plate and began to wipe the table. Stavros reached for the rag.

"*Ela*, relax," Hero said. "You clean the tables in your house, I'll clean the tables in mine."

But Stavros went on to wipe the table next to him, and the one beyond that. It was not because he could not pay for his *galaktoboureko*. It was not just that he wanted to hide his custardy eyes. What was this new feeling?—ah, it was that he could wipe every table for the rest of his day and still feel indebted. Stavros scrubbed at a sticky spot. He collected all the napkins and silverware onto a dirty plate. He could feel the Greek staring at him.

"Hey, Cretan," Hero said. "You ever work in a restaurant before?"

Stavros nodded without nodding. He said, "I ran two *kafenia* back home."

Hero laughed. "Didn't we all."

"I can run a kitchen. I can cook."

"I run the kitchen. I cook. What I need is a dishwasher. Can you do that?"

He could. He could wash dishes for a man who by kitchen alone could convince everyone that he was their Greek mother, who wanted to share his *galaktoboureko* with other Greeks, who was respectful enough to stand when another man was starting to cry, who was here at the right time, when Stavros was at the end of his money and courage. Stavros said, "I can do anything you ask me to."

ζ

The next few weeks, Stavros was good to Dina. They took walks at night, they held hands through the park when no one was around. He talked about his job as if it had been the plan from the start. In America, *kafenia* did not have prestige or authority. They were convenience stores selling Twinkies and cans of Shasta; they didn't even serve coffee, it was just cloudy water. Stavros wanted to open a kind of business that would get him respected and paid. He would become an innovator, like Hero. He would show everyone, most of all his mother. He would open a diner.

"There's something in the corner of his eye, when no one's looking," Stavros said excitedly. "He can tell that I'm no dishwasher."

"He's going to give you a raise?"

"Right now, I am giving him the cleanest pots he can imagine. They come out more *oraio* than they were when he bought them brand-new. He will see what a good job I am doing, and he will give me the chance to earn more."

Dina tucked her head into the crook of his arm. She said, "You always do a good job."

He liked that. He liked how they looked, man-wife, against the chilly copper sky. He liked that she was proud of him, that she believed in him. "*Agapi mou*, I am doing all of this for us."

She looked up and smiled. Her left eye wandered, then found him again. Stavros laughed and kissed it, his mustache tickling her.

They went home and made their first Greek baby.

Over the next few months, while Dina picked up extra weight, Stavros picked up extra hours. He would wash dishes for the morning shift, then wash dishes for the afternoon shift, then scrub the floors, then sleep on a cot in the back room, then wash dishes for the evening shift. Washing dishes became such habit, sometimes he got up from dinner at home and started scrubbing the ones in his wife's sink. His hands were not the callused hands of a workingman; they were the bloated, worn hands of a sailor.

It was exhausting, yes, but it was life-making. He was bringing home every-week paychecks without having to feel abused. He was bringing home full-cooked meals for his wife, who was eating for two.

He was working with a man who respected him, a man who had come from Corfu when he was just sixteen.

"What the man can do with potatoes," he said to his mother over the phone in one of their monthly conversations. "He makes them taste like they could never have come from the ground."

What Stavros meant, but could not say, was that Hero made it seem as if nothing he touched came from the ground. Not his business, not his customers, whom he coaxed with recycled compliments, not his beautiful and smart and pleasant wife, not his son who was growing up to be the head of business. Even Hero—Hero himself—was made of much more than humble clay. No matter what came, Hero was smiling, acting as if each morning were one big *galaktoboureko*.

In the first weeks of employment, Stavros saw Hero terminate two waiters. "I wish you were my wife's family, so then I would be forbid from firing you." Then he gave them each a free meal and sent them to his cousin's place, where they could apply to drive trucks. Then he hired two new men, whom he loved just as much. "These men, these are my family," he said. The same thing he had said to the men they were replacing, the same thing he had said to Stavros on his first day of work.

In ten years, Stavros planned to be him.

"How fat is that woman of yours?" Hero said. Stavros with his feta stuffed into bread and his Saratoga, Hero with his American coffee and Greek sweets. Stavros on an overturned mop bucket, Hero on a three-legged stool that should have had four. He spoke in English.

Stavros answered in Greek, "Getting fatter."

"They are wonderful when they are fat."

"She farts these ugly pregnancy farts. They are just terrible, because how is my son not suffocating in there?"

"Is this your biggest problem, that your pregnant wife farts?"

"Hero, I'm choking. I am at the point where honey mustard smells exactly like fish."

Hero took pleasure in this. He got up and rummaged through the pantry. He came back with two jars of honey mustard. "Tell Dina she can thank me in the future, after she names her son Hero."

"You are a *malaka*, you know that?"

"Pregnancy taught me somethings important, Stavro. First, the mother is always number one, because the baby is always number one. Second, whatever the mother craves, she will hate once the baby comes: she will not even be able to smell it."

"No more honey mustard, Hero."

"Happy mother, happy baby," Hero insisted, pushing the jars across the table. "Bring these home, you get to be happy husband."

Stavros brought them home. The next day, he got a promotion. Dishwasher-busboy.

The problem was that the new Dish that Hero hired was Hero's wife's lazy cousin and did no work, so when Stavros came back to the kitchen, he was stuck with the same load he had bused the hour before. Hero wasn't pleased, and he blamed Stavros.

"Think of these dishes each like a crying baby," Hero said. "They have to be picked up, washed, and put to bed. You don't just leave them lying on the floor with dirty diapers."

Stavros was not going to lose this dishwasher-busboy job because of some no-initiative immigrant, and he was not going to keep it out of pity. He was going to earn it.

At home, it was also getting harder. Dina was another lazy. All she wanted to do was stay on the couch with her arm on her belly, sometimes throwing up. Or else she took walks alone—good for the baby, she said. Her mother came by once a week to help. Dina said it was not enough. Stavros did not understand how it was not enough. How could one woman not take care of one apartment, when that was the one thing she had to do? But Dina complained so much, she got him to hire a "helper"—her friend Stephanie. All Stephanie gave help with was eating food in his cabinets and bringing in the mail from the mailbox, which was practically in his house.

"She does not even vacuum. She does not even touch the laundry. I work all night running a restaurant, and I have to wear dirty clothes," he said in Greek.

"The vacuum's broken," Dina said in English.

"She is not a helper. She is an unhelper," he answered in English.

"It's too hard to be here by myself."

"What does she do for you that is worth thirty dollars?"

"She helps me get through the day," Dina said. "She takes me to the doctor."

She did take Dina to the doctor. She also brought Dina daily medicine. She spent days with Dina as if they were sisters, and they spoke English so fast, like the people on television, that Stavros could never understand what he was doing that was so funny. But he kept Stephanie around because his mother told him that Stephanie was doing for Dina what Dina's sisters-in-law would be doing if Stavros and Dina still lived in Greece.

There were other problems, ones he did not tell his mother about. Money problems, which were Lying problems, which were Wife-Husband problems, which were Future problems. He gave her money for electric, for phone, but somehow the bills remained unpaid. They are processing, Dina said. For two weeks, they were processing, twenty-four hours a day processing, and at the end of the process, the woman on the other line told him that their balance was still $78. The dollars for the electric, which he cut off from the skin of his palms, were gone. The money for the phone, which he skinned off his knees, was gone. The groceries, there were no groceries.

"You work at a restaurant," she said. "All of your meals are free."

"I gave you almost a hundred dollars," he said. "What did you spend that on?"

"Baby stuff."

"Show me the baby stuff. Show me where it is."

She lifted her shirt and smacked her belly. "This is not just a snack, you know."

He did not hit her. He raised his hand, but only in sternness. She had learned to shield her face and turn her body in a way that showed him the shape of his child. He felt shame. He could not hit his son. He did not want to hurt his wife. He was frustrated. He went to work so that she could deal with the electric company and the phone provider and the grocery clerk. He needed her to be his English mouth and his paying hands.

Hero could read Stavros's temper, even when Stavros had never really let him see it. "Just because you have to crack some eggs doesn't mean you have to break the yolks," Hero said, which was somehow supposed to mean that Stavros was too hard on Dina, that Stavros had to be more patient and understand that his wife would one day be his children's mother. In Hero's world, a man was the ruler of his house but he never had to show it. Meanwhile, Dina ignored his wishes. Stephanie was at his home when he left in the morning and at his home when he came back at night. Stephanie was one time sleeping in his own bed, so Stavros had to lie down on the couch without even a blanket. "Gentle, gentle," Hero said. "*Siga, siga.*" Meanwhile, there were more medicine baggies on the table. Meanwhile, he found an exposed razor under the coffee table and was told by Dina that it was to cut capsules in half so she did not take too much at a time, so that the baby wouldn't be up all hours and she could get some sleep. Meanwhile, all this medicine was costing more money.

"This spending trouble, it will all go away when the baby comes, and then it will all get worse." Hero laughed, continued to laugh when Stavros wouldn't. "You have to learn to relax, Stavro," Hero said. "You have to be more like me."

"Hero, Hero, Hero, Hero, Hero, Hero. The world is not all Heroes. The world is Stavros Mavrakis, also. I go home to problems, they are not Hero problems, they are Stavros Stavros Mavrakis problems, they are baby and Dina, they are money problems, they are dish problems, they are the only troubles of Stavros Stavros Mavrakis."

It was his first outburst in English. The plating and washing stopped. Stavros felt pinned between the cruel curiosity of the kitchen and the firing he felt coming. His face was hot with anger and grease. He would have to go back to Mihalis, to Andonis, to jokes in his shoes, to life without his friend Hero.

Hero laughed, clapped him on the back, and everything started up again. "Poor Stavros Stavros," Hero said, "sounding like you have more problems than dishes."

STAVROULA MAVRAKIS

In her mind, what Dina was carrying was not a baby but a car battery. Being pregnant, like being high, was just another way that electrons zigged from negative to positive back to negative. When nine months were up, what she would push out would be a black box of energy. Still, Dina told herself, "When she gets here, it will all be about her." In three months, when her firstborn arrived, Dina would go from idle to forward. No one ever told her she could do anything, but this—this, everyone said, was automatic. It was natural for her to make children.

"A woman's thighs, there are only two reasons for them: men hold on as they're going in, and children hold on as they're coming out." She could not remember which man in her life had said that—father, husband, father's friends, husband's friends, strangers over Greek coffee. They had probably all said it at some point.

The wonderful part about being a mother, though, was that no one treated the thing inside her like a battery and no one treated her like the broke-down car. She could feel the pride and warmth radiating from her father. He rubbed the bump of her belly as if it were the back of his grandson's head. Her husband kissed her belly button as if it were his son's sleeping eye. Her mother was over all the time, calling the baby Blessing. And then she started calling Dina Blessing, and then she used Blessing interchangeably so that Dina wasn't sure which of them she was talking to. The real blessing, Dina thought, was how happy they all were because of something she was. A state she was in: with child. All she had had to do was lie back and it happened to her, their happiness. She had never been able to do that before.

Being pregnant had softened Stavros, too. They had fights still, but the bigger she got, the better he got. He came home straight from work to lie in bed and massage away her heartburn. He rubbed the fuzz at the top of her belly and said, "I don't think it's a child in there, I think it's a goat. You have my milk in there, little *kri-kri*?"

He talked often to his mother now. Dina would wake at two in the morning to robust Greek. Their hot personalities had a chance to cool over the thousands of miles of telephone line, their voices full of excitement rather than bullying. In Crete, the animals and fields had already been watered and fed, and his mother was gossiping about the village and prodding him about Dina and work. From the bedroom, Dina watched Stavros pull at the strings on the apron folded on his lap. She heard him say things like, "There is so much land here, but they carve it up into little pieces," and "She looks fat and beautiful."

Yes, when the baby came, Dina was going to change. She was going to keep this Stavros.

She did not have the heart to tell him it was a girl. He was convinced—they all were—that he would have a son. Dina had passed all of his tests. The Key Test, she picked up the fat end of the key. The Dream Test, she told him it was all snakes and stairs, when really it was moonbeams turning into moaning whales and lizards simmering, their tails hanging over the pot. At one point he was discouraged, saying, "You are carrying too high."

"This is not high. I am just short."

A Sunday morning, he pulled her out of bed early. The moon was still a chip against the brewed sky. She wiped her eyes and padded out to the kitchen. Sleep was ringing in her ears, but she could sense how excited he was.

He said, "You are far enough along now. This will tell us for good." He had a *briki* going. He poured her a steaming cup of thick Greek coffee. "Drink, please."

"I won't be able to get back to sleep."

"Of course not. Now drink, and hang the question up in your mind: Is this a boy?"

She took a sip. She couldn't stand Greek coffee, the way it left grains in her mouth. She said, "How do you know how to do this?"

"My grandmother, when I was small. I watched her read *kafeman-teia*. Any Greek can do it, if he knows what he's looking for."

He picked up Dina's cup, even though it wasn't quite empty. He said, "Whenever a girl got engaged in the old days, the married women of the village would come banging spoons against their copper *brikia*, all the way up the hill to my *yia-yia*'s house. They would shout at her—like a little song—Come Out Cup-Woman, Come Around Our Coal-Fire and Look Into Your Private Cup. Yia-yia sat with them in the dirt and said somethings like, *Watch out for a bird that presents itself three times*, or *Children with speckled eyes bring good meat to your kitchen*. Also, *There is a white rat near, keep it nearer*—that one she said a lot. I used to watch them from a corner."

Dina wondered what his *yia-yia* would have been able to determine about her in the coffee grains.

Stavros held the cup out, turning it three times clockwise on its side, so the sludge coated the inside of the cup. He turned the cup over on a napkin and closed his eyes. She said, "What are you looking for?"

He opened them. "Anything, but especially animals, rivers, initials. Yia-yia always wanted to find a face, but it never came up."

"What face?"

"Let me concentrate." Less than a moment later, he was setting the coffee cup upright. He pointed at the inside of the mug. "Symbols on the bottom are the past. Symbols on the sides are present. Anything near the top is what is approaching."

"What's approaching?" Dina pushed herself up to see. In her head, she said, *Show him whatever he wants to see. Show him three boys, if necessary.*

"This is what's approaching." He held the mug out. She saw a smear at the bottom, where his finger touched the grains. "You see the square?"

She nodded.

"That means a new home, like a foundation."

"So a boy?" she said.

"Yes, of course. What else could be foundation?"

ζ

The baby came two months early. Stavros raced from work to the hospital, saying to himself, "We're going to lose him." Speeding, treating stoplights like the flat, dumb faces they were, he made a deal with God about keeping the baby safe until he got there. When he made it to the lobby, he made a deal with God about keeping the baby safe until he could pick him up.

A nurse told him that Dina was sleeping, but did he want to see his daughter?

"Daughter?"

"She's small, but she's a fighter."

The nurse brought him to the NICU, where the preemies were lying on their stomachs, wearing diapers the size of their whole bodies. Some were more robot than human. Some had skin that was not skin; he could see shadows of organs that he should not have been able to see. He averted his eyes until they came upon the one marked with his name. A day ago, his baby had been just a bump on Dina's body. Now here she was in the world, trying to breathe with a tube taped over her mouth. Her legs were tucked under her body. Her thigh was the size of his thumb.

Stavros put his face into his hands and squeezed. His son Stavros was not in his wife's belly as he should have been. His son was a girl who had been ripped out too early and put inside a glass box to incubate, the way a baby chick might. Oh, this was not a baby. This was 3.1 pounds, this was an egg. How would she ever stand, with legs so small as that?

"You're the father?"

Stavros looked up. It was the doctor. Stavros could tell, because he wore a white coat and glasses. "Yes, I am his father."

The doctor came around with a clipboard, rested his hands on the glass case. If there had been no glass, Stavros observed, his hands would have taken up his daughter's face. "What's her name?"

Stavros blinked. "Stavroula."

"We're giving Stavroula two liters of oxygen until her lungs have a chance to develop."

Stavros nodded. He could see now she had only a little bit of lung, not strong enough to take breaths without the help of some machines. "What happened? Why is she alive so early?"

"That's what I'd like to talk to you about," the doctor said, and led him to the hall.

"Dina, she is OK?"

"At the moment, resting."

The doctor's office was filled with plaques and degrees and he sat in a leather chair, which made it easier to listen to him even though Stavros did not understand many of the words he used. The doctor said that their "goal" was to "minimize complications and promote normal development." Stavros nodded. He liked the word *normal*. He crossed his legs. He said, "But this does not explain me why."

The doctor took his glasses off. He said, "How long has your wife been addicted to drugs?"

Stavros uncrossed his legs. "I don't know drugs." He had seen her drink, not too often. Cocaine, he knew nothing about. Ten weeks early, he did not understand.

"We need to talk about getting your wife help. If she's going to be a mother, she belongs in a rehab facility."

Stavros did not understand rehab facility, either. The only place he saw Dina belonging was a hole. A deep one, so she had to dig herself out the way his daughter was digging herself out. He said, "How do we fix Stavroula?"

"We're monitoring vitals and weight gain. She'll need to stay here for a while."

"Can I see her again?"

"Yes. Would you like to see your wife first?"

"The baby, please."

He could not take this. He could not have his baby be so small. He could not accept feeling so stupid in front of this man, in front of all the hospital people, because all that time he thought that the baggies from Stephanie were baggies from the doctor. He reached the door and again was let in, and again was alone with the infants too small to be real. He took a deep breath, the first since entering the hospital. He put his hand on the glass top, exactly where the doctor's had been.

He said, "Stavroula, don't be shy." The baby did not move. He stroked the glass.

He whispered, speaking in Greek. He said, "We all have a job to do, Stavroula, in this life. I will do mine, if you will do yours. I will protect you from her, from anyone. All you have to do, little goat, is survive."

Dina's parents came and went. Her lunch tray came and went untouched. She watched them take away the baby. She was missing her child, she could not stop missing her, but she was afraid to hold her: a baby the size of a key. A keyhole. She tried the fit of the name on her tongue and was surprised to see that she could do it. "Stavroula."

Dina sat up. Her feet worked, they were moving her toward her child. They were stronger than her fear, they did not care about her fear. She stopped at the entry to the NICU, took a step back so she would not be seen. At the door were Stavros's shoes. He had left work to come hold their daughter. He was here, in a green gown, in his socks, kissing Stavroula, letting only his bottom lip touch the very top of her forehead. He was not afraid of how small she was. Dina wanted to rush to him. She wanted to hold her baby now, instead of him, beside him. She was going in, she was ready. But she stopped. Stavros had begun to weep. He did not stop himself from crying, which was what she was used to seeing. He kissed the baby again, and a second, a third time. Each time, his lips barely touched her. She could not break this. She could not interrupt this moment where he was seeing, just as she had seen, how small and vulnerable their baby was. And yet—he was here, holding her.

At seven, Stavros returned to the hospital a second time. Hero forced him to go, upon penalty of firing. In his pockets were cigars, which Hero had made him smoke, and a cash bonus, and in his arm was a baby doll with a plastic head full of plastic hair. There were clouds under his eyes, which made it difficult to see. The only sleep he had gotten in the last twenty-four hours was in the backseat of his car. After the hospital he would rest, but first he had to see his child, and then he had to talk to Dina. He would check on his little goat in the NICU, and then he would tell Dina that she was no better than a goat—no, worse.

He got to the NICU in time to see them take her out of the incubator. They did not notice him come in. The nurse who called his daughter Honeysuckle was placing his daughter in his wife's arms. For a moment Dina looked young, scared. He was not sure she would take Stavroula. Then her chin tipped forward, and her eyes discovered the baby tucked in her arms. Her hair fell across her face, he could only see her lips moving. It surprised him, how seeing this squeezed his heart into a lemon.

The nurse brushed Dina's hair behind her ear and said, "That's right." Then she saw Stavros, and said, "They're getting along better," before stepping out.

Stavros came close. The eye was still the size of a baby's pinky nail. It surprised him that what came out was more sadness than anger when he said, "You look forward to nine months and a son, and what you get is seven months and a daughter, and maybe not even that."

"She is stubborn like her parents," Dina said. "She will only get bigger from today." The baby seemed to barely move, but if they watched carefully, they could see the smallest, most powerful twinges of life. "This is the smallest she'll be."

He understood what she was saying. She was making a promise. She had been making errors before the baby came, maybe because the baby was not real yet—it had not been real to him, yet, either—but now Stavroula was in their lives, and Dina was saying that she was going to do whatever she needed to do to make sure the baby was cared for. He did not trust her but, because he had his own promises to keep, he would make sure she kept hers.

"Do you want to hold her? She has to go back in a minute."

"No," he said. "You hold her."

They stood quiet until the nurse tapped the glass window. Dina put Stavroula back into the incubator. The baby kicked her duckling leg, then settled. Stavros liked that. He wanted to see her kick again. He tickled her foot so that she would kick again, and she did. Stavros took the doll from his arm and put it into the incubator, on the other side where it would not bother the baby, but where she could see she had a gift from her father. The doll was larger than his child. The doll looked stronger than his child, but the doll was not stronger than his child.

The baby stayed in the hospital for two months, and it grew. They took the baby home, and Dina was happy. The baby was bigger. The baby was her, a better version. But then Dina found herself alone for the first time with a tender newborn entirely dependent on her. There were no nurses to help, no wires connecting the baby to a machine that blinked out vitals and made sure everything was OK.

She tried to give the baby a bath while Stavros was at work. She had the baby next to the sink, she got that far. In the sink was the special blue tub. She turned on the faucet. The faucet ran for an hour. She picked up the baby, played with the baby, gave the baby some milk from a bottle. They could take this slow, slow and easy. She tried to lower the baby into the metal sink. There was a suctioning noise in the back of Dina's head—a sucking, a draining—and it was getting louder. It predicted that she was going to drop the baby, glug, drown the baby, glug, burn the baby with scalding water, glug. Next to the sink, the baby's bare arms and legs quivered. No sound came out of her mouth, but Dina was sure that the baby was suffocating from crying. The baby was shaking so hard from the cold air that its neck was going to break.

"Stop," Dina said. "Stop, breathe."

She laid Stavroula back in the crib. She could not do it.

She called Stephanie. Stephanie did not answer, did not call her back.

Sometime later—days, for Dina—Stavros came all the way into the house without taking his shoes off, that's how excited he was to be home. He picked up Stavroula and brought her to the nape of his neck. "She is crying so much," he said. "She must miss her father." The baby stopped. "See?"

Dina said, "I was about to give her a bath. Do you want to do it?"

"The water is supposed to be ninety-nine degrees. It's freezing."

"I know that." She dumped the water.

He filled the tub, then checked with his elbow as the nurses had instructed. He picked his daughter up, one hand supporting her head and shoulders, the other on her back and lower body. He made it look so easy. He waited for the baby to relax. When she uncurled into the water like a petal, he relaxed, too. He used a cotton ball to wipe one eye from the inside corner out, then used another cotton ball for the other eye.

She leaned in, said, "Don't swipe back and forth."

"Does it look like I'm swiping back and forth?"

He was careful with the creases in her arms and legs, the folds in her calm neck. Not one tear. Dina said, "She likes it."

"Of course. You just have to be natural." He filled a plastic pitcher. "You do this part."

"You do it."

"*Re*, just rinse. Don't get it in her eyes."

Dina took the pitcher. She was not going to pour it over the baby's face, no matter what he said. She poured water over the baby's waist. The baby trembled, but not in a way that meant she was afraid. Stavros smiled at Dina. "You see," he said, "we are a good team."

Dina looked forward to bath night. She looked forward to dinner with Stavros, which was Tonight's Hero Special. She did not mind that her baby was Turned Off, as they called it in the NICU—sleeping all day, shutting out stimuli. The baby was nice and quiet, and when her father came home, she came alive. The baby was growing, the baby needed her.

But not even this could stop Dina from using.

LITZA MAVRAKIS

During the Year of the Broken Yolks, Dina dropped days off the rooftop with the belief that they would fly. She let them drop one by one in singles, then in full calendars. The unborn days cracked open on the pavement. Dina, from far above, watched their yolks drain.

Litza was born. The baby was using teeth to get out of the birth canal. Dina cursed Stavros Stavros Malaka Mavrakis for doing this to her.

Stavros got a second raise. It gave him another inch, all of it in his mouth.

Dina discovered she could keep her stash without him finding anything.

A woman came to show her how to nurse, because she had been unable to nurse Stavroula. "Her mouth should be moving like a fish," the woman said. "You should feel her chin on your breast." Litza's eyes were closed. Her temples and jaw working furiously. Dina felt the constant pulling as a repeating question. *Will you? Will you? Will you?* Litza wanted so much from her, wanted it all right now, and Dina wasn't sure she could. Her eyes teared. "She's biting."

The woman said, "She's got no teeth."

"No, she has teeth."

"It's just pressure you're feeling." The woman said, "Give it a few hours, try again."

Dina said she would try, she did try.

The babies grew, inexplicably. If she added pounds the way the babies did, she would have devoured Stavros by now. She would have eaten her own mother.

Dr. Marone prescribed Valium.

She saw Stavros watching her, so she picked up the baby. This new one, which made the noise of two babies.

Stephanie sent a card from California, and in it a folded dollar bill with some sleaze in the crease. It said, Stop getting pregnant, Come Visit.

Dina wondered what noise Stephanie would make dropping from the rooftop.

Stories below, the yolky flecks of days hardened.

Fat Lisa and Jermaine from next door invited her for cocktails. These were her real friends, because they were here, and they were as ready for something else as she was. She shook the vial of tiny brown rocks, which was both lunacy and universe. This was her favorite part, right before, the part where Jermaine leaned over and Fat Lisa put a flame hat on top of the candle. The spoon was a charmer. Then it was her turn. For once in her life, her turn.

You know what those moments were like? They were like finally getting that baby elephant, stringing it with lights, strutting it through town, and delivering it to Papous's doorstep, where he would come back from being dead just to give her a thousand kisses. Though of course she always came back to this shitty room before he could get to her.

Stavros came home, yolk after yolk, and said, When was the last time you changed them? And each time she said, I Just Did, no matter how pulpous their diapers. It was not uncommon for Stavroula, un-supervised, to smear her own shit on the wall. Good thing he did not find out about the iron, which she left on, which she had turned on be-cause she wanted to smooth out the walls, and which Stavroula almost pulled to her stomach like a stuffed animal.

Stephanie's final card came. Dina knew it was the last, because in place of a return address was Dina's own apartment number, plus the admission, *I said Yes to Vegas.*

Dina turned twenty, and Fat Lisa and Jermaine baked her a bake-less birthday cake. It was the nicest thing anyone did for her that year.

Dr. Marone said No more Valium, I'll lose my license. Then he called Stavros so Stavros could drive her to rehab. Stavros, her small

Greek husband who mislearned Valium as a word to describe bravery. (Well, he was right, wasn't he.)

Six rehabs in eight months, talk about dropping days. The days did not even pretend to be days. In places like the ones visited upon Dina, days were shells. Days would not poke their beaks out into the world. Days plummeted when you let them go. They got thrown from the rooftop—if you were Dina and Renee, Dina's new friend—where they cracked against counselors' windshields.

There was more hope than this. In the first rehab, there was hope. Dina did an uncommon thing, she stared at herself in the mirror, she studied the slippery hair and the face the color of cigarette filters, the skin on her nose that always reminded her of cooked turkey, and the weak, untamable eye. She told herself, "Dina, for the first time in your life, don't fail. Do it for your girls."

The second rehab, she told herself, "Dina, don't fail."

The third one, "Dina, your girls."

The fourth, she said, "Dina, for the first time in your life," with Renee egging her on. From a pay phone, she called Stavros to tell him she had fallen in love, and it was not with him, and it was not with his children. Renee had kissed her, a real kiss, and it surprised her enough to shove Renee off the bed. But then she had joined her on the floor, and then back on the bed, and now she was leaving him to go live her life.

He was so upset, he was conducting his whole plea in English. He said, "Pregnancy is just the waiting hour, now is where you show up. Now is when you must be the mother."

"I learned something about myself this year," Dina told him. "I'm nobody's mother."

"You have two babies, which is Stavroula and Litza."

"No, what I have are eggs."

"What do I do, *re*? What does a man do with two babies?"

"Drop them from the roof!"—this from Renee, laughing enough for Stavros to hear.

"I can't protect these children by myself. You hear me? I can't promise to them one thing."

She was tired of people demanding sacrifices of her that they them-selves had never made. "I never got protection, Stavro. I never got a life."

Dina checked out of the fifth rehab, court-appointed, before her release date. She did it because Renee did it. A few days later she watched paramedics turn Renee on her left side, slip a lubricated en-dotracheal tube down her throat until it reached her stomach. They washed out the yolky fluids with salt water until what came up was clear.

By rehab number six, Stavros had sole custody. He was shipping the girls off to Greece. He was expecting her to change her mind and come home. She did not.

The day Stavros buckled his two girls into seats 21 D and E, Dina stood on a rooftop and wondered what noise her babies would make if they were dropped from the plane. Would they be pats of butter hitting blacktop? Would their instinct be to call for her, still?

Stepping onto the ledge, putting one foot out, Dina wondered what noise she would make if she fell from this rooftop right now. That one was easy. She would make no noise. She would make no noise.

Hers was the face We lost first. Hers was the face that turned to glass whenever she looked at Us.

The Day She Left happened much, much earlier than The Day She Left.

Twelve times what a mother gives, when that mother gives zero, is still zero.

THE REBIRTH OF
STAVROS STAVROS MAVRAKIS

Six months after Stavros left his girls in Greece—first with his brother, who spent Stavros's money and fed them coffee and bread, then with his mother—he opened a diner. The single-room building had been a salt shed, which was good, because sprinkling salt in a Greek house got rid of an unwanted guest, and his unwanted guest was his past. Before the salt shed was a salt shed, it had been used to store coal. Its one real window opened to a brick wall not more than four inches away; the rest of the windows lined the very top of the wall. There was one cracked fluorescent lamp. Some fool, some immigrant, had installed a half-attempt sink and grill. They were both in decent condition, which meant that business had been bad for the previous owner. But that did not mean it had to be bad for Stavros.

Cheap, cheap enough for a man still learning English. Cheap enough for Hero to lend him the money.

"No," Hero said. "I'm giving you money only to bring back the girls. That's the only money I'll give."

"I bring the girls here, I have to send them back the next day or the next year. Hero, you know how these things go. A man will fail from a lack of something to stand on."

"You are a family man first, Stavro. Then a businessman."

"Yes, I am a family man, but to be a family man, you have to be a businessman."

There was no point for Stavros to explain the apartment that still reeked of Dina or the trick of making a diaper work the way it was supposed to; the problem with turning a father into a mother. There was no way for Stavros to explain that without his own diner, everything he had done was a waste. He would think of nothing but his children, but first, he needed to make his diner a success.

Hero tapped his chin with some papers. "I don't think so."

"Charge thirty percent interest. Give me two years, I pay." This he said in English.

"It is not about the money."

"Yes, it is about the money. For me, for you, for them, it is about the money."

Yes, for some days he held Hero's money in his hands. Yes, for some days he thought about using money at Hero's twenty percent interest to go get his girls. It was a question he ground between his teeth. How many times he bit down on it, flattened it to a penny. But then what? Go back to dishwashing? Give all of his spit and nickels to the woman downstairs so she could barely keep her two eyes on his two daughters? No, these were not options. He bought the salt shed. He unlocked the latch on his very own *kafenio* and swept clumps of salt into the drainpipe, where it got foamy. A salt shed was not supposed to be the dream, but suddenly it was.

The first month, disaster. He got only some single customers, which meant he could expect only single money whether he was in the kitchen morning till dawn, which meant he could not afford to stock supplies and so was forced to send out his only waiter/host/busboy for ingredients when another single customer came in. When he had enough chicken, he found loafs of bread already at their ends. When he had enough olive oil, he panicked over the cucumber-less cucumber salad. Worst, his cooking was bad. He knew it. Everything, everything with too much salt. He could not get it out of his hair, his kitchen, his life. It seemed to fall down from God's mouth and into his recipes.

Close to default, close to putting on the apron in Hero's kitchen once more, but not close to defeat. Not close to going home. Never was he going home. Home did not exist. Home was this salt shed, the Galaktoboureko, which his six returning truckers called the Gala.

Then the *pappas*'s daughter walked through the door. He did not see her, he was too busy scraping black gunk off of the grill. He said without looking, "No more Trucker Special today, we are finished," because the only thing he could serve right now was coleslaw, bought in buckets and scooped out soupy. The men who came to the Gala were crazy about their cabbage and mayonnaise.

"You refer to all women as *karagogeas*, or just the ones who've seen you with your pants down?"

The Greek made him snap his head up, and then he realized who it was. Marina, with her shoulders and plank neck and runaway mouth. Marina, with her eyes and words full of sand, no matter what anyone has to say about it. Marina, more καρραγωγέας than any woman he had ever met, except maybe his wife. Marina, who had been watching from the wire fence the day his brothers burned off his *peos*. In public, Stavros had called her *keftedaki* like everyone else—Marina Meatball— the only villager with a worse nickname than his. She did not help things, chewing on garlic during recess, or so people said, so that none of the children talked to her. Except Stavros did, sometimes, when his brothers weren't looking. He and Marina threw olive pits to see whose would land farther; each time, they both insisted their own.

All that shared history turning up in this country made him yelp. He came around the counter.

She put down a suitcase the size of a grocery bag, and they hugged. She said, "You would think in a country this big, it would be difficult to locate a Greek. But talk to a Greek, and he will get you your Greek."

He said, "Sit, sit." He was overjoyed to see someone from home. He had seen his family recently, yes, but having a guest from home in his establishment, it thrilled him. It made him remember he was a person with dreams that people were watching from afar.

She sat. She took off the scarf tied around her neck. She looked around, said, "They said you were starting out on your own, just like an American."

He had told his mother about the new business. It came across as much bigger than this saltshaker. But to Marina, he said, "This is how it works here. You start small, prove yourself big. Smart, if you think about it."

"If that's how they do it here."

He jumped up and began to make her coffee. He was a little shy because it had been a long time. She had gone to live with her father's sister when they were teenagers, because her aunt had three sets of twins and needed help cooking. She did not move back to the village until after Stavros left for America.

Marina accepted the mug from him with a thankful "Beautiful." She said, "You have some pastry for this?"

He hadn't. They weren't on the menu yet, because he had no time for phyllo dough. He said, "Baker comes in the morning," which he didn't. He said, "How long do you stay?"

"As long as it takes to make a life." She took a sip, and a pleat of pleasure softened her face. He recalled this pleasure—a cup of *kafe* after being in transit for two days. It felt good to give that to her. Him doing something useful for a compatriot in need. He would not charge her. He said, "You are visiting someone?"

"No."

"*Ela*, your father isn't here, is he?" He tipped his head to look out at the parking lot, but of course there was no real window for him to see through.

"He is not."

"How is he? Your father."

"The same. Running other people's lives."

In English, Stavros said, "You must call him. He will be waiting to know if you are safe."

In English, she cut back. "I didn't fly a hundred thousand miles from my father just to get a new one, Stavro."

Gamoto, her English was better.

Stavros sat back. He looked again at her suitcase. He had seen dogs bigger than this suitcase. It told him that she could not be planning to stay, but the look on her face, the way she was settled in the chair but also unable to settle into the chair, told him, yes, she was an immigrant. Yes, she had a time line that offered no comfort, because it offered no return ticket. And she was clearly alone. Probably, she had taken a bus directly here from the airport. Possibly, she had nowhere else to go and had actually gotten this address from his mother or some other onlooker. A glimmer of a plan worked its way into his eye—he could bring his girls back for Marina to watch, and in exchange he could give her a place to live. He could stop thinking about the things that were out of his control and get this place running, even if it ran miserably, no better than his father's wagon.

He said, "Do you have a place for the night?"

Marina returned the mug to its saucer. "My aunt's friend is renting me a place."

"Are you looking for work? The best money is in child care."

Marina guffawed. "Don't be stupid. I'm not here to raise your girls, Stavro. I'm here to cook for you so you can run this mousetrap."

"Cook for me?"

Marina stood. "*Nai*. I'm going to make you a meal you believe in, and you're going to hire me to operate your kitchen."

Stavros could not protest when she pushed her way through to the counter, because anything that would have stopped her would have been too hard for him to say. No, Marina, I can't hire you because I have no money. No, Marina, because in just a few days this failing business will close up its one room and turn back to salt. No, Marina, because I have been cooking food that tastes like sponge and you won't do any better than me because America is lousy at growing anything meant to be eaten. No, Marina, because the ingredients you are going to find are scraped to the bottom of the jar and it is impossible to make even a single good meal from the snakeskin options of my kitchen.

Ela, she was so dumpy in his diner, the *keftedaki*. It was depressing him.

Marina was back there with her fat elbows in his refrigerator. Marina was making a quick pile of food too insignificant even in weight to count as a meal. He spotted a fourth of an onion, a tomato, a diamond of animal fat, a leftover bone that she was roasting in the one-foot-wide oven for almost fifteen minutes now. Then she toasted a stale piece of bread. She whisked together a soft lemon, the last drips of olive oil, some kind of green herb that she picked out of the garden of her pocket, and she poured it all over the marrow that she scooped from the bone. Everything went on the toast. On the side, an onion marmalade, plus a squash he had thrown out, which she skinned and revived.

She said, "Eat." She would not sit until he broke off a piece of the bread.

He put it in his mouth and chewed. The bread, crispy. The marrow, like the best parts of a leftover stew. Salty and congealed. Like he was getting to dunk his bread in his mother's pot while the whole house was sleeping, like the flavor could make him drunk if it got loose. Only, it was too salty. He wanted to ask where, where did this come from. He said, "*Ela*, it's nice. But I don't know if anyone could believe in it."

Marina broke off a piece of the bread, tasted. She chewed. "Maybe your head doesn't want to believe in it, but your mouth is already converting your stomach."

"Americans don't eat like this, Marina. When you get into the business like I have, you will realize that."

"You and I will show them how to eat."

He ate more, not too fast, not giving her the wrong idea. But he was starving, and it was nice, the nicest thing since Hero's *galaktoboureko*. It was wonderful to be given a meal by a woman who knew how to make meat out of bones. His mother had been like that. Something he wished he had appreciated as a young man.

Marina said, "You are no fool, Stavro, or else Marina would not be here. I know you—if you have any sense, it's business sense."

She was buttering him up like a fat leg of lamb, and he was enjoying it more than the marrow. "OK, one good meal. But how do I know you have the training to excel my business?"

Marina uncrossed her arms from her safe of a chest. She broke off another piece of toast. She chewed the way a man chews, the way a priest chews: everyone could wait until she had formulated her thought. And it was this: "Stavro, while you were here making babies and trouble for yourself, I was with my aunt in Crete. Making breakfast out of trees and lunch out of nests and dinner out of smoke. You learned some things, I learned some things. I can do this for us."

"Don't pretend this is for me. You're trying to get fat on the riches." He could talk to her like this, so far from the *pappas*. If she wanted to be in America, she would have to get used to hostility, even from other Greeks. Especially from other Greeks. If she wanted to work, she had to prove she could handle it, move up the greasy ladder like he had.

"Marina wastes nothing. Every part of a goat, every leaf of a vegetable. It all gets made into money."

He could tell she was not lying. Or lying like a Greek lies, which is exaggeration, which is not lying at all, really. Marina took the last toast and caught him looking at it. She pulled it apart, a piece so small it would not have given hope to a mouse, and gave half to him.

It was the wrong thing to do. All he could think was, *She sees how I am desperate.*

"I will be in at six in the morning tomorrow. You will come in at eight. You make a big, fat sign to call in your truckers. I will cook them a meal that leaves them hungrier. You don't pay me until that toy register of yours hits four hundred. At four hundred dollars, we buy ingredients, and we split what's left. We make this place more than what it is."

He heard what she was saying, and shame filled the empty cup of his life. This village woman, this spectator, was telling him that without her he had nowhere to go but further down. Nothing could have made him angrier, except the ugly face of his wife saying it. He wanted to make Marina leave, even as he was already missing the promising children and grandchildren of the meal he had just eaten, even as he wanted to weep, *You've come too late. I would, but it is just too late.*

"I am not giving you a job. Go wash dishes, if you want to be in the business."

Marina pushed the saucer toward him. "You men, always thinking there is room for your *phallos* in the profits. Stavro, take it out of the discussion."

That was it. He picked up her suitcase, put it out the door. It was bad manners to keep a Greek from finishing his coffee, so Stavros picked up the mug, too, and he left it at the doorstep. She watched him lock her out. He was alone again in the darkness of the restaurant, trying to take a breath. He could at least have called her a cab. But he was not going to do favors for anyone who came to his establishment to tell him he was a failure.

He picked up the plate and brought it to his nose. It was commanding him to put its final morsels to his lips, where they melted in seconds. The remaining juices he scooped up with the only thing left on the counter—a citrusy rind—and he sucked it until it was like papers in his mouth.

The next morning, Marina was in his kitchen. She had arrived much earlier than six, with foodstuffs from who knew where, orders lined up from who knew who. Bacon and eggs for the salesmen? Pancakes with berries the size of bumblebees for the steelworkers? Lunch boxes for the truckers, so they could get two for the price of two? Yes, customers were today's special on Marina's menu. More customers than he had ever faced alone. Most of all, the place was clean. All the salt in the crevices, all the thick salty paste coating the burners and the boards and the counters, it had been wiped clean. She had scrubbed it all away, she had kept it out of the cooking—something that in his overworked, alienated state, he had never been able to manage.

"How did you get in?"

"Front door."

Vlaka, he knew how she got in—that lock was more a suggestion than a law, as was, apparently, his refusal to hire her. But they were so busy, such a rush, how could he dismiss her? Look at the amount of lunch boxes that were going out. (Lunch boxes? He had never made such a thing.) Look at the amount of people coming to sit in his salt shed, knowing Marina by name, waiting for an empty seat to flash its big welcome smile. One man, a trucker who stopped by on Fridays, said, "This must be why all the foreigners keep their wives in the kitchen."

"He's not my husband," Marina said, waving her spatula. "I don't marry ugly men if they aren't American citizens."

The truckers liked that one.

Stavros was not used to this, someone being commanding and irreverent in his business. He saw that the truckers liked the way Marina pushed around the place, and he privately decided that tomorrow—Marina or no Marina—he would make jokes with the men, too.

Stavros put out menus and glasses of water. To keep from losing business he turned an unfixed cabinet on its side and made it into a third table. He grabbed his keys to buy more eggs, which were always running out by this time, only to find that Marina had three extra cartons in a refrigerator behind the building. (The refrigerator, who knew where that came from.) He took off his *jaketa*. By ten thirty, he realized his waiter/host/busboy wasn't coming in. This employee had never even been two minutes late. Stavros had made sure of it, telling him he'd lose not only this job, but the one at Hero's, too.

"I sent him home. All he was good for was being in the way."

"But he's my server."

"Actually, you're your server," Marina said. "And now, one less mouth to pay."

By lunch, Stavros told himself. By lunch, she will be gone. But lunch was busier than breakfast, and dinner was busier than lunch. This was because the men who had come at 6:00 a.m. had told their buddies to come at twelve, and those buddies had recommended the evening shift at seven. It wasn't the bite-wait-bite that Stavros was used to. At the end of the night, Stavros opened the till. Six hundred and thirty dollars. Seven times what yesterday was worth. But now there were two of them, and he would have to split the profits. He would never have agreed to fifty percent, but look what she had brought in. A business. He would get her down to twenty percent, plus maybe some days off, his mentorship.

Marina was cleaning grease off of the stovetop. Her hair was wet against her head. "Come have some stew," she said, "the tomorrow special."

He sat down with her at the cabinet table. She scooped out a pailful, and he started eating even before she got him a spoon. Neither of them had taken a break all day, not even a white cracker in their mouths.

"Good day," she said. She was eating with her mouth open, too, she was just as unworried about being polite. This was kitchen, not dining etiquette. This was eating as hungry equals.

He nodded. "Better than average."

From her pocket, she pulled out a crinkled paper. "Here is a receipt for the food," she said. "I will take my half of what's left."

He kept eating. He used his collar to wipe his mouth. "Marina, I wouldn't give my own father fifty percent."

She kept eating, too. "I wouldn't give that to my father, either."

"You think I can afford any villager that knocks on my door?"

"I'm no villager."

The stew kept opening and shutting drawers for him, like he was searching for something and finding it, then looking again, rummaging not with his hands but with his tongue. He figured out, finally, what it was. A blanket his grandmother had made out of rabbit. That was what Marina had added to the stew. The knowledge of that blanket, as if it still existed.

Still, this was about money. He had children. "Two hundred for food leaves two hundred for you, two hundred for me. Why would I open a business just to pay my staff the same amount that I make as boss?"

"Partners, not staff."

"Staff, not partners." He pushed away the bowl. But he was too hungry, too eager to pull the blanket back up, and he returned the spoon to his mouth. "I have to start my life, Marina. I have to get going. I can't be kept down fifty percent of the time."

"This is your life: you are having a life. This counts. And six hundred dollars is a nice shove forward, considering yesterday you pulled in eighty-three dollars."

How did she know?

Marina leaned in. She took his hands in her own damp ones, something that surprised him, something she would have never done before today, and suddenly their acquaintanceship was more like roots. Suddenly their shared meal was a shared meal.

She said, "I know what kind of problems you're having with the Galaktoboureko. No one else knows, and no one needs to know. But I am telling you, Stavro, we can fix it. Marina does not make promises that go teethless. Marina's words leave marks."

He closed his mouth. Still, it quivered.

"Six hundred is just day one. Day two, it will be eight hundred. Day seven hundred, it will be eight thousand."

How was she giving at exactly the same moment that she was taking? How was this, again, the place where he found himself to be with the woman in his life? Still, he nodded. The nod was made of bone, but it was an agreement.

"OK, you get a big chunk of the profit. I will give you that. But the business is mine. The business is always mine."

Marina sat back. She patted the top of his hand.

Stavros let his spoon sink into the stew and crushed his face into his hands. Always, one step up, one step back. Everyone in his life, letting him keep his arms so that they could turn around and steal the legs. Taking away sons to give him daughters. Taking away even daughters. He could not help it, he began to weep.

Marina was quiet. To keep them from embarrassment, she continued to eat. She said, "You will bring them home, Stavro. It will not be the last thing you do."

For the first time, he felt he could speak the pressure out loud. "Every month, I think I am one month closer."

"That's exactly what you are. Because if it's one thing I know about Stavros Stavros Mavrakis, it's that he was born a stubborn Greek who gets what he wants."

"Stubborn? You calling me stubborn?"

"Like my father and my father's mule and my mule's father."

Stavros's face slipped, and he laughed behind his hands. "Good thing it takes two stubborn Greeks to run a diner."

Marina ladled them each another cupful, then said, "No more eating the profits."

They cleared the table, chopped onions, mopped the floor. At the end of the night—too close to the next morning—she returned the scarf to her neck, as she would every night when work was done. Knotted tight around her neck, it made Marina ten years older. A woman unable to relax, an immigrant with money on her mind.

That made two of them. Here they were, two foreigners and a salt shed, all trying hard to be what they were never, and always, meant to be.

We were told He Will Come Back Tomorrow. Tomorrow We Were Told, He Is Working, Always Working. He Is Coming with Christmas. He Is Making a House for You, Plank by Plank. He Is Cooking Tyropeta, *and When He Makes Enough to Feed the New York, He Will Come for His* Kouklares. *He Is Helping Your Sick Mother Get Better. He Has Shingles, Very Painful, Very Worried for You and Wanting the Best. Soon,* Koukla, *Soon. He Is Coming after You Finish Your Porridge. He Is Coming When You Stop Crying and Stomping Your Feet. He Will Be Here the Minute You Don't Pee the Bed Anymore. He Is Coming When He Can Come for Good Girls. He Is Coming When You Answer Back with English & Not the Angry Spoons of Greek. He Is Coming When That Star Moves to That Black Space. See Him? He Is on His Way. He Is Just Greetings Away, One English Word Away. He Is Never So Near, He Can Hold the Rain Back with Nothing More than a Shrug. He Is Not Afraid of Nightmares, He Will Conquer Them for You. He Is So Close, You Can Touch His Strange Animal Beard. You Can Hear the Approaching of His Footsteps in Your Own Throat. He Is Coming. He Is Coming. He Is Coming. He Is Coming.*

PART III

DAY 2

Acceptance

CHAPTER 20

Marina has a story to tell, too.

Marina has her own dream.

Marina comes to work today, every day. Marina misses no work. Work is the moon that hangs the day. The moon is the crescent sickle that hangs the day. The moon tells Marina, Get up, use your fingers and your rosy brain. Even when the wake-up moon is shrouded in coal, Marina gets up. Summoned, chosen. Work helps you understand that a day has just happened to you, that you have been lucky enough. Work, not sun, marks our orbit.

Marina prays before the sun can make its interruptions. When she was younger, the prayer had words to it, but now words are not necessary. The prayer is in the breathing, which she says *Pay attention to, because the prayer keeps each of you between its breaths.* When Marina prays, she thanks for many things, which includes the pig she will kill today. Marina pats the hind of the pig, which sounds like dough being slapped onto a board. Each day, for sixty or more years, a pig's hindquarters have sounded like this to Marina. The quiet is nice, too, for Marina. The moon. Maybe one time it reflected the things missing, and one time reminded her of someone she left behind, someone whose skin feels like cork, but Marina is not a lonely woman these days. Look at all she has built, all the life that she has come by. Even this person she has left behind, the one who could massage the stone out of her chest, even this person would be honored and hold no regrets.

The dream-sky gets clearer, and Marina knows that it is time for *kafe* with Stavros Stavros. She knows that he will come down from his apartment, and that if it is not raining or very cold, and today it is not, they will sit on each side of the picnic table and make lists and ask each other the names of the customers they are continuously forgetting, and Marina will prod Stavros Stavros to tell her what is new with the girls, and he will remain vague because he does not have a head for it, and she will craft her own understanding of their lives from the shavings of detail he gives. Her girls—she's watched with growing pains. She will think of them through his complaints while he makes the *kafe*, the one thing he does for the two of them because it is his kind of prayer, Marina has come to realize. Marina will shake out her apron and tie it to her, and then Stavros will retie it as he walks by, almost without thinking, because her hands, which can fillet a bulb of garlic, have trouble with knots these days.

Stavros Stavros thinks of work the way she thinks of work. Not even when his youngest was born did he take a day off.

Because at their core people are always who they were, Stavros Stavros will tend to the goat, which is standing in the corner of the lot and scraping against a tree. The day will be getting louder, it will be full of crispy promise for the simple fact that it is a day, and then they will talk business and ingredients very close to spoiling, which must be turned into specials.

But, of course, Stavros Stavros does not come.

It is four days, Stavros missing.

Until now, she has only laughed about living until we say goodbye.

Marina boils the *kafe*, cuts two thumbs of cheese, and spoons out a clot of honey. This happens very fast, all at once.

Marina takes the wooden stairs to the apartment. She stands on the top step, which is larger than the others, and which has one flower in a pot. Marina knocks on the glass, which is obscured by a shade. Marina tries the door, which is unlocked. She feels already that it is an empty place, that it is like a carcass rather than an animal; she will not find her boss and partner here. Foolishly, Marina enters calling for Stavros Stavros, and because it is a trembling voice, she does not believe it belongs to her.

The bathroom, it is empty except for a wet towel curled on the floor like a dog. The bedroom, it is unmade, but she can smell cologne on the collars of hanging shirts. The hall is dark. The kitchen—the kitchen.

This is Marina's fear, because the kitchen is where Marina was born, and the kitchen is where Marina will die. So Marina feels for the light switch before she looks. Marina turns her face to the particleboard cabinets before she will look at the table or floor. She tries to feel, rather than see. She trusts her peripheral vision to tell her what is to come, what there is left to work through.

Nothing. Nothing she can foresee, except a blackness.

The dream, it gives Marina a chill.

"Which is why Marina has asked for you today, which is why Marina has brought the two of you together."

Something troubled Stavroula. Marina's story, but also the story being told beneath Marina's story—it went *clang, clap clap*. It was outside, tied up: the goat. It continuously pawed the metal doors leading to the basement, as if there were a dent it was compelled to bang out. *Clang, clap clap*. She felt her stomach lurch. She looked at Litza to see if she could hear it. She couldn't tell.

Litza said, "He has a dream about dying and wants everybody to jump. Now you have a dream, you expect everybody to run."

This morning, Stavroula had awoken and stared at herself in the mirror. What she saw was Dina. Dina's square face, her whittled, selfish eyes. Dina's short short hair, yes; that, she had given to herself willingly. Staring into the mirror, Stavroula said, Four days. There were no traces of her father. Where was her father in her?

Litza had taken care, extra care, with her clothes. Her black shirt was ironed, and she wore a silver necklace that repeated itself in loops. She had on three pretend-silver rings. Or, what did Stavroula know, maybe they were real. Litza had dressed carefully, but that did not hide that there was something clammy about her face. Her makeup was slipping. The eyeliner was a blue scrape. If Litza had slept at all, she had slept too much.

Something was wrong with Marina's face, too. Moist darkness beneath the eyes, like mushroom. Stavroula wanted to wet the bottom of Marina's apron and wipe them.

"He is not with you, he is not with me, he is not with your mother, he is not with your sister, he is not with Hero. Not with customers nor vendors, his car is here." Marina clapped her knife on the board. "You must agree, your father is gone."

Frail. This was how Marina looked. It suddenly hit Stavroula—Marina had brought them here to plead with them. Stavroula said, "Should we call the police?"

Litza snickered.

Marina slapped Litza. Right in the face. Marina's mouth trembling. "For once, stop being an animal."

Stavroula waited for the explosion. Litza, who had told Marina off over far lesser insults. But Litza was not yelling or fighting, and Litza was not running.

Clang, clap clap. The kitchen gone silent, uneasy.

Anger crowded out the fear, put Marina back inside Marina. She flung her apron. "You are not children anymore. This is yours to deal with, like it or not." Then she was moving through the kitchen and into the dining room, telling them about their Mother's Ass and Where They Could Find Their Father's Unwed Whores, who were nearby in Hell and Reeking of Plant Decay. The kitchen, relieved, got loudly back to work.

All this time, Litza held her palm to her cheek. Standing beside Stavroula. Listening—Stavroula was sure of it—to the *clang, clap clap.* Admitting, for the first time, that she heard it, too. Litza's breaths coming quick, just as they had on their first day in America. Little Stavroula entering this country holding her breath, Little Stavroula, looking straight ahead, taking her sister's hand. Saying, *Myn AnysykhYte, Don't Worry, Never mind.* Then slipping a stone—not a stone, a blue Evil Eye to ward off bad spirits, which she had dug out of the ground—between their palms, and holding it there, between her hand and her sister's. Encouraging Litza to be brave, because what did Little Stavroula know about what was to come?

Stavroula said, "You OK?"

And, finally, Litza running.

CHAPTER 21

Litza went looking for her father, alone. It was a familiar feeling, seeking someone who didn't want to be found. She drove. She tried to imagine where he'd go, but she could not create a route that reminded her of him. Only the roads themselves, speeding up and turning away from her, escaping to other towns, other countries, barely looking back, reminded her of her father.

Dear Dad: What am I looking for?

His philosophy had always been, *If you make a wrong turn, don't expect me to come find you.* Alternatively, *Always take the high road, and you won't be in the dark with the mud or bums.*

What she wished to hear was—*It's OK if you make mistakes, even if they hurt other people* and *You have the right to be happy.*

At the pizza place that he went to when he wasn't having Marina make him a meal, they told Litza that he hadn't ordered anything in days. She drove to the Greek church, taking the back roads, which she imagined her father taking, too. He was not at the church, she knew he would not be. She went to the mistress's house, an address she had found in his office when she and Stavroula went ransacking, even though Marina said it was over between them. The mistress lived in a development where one house looked exactly like the next, but the cunt couldn't hide from her. Litza had no shame, Litza didn't care, she looked through the windows. She shouted through the door, "Is he in there with you?" She pounded on the glass and appreciated how it shuddered in response.

The yellowing blinds went up. The cunt's voice came through, muffled. "I haven't seen Stavros in a week."

They stared each other down through the glass door. Litza was surprised. This person seemed to have almost nothing in common with her father. OK, she was black, but she also had to be twenty years younger, and she was big—she looked like she was built for nesting. Her father's mistress looked like she had more in common with Mother, truthfully, which was fucking hysterical. He clearly had a type.

What type was that, exactly? What was Rhonda? A 303? 304? And whatever code there was for *Gold-digger, Taking Advantage of a Man Who Has Cut Himself Off from His Children.*

The mistress gave in first, and the blinds fell. Then came the unlocking of the door, and the opening, because she must have been warned it was better not to fight Litza.

Litza sat on the stoop. She stared at the two cars in the driveway. One was older, a sedan. The other was new, an SUV. Black. She guessed that her father had paid for that one.

When the mistress came back—Rhonda—she had two mugs in her hand. She sat next to Litza on the step and gave her the mug, and when Litza did not accept it, set it next to her. She had taken the time to put cream in Litza's cup, though she had not bothered to ask if Litza would care for any coffee.

"Can you tell me what makes somebody so desperate that they have to go looking for a married man online?"

"I wouldn't know," Rhonda said. "He came looking for me. And you're at my house, so remember that when you open your mouth. I know your father taught you as much."

Litza didn't begrudge this. She tried to imagine her father keeping up with this woman and couldn't. Maybe that was one of the things that attracted him to her. She tried to imagine them doing things like walking hand in hand. She never thought of her father's hands as small, but they would be small in Rhonda's. She tried to imagine them dancing together—her father liked to dance and was good at it, he had decent rhythm—and figured she'd be the one woman he let lead. She imagined her father being unable to help laughing at himself when Rhonda lugged him around the floor like a sack of flour.

Litza said, "I bet you're sorry now that you answered his email."

"It takes two people to make a mistake. But I should've seen him coming." Rhonda held the mug close. "So you know, he said he wasn't married."

Litza shrugged. A technicality. Maybe he said he wasn't married, but that didn't mean she should have believed him. Litza could tell that Rhonda was shrewd, and "unmarried" was the story she wanted to believe because it was convenient. The truth, though—even Litza could acknowledge—was that his marriage had been gutted by that point, anyhow. Long before he ever made an online account to date black women, Litza had judged him for being unfaithful. It had almost nothing to do with Mother, and even less to do with a mistress. Add cheating on his wife to his long list of infidelities.

"I'm not proud of it, all right?" Rhonda said. "I should've cut him off as soon as I found out. But it was too late by then." She took a sip from her mug because there was awkwardness between them, because all of a sudden this was a real conversation, and neither of them had expected it to turn into that. She said, "How is he?"

"I wouldn't know."

"Last I saw him, he didn't look too good."

"What, like sick?"

"Unh-uh. More like troubled."

Litza laughed. "Maybe you're the trouble."

Rhonda cracked a smile, but it faded quickly.

Rhonda had no idea he was missing. She believed Litza was here to confront her about being a mistress. It delighted Litza that she could withhold this critical information from someone who was firmly inconsequential to her family. More inconsequential than her. Even if the cunt had received a new car and Litza hadn't.

Litza tried the coffee, which was very hot. And tasted burned. "What is this?"

"Starbucks."

Of course. Probably, he had gotten it for free from Mother, and then passed it on as a gift to his mistress. How Litza hated Starbucks coffee, almost as much as Greek coffee.

There was something about Rhonda that reminded Litza of

Mother. That is, a woman who had been presented a vision of a man who pretended to be one way but really was the opposite. Stavros pretended to be a man of courage and sympathy and someone who opens a door for you because all he wants is to cherish you, when in reality he is opening the door so you can cherish him. When, in reality, he is giving you gifts so you can praise him for being such a giver. When he looks at you, all he sees is what you can do for him. This much Litza could read on Rhonda's face. But there was something in the way that she shook her head that reminded Litza of herself, too: she and the mistress were the kind of women who both accepted, but resented, that they had to take what they could get.

Rhonda said, "I can't be with someone who's looking over his shoulder all the time. I need someone to be *with* me."

"Bullshit. You got what you wanted, and you got out."

"Have you known anybody to get what they wanted from your father?" Litza let her have that one. "Your father can't give what he don't have."

E883.9. *Falling into a hole or cavity or other open surface*, such as a pit or a shark tank. Rhonda had actually loved him, Rhonda had fallen for him. Or, more realistically, E886.9, he had pushed or collided into her or shoved her into caring for him. Rhonda, like Litza, had had to find out the hard way how disappointing he was.

"Did he get you that car?" Litza asked.

"No."

"Yes he did. I saw the receipts." This was a lie.

"Then he bought himself the same one." Rhonda turned to look at Litza. "What did you come here for? A fight?"

"I can get that at home."

"So what, then? You want an explanation? 'Cause you should go to your father for that."

"I just came for the coffee."

Rhonda snorted. "If it's one thing you can get from your family, it's coffee. Why are you coming around now, Litza?"

It was surprising to hear her own name. It was validating, in a way, and it somehow made Rhonda more real, too. It meant her father had talked about Litza, but also it meant that Rhonda, as a potentially objective outsider, had been listening and might have made up her own mind about her. And maybe could be fairer about Litza than any of them. It was strange to have an ally in someone who, for all intents and purposes, didn't matter but wasn't meaningless. It meant something to Litza to be seen, truly seen, by her father's mistress.

"I don't want anything from you." Litza stood. "I'm just looking for him."

"Why?"

"He owes me money."

"That man doesn't owe anybody money."

Rhonda didn't stand, which was a power move in itself. She looked out at the street. "Your father is a good man. He stuck by his family, even when things got tough. He made hard choices 'cause he had to. You think I don't know, but I do. I was paying attention the whole time. He told me all of it. You girls don't know him. You don't see all of him."

"Neither do you."

Rhonda shrugged. She wasn't willing to say so.

"He just tells you the version he wants you to hear, and you eat it right up."

Rhonda stood, finally. "I know how to read between the lines with people like him. And people like you, too."

Litza dumped her coffee into the sliver of a garden bed next to the stoop. There were no people like Litza, cunt.

Rhonda poured her coffee out, too, in the same spot. But then she said, "He wants the best for you. That's what any parent wants. Even the shittiest ones can't help themselves, and believe me, I would know."

"How does it feel to know he's tired of you and moving on?"

That was true. The letter spoke that truth. The mistress had been left out completely.

Rhonda smiled. It was real, insofar as that it saw right through Litza. "Honey, if I had the time to wait around for your father to catch up, we'd be having this same conversation, only you'd be calling me Mom."

A snort. "Yeah, that's not what I'd call you."

Dear Dad: Did you leave it all to this cunt?
Dear Dad: What could she possibly see in you?

Litza was driving in circles. There was no one else to call on, because there was no one he was good or loyal to. She didn't contact Ruby or Mother. She had not told them he was missing, and she was willing to bet Stavroula hadn't, either. For the last two days, Stavroula had been holding the knowledge of their father's disappearance at arm's length, away from herself. Litza felt she could keep the truth of her father's disappearance in a cage, bottle-feed it, make it hers. She would be first to find him. She was owed. She would face him, whatever state he was in, and demand to know, *Where have you been?*

Litza did not expect to run into her father's oldest and possibly only friend playing *tavli* in an ice-cream parlor owned by a young Greek. Hero, who only played with bosses, let Litza in on a game once or twice in her life, because he saw she was a boss. She had not seen him since her wedding. He had gained a few pounds, and he had finally given his hair up to gray. The mustache was gone, but the skin looked heavy there, like a horse's lip. Her father's would look the same, no doubt, if he shaved.

Hero shook his die, said, "Are you bringing good luck, or bad?"

"Always bad."

"Who needs you, then?" He stood, kissed each cheek but landed on her ears. Pulled out a chair. He had always been sweet with her, fair. If he had been her father, he would have been more forgiving. But, maybe not.

"Ice cream changes your luck," the other Greek said, no accent. "Have some with us." His hair was a stiff wave. His red shirt was un-collared but crisp. His father had probably given him this shop, easy. Like Hero, he was probably one of the lucky ones, no ICD code to his name.

Litza did not sit, because she knew it would obligate her. "I'm looking for my father."

"That's an easy guess," Hero said. "Your father is working."

"He's not. He's missing."

"Your father's missing?" The boy sat, straddling the back of the chair, his shoes slipping from their brown dress socks. The pants stiff, as if never worn before, just like the shiny, uncreased belt. Stavros Stavros would have said, *How can a man who dresses like this know the cold of his own ice cream?*

"Stavros is not missing, *re*. If his diner is here on earth, he's not going anywhere." He took the die, shook it, but didn't toss it. "How long he's missing?"

"Four days now."

"You've called the police?" the boy asked.

Litza looked down on Hero's head. She remembered her and Stavroula, young girls, trying to hide packets of sugar in his blond hair. Now it was so thin she could brush it away with the back of her hand.

"You are worried, *koritisi mou?*"

The boy pushed back his chair. "We can help you look."

"I'd rather go alone," Litza said.

Hero stood. She didn't see it coming, his warm, padded hands on her face. He was whispering something possibly meant to be reassuring, but she couldn't make it out. She could not look up.

Mercifully, he let go.

Litza sat in the parking lot of the funeral home. She stared at herself in the vanity mirror. She dipped a crumpled tissue into an old water bottle and dabbed at her cheek. She brushed her hair. She tried three times to open the car door. Gabriel had promised to be there, if she needed him. She pictured herself as part of a painting that Gabriel was both creating and inside of. She thought about his eyes, which were parchment. He would be standing inside the funeral home with his hands behind his back; he would comfort her, smelling of bath and broth, and offer refreshments intended not to fill her but to bring warmth.

She adjusted her chair, reclining, trying to feel what it would be like to lay her head against his chest, and she felt her fingertips graze *To Live Until We Say Good-bye.*

She opened the book, somewhere in the middle. She turned the page, the one after that. The pictures of people dying, chapter after chapter, were like watching a bonfire slowly succumb to a scalloped sky—watching the brilliant breaking down of wood, the wood fiercely facing its moment of burning even as it crackled and ashed into less than it ever thought it could be. And the color gray. How brave, and yet scared all these people were. They were all experiencing the greatest betrayal of all: the body's refusal to forgive, the body unable to remember and protect, and, ultimately, the body abandoning the body.

I used to wish for death A lot of the time. Then I died. For a little time. Now I wish to die Some of the time. But, now I know, I know It will be For all the time. The woman on page 48, this beautiful model whose face at once stood up to and became disgraced by cancer.

Whatever they had been in life—the woman, everyone—they were all 000.0 now. Nothing but a fading memory, a faint bit of writing.

CHAPTER 22

Stavroula heard a commotion outside. She dropped two lids. She threw the dish towel over her shoulder and flung open the back door, half expecting to see her father at the bottom of the stairs, Marina having missed the spot in the apartment, as if he were a loose hamster. Stavroula searched the blackness for something she could assign to the noise. A strangely tall man, taller than his shadow, stood with the goat. He petted its horns. Nearby were barrels and some clay pots, knocked over.

Stavroula shut the door behind her and called, nervously, "Is this your goat?"

Her eyes adjusted to the light, and she saw that the man was tall, but not as tall as she first thought. His hat made him look taller than he actually was. "Hello?" She came off the step. "Are you here for your goat?" He continued to pet the goat's horns, something she did not think people did. He was clucking at the goat. She came close and he stopped. She saw that he was wearing a black cloak as well. That he was a priest. He lifted his head and smiled at her and looked familiar.

"This is not my goat. My goats are the ones you can't see—the ones maybe your father has told you stories about. The elusive *kri-kri*."

"No, he never told us."

"Ah, well. Elusive. At least your father shared with you his big nose."

She realized how she knew him. He was Marina's father, from the face.

"But not the eyes," he said. "They must be yours alone. They are not your mother's, either."

"You know my mother?" She didn't like to call Dina that, but with this man, it seemed that they were speaking of history that predated her.

His face was pockmarked all the way down to the neck, looking the way a firecracker sounded. "Eczema." He rubbed where she was staring. "Got me in my best years. Marina does not look so bad as me, I hope?"

"No, she's just fat these days." Marina, calling from the top step. She said, "What's wrong with you, you can't use a telephone anymore?"

"*Ela*, I was already on the plane when that thinking came to me," he said, his voice hoarse. "Thoughts take their time to get to the old."

"Liar," Marina said. To Stavroula, "He knows I would have told him to stay home."

"She doesn't let her poor *pateras* visit, so close he is to making death a professional acquaintance. To kicking the dust." He twittered his fingers. "Come here, little bird."

Marina came out, but not as far as he beckoned. "You don't know to use a front door? You creep around the back like a thief?"

"The things you learn from a man's back door are valuable. For instance, I discovered this goat."

They did not hug. Marina gave the *pappas* two obligatory kisses. Then she gave two more. She kneaded his hands. She said in a chiding voice, one Stavroula had never heard before, "You did not tell me in your emails that all the time I was getting old, so were you."

Stavroula recalled a single photograph, a memory she did not know was hers—and maybe it wasn't, maybe it was her father's or Marina's—of the *pappas* at a wedding. In the picture, he had weepy eyes and a robust black beard, and he looked as if he were celebrating everybody. In his arms, tucked against his black robe, were four spotted baby goats, all staring at the camera, all squeezed together in a hug. This man in front of her was just like him but more svelte, and the beard white, not so insistent. The skin of his eyelids was finely cracked.

They were trading some words in Greek that Stavroula could not follow. Their voices turned crucial. Then the *pappas* leaned over, reminding Stavroula of a swan, and folded Marina into his arms. He put the bottom of his cheek to her forehead. His eyes were wet. He said, "My fat Marina."

Marina took Stavroula's arm and pulled her near. "This is his oldest. A beautiful girl."

Stavroula put out her hand, and he took it in both of his. She said that she was pleased to meet him, and she felt shy. He said, "*Hairo poli, hairo poli.* Your father should be proud."

"He is," Marina murmured.

"You know what happened to him?" Stavroula asked. She felt the *pappas* searching her, understood instantly that he did not. He and Marina traded more quick words.

"But I am here for the final rites. I was sent a package, a very specific package."

They brought him inside. With a wet cloth, he wiped his arms up to the elbow. He refused to sit in the dining room. He said that dining rooms were for outsiders, kitchen for everybody else. He chanted some prayers over the stove, accepted a metal chair. He wore blue jeans under his cloak, also sneakers with Velcro, and his ankles looked mossy and thin. Like a girl's. Marina fixed a salad and toasted some bread—he didn't want hot food. The *pappas* took an olive with his long fingers. He tucked it into his mouth.

Stavroula brought coffee. He said, "At my age, this is not what a man drinks."

Marina pulled a bottle of raki from the freezer. She poured a shot and said, "We will get to the truth faster this way, anyhow."

The truth was that the *pappas* had received a letter in the old-fashioned way. Not through email, the way Stavros periodically wrote him, which he checked every few days at the internet café. No, the letter came by donkey. An old farmer, as old as the *pappas* himself, rode side-saddle to his porch to deliver it. It was a surprise, what the letter shared with him and what it kept from him. It included a packet of some money and a plane ticket to the United States.

"Stavros Stavros and his letters," Marina said. "You'd think Marina would receive one by now."

"Can you tell us what it said?" Stavroula asked.

The *pappas* reached into his pocket and pulled out the letter, which had tired of traveling days ago. "The letter is private, like a man's soul. It says things like a confession. So I cannot read it to you." He skimmed the letter, which was in Greek. "He whines a lot, the whiny *malaka*."

"Say what it really says," Marina said. "Say what it means."

The *pappas* read:

"'So, Pappas, I ask that you deliver this man, who is both more and less than a son to you. I ask that you guide me to the next place, where the soul can fit inside a palace instead of a shoe. I ask that you forgive my sins, which are more than I am capable of admitting. My family, my daughters, they will need you. Marina, and, yes, even my ex-wives. You have always told me, Stavro, you can be reborn. Well, Father, this is what I am asking you. I am asking, Can I be reborn?

"'The plans are in place. The arrangements are made. It is urgent you come now.'"

Stavroula entered her father's office. The papers on his desk appeared both important and outdated. She revisited the yellowed articles and dollar bills on the wall. She unpinned them to see what was beneath. One of the pieces of yellowed paper she recognized—her own handwriting, the phone number of a Mr. Cown—from when she was fifteen or sixteen. She could not believe it still hung here. Why was it not in her father's Rolodex or, more recently, his phone? She remembered him demanding to know everything she had said to the caller. Had she made herself sound like salt during the conversation, or pepper? Stavroula could still feel how nervous she was then, worried she had embarrassed herself and the diner in front of someone very important in the food business, someone who would write about them and publish it. Days later, her father told her it was a plumber. Only a plumber! But did that matter? Shouldn't she always make herself with as much dignity for an idiot as for a king? Because who does she think the king takes for company when he wants to laugh?

In their search for answers, she had not been honest with Litza. She had not really been looking—was it really just three days ago? Litza had been the one ransacking his office, Stavroula had only been playing. Now, using her father's birthdate, she opened the safe. She knew where he kept the cash in case anything should happen to him. Inside, three thousand. Also, his passport. He had not run.

Her father's sweater was draped over the back of his chair. It felt worn and familiar, scratchy but warm. Or almost warm. It must have been the smell that was familiar, because it stank of Saratogas. He only ever wore this sweater in the office. He didn't even hang it on the hook behind the door but left it on this chair. He wanted to be a man who only ever appeared in a suit jacket, but as he got older, he found sweaters tending. Stavroula could tell this embarrassed him.

What did it say about her, a daughter who knew for days—in her gut—that her father was gone? What did it say about her that she declined his invitation to dinner, knowing he truly believed it to be his last?

Marina and the *pappas* were loud, suddenly. She peered through the portal to see them arguing. The glass blurred their faces, but she could see waving arms. In disputes, all Greeks become their hands.

Stavroula leaned back in the chair. She pulled the sweater around her shoulders but did not put her arms in the sleeves. When her father's voice came to her in a furling accent, it said, *I don't like to be so chilly.*

She closed her eyes to that voice, but smelled it anyway. The smoke.

The day he caught her and Litza in the office with the will, he cornered her. Litza escaped, taking her copy of the book on grief, but Stavroula stayed to see what he would say to her face. In her own way she was being confrontational, because she made herself a brick wall. What she got was *Oh, Stavroula, your poor father, Oh, Stavroula, help me pick out my coffin, it is nothing more than a box and would take only a few minutes of online shopping together. Then you be my date and we go to a special restaurant for octopus and you can whisper to me if the cooks are as good as us.* She simply said, No. No, I can't help you. He tried this, he tried that. Kindly, severely, each time she said no. She would not give him what he wanted. Her reasons were unclear even to herself. Old redresses, things she could not or did not want to remember.

Part of her considered saying yes, the part of her that had always wanted a father, someone who knew what she liked to eat and encouraged her to pick the place. Though, of course, he did not realize that octopus was her favorite: coincidentally, it was also one of his favorites.

Nonetheless, part of her was thawing, warmed by pity and concern. This man—*her father*, she told herself—was so sad at this stage in his life. So alone. He was cured meat, but still you could tell what he once was. That he once had roiling hot blood in him.

Are you on your Woman Thing? he asked. *Don't be bitter, I only ask because your No is like an ax to my face.*

"Your mistress got rid of you, huh?"

She was not trying to be hostile, but this was how he took it. Well, yes, she was trying to be hostile, and that's what made him get mean. He said, *Do you know what is a man? No, just because you look like one you think you do. You are not a man, you are only a woman with mannish hair.* He had said things like this all her life, so she knew how to be brick. He shouted, but she did not relent. That was the victory, not giving in, and he saw she was winning. The only thing she could not help, the smile that uncurled itself. It made him mad. Out of the kind of desperation she had seen in animals giving their last futile kick, he shot back at her, *I should have walked away from you in your box*, re, left you for good from *the day you were born*. It did not surprise her to hear this. It made it easier to walk away, herself. She was glad—so glad—she had never taken anything from him.

But these were a father's last words to his daughter? Even he would regret them. Or did she just want to believe so?

Stavroula touched the mouse for his desktop, gently. The screen came to life. She did not know his password. She thought for a moment, then typed STAVROS. That was all she needed, the computer took her to his email account.

There was a message already open. It was from the day before his disappearance—Day 6, according to the subject line—but had never been sent.

It was addressed to her.

Dear My Oldest, My First. My Stavroula.

You know the story of your birth, I have told it to you many times, how you were only three pounds. But you cannot know that I hold you in my hand, very new, very small. Like a paper clip, the way your body came folded up. Your leg was the same size as my thumb.

Which it is big for a thumb, not for a leg, no. For a leg, it says,
This child will not survive. But you do. Like your father, you live to
survive.

There is so much more for me to explain you. But we don't have
all the time in the world anymore. You look for Your Father on the
ground as a seed, but he will be in the sky as a tree.

Stavroula, like your father, you make your own path in a way that
maybe others cannot. Ruby, your sister, cannot go out so far on her
own. Litza, your sister, goes out so much that she is like one of those
planets you cannot even see with your naked eye. You ask, always,
Why is the father so hard on Stavroula? But what is hardship when it
makes us who we are?

Some things, Stavroula, I should never say.

Remember me, Stavroula. For yes, my pride. But also for you,
because Stavroula is deserving of a past as much as anyone. The only
thing I am asking, yes, I dare to ask, is How can you bury me? And
help your sisters and your mother and all of the people who love and
refuse Stavros Stavros Mavrakis, to bury him? I am asking, How can
I be present, future, but especially past, as you are my present, my
future, and especially my past?

It is no little burden to carry your father to the end of his day,
because it also means carrying him to the end of yours. And in this, I
cannot walk with you.

But I can tell you what to do. And, for once in your life: listen.

Here is my last last request:

Gather everybody here, Sunday at 12:00. Tell them, Take this, It
is my father's daily special. It is very good. Give them wine and tell
them, Take this, it is my father's sweat. It is all he has built of his life.
Say to them, Eat with me, and you eat with my father/

That was it. The cursor blinked on *father*, as if waiting for him to
finish. She scanned the letter once more. His last, last request. Something told her there would be another letter tomorrow, and another
one after that, and she would wake up to letters for the rest of her life.
Requests she had not fulfilled. His Oldest, his First, the one he should

have abandoned at birth. Her head was fizzy with the sweater's stale smoke. It was too much. She covered her face, and began to take deep, gulping, smothered breaths. She wanted to escape into the cold air.

And in this, I cannot walk with you. But wasn't she always on her own?

Stavroula sat a minute, two minutes. She listened to the *pappas* and Marina still arguing. She thought about Litza. What would Litza do with this plea? *Say to them, Eat with me, and you eat with my father.*

She adjusted the sweater so that it covered more of her. Her chest relaxed. Her throat was sore with the residual smoke.

She opened a new file. She typed:

In Memoriam,
Please join family and friends in celebration of
the life of Stavros Stavros Mavrakis.
Sunday, The Gala Diner II
The Mavrakis Family

She printed the invitations on glossy paper that she found in a drawer. She cut them to size, arranged them in a stack. She would give them to the hostess, and the hostess would fasten them to the cover of the menus. The memorial would be tomorrow, and the right people would come. She pocketed one for herself. She exited the office, wearing the sweater.

Marina said, jovially, "Don't feel too sorry for the *pappas*. Tonight is the longest we have ever gone without a fight."

Then her face dropped.

Stavroula turned around, and there was Ruby. She was in the kitchen, where she had not been in years and years. Litza was standing with her, almost holding Ruby up with her arm—Litza, who had come back.

Ruby, her face bruised with worry, said, "Stevie, is he gone?"

Our father had three daughters. The first, as dear as gold. The second, as dear as wood. The third, as dear as salt. The daughter as dear as gold, he addressed from a golden throne. The daughter as dear as wood, he summoned from his wooden throne. The daughter as dear as salt, he looked down on her from his pillar of salt. He sent them each letters that they had to crack open with a spoon, as these letters were made of eggshells and could not be sealed once they had been read. The letters required the daughters' attendance and told them each about themselves.

"But Father, why am I as dear as gold?" the first daughter asked. She wanted to know, because she did not believe him, because Our father was often unable to say what he was actually thinking and instead tried to make his heart feel what his words announced.

"Because, Daughter, you are of great worth to me." He showed her his many rings and amulets, the golden throne, the cloth that had been woven golden hair by golden hair, the studded crown that proved how far he'd come. "You see how much I like gold."

She said, "Is that all?"

"You are as dear as gold," he told his daughter, "because you stay in places deep and dark, as warm as a skull, until the sun transforms you into precious metal."

The daughter as dear as gold was satisfied.

The second daughter came and had to raise her head high, for Our father's throne was in the canopy of a tree. It was hard to hear him, and the words took their time traveling down the trunk and over the chirping of squirrels and the plunkings of woodpeckers. She waited to hear why she had been summoned and then dismissed and then summoned. She asked Our father why she was as dear to him as wood.

"Better to burn you with," he said, but this was a joke. What he said after many laughs, which he shared with the woodland creatures, was, "You are as dear as wood, because wood can build a house or make a fire or hang a hat or succumb to paper."

"Is that all?"

He chose not to tell her other indelible truths about wood. He said, instead, "You can burn wood and turn it into something new."

"Is that all?"

Our father took his time answering, and by now the second daughter was used to this. She could wait a long time for his answer that might never come, or it might tell her more of the same, which was that to matter, she had to be consumed. What she heard was, "Wood breathes, even after death."

She left with this power, which was a self-knowing, and a hunger for chopping down trees and milling them into paper.

The third daughter approached her father from a distance and found that she could not tell where the throne of salt began. It was a pillar, yes, but it spread finely over the floor. She felt the grains beneath her bare feet. The slightest disturbance caused an avalanche. Each breath, the salt was burying her feet. Someone eavesdropping sneezed, and the salt sprayed over her ankles.

"I will deliver a riddle," Our father said to this one, the salt reaching her calves. "What is essential in small quantities but deadly to animals and plants in excess? So harmful it can leave you with muscle cramps, dizziness, death, even electrolyte disturbance?"

"Salt," the daughter as dear as salt answered. The salt coming now to her knees.

"No," he corrected, "daughters." She attempted a step back, but he required that she come forward, as did the salt. It sunk her thighs.

"Salt is money," the daughter as dear as salt answered. "Salt is blood. Salt is water." Her voice caused a dramatic avalanche. Her waist disappeared beneath the white mountain. "Salt is work and salt is sweat. Salt is making home and leaving home." Her chest, her shoulders. "Salt is yesterday and tomorrow. Salt is point-oh-four percent of the body's weight at a concentration equal to that of seawater." Up to her neck in salt, but at least she and Our father were now eye to eye.

"Is that all?" the father asked, and the salt rose to her chin.

"You cannot escape salt, just as you cannot escape me."

"Just as you cannot escape me," he said, and the throne of salt buried the daughter as dear as salt.

CHAPTER 23

The *pappas* himself takes hot chocolate to the three beautiful girls. He carries the mugs one by one, because he is half blind and the eczema worm has eaten his hands. No matter how many prescriptions she sends, he prefers myrrh and eucalyptus. In the booth, the girls are obedient. They accept the mugs because he asks them to. In booths, all children of all ages wait to be told where to go next; even Marina. *Pappas, if you call, I will come to your table, and I will take some chocolate to drink, too.* But, no, the *pappas* is not her father right now. The *pappas* is a consoler, and he is a meanderer, and he is a poet, and he is a priest, and he is a bird tracking the crumbs to the missing Stavros.

Marina feels very unwise tonight. Her heart is a king with many heads and tigers, and she cannot trust it. Tomorrow is the conclusion for Stavros Stavros Mavrakis, her friend and business partner. Tomorrow ends the story that Stavros began in nonsense letters to his family. Impossibly, tomorrow is Easter Sunday, and tomorrow morning is the scheduled Memorial of Stavros Stavros Mavrakis. This gathering of the girls tonight, this *koinonia*, it has nothing to do with the father. This is their wish, not his, even if he would wish it, too. This was not in your plans, Stavro, but here they are, anyhow. They make their own way. Tonight the girls have their own kind of memorial, which is in one way more a communion about being sisters than daughters.

Her Stavroula is so brave. All night, she has been answering her father's last final letter. Stavroula has been inviting customers and employees to come tomorrow to pay their respects. She has been taking care of food and seating arrangements. Now Stavroula is making the table into a triangle that points back to her as the head, so that her sisters will know she has the eyes to see them through this difficult period, and whatever difficulty follows. She is as brave as she was when she first entered this country. Marina remembers, Marina was there to bathe her, because Marina spoke Greek; and after she bathed her, she rubbed olive oil on little Stavroula's bare *koulo*. *Why?* Stavroula asked. *Because oil is the fertilizer that helps you grow*, Marina said. After a breakfast of warm rice pudding, she sweetened a teaspoon of oil with honey and brought it to Stavroula's lips. *Why?* Stavroula asked. *Because you think not in thoughts, but in bubbles of oil. Why?* Stavroula insisted. *Because it is oil that makes your tongue as slippery as it is*, and Marina caught her tongue between her greased fingers.

Marina, knowing it is both a right and a flaw within herself, cannot help but hold disappointment in her heart for her dear Stavroula. Stavroula senses this, and that pains Marina. Who could believe that Stavros Stavros's letter would speak truth? Marina knows now that he is right about Stavroula, that Stavroula desires things no woman is entitled to—a kind of happiness that should disgust Marina, but mostly it saddens her. Stavroula, a horse that refuses to break, even if domesticity would make life easy. After too many years, even Marina, whom no one could break, had finally broken. Not Stavroula. Her daring Stavroula, this much in her she can admire.

Stavroula meets her eye; Marina taps middle finger to thumb three, four times. A kind of quiet clapping that says, I love you. I see you. Stavroula smiles, turns back to her sisters.

Now the *pappas* is telling a joke. It is either about the goat girl, the snake tree, or he is trying to have them guess at what is the quickest thing on earth. Somehow, the joke becomes a joke about their father. It is Ruby who laughs the easiest. Stavroula, like Marina, laughs with her mouth open. Litza laughs only when Marina catches her not laughing. Of them all, Marina knows, she is the one feeling the hole of her father's absence—because it is a larger version of the hole she feels at all times.

Litza sits across from the *pappas* and the sisters, alone. If Marina were asked to join them, she would sit on Litza's side.

Yes, Marina loves Stavroula, but today maybe even more Litza, because Litza so much needs love. Is broken over it. And Marina, in her own way, can give it from afar though she knows that will never be enough for Litza. As well as, Marina sees some of herself in Litza. They two are the kind of rock that continues to appear in your yard after you sweep it away, more weed than mineral. The kind of rock that has always been in Marina's throat, and, yes, Litza's throat as well, because they both insisted on relying on themselves at such an early age. Marina knows Litza's pain; Marina knows Litza must rise above the pain, as Stavroula has learned to do. Must chew on the rock. Women like them chew on rocks all their entire lives. Which is why Marina cannot offer Litza leniency, but she can offer love, from afar.

The *pappas* says something that Marina, wrapping pastry at the counter, cannot hear. All three girls blow diligently into their cups. Marina knows this trick: it is the sailboat. Whoever blows the sailboat fastest—the *pappas* says to all the children in the village—wins the race. Marina knows there is no sailboat. *That does not stop us, Pappas. That makes us try harder.*

The mother will come soon, and then Marina can call the *pappas* back from the family. Marina can say, *Come away, let them think in peace with their confusion*, once Carol arrives. Until then, Marina takes care of the bakery case. Marina uses plastic wrapping for the pastries and does not get too involved in the condolensing that is happening at the table.

Marina does not know if Stavros Stavros will die or will he live. Marina is not someone who can see into the future. Marina trusts that what must happen will happen, just like the hen under the knife bends her neck to what's to come.

So Marina tells herself. But Marina does not trust Stavros Stavros or his brain, thick as cow tongue these days, or his disappearance.

Stavros Stavros is the kind of man who will arrange his own funeral and not die, but he is also the kind of man to arrange his funeral and then go ahead and die.

What will happen to the three beautiful girls? Ruby, who does not yet know how to read the world, and maybe never will, or could it be that she is fortunate enough that the world will more properly read her? Stavroula and Litza, think how far apart they already are, one an ocean liner, one a satellite. Marina loves them both, dearly, as if she thought up the idea of them. Marina understands that Stavroula and Litza—and you, too, Stavro, and you, too, Dina, and you, too, Marina, and you, too—belong to a race of people who must carry everything they own in their mouths. All of their luggage, they squeeze into their mouth. You can only fit so much of the old place, Marina, or so many words, or so many exaggerations, or so many stories, or so many people, or so much soup before you must spit and take a breath; and then a very different world fills you up. It is not unwelcome, it is just reinvention. This is immigration, even so many years later.

Marina wraps the pastry with three easy folds. Plastic on plastic on plastic, so that it is no longer clear, it is cloudy. The *pappas* calls for a round of milk shakes, the girls not quite through with their hot chocolates. Every flavor, he says to the waitress. It is a reason for everyone in the diner, even her, to love him.

The beautiful girls do not understand their father. They don't know what a stubborn man he can be; for years, stubborn enough to resist all the forces ripping his family apart and then stubborn enough to rip it apart himself. Marina watched without giving advice or getting involved. She told herself that he would have cracked her advice against the side of a rock. Marina, without children, without family, without any troubles besides the ones that get stirred up in pots. What does she know?

That is not true, Marina, and you know it.

All those years, Marina's greatest sin, talking too much and saying nothing. Yes, Marina, you had your say for how to fillet the flounder, and you had your say in keeping vultures out of your kitchen, but what did that matter? What life did that change? Your *pappas*, who has never met these children before, is offering the easiest word of all—silence. He kisses them all on the forehead, his face grazing theirs like a sheep's. Marina's heart breaks, and also she feels relief when the beautiful girls seem consoled. What she has failed to do for so long, the *pappas* has done in minutes.

Now, Marina is brave enough to say what she could not say for years. A prayer in the diner is as good as a prayer anywhere:

Father, take care of the girls.

The milk shakes come. The *pappas* fashions farm animals out of the straw wrappers and makes them walk.

When he begins to sing, too low for many people to hear, Marina cannot go on with her prayer. She cannot go on with her work. She watches and listens. The song tells about an apricot tree and a shepherd who falls asleep only to wake up and realize that his flock never left him, they are just on the other side of the mountain with the girl from his dreams. It is when he sings the refrain, "The girl of his dreams," that the *pappas* looks up at Marina, his eyes glossy. It is when he sings "I could see you for the apricot trees," that he beckons her.

Marina is the little girl holding her milk jug. Nothing lost but the bottom. And instead of scolding her for the spilled milk, he laughs; she makes him laugh.

From behind the counter, Marina joins her *pappas* beneath the apricot tree.

CHAPTER 24

Dear Dad.

Are you in hell?
    Are you in heaven?
    Are you in hell?

Hell was one clean plate, one fork in the drain board, two mugs on the counter. Hell was three in the morning, Dina at the stove in a green robe, supervising a kettle. She was digging the crescent of her thumbnail into an eyetooth, sleepy but not irritated. If she had seen Litza from her window the day that Litza followed her father here, she said nothing about it.

Dina did not complain about Litza's banging on the shuddery glass window, and she had not been nasty about being pulled from the couch, though it would have been better if she had. Instead, she said, "I knew you'd come. A mother senses when her girls have unfinished business." She was forever saying shit like this anytime Litza gave her the chance—things that exonerated her by insinuating that she could mother from a distance, that she could be forgiven, when a) she was not exonerated; b) she was not mothering; c) this was not distance enough; d) even now, Dina mistakenly believed in redemption.

She did not ask if Litza wanted cream or sugar—either because she didn't think to, or because she remembered that Litza took it plain. She said, "You were never this quiet."

"I'm changing."

"That's good. I hear you're fixing your mistakes lately. Living better, living like me."

"I'm not here to talk about my mistakes."

Dina crossed her heart. "Good idea, we won't talk about your mistakes, and for a change, we won't talk about mine. Let's promise."

Litza pulled at the string of the tea bag. She was going little by little, the way you did with a stranger you didn't like but suspected might be helpful. She gave this much—we've been searching. She gave nothing more because—what good was Dina to her? She was sure that before she knocked, Dina was sitting with one thumb over the other, staring from one flowerless vase to another, waiting for her opportunity to die. The only thing delivering her from that, for a few minutes at least, was Litza.

"Your father is crying in some woman's lap."

"Whose?"

"Anybody's, that's how your father is. He will cry to anyone with a tissue and tits."

Litza nodded, though that was something he and Dina had in common.

Dina reached behind her to a messy shelf and pulled a book. *To Live Until We Say Good-bye*, fucking again, fucking everywhere. The cover, gray and cracked. Dina put it on the table. Litza turned Elisabeth Kübler-Ross over; she was tired of looking at this old book and its unnaturally sympathetic author.

"He gave you a copy?"

"Of course. He wants everyone to grieve his way."

Litza had been doing grieving of her own, thank you, grieving that completely obliterated her father's. Did he really believe she could be contained in just five stages? Did he think her sorrow was simple, a linear reflex of denial and acceptance? Her mourning was supposed to be explained entirely by his death? How about she mourn all those years he was alive and dead to her? No, fuck you, she had been grieving so long, her grief had become immortal. Her grief was porous and residual, as one J. William Worden understood. The healing, Dr. J. William Worden explained in his book, which she had found in the library where she could be anonymous and unbothered, begins only when things look like they've gone back to normal. It's at that point that you TEAR, and the four tasks of mourning begin. Litza did not read Dr. Worden's advice as *tear*, to cry: she read it *tear*, to be torn in half. *T* meant she had *To accept the reality of the loss*. *E* meant she had to *Experience the pain of the loss*. Then there was *Adjust*, forever *Adjust to the new environment post-loss*, and finally *R*, *Reinvest in the new reality*. It was the *R*. That tricky *R*. She couldn't do it, she could not root herself to a new world knowing it might be wrenched away any day.

Dina said, "I have something better."

Litza didn't react, so Dina went off to a dark spot down the hallway, what could only have been the bedroom in this shitty apartment no better than Litza's. Litza imagined it was made of leaves, a warren with the bones of baby rabbits in piles beneath the bed, which Dina munched on. Litza rubbed her own belly. She whispered, "If you're in there, I want you to know that I will never eat bones the same size as you."

Dina came out with an e-reader. She had loaded *Taming Your Outer Child: A Revolutionary Program to Overcome Self-Defeating Patterns*.

Fuck her.

Even if she was right, fuck her.

"This is a great resource," Dina said. She offered it like a pamphlet. "Relax, read a page. You can stretch out on the couch. Read a chapter."

Living with Dina during her teenage years was worse than life with her parents. She hated admitting it, but everyone knew. Dina had never wanted her for a daughter, had wanted instead a playmate. If her father died tomorrow, this is what she would be left with. The same motherly nothing.

She let Dina see her press the power button and then she put the device down when Dina opened the oven door. She expected it to be full of books, books about reclamation and healing and abandonment, or pages and pages of Dina's own writing, a diary that offered not explanations but some sort of inventory of excuses. Instead, Dina retrieved a pie, and Litza realized she had smelled something baking this whole time and had dismissed it as coming from the adjoining apartment. It was the most ridiculous thing to her, a pie in Dina's house. The few years she'd lived with Dina, never once had there been pie.

Dina used her fingers to scrape chunks of berry from the serving spatula. She delivered the plate, friendly. Filling was darkening under her nails, and she sucked it out. "Read the introduction, at least. Don't be shy."

It was a careful pie, as if Dina had never spent generosity or tenderness on anything before the idea of pie came to her. Litza's slice, other than a small dribbling at the thinnest point, came out perfect. Litza imagined Dina crouched in front of the oven, looking on as the pie went from soft dough to baked, flaky crust, and wet filling from loose to firm. Dina baking pies day after day for the last ten years, getting it just right every time. It looked perfect, yet each time she started a new one, because it was not perfect, because Litza was not here to sample a blessing.

Dina liked how Litza was admiring it. "I can bake you your own, if you'd like. Which is more than your father can do." She laughed. It was the workman's laugh Litza remembered from childhood.

All night, Litza had sat in the booth, burning candles across from her sisters. The candles were long, white, and they held them at the *pappas* insistence. Her sisters glanced up anytime a door opened, but Litza resisted and resisted. Litza focused on the wax, the way it spilled out of itself, made itself from itself, and stopped just before her fingers, just before she wanted it to. Her fingers scraped the wax until it clumped like fat beneath her nails. He did not come.

She had no intentions of eating the pie, but she was eating the pie. While her mind was back with the *pappas* in the booth, her mouth had started without her. The crust loosened into buttery silt. The filling warm enough to drink and the berries held up until she bit down. It was exceptional pie. Like folding up a silk purse and holding it in her mouth, the kind she coveted—then stole—as a child. She would have eaten more, if Dina had offered. She would have used her fingers.

"Do you like it?"

"Yes."

Dina's face flooded with gratitude.

"Who did you bake it for?"

"Myself," Dina said. "My friends."

Dina used the table to push herself up and went to the counter, where there was an unmarked white box, its corners taped. Dina opened a drawer and removed a black ribbon. She strung the ribbon along the top and then, without looking, ran it along the bottom. She knotted the ribbon, simple and clean, and then cut the extra at an angle. Litza had never seen Dina proficient at something like this, or at anything.

He did not come and did not come. Litza would have known, Litza the last awake in the booth, her candle squat and hobbled, grown older by disappearing. Mother had come for Ruby, but Litza and Stavroula stayed on with the *pappas*, which felt right. But then even the *pappas* fell asleep, Stavroula on his arm, his head back and his eyes closed. He was still, so still. Watching his chest barely rise, Litza took deeper breaths. His thin, matted hair. The skin on the back of his hand, more translucent than a wet napkin. She did not dare shake him. When the door opened—Marina coming for him—he opened one eye.

Dina sat, interlaced her fingers. "Stavros is a mean little cockroach. Trust me, I know him best. He's not going anywhere. But just in case." She slid the box over. "You can take it with you, or I can bring it."

"You're coming to the service?"

"I am the *executor*, aren't I?" She said it in the way of executions, which was confusing and creepy. Dina, always sounding off.

Litza stood.

Dina cut a second slice of pie and put it on the other ceramic plate. This piece was messier, broken at the bottom. She placed it on top of the box.

Dina said, "I should have said, when I answered the door, you look better than ever. I couldn't believe it was you. You look—healthy." Her eye blinked furiously. Litza wanted to cup it with her hand until it stopped, but she felt the other would start up, and then she would need to cover her mother's eyes with both hands. She had not touched her mother in years.

Dina shut the door and did not look through the curtains, as she had when Litza first pulled up. Litza put the pie box on the passenger seat. The extra slice, the plate, she left that on the steps.

She touched the black ribbon. It was somber, but somehow festive without being offensive.

On the console between the seats was *To Live Until We Say Goodbye*. She stared at the cover for a long time, its glossy title. She turned, finally, to the page her father had marked with a business card. She had resisted it until now, believing he had intentionally marked it for her, then believing he had not. Neither was satisfactory. She did not want this passage to be some sort of explaining excuse, making up for everything. But at least it could try.

Litza's eyes fell a third of the way down the page—

> *. . . she could express her rage, her sense of unfairness about the many losses that had befallen her, and where she could question God and express her rage without someone judging her or making her feel more guilty . . .*

> *Dear Dad: What the hell are you leaving me with?*
> A foot-and-a-half-length of rubber hose.

> *We use a rubber hose because, first of all, it is inexpensive, is easily available, and can be tucked in any bag, can be used in any place. It also enforces the power in our arms when we feel like striking or hitting someone in rage and anger. If no rubber hose is available, it is very easy to take a bath towel and fold it, or, if necessary, we can use our fists. But with a rubber hose the worst thing that can happen is that we will end up with a few blisters on our fingers. . . .*

By the time she was finished, the box was pulpy and crushed, the crust destroyed. The funereal ribbon, frayed and ripped away. Warm berry filling oozed onto the passenger seat. It was wet and darkening. Less like blood, more like smashed, very tiny organs.

CHAPTER 25

Stavroula was not herself. She was wrapped in clothes that did not belong to her, and someone had covered her in a gray wool blanket. She was lying on a bed that felt like it was made of canvas, with a little bit of padding. A cot. She blinked until she understood that she was back in her father's office. That he had been missing now for four days going on five. That last night—just a handful of hours ago?—she had talked to a police officer who took down notes about her father's physical description, the last outfit he wore. She remembered being asked about her father's medical conditions, which she did not know. Afterward, Stavroula went through his medicine cabinet and found remedies for surprising ailments. High-cholesterol medication? Suddenly her father was an unwell man.

Her memory felt like a fish, and all she was left with was the cooked, blackened eye.

The diner was quiet, unnerving at three in the morning the night before her father's funeral. The diner had never closed before, not even on Christmas. It was dark now except for the bakeless light of the street lamps. She did not like waking alone in a place that was meant to be warm, filled. She imagined that this diner, exactly as it was now— solitary, unpeopled—was what the first few minutes of death would look like before her eyes adjusted to the afterlife.

Stavroula lowered herself onto the tile floor from the cot. She rubbed her arms through the sweater—her father's sweater. Mother had taken Ruby home, and Marina had taken the *pappas* home. Litza—Stavroula did not know where Litza had gone. Litza had stayed as long as Litza could. Stavroula was not mad. She just wished Litza had taken her along, too. Litza—was Stavroula remembering this right?—let Marina read her palm. Stavroula could only make out some of the words, because Marina was whispering them to Litza. Litza was listening intently. Stavroula heard, *Litza* mou, *what this line in your palm foretells is that you have been picking up stones for a long time now, and soon, after so many years, you will begin to build a castle of them, you are already building a castle, and soon Marina will stand on the highest tower, and nod in appreciation.*

Then Marina read Ruby's palm, and it was a show; this *was* a spectacle—for the girls and the waitresses and the *pappas*, all of whom were drinking ouzo—Marina naming all the men who will try to take Ruby by the hand even with Mr. Dave in the way. "But Ruby will not give them the satisfaction. Ruby will say, No, Peter. No, Josh. No, Michael. No, Rick. No, Stavros. No, John. No, Joe Blow. Ruby will find her own path, Ruby will sacrifice what is necessary when the time is right, when she knows how to listen to herself as she truly is and not as she is imagined to be."

Ruby read Marina's palm in turn and said: "I see a fat old lady who gets into everybody's business until one day she finally finds a boyfriend, somebody who doesn't give a shit about Greek food." Marina took back Ruby's palm, claiming she hadn't finished: "Actually, I was wrong, *koukla*, the fates say for a little *poutanaki* like you, it will be Yes, Peter, Yes, Josh, Yes, Michael, Yes, Joe Blow." They were laughing, getting loud and using their hands to talk over each other with their predictions; even Litza was playing, claiming what she foresaw was a fat old lady with *no* boyfriend, choking on a turkey bone.

Marina did not read Stavroula's palm; what she did, over the course of many hours, while the candles were burning, was to keep Stavroula in the corner of her eye. It was as if she were saying, *Your future is beyond me,* koukla; *your future is in your own hands.* Marina, at the end of the night, must have been the one to put the blanket on her but Stavroula could not recall this. Nor her walk, half asleep, from booth to office. What she felt was Marina grazing her arm with dry fingers, which felt like fish scales. Marina putting her to rest. Marina standing over her with an unlit but smoking candle, saying, *It was a very good menu. Not to Marina's tasting, but Good because it was Brave, and Brave is the deepest of all flavors to cook with.*

The menu was here, next to her.

I would be proud to eat from this menu, koukla. *Marina would be lucky to.*

Stavroula's phone beeped once to remind her that a text had come through. She thought it was Litza. It was July, at three in the morning, saying <HOW ARE YOU?>.

She had texted July earlier to explain that her father was still missing. That she needed more time to sort things out. She was sorry. For missing another shift. July answered with sympathy and questions, but Stavroula didn't respond. She responded now <YOU HUNGRY?>.

In one hand, the fanciest food in the world: lamb ribs, uncooked, untrimmed, wrapped in parchment. In the other, the humblest: four eggs in burlap. Plus a bag of her own spices and cookware. She rang the doorbell. July answered the door wearing jeans, but it was clear she had just gotten out of bed. She hugged Stavroula around the packages, a sympathetic hug.

Stavroula followed her into a large, very white kitchen that masked its emptiness with plants and unopened bottles of wine. Down the center was a bar and on the other side, where the dining room began, were stools. The appliances were a microwave, a refrigerator, and an espresso machine. No knife block, no canisters of flour. The room existed as one large space for storing, not for making.

This was the closest they had ever been—this home, intimate space.

"You want to talk?" July asked. "I can make tea. Or get us some whiskey."

"I prefer to cook."

From her bag, Stavroula removed her own apron, a set of knives, twine, and a flowerpot. She washed her hands. She tied the apron.

July washed her hands, too. She said, "What do we do first?"

"We get to know the animal we're about to eat."

Stavroula gestured with her knife. The lamb rack is a primal cut on the back between shoulder and loin. A hotel rack, she explained, is two joined racks. I used a band saw, split them from the chine bone. Then: American lamb is larger than New Zealand lamb, because it comes older to market. American is better. Then: Americans don't like their meat to taste like meat, they think cooking lamb smells like a peasant hut. But that's just an untrained palate. Then: No culture, no religion bans the eating of lamb. Lamb has evolved right along with man for thousands of years.

Then: This is my father's favorite meal.

July's pause. "We'll save him some."

"Here, pull this," Stavroula said. July did and, little by little, the fat gave way to the meat.

Stavroula showed her how to cut out the fingers of meat between the ribs. "You move the rib across the knife, not the knife across the rib. The meat is boat, the knife water. You want it under you, still, at all times." She offered the knife to July, feeling self-conscious about her food metaphors, but also proud because they were honest. "You can't mess up. The bone stops you before you make any mistakes."

July made fairly even strokes, and when she sawed instead of cut, Stavroula corrected her. Never touching her.

Stavroula lifted the flowerpot. It contained a cylinder spool. "Know what this is?"

"String?"

"Not string."

"Thread?"

"Not thread. Thread's too fine."

"Hemp."

"Never hemp, hemp leaves fibers. Nothing coated in wax, not polyester. Linen—that's the only kind of butcher's twine you want." She showed her how to use the hole in the pot to dispense the twine. Stavroula wrapped it around the ribs at the base, cleaning up the meat. July tugged the twine, hard, the muscle in her bare upper arm blinking.

Stavroula said, "We just frenched."

It got her a laugh.

They made a paste of olive oil, coriander, garlic, black pepper, thyme, salt.

From her bag, Stavroula removed the final instrument, a Bundt mold. She instructed: Tie the ribs of each rack together with the twine. Now curve the two racks around the middle to make a semicircle and wind the twine three times around. That's it, see how simple? They took turns rubbing the paste on the meat. They placed it in the oven at 130 degrees.

"Lamb lacks internal fat," Stavroula said. "The way you mess it up is to cook it too high too fast. It demands patience."

Stavroula said, "My father taught me that."

They watched the oven. July took off the green apron. She wore a sleeveless yellow shirt with a low neckline, which Stavroula couldn't help but think she had put on because she was coming over. There were many bangles around her arm and layers of gold necklaces hanging at her throat. It was a throat like a very pretty glass pitcher that Stavroula, in her childhood, knew not to reach for.

July brought them glasses of orange juice. The juice was cold, sweet, and sharp. Stavroula drank hers and asked for more.

Stavroula said, "What was it like when you lost your mom?"

July, searching for words. "Afterward, you're a different person."

"That feels true already."

July nodded. "They'll find him."

Stavroula was no help to the police, because she could not accurately describe her father. Her father's eyes were brown, but the brown of hazelnut or the brown of liver? His hair was black and streaked with gray, but was it really as short as she said? Was his nickname Steve? Was there actually another nickname that better described him, that he had never been able to share with his children? Only the inoculation scar on his arm, only that was definite in her mind. She could trace it with her finger in the air and make it appear just like that. The same ridges, the same circular outline as a bottle cap. The police would find her father immediately if they could just go around matching the scar in her mind to the scar on his arm.

She was not going to use the word *suicide*, not even with July. That wasn't what happened. One thing was true, it was her father who had taught her about resilience.

She could not face the thought of him dying alone.

They sat together at the counter, drinking juice and watching the minutes on the timer. "I'm sorry," Stavroula said, "about the menu. Sometimes I forget I'm just like him."

"Stevie, you're not like anyone."

Stavroula shook her head. "I can't help what I cook, it just comes to me. I can't water it down. I'm sorry if I embarrassed you." What came to mind was an expression, handed down by her father—Εφαγα τον κόδμο να δε βρω. *I ate the whole world to find you. I've been searching everywhere for you.*

July smiled, kindly, but as if maybe she had been embarrassed. Then she reached up and rubbed the edges of Stavroula's hair where it was shortest. "It's funny," she said. "It was like seeing a reflection of yourself, only in food."

Stavroula surprised herself by leaning into July's hand, into the hospitality of it. What was so unexpected, delightful, was that July's palm opened. Stavroula closed her eyes, and the faint whirring of the oven sounded like it was coming from the touch. July's hand moved across her hair to just below her earlobe, grazing her neck with a single nail. "You're good at what you do, Stevie."

She was a sucker for flattery. Just like her father. She opened her eyes.

July took back her hand. "You're the only zealot I've ever been fond of."

"I want everyone to see the real you. The one I see."

July stood eye to eye with Stavroula, the oven beeping and neither of them moving to check it. "The one you see."

Stavroula nodded. Fond was good. Fond was a start.

July perched her arms on Stavroula's shoulders, she pulled her close. The hard, cool jewelry, July's slim neck the smoothness of wax paper, her solid arms. Stavroula was expecting something delicate, like the body of a game hen, and got something even more delicate, a quail. Except for those arms, which both drew her in and kept her out.

Then the overwhelming feeling: this was kindness. A friend, giving her shelter.

Tomorrow, she would be on her own. Would have to face her loneliness, once again.

Would go back to the menu, start from scratch until she got it right.

Stavroula pulled herself from July, began poaching the eggs.

Some minutes later, they were dipping crusty bread into the drippings and licking their fingers.

DAY 1

Denial

CHAPTER 26

Stavroula pulled up to the diner. It was five in the morning, still dark. Just a few hours before her father's funeral, which they had all agreed to observe. The wet pavement glowed pink from the Gala's neon sign. Someone was standing across the street. Stavroula could tell who: Litza, nocturnal as usual. Her arms were crossed, and her hand trembling a cigarette. A blinking amber streetlight lit up only part of her face, as if the darkness were protecting the rest. Litza crossed, leaned into Stavroula's driver's-side window. She had been crying and the crying had made her angry—not the other way around.

Still, Stavroula said, "You want to get in?"

They sat in the chilly darkness with the windows down, Litza taking puffs of a second cigarette every now and then. Her eyes glassy. "I need coffee."

"Know a good diner?"

This made Litza snort. Then, "Let's get away from this fucking place."

They drove.

"Nothing's open."

Stavroula stopped in the middle of an empty intersection and reached back for the paper plate covered in tinfoil. Litza picked off some of the lamb. She nodded in appreciation. "You got really good. He taught you right."

"Thanks."

She lit another cigarette and closed her eyes. "At least one of us learned something." She meant it, she wasn't *Digging around your palm with a spoon*, as their father would say. For the first time in a long time, she didn't sound bitter.

They went to the playground where their father had taken them a couple times when they were young. On both occasions, he sat on the bench for fifteen minutes while they played, him all bunched shoulders and coat, smoking a Saratoga. He told them *No, push each other on the swings, first one and then the other. It can't be both at once.* The first outing they just sat there waiting, but he never got up. The second time, Stavroula pushed Litza and Litza pushed her back. They never got very high before one had to slide off the seat, take a turn at pushing. Still, they sang *eeska deeska bella*, and having to get down did not deter them. Their father, he didn't understand the bastardized Greek rhyme. It was like a secret between the two sisters.

Litza said, "When I have a daughter, I'm going to take her to the park every day. I'm going to teach her things we never learned. And give her everything we never got."

"You want a girl?"

"It's not about want. I can feel her pushing to come out. She's fighting her way to life."

Stavroula found herself admiring this. Though Litza would be a terrible mother.

They drove on. Litza took a drag with her eyes shut.

Without intending to, Stavroula took them to their father's first diner. The Gala 0. She slowed but did not park. There was nothing to see. It was not a diner anymore, not even a salt shed. Just paved over. Extra parking for the car dealership next door. The salt shed had been here when they were young, but by then it was a pulled-pork joint. Small as they had been, they thought the building so tiny. That didn't stop them from feeling awe: this was the place where their father first dreamed of bringing them home.

Stavroula put the car in park in the middle of the road. They stared at the lot. Every few minutes, the traffic light ahead changed from green to red.

"Stavroula. He's dead."

"We don't know that."

Litza turned her face to where a tattered yellow tape, tied to a post, was flapping in the wind. Stavroula put her hand on Litza's leg. She had not done that maybe ever. She saw something else come over Litza's face, a flicker. Too jagged and abrupt to be a smile.

They ended up at the airport in long-term parking and watched the sun rise. This was how their father had entered the country, and where they entered too. He came with three hundred dollars in his pocket, a beard, and a wife. Was he leaving with more, or less? At least a bright cloudless day, a pink sky. It brought the girls out of the car, though it was cold, and they perched on the hood and tracked the planes that approached from varying distances.

In the promising daylight, Litza was already shrinking back into herself; another shitty cigarette in her shaky hand. She was crying.

They had been doomed from the start. It had always been Stavroula's task to carry her sister, but Litza was gallons and gallons of water, and all Stavroula could use was her hands. So she kept losing Litza, kept scooping her up, kept losing. She could cup her hands and hold her close, but what good would that do? She could never have carried enough of Litza to make a difference.

Suddenly, a plane rushed overhead so close it loomed like the belly of a shark. And where was he? Where was he? Stavroula began to scream. She was shaking and swearing. None of this could be heard because of the shriek of the plane. Was she weeping for him? Weeping for her sister? She wouldn't go back for Litza. She'd go forward, just as she had all her life. Because, if they made her, she would do it all over again: she would save herself first. Still.

Litza yelled something over the roar of the plane.

Stavroula shook her head. The roar was dying down.

Litza said, "You hate him, too?"

Stavroula laughed. She wiped her face on an old napkin and passed it to Litza, who also wiped her face.

"Stevie," Litza said, "it was me. I broke your window. I shouldn't have, but I did it."

Stavroula slid off the hood. "I know. Let's go."

ζ

They ended up at the diner, of course. Instead of smashing the bakery case, they opened it with a tiny silver key from the register. They pulled two stools up to the counter and surrounded themselves with trays of dessert, and Stavroula made coffee. She sweetened Litza's for her and left her own black and strong. They went down the line of cakes, all looking more like costumes than food. They used forks, not plates, and left tracks in the frosting. Litza picked up an untouched sheet cake and took a bite of one of the corners. White and pink clumped to her chin. Stavroula wiped it off for her with her arm, and frosting stuck to her shirt. She slid the sheet cake back into the bakery case and said, "That one's yours." Meaning she wouldn't touch it, and neither would anyone else, and it would stay there, imperfect, through the memorial.

They were becoming dangerously full.

"Chocolate cheesecake, to Dad."

"Lemon meringue. To Dad."

"Carrot cake: to Dad."

"Strawberry shortcake, Ruby's favorite—to Dad."

Then Litza, taking a bowl from behind the counter, poured some cornflakes. She spooned chocolate cake on top, and then she covered it with powdered hot chocolate, poured milk over it, and then put it in the microwave for a minute. "Toast: to us."

Toast was disgusting: like eating a sweet swamp. They went back to cake.

Then Stavroula reached for a lined notepad, the kind the waitresses used, and said, "To Dad." Litza clapped. They began the letter, *Dear Dad.*

Let We *explain* You *something.*
Writing, it is not satisfying. It does not get close enough to what must be said.
We write one draft that blames You *for everything;* We *write another draft that saves* You *of everything. We absolve* You, *saying to Ourselves that We do not begrudge* You Your Mistakes.
But that is not true, either.
How can We say exactly what We mean?
We say it over and over.

CHAPTER 27

If Marina does, it means death. It means that Stavros Stavros, a man voyaging between two worlds, will no longer be reached. Doing what Marina has been asked to do means: Marina will be shoving Stavros Stavros off on his last boat, shrouded in dark water with light fading fast, and light growing, too.

Granting a man his final wish means closing his coffin door.

But if Marina does not, it means denying a dying man his wish.

And depriving the world of the last, last supper, perhaps the most glorious meal of Marina's life. A meal, after all, of thanks. A meal that may have nothing to do with Stavros Stavros and all to do with her, the blessing of living, the life that she has lived alongside him.

A letter has come to Marina, after all. It is in the common language— not Greek, but rather in the communication of food. And it is staked through the heart. The letter is not a letter; it is an order, written on the lined green pads the waitresses use. It is posted on the chef's planchette as if it may have been there all along. It was not: she would have known.

It is there now.

It is insistent: *goat.*

What she can make Stavros Stavros is meats, cheeses, a feast, a tray of just grapes, her best recipes and the ones they discovered together, bread, three salads, pork.

But the letter demands: *goat.*

Cannot. Marina cannot. Yet must.

And does.

At seven in the morning the girls feast on desserts, Marina can hear them. It is good, finally they are forced into a single boat and will row, row together. Marina, alone, goes outside. The back door clatters behind her.

Marina, with a curved knife, displays the goat's mysterious throat.

It is done.

The animal collapses, shaking to the earth, and Marina coos it to its death. Marina, always, always, holding the parts of the animal that cannot be held, that have been spilled. They bleed through her fingers.

This is a compassionate killing, Marina hopes, she hopes to God.

She scatters salt, excising evil, blessing this place.

In her scattering, Marina's wrist mimics the sputter of the goat's willful, lifeless kicks.

The day of mourning stretches so long, it will be a surprise if it does not reach everybody.

The letter demands goat. OK, goat.

But Marina demands: marrow. Great knotty logs of it, which she will roast for the here and gone, and they will eat at first with a spoon and some bread crust, and then plunge their tongues and fingers in it, and suck on the bone until they realize: there is no going deeper than this.

CHAPTER 28

Blessed are those whose way is blameless, the *pappas* chants.

Incense clouds the air at his knees.

The *pappas* wears a thick gold cloak and square black hat, shrouded in black and circled in gray.

The *agia trapeza* is a table with gold crucifix, the saints, and a hundred beeswax candles, placed there by the faithful.

The diner tables are cleared. There are rows of chairs facing the *pappas*, and they are filled with familiar, nameless people. Hero is there. The mistress is not. Dina is not. The family sits in a booth, Stavroula and Litza on one side, Mother and Ruby and Ruby's new husband on the other.

The *pappas* intones the Small Litany. At the third stasis, on the verse *early in the morning the myrrh-bearers came to thee and sprinkled myrrh upon thy tomb*, the *pappas* sprinkles rosewater.

He offers the Amomos, the *blameless*.

When he sings, the skin of his face becomes smooth, like a page.

When he begins the memorial service, the *pappas*'s English is as cracked and elegant as driftwood. He asks, "What does it mean, really, to lose someone? What does it mean to say they are no longer with us?"

The *pappas* never stops swinging the censer. He offers hymns, prayers that Stavroula does not understand. This does not feel like a funeral— or a memorial, whatever it's meant to be. It feels like the *pappas* is a man reading foreign poetry, and all of these people are indulging him because they sense he has lost someone very dear. Patiently, they are waiting for him to stop speaking so they can return to their meals and conversation, joyous cutlery. They will buy his red carnations out of pity, if he would only let them and be gone.

Stavroula smells myrrh, also cigarette through the clean shower scent on Litza. Both sisters have their hands in their laps, and neither of them cries. Stavroula's eyes are cooking, and she thinks Litza must feel the same. How many days have they gone without sleep? Stavroula has trouble listening to the *pappas*. This is not the way she feels things, out in the open. Rather, she feels things in small cuts, with fine tools she holds close to her body. Otherwise she feels: nothing. Stavroula would like to go back to the kitchen with Marina, who, to nobody's surprise, is avoiding the *pappas*'s poetry. But Stavroula cannot leave, Stavroula has brought everyone here. Mother is taking turns petting their hands and smiling kindly on the girls. She is nicely dressed, with tasteful jewelry, but instead of the black he demanded, she is wearing a bright pastel shirt in the spirit of Easter.

The first thing Mother said when she came in was, "It was just an email." As if she expected one of them to disagree. When they didn't, she took them in her arms. Stavroula did not think they would all fit, but they did, coming together in an amorphous shape that seemed to spill out of itself. Mother would not let them go, even when Stavroula tried to pull away. Mother was crying, ruining her makeup. She kept saying, "My girls. My little orphans."

Ruby, who was crying without shame, said, "He won't be here to see our children."

Stavroula, lighting her own candle at the *pappas*'s request, is realizing she may have the most hope. Litza, the least. Litza, drifting through the last few hours. She is lifting the dark material of her skirt and scratching her thigh, the same place. It is becoming raw. She's wearing sunglasses and has not cried since this morning at the airport.

The *pappas* interrupts his own service. In English, he explains that he has been called to do a job he cannot do. "I am summoned to give repose for the dear departed, but who is departed? Who is here for us to give our goodbyes?

"How do I, a humble messenger for the Lord, give comfort when we cannot even point to a wound? How do we forgive what we cannot see? How do we let go of someone already gone and yet still so here?

"Ah, *paidi mou*, that is the mystery of faith. We accept that there is truth even in knowledge that is kept from us.

"Even if we cannot wash Him and dress Him and lay Him to rest and watch Him rise on the third day: we must relent that He died for our sins for reasons we, his children, can never understand.

"You believe that just because God is invisible to you, He is invisible to your pain? No, you are not alone. He will be with you always. He was there at your birth, only you can't remember. For your first breath. He will be there in your last, for your suffering."

Stavroula has been trying to quiet her sister's hand. Litza pulls the material of the skirt tight around her legs.

"The time it takes for a glass to tip, and one drop of water to spill.

That is the brevity of life that I am talking about.

That is what God asks me to remind you of, His children.

At the end of this service, you must all extinguish your candles. And you will think to yourself, this is all there is: one strong wind comes, and I am blown out. At the end, I have to surrender my soul.

"But before that happens, you must claim it."

The little bell above the door rings, and the door opens. Stavroula turns and cannot believe what she sees: her father, wearing a light-blue shirt and gray pants, sunglasses. He still has the beard that brought her into this country, a beard she mistakenly believed as a child that she could hang on to, not realizing that it was like tree bark in that it only looked strong. His arms are raised, and he is coming for them. Litza sees him, too. Litza takes Stavroula's hand beneath the table.

But it is not their father. It is only a man who looks like him.

Litza wrenches her hand away. She leaves the booth. The kitchen door is swinging shut behind her, and for a moment, Stavroula thinks to follow.

But the *pappas* summons. She must deliver the eulogy, the ἐγκώμιο, which roughly translates to "praise." She has taken it upon herself.

Dear Dad.

Litza knows something isn't right. She pushes through the door and goes directly to the sink in the Slop Room, and she drinks water. The glass she has chosen is not clean, but she doesn't realize that until she is halfway through four airless gulps, and it isn't making her stop, anyway. Water feels like the antidote to everything the *pappas* is saying. It wasn't the man who entered—it was her thirst that drove her here. But the kitchen is eerie and quiet, a fan murmuring somewhere unseen. It feels like this is her father's tomb, and all she has to do is go behind these shelves and she will see his body on ice; see him floating in water; all she has to do is go around a corner, and she will see his body lying on top of all the letters he has written—even the unwritten ones. *Dear Dad: What do you have left to say?*

What is behind the shelves?

It is something, it is something.

There are gaps where stacked pots meet the handles of other pots. She could put her eye to a hole and see. Is it the man with the beard? Has he followed her back here? The man too carefree to be her father's ghost, because even a young ghost must carry the burdens of a man's whole life. If it is her father's ghost and he has followed her here, she will not know how to scare it off. She has never known. Would Stavroula know how? No. Stavroula would not believe in their father's ghost, she would keep looking past it for the man she secretly thought existed. She has hope, still. But Litza does not have hope. Litza feels dread.

Plip-plop, a drip. It is coming from the sink behind her. *Plip-plip-plop*. It is followed by a kind of moaning that Litza has heard before. She thinks of the wooden man made of clothespins, the one she broke and broke more, the one she buried as a child. The one that showed her the small frog sounds of her father's throat, so gentle they could exist neither on land nor water. This is the sound her father is leaving her with.

Litza braces herself and looks. She sees a wooden spoon. Next it is a trail of brown, like a dribbling of gravy.

It is Marina. Facedown, the apron pulled beneath her right knee as if that was what had caused the fall in the first place, and she will fix it as soon as she gets up. She is lying on the tile as if she knows what she is doing, as if there is some business here she must tend to, something secret on the kitchen floor that no one but her is meant to see, and she will get up, soon as she is done. She is facedown as if she knows how to do this better than anyone. But she is not getting up.

Next to the body of Marina is Stavros Stavros Mavrakis. Crouching on his haunches, his left hand over his face, his shoulders shaking. As if he has been here all along, the one place they forgot to check. He is crying. His hand is squeezing Marina's shoulder, over, over, over as if to say, Not yet.

When he finally looks up at her, his daughter, he holds out one hand to say, Come.

CHAPTER 29

Today I address to you with a whole, and heavy sadness.

We lose the person, Marina, that never we should lose.

I never believe, in all my life, that this woman of miracles could die, or that I, Stavros Stavros Mavrakis, known to you as Steve, could give up my partner of thirty years. Or that I, Stavros, would stand before you to ask that you memorialize her.

Do you understand that she made meals out of bones?

Do you know she fed you, all of you?

I had a dream exactly ten days ago. The dream was a goat, and the goat was Death, and Death was promising to Stavros Stavros Mavrakis that he was coming. The leash on the goat would become the leash on the man, and the goat would lead me to a final resting place. Under this kind of stress, I did what any man would do: I tell my family of this warning, I ask them please to keep me in their prayers. I say to them, Look, here are ways of pain in life, and here is how, according to your father's wisdom, you can avoid pain, at least for a little. I give them fatherly advices.

You tell your children what to do with their lives, do you know what they say back to you? By your laughter, I can tell that you know the answer: Get your own life, Dad.

So I did that, exactly. I say to myself and to my goat, my real goat, Am I the type of man to wait around for the Goat of Death? No, I am not. I am a man of two lives—one in Greece, one in America—and who says I cannot be a man of three?

I decide to go meet this Third Life, or meet Death in the process and bargain. I walk. I walk only. I feel that Death, if it wants, can catch up to you quickly. If you are on a train or you drive cross-country, Death has many obvious ways of running you off the road. I would make Death slow down. I would make Death walk with me on my journey. Then he would understand Stavros Stavros Mavrakis and offer forgiveness.

Do you know the elusive *kri-kri* of Crete? He is a goat that is never seen, never, even if he is nearby. His own shepherd cannot find him. Death, he is like that.

Together, Death and I walk through America. One diner to the next, eating meals with strangers—for free, some of them. Some things we see, I can share with you, and some places I keep only between me and my Death. We take the road through cornfield and over mountain. Even desert. There is desert in America? I think I will see a world of mud, that this is what Death will show me, but over and over I am shown fields and sun. Enough to feed us forever in America if we let it.

A funny thing happen then. This man who is traveling with Death meets a lady on his travels. She is in a field carrying very large sunflowers and a bucket of water. She does not slow, so I follow her. We talk on opposite sides of a wooden fence, where she cannot see Death at all, and she says to Stavros, "You take your dreams too seriously." I answer to this pretty lady, which she is from Eastern Europe and speaks not even so good English as Stavros, "I am an immigrant. Of course I have always taken my dreams seriously." She answers, "Maybe it is time to stop being an immigrant."

I think to myself, I will like to see this pretty Eastern Europe lady again, who is so impressed by Stavros and has agreed to friend him on Facebook.

I leave the field and begin my journey with Death again. I miss the pretty lady's watery voice. Death is a quiet companion, with no answers, so Stavros the man thinks on life. He thinks and thinks of the last ten days, including today, and tells Death:

I will face you here, Death. Death, you will answer. Because I am not finish with my life.

Death listens without speaking. Stavros waits, but Death will not respond. Stavros waits some more. Stavros demands, thinking about the pretty lady in the field, I still want more. Will you give me more life? Or will you take it from me here and now?

Death will not take Stavros here and now.

Death's answer is to bring Stavros Stavros home.

Death's answer is Marina, on the tile floor.

So today, in honor of the greatest cook that not even Death could spare, I ask that you eat, eat with me, with my family, for Marina who loved my children, for the *pappas* who has lost his only daughter.

We raise bread for Marina, who raised us all and filled our plates and gave us more.

In honor of you, Marina *mou*, I raise bread: I say something that Stavros Stavros Mavrakis learned on his long walk with Death. Something Stavros Stavros has never before been able to say.

I am a grateful man.

I thank you, I thank you for listening.

EPILOGUE

—

The Letter that Stavros Stavros Meant to Send. The Letter Stavros Stavros Wanted for Litza. The Letter Litza Wanted, herself. The Letter Stavroula knew could be hidden inside the Mouse Hole of her father's heart. The Letter that said, If I could replace me for another me, For You, I Would. The Letter that said: Dear Daughter, Our Letters are like bandages, always trying to mark the wound.

The Letter That Could Not Be Written Because It Was True. The Letter He Did Send, with No Way to Open.

Dear, Family.
Dear my cherish ones,

Let Me Explain You Something:
A man may hold a child, like if she were a fish.
Did this man want fish? No, he wanted sons.
But in his palms are three fish, given by God. One is beautiful, one has gills so small it is a miracle that she survives, and one is so fierce she is like a dark star exploding.
The man is up to his knees. He is in a current that remembers every time it goes out and forgets each time it comes in.
He keeps his beautiful fish in his pocket as long as he can. The beautiful fish is a delight to anyone who holds her. But a pocket is no place for a beautiful fish, or else a beautiful fish becomes nothing more than a beautiful shell. The father, he gives little by little until finally the little fish is swimming on her own.
To the next fish, the miracle fish, he tells her, Your gills are so

small, how can you hope to live just the way you are? The miracle fish splashes over the lifelines of his palm. She is a stubborn fish, so she says to him: "I only need to hold one breath at a time." Yes, the man says to himself, this is wisdom. Like so, she could swim forever in the fearsome ocean, the Atlantic.

OK, so the man addresses to his other fish, in his other palm; this one, she is more like a sea urchin, with black spikes for skin and a pink mouth she keeps hidden. If a diver steps on this type of fish, he will feel a spike through his heel. So the man tells her, his little black fish-child, This is a way to hurt others, this way to be. In return, black fish-child says to him: "This is a way not to get eaten." She is right, too, in her own way. She swims in the ocean of fearsome in a different way.

The miracle fish, the dark black urchin, and the littlest beautiful one. What choice does the father have but to give his children water? This is how they must live.

The man is up to his knees. He is in a current that remembers every time it goes out and forgets each time it comes in. His palms are empty. His children, gone to the same sea.

Over a lifetime, a man becomes a whale, very large.

He wants only this.

When he dies, his body sinks to the floor for his children, his fish, to feed.

AUTHOR'S NOTE

While I've drawn inspiration from family and friends for *Let Me Explain You* and some resemblances may emerge, this work is a novel and not a memoir. The character eccentricities and personal conflicts portrayed within are fictional and in service of the central narrative. I realize that this comes as a shock, but we may be the only Greek family in America not to own a diner. And among many other things, I don't have a father who makes prophecies about his own mortality, no one in my family participates in petty vandalism, and there is no Goat of Death. What the Mavrakis family and my family have in common is that they are all warriors, and I love them for it.

ACKNOWLEDGMENTS

Thank you, Sara Nordstrom, my partner and my best friend, for believing in me. This book is for you: every book will be for you. I know I can't build you a house, but at least I can try to make us a home out of words.

Who's gonna stop us now?

Thanks to my family. I want to applaud my mom, Michele Liontas, and my sisters—Damara Burke, Angie Liontas, and Alexis Liontas. You are models of resiliency and strength—and you have each, in your own way, inspired this novel. While *Let Me Explain You* is of course a work of fiction, I hope that something in these pages speaks to you. In many ways this story was written as much for you as it was for me.

Thank you, Judy Baker, aunt and PR extraordinaire, for reminding me always that I am a writer. Thank you, Marissa Baker, for teaching me how to write a child's resilience.

Thanks to my editor, Kara Watson, for helping to shape this book into the best expression of itself. My appreciation extends to Kate Lloyd and the entire team at Scribner. Thanks to my agent, David McCormick, and to Bridget McCarthy: truly, I could not ask for better readers.

Thanks to Syracuse University and the National Writing Project @ Rutgers for the space and time to write. Thanks to Maggie Devine for her encouragement.

My greatest appreciation to: my *mentoh* Arthur Flowers, who taught me the novel and demanded to know whose story this was; George Saunders, who explained me what it means to write joy as well as pain; Christine Schutt, for her honesty; Dana Spiotta, for showing

344

ACKNOWLEDGMENTS

me myself; Ellen Litman, for her guidance. I am especially grateful to my compatriots, fighting their own fight to say it better. Joyfully, there are too damn many of you even to name. Thank you to my workshop— Oscar Cuevas, Danny Magariel, Jessie Roy, and especially Caitlin Hayes and Alex Barnett. Your killer insight gave this book a second life. Thank you to my friends and brilliant readers, Christi Cartwright and Cate McLaughlin. Your love and support are humbling.

Thanks to Katherine Kourti, my Greek teacher, proofreader, and wonderful maker of *gigantes*.

I want to thank the people who helped make Marina who she is: Marion Hodum, my very first mentor at Mt. Ephraim Public Schools, as well as Audubon High School's John Skrabonja, Sue McKenna, and Mme Susan Parker. I can finally acknowledge your generosity by dreaming up a character as beloved as you are.

Deep and belated gratitude to Siobhan Gibbons, Rutgers University. If only the bottom is broken, Siobhan, not all is lost. Thank you for your obstinate, loving hope for me.

And eternal thanks to the reader who gets what it means to be foreign.